OVERCOME
BY PASSION—
THEY PLEDGED THEIR LOVE.

His caresses this time were gentle, as subtly insistent as before they had been brutal. He kissed the bruises that flowered already on her breasts. Once more her desire flew up to meet his and she parted her thighs for him with a sigh of delight, arching her back so that there should be no part of her that did not touch him, please him, worship him. She was a part of him now, as he was of her: they could never again be separated by life or by death.

MY LADY'S CRUSADE
by Annette Motley

MY LADY'S CRUSADE

Annette Motley

BANTAM BOOKS · TORONTO · NEW YORK · LONDON

This low-priced Bantam Book
has been completely reset in a type face
designed for easy reading, and was printed
from new plates. It contains the complete
text of the original hard-cover edition.
NOT ONE WORD HAS BEEN OMITTED.

MY LADY'S CRUSADE
A Bantam Book | published by arrangement with
Futura Books

PRINTING HISTORY
Originally published in Great Britain by Futura Books 1977
Bantam edition | March 1978

Bantam Books are published by Bantam Books, Inc. Its trade-
mark, consisting of the words "Bantam Books" and the por-
trayal of a bantam, is registered in the United States Patent
Office and in other countries. Marca Registrada. Bantam
Books, Inc., 666 Fifth Avenue, New York, New York 10019.

PRINTED IN THE UNITED STATES OF AMERICA

MY LADY'S CRUSADE

CHAPTER ONE

Hawkhurst

The torches flared and shuddered in their dozen sconces about the walls and the candles flickered on the long table as the sudden draft gusted down the hall.

Eden knew there would be a storm. She signaled to Rollo, stretched on the straw beside the two great dogs, content and dreaming after his meal. The serf got up at once and took the long curtain-pole from its place behind the settle; he drew the heavy, hide-backed russet folds across the tall, shuttered windows, his shadow scaling the high, stone walls to reach them unaided.

"Shall I feed the fire again, my lady? It'll be a cold night. Snow, mebbe."

Eden shivered and drew her cloak of fine, dark-green wool close across her breast. She hated the winter. It seemed that she had always been cold since Stephen had left. It was at moments such as these, when the demons took their spurs to the winds outside, and the doors and shutters creaked and rattled their hinges, that she felt her isolation most.

It was small consolation to her to be the sole mistress and sovereign lady of Hawkhurst, if she must keep her state alone at her board every night, with nothing but the prospect of a cup of wine with her chaplain or a game of backgammon with her bailiff to call her pleasure. True, they would speak to her of Stephen, calling up visions of the Holy Land as if it were a country in a minstrel's tale. They did so to bring her comfort, she knew, but as she listened, it was as if her husband had gone from her into the flat dimensions of a map or the exotic scene of a tapestry,

1

so far from reality were their pictures of turbanned
knights and veiled women, of silken luxury and barbarous cruelty.

At first, she could not believe that he had indeed
taken the Cross. Stephen had lived with her, here at
her manor of Hawkhurst, since both of them were
children. She had been her father's only heir and was
betrothed to him at the age of seven. He had entered
the household, when she was ten, so that he might learn
the virtues and responsibilities of his future inheritance.
To the lonely girl, by now motherless, the handsome,
thoughtful boy became the adored elder brother she
had never had. He was sixteen and he came to repre-
sent to her all the heroes of her favorite legends; he
was Launcelot, Roland, Tristan, all in one. They had
married when she was fifteen and there had been three
years of this changed state of existence; just three brief,
ecstatic, confused years of darkness and brightness, and
then the cry had gone up for the Crusade. Stephen,
idealistic, fervent in his Christianity, in love with the
concept of Chivalry, eager to serve his great, golden
giant of a King, had been among the first to sew the
white silk token on his shoulder.

He had been gone for nearly two years. There had
been no news. It was scarcely expected. It was known
that his troop had been present at the seige of the great
city of Acre; it was possible that he was still in that
region and alive; the city was still beleaguered. No
news had come of its relief . . . and some men must
live on when others die.

Eden prayed nightly for her husband. At times,
when the task of maintaining the well-being of six
hundred acres of land and some one hundred and
twenty souls became overwhelming, she wept . . .
though whether for his absence, for his return or simply on account of his desertion of her, she hardly knew.
There had been, there would be, too many nights like
this one. She was not formed to sit and stare into the
fire, feeding her cold heart on memories, like a woman
three times her age. She was only twenty; she was
bold and bright and quick as sunlight, and her body

cried out with her spirit for rescue from this penance that had been laid upon her . . . for no sins of her own. Why should she not dance, run, make love, bear children, enter into all of life's rich rhythms, as other women did? Granted she was clerk, steward, justice, overseer of her lands, ruler of her household, but she was no longer a woman; she felt herself almost anonymous, a wraith without a sex. She did not think she could bear it much longer. As she did so often on these lonely evenings, Eden sent away the serfs and tried to arouse her tired senses with music. She was learning to play the lute, an accomplishment which, she had heard from a pilgrim last month, was much admired among the ladies of Queen Eleanor's court. Her father had used to promise that one day she should go to Winchester or to London and see the wonders of life among the Plantagenets for herself, but time had passed, and more time, and the promise had never been kept. Perhaps, one day, when Stephen returned . . .

She swept the soft strings of her instrument, caressing its swollen belly with loving hands. "My love rode away to Jerusalem," she sang, determined to allow no break in her voice. She finished the verse and poured herself a brimming hanap from the pot of mead that was simmering on the hearth; it was spiced with some of the precious cinnamon brought by Sir Godfrey, her father, from the second Crusade, so long ago; it was still fresh; she had wrapped it in leaves and kept it in a box with a firm lid. Thus seasoned the mead became metheglin, the fairy drink, beloved of King Arthur and his knights, balm to the weary bones and the humorless mind.

She watched the flames leap and dart, sending the nameless troops of unquiet shadows out into the long room where they climbed the walls and hid behind settles and swarmed across the board where none had supped tonight except the lonely Lady of Hawkhurst. It was a fine, high-roofed hall, made for feasting and dancing and the cheerful companionship of friends and neighbors; its efficient and elegant hearth and

chimney were the envy of the entire county of Kent.
There were tapestries on its walls and warm wool-
sacks on its seating. There was good pewter in the
kitchen, to dress the board, and a wealth of fine wines
from France, down below in the undercroft. Eden felt
its emptiness as she felt her own.

She was tired to the bone; she had ridden twenty
miles that day, to the house of Isaiah the Jew, to ask
for a further loan against the next season's wool. She
had got her money, but the interest had gone up; she
didn't know where she was going to find it, but find
it she must.

She drowsed, only half aware that she had drunk
more deeply than usual. Her head drooped sideways
and rested upon the carved back of her tall chair; she
scarcely noticed how hard it was as she drifted willingly
into sleep.

Outside, the storm furies lashed the winds to a fine
frenzy and the rain fell mercilessly upon the cowering
earth, making flooded trenches of the farm furrows,
tearing at thatch and croft and turning the roads into
rivers. It was not a night on which to ride out. Nevertheless, while Eden slept a heavily cloaked and booted
troop of men were directing their unenthusiastic
horses along the almost indistinguishable path to Hawkhurst. Their leader crouched low in the saddle, turning
now and then to hurl encouragement at his followers,
cursing as his mount stumbled over a loose rock.

"Not long, now, lads! We'll soon be home and
dry! And remember . . . not a sound, do you hear? We
want to surprise the Lady Eden! The storm will keep
our secret till we gain the house!" His laughter scattered before him on the wind as he spurred his
horse to greater effort.

As the Lady of Hawkhurst slept on in exhausted
ignorance in her great hall, the cloud of dark shadows
rolled toward her with the storm. She did not stir as the
broad gates opened to them, nor did she wake at the
sudden outcry from the undercroft, where the serfs and
servants caroused to keep out the weather; she heard
nothing as the leader of the sodden and weary troop

gave curt orders which were immediately obeyed, nor when his henchmen stole like ghosts through the quiet chambers, going quietly and efficiently about their several duties.

Their captain, having assured himself of their obedience, left them to stride purposefully toward his own object, though taking the time to make an interested inventory of the eye as he passed through the great kitchen with its silver and pewter, up the twisting stairway, warmly tapestried against the cold, through the small family solar, where hung the late Sir Godfrey's treasures from the Holy Land, chased and jeweled swords and scimitars, exquisite metal and enamel vases and cups, hangings whose colors sang in brilliant silks, and the strange, flat, deeply-hued paintings of slant-eyed virgins of the Greek church. He smiled, his look satisfied and proprietorial as he looked upon them. Then he passed through the curtained doorway which lead to the heart of the house and looked, at last, upon its lady herself.

She presented an exquisitely vulnerable picture as she slept. Her face had lost its tension and her skin gleamed, translucent in the firelight. There was strength there as well as beauty; dark golden brows curved boldly above long-lashed, heavy lids; the full, red mouth held a resourcefulness that its owner would not have recognized and the memory of a sensuality now suppressed. The fine bones were beginning to reveal their line beneath the rose-gold surfaces of her skin, the cheek high and proud, the chin resolute. Her mouth had fallen open slightly and her small, well-shaped teeth showed white and strong. A yard of deep gold hair, unbraided and left loose, spilled over her lap and gilded her blue-green gown. The darker cloak had fallen from her shoulders and framed her body in graceful folds.

The man who stood before her derived a slow and sensual enjoyment from the sight. He was tall, broadly built with powerful shoulders and strong limbs, heavily muscled. His face, as he stared down at Eden, was cruel and clever, its structure half buried in coarse black hair. His eyes, too, were black, and sparkled like sea-coal. His red cloak clung, soaking, to his tunic. He let his eye roam delightedly from the parted lips to the full, round breasts beneath the soft, woollen dress; he followed the line from small, neat waist to splendid, flaring hip, from long thigh down to a slender calf and tiny elegant foot. He noted the mud on her green leather boots, the heavy keys on her woven girdle, the callous on one finger where her rein had rubbed it.

"You give yourself too much work, lady! It becomes neither your position nor your beauty."

The voice was crusty, deep and filled with confidence. It brought Eden back to herself swifter than a cold ducking.

"Sir Hugo!" She sat up, pulling her cloak around her again.

"I sorrow to disturb your sleep, lady, but I told you I would come for my answer." The pleasure had left his face, a deeply etched, customary scowl taking its place. Heavily he waited. Eden stared at him in distaste, forcing herself fully awake. Sir Hugo de Malfors, who had so arrogantly thus availed himself of her house, was not the least of her present problems. Importantly, and unfortunately, he was her overlord. Baron of Stukesey Castle, to whose honor the Lord of Hawkhurst did homage, he, in turn, held his lands as tenant-in-chief of King Richard himself; it was said that the King was also his friend.

She sighed briefly, with a tired impatience. "You have had your answer, a dozen times. It has not changed. It will not do so." She was careful to keep her voice level and pleasant. "And I wish you will cease these importunities; they add no dignity to the relations we must have with each other."

The frown deepened between the black brows. "You speak as though I sought to do you some dishonor! You are harsh, Eden. All I wish to do is to offer you my hand and my name." He laid one fist over his heart in a gesture that, knowing him, she could only understand to be sarcastic.

"As I have repeated so frequently," she said, her voice very slightly unsteady as her anger rose, "I already have a husband."

Sir Hugo shrugged. He dragged forward a broad, low-backed chair and made himself comfortable, stretching his black-booted legs to the fire. "Your father gave you to the wrong man; now he is gone, and likely will not return. It is time to right the matter. You know I wanted you, when they married you to Stephen! Your father was a fool!"

"How dare you slander his name in his house!" Eden's control had broken its leash. "He preferred Stephen because he knew you to be the man you are!"

There was silence. Then, "Indeed?" said Hugo quietly, his eyes dangerous. "And what kind of man is that?"

But she would not be drawn. "He did not think you would ensure the welfare either of Hawkhurst or myself. And besides," she added, remembering suddenly, "you had recently buried a wife."

"A green girl who had not the strength to bring a healthy child into the world! I was well rid of her. A man without an heir is like a tree without a leaf."

Eden recalled the small, unhappy figure she had once seen at a church festival. "She was too young to bear; you could have left her to grow," she said.

He grinned, then spat.

"What use is a wife, if not in bed?" Eden shuddered.

Sir Hugo was becoming restless. "I'll speak once, for the last time of asking. Our lands march; you are my liege-woman; it makes good sense that we should marry. Will you be my wife?"

"For the last time, Sir Hugo . . . and right glad I am to have your word on *that* . . . I will not!"

The black eyes glittered and a certain satisfaction appeared in them. "Then I have to inform you, lady, that I rode here tonight with thirty armed men at my back. I have become tired of asking. I have courted your vanity like a lovesick squire for overlong. Now I shall *take* what I want."

She stared at him, unbelieving, her hands clutching at the arms of her chair.

He nodded, the truth triumphant in his smile. "I admit that I had a little help from within your walls. One of your men had a mighty fear of losing both of his hands . . . if he did not employ them in opening your gates to me."

She ground her teeth to prevent the cry that welled within her. She could not bear to face the treachery.

Hugo looked at her in mock regret. "Alas, even so! Loyalty is a mere, fleeting thing. I verily believe I will take off his hands anyway, to teach him a better morality. What do you say?"

Her look of disgust was his answer.

Sir Hugo's mood changed, the amusement fading from his eyes. "I've not come here for conversation, lady. I've come for what is mine. I have Hawkhurst and can hold it . . . and I will have you, too . . . tonight. Make up your mind to it, and we shall do very well together. I'll marry you as soon as may be."

"I am married to Stephen," she shouted furiously then, losing all reason as the full wretchedness of her situation was borne upon her. Married indeed, and to a man who had taken every able-bodied man off the domain, leaving her with boys and well-meaning graybeards to guard what was hers.

His contemptuous laugh dispersed her fractured syllables like blown leaves. "Are you so?" The dark amusement and unholy pleasure returned to his face. "Then why," he asked with quiet obscenity, "have I heard it said that Stephen de la Falaise was no true husband to you? I can have it attested before the Shire Court that there was no blood on your fine, white sheets, after your wedding night . . . nor ever."

He grinned, satisfied with her incredulous gasp.

"Poor Eden! Your miserable clerk of a husband could not do a man's part by you, confess it! He was fit only for the monastery. And my good friend, the Bishop, will therefore take pity on such a lusty young woman as yourself . . . and grant you the annulment of this mismatched marriage . . . on the grounds that it was never consummated."

"It isn't true! No one would believe you!" she cried, distressed beyond measure.

"Would they not? You've been wed nigh on five years, Eden. You should have three or four fine sons by now. Where are they?"

She could not bear his triumph; he had sought out her secret sorrow and now defiled it with his ridicule. She had hoped so agonizingly to conceive before Stephen left; she had hoped, also, to bring forth the heir to Hawkhurst while her father still lived. He had enjoyed no son; she had greatly longed to give him his grandson. But it had not happened, not then, not now.

She hated Hugo de Malfors with all her spirit. She summoned her strength and spoke coldly and clearly. "No Bishop would put his soul in peril to do what you suggest."

"You would be amazed at what even the Pope might do, if he were offered a great enough inducement," said Hugo dryly, shifting his bulk for a moment to lean and help himself to a cup of metheglin.

He gave her a grin of encouragement. "Put off that whey face! You'll change your tune, right enough, when we've made a proper marriage of it, as we should have done long ago. Why, I'd have tupped you like a ram every night of your life. You'd have those four strong sons by now, and your breasts filling with the next." His eyes raked her body and she began to be afraid.

There must be something she could say that would turn away his purpose. Her throat was dry; she swallowed. No words came.

"You are lax in your duty as a hostess," he complained, holding out his hanap for more of the mead. "I don't like to see that. I trust you will not see my friends go dry when I am master of this excellent hearth."

"That will never be!" she raged, finding her voice at last.

He opened his throat and sent down the wine in one long stream, then wiped his mouth with the back of his hand. He belched.

"Indeed! Will it not? I think it may already be accomplished!" He rose from his seat. "Now, my lady . . . you will show me the way to your bed. I have a mind to take my pleasure of you . . . most thoroughly."

She made no sound, but sat rigid in her tall chair, confounded by an incredulous horror.

"You were Stephen's friend!" she whispered, loathing him from the very core of her being.

Hugo nodded agreeably. "I was his good lord, and as such, gave him wondrous good advice. In truth, Eden, I cannot understand why you insist on remaining so pitifully loyal to the memory of one who was so eager to forsake the pleasure of your person for those of Outremer."

She understood him well enough. "Your 'good advice' told him to take the Cross?" She already knew the answer; it turned in her like a sword.

Hugo's strong teeth showed in his wolf's grin. "He was remarkably easy to persuade. He had a true devotion to his Christian duty."

"Christian duty!" she spat. "What do you know of that . . . who are as much a Christian as Saladin and all his race of devils?"

"My friend the Bishop would take issue with you," he replied amiably. "It was, perhaps, above all, his sermon that tipped the balance with Stephen. Who could resist that ringing eloquence, filling the vastness of the cathedral at Canterbury? The great call to all faithful knights of Christ to wrest his Holy Sepulchre from the violation of the Infidel. Most moving! Why, when I saw Stephen sink to his knees and cry 'For Jesu!' . . . I nearly took the cross myself. But then he would have had none to look to his lands . . . and his lady."

"Blasphemer! You are very bold in tempting the wrath of God! You will be less so when He sends your punishment. Be sure that if you do harm to myself or to Hawkhurst, you will die at Stephen's hand when he returns!"

There was a guffaw of genuine derision. "Stephen will *not* return, my lady, believe me! It is most likely he is already dead, of a Saracen arrow or his own incompetence. If not, you have my promise that, in any event, he will not reach Hawkhurst again . . . alive. So put him from your mind, Eden. You will soon have much other matter to fill it . . . aye, and other parts too."

At first she thought she would vomit. Then, with a cry of rage and hatred, she seized her heavy pewter hanap and hurled it with all her force in his face. The black hair dripped wine upon the floor. He dashed the liquid from his eyes. His movement was controlled but his look struck terror to her belly.

He hung over her and she was instantly reminded of the first time she had set her eyes on him. A child, she had sat dreaming by the river; he had ridden up and reined his horse in close to her, a red-lipped scowling boy who had subjected her to a minute's discomforting, brooding scrutiny before she had leaped to her feet, and, following some deep, uncomprehended instinct, she had taken to her heels and raced back to Hawkhurst as if a devil were after her. He had not followed but his black, speculative look had troubled her dreams. He bent this look upon her now.

"Get up!" he ordered her thickly.

She did not move. Her heart raced like a rabbit's.

He took her roughly by the wrist and jerked her to her feet. "Do not think yourself too fine for me, lady. You are not. There are many who would envy you this night. I have bastards enough about the county to prove it."

She stood, helpless, pinned beside her chair, the tears gathering and falling down her cheeks. Her sense of desolation was greater than anything she would have believed possible. Hawkhurst had always been her ultimate security, her pride, the warm place at the heart of her life; now the knowledge of its vulnerability, as great, it seemed, as her own, tore at her heart.

She stared at Sir Hugo and drew back her hand into a seeking claw.

Without knowing it, she screamed, then found herself reeling back from his sickening blow to her mouth. She steadied herself on the back of her chair, tasting blood on her lips. He came, scowling, toward her.

"Take your taper, Eden, and light me to bed," he commanded.

She shook her head, unable to speak.

With a foul oath he hauled her toward him and threw her across his shoulder. Seizing a candlestick from the table, he held it uncomfortably close to her swimming head. "If you struggle or seek my harm, I shall set fire to your admirable hair. I can quite well do my will upon you without the added pleasure of winding it round my fingers."

She shuddered and kept still, hopeless tears salting her hurt mouth.

He carried her deliberately into the solar, where he flung her onto the bed with a force that winded her. She longed to cry out, but who, even hearing, could aid her? Although shrill sounds of conflict came from the kitchen and outbuildings, she knew that thirty trained men must have made short work of her poor serfs. By now they were doubtless merely amusing themselves; there were two or three pretty girls in the household and a great quantity of wine.

Sir Hugo threw off his cloak and came toward her, unbuckling his belt. She moaned and shrank back as he knelt heavily upon the bed. His smile was terrible to her as his dark, feral face closed over hers, and as the massive body pinned her down, she felt that she would suffocate. She found herself cursing again the faithless serf who opened the gates, and then, somehow, it was Stephen she was cursing, for having left her to come to this pass. "Sir Hugo has promised to look to you, my love; you may trust him in everything." He had said that on the day he left! Black anger rose in her throat, to be choked by the hot, seeking tongue that forced into her mouth. His breath reeked of the spiced wine, and his muscular body of rank sweat and sickly sweet civet. She cried out involuntarily as he bit brutally into her bleeding lips, her hands pushing uselessly at his great bulk as he tore at the neck of her gown, finding and baring her breasts; his lips fastened hideously upon them, biting and sucking at her like some monstrous infant giant. Then, as he reached down to pull up her skirts about her waist, she made a desperate move to escape.

There was a low growl of fury and his fist cracked into the side of her head. She fell back in a haze of pain and nausea, only half conscious as he pulled her thighs apart and wedged his panting weight between them. His hands clamored at the soft entrances to her body; she felt the vomit rise in her throat and arched suddenly, desperately seeking escape; then his arm came down like an iron bar across her throat and she felt him thrust deep into her. He closed one hand greedily upon her breast, his elbow, still beneath her throat, preventing her from moving while his other hand kneaded at her buttocks to aid the energetic rhythm of his working thighs. His mouth possessed hers, the black eyes gleaming like a hog's; she closed her eyes to shut them out, but there was no escape from the hot, thrusting reality that moved between her legs.

At last he had done and she knew that he had left his foul seed within her bruised and shrinking flesh. His sweat came then, strong and fresh. He rolled away from her, leaving her shocked and motionless, unable even to weep, so deep was her sense of degradation and loathing, both of his vile body, for what it had done to her . . . and of her own, which had not died rather than suffer such ignominy.

Sir Hugo slept almost at once, well satisfied. He snored regularly and loud. Eden lay awake until dawn, unable to find either expression or acceptance for her misery. She thought of killing herself, but knew that God would count that worse sin than this terrible act of violence had been.

She lay quiet, staring into the half light, afraid to move lest she wake the monster who slept at her side. If he should take her again, she knew she would become a madwoman like the girl who had been taken away by one of the mercenary bands, idle before the Crusade. They had brought her shamefacedly back to her village, a poor, driven shell, who would not look up from the ground and could no longer remember her name.

As the birds began their ironic welcome to the dawn, she heard him stir at last. Instantly she feigned sleep, breathing regularly and deeply. She felt his heavy movement around her and then his breath, close to her face. She prayed.

Hugo pulled back the sheets. She knew his bright, black eyes were traveling the length of her body; with an enormous effort of the will, she lay still and relaxed, though every fibre shrank within.

She heard his lips part, wetly, and his hand was heavy on her flank. "You've a fine body, lady. I can't remember when I was last so lusty. Well . . . take your sleep; we've many long nights ahead of us. I'll get a child on you within a week, by Saint Thomas, I will!"

Thankfully she felt the covers tossed back across her shoulders, and heard his swift preparations for leaving.

As soon as he had gone she opened her eyes. Left alone with the realization of what the night had been, she gave way, at last, to great, rending sobs that shook the wooden frame of the bed.

"Holy Mother of God," she prayed, "let me be forgiven. I will do penance. I will make endless reparation. Do not let me forfeit my eternal soul!" When she had sobbed herself into exhaustion, she began to think more coherently. She had committed a dreadful sin, but she had been unwilling. God would not punish her. He would forgive. He was all-merciful.

Suddenly, after her storm of weeping, she realized how tired she was; she had not slept; she must do so, or she would not have the strength to be able to think what she must do. For she must do something . . . she must not accept this evil in her life . . . she must combat it. Worn out, she slept.

Later, the woman Hawisa crept into the chamber. She had been Eden's childhood nurse and had taken over the ordering of the household on the death of the girl's frail mother. Her kindly, lined and practical face was softened with sorrow for her mistress. She knew well enough how it had gone with her. So did every serf in the household. Sir Hugo had swaggered into the hall at daybreak, calling to his ruffians to make ready for hunting, and had demanded meat and ale and the presence of all within the house, forthwith.

"Your lady has consented to be my wife as soon as may be arranged," he had announced, grinning impudently at their horror. "I am your lord now, even as I have ever been your overlord. See to it that you obey me in all things, and you'll not find me cruel. Displease me . . . and you'll not live long."

He had eaten and drunk, then struck the board with a cheerful oath and ridden off with his scoundrels to his day's hunting; he was a man of habit, and let nothing come between him and his daily sport. He had, however, left a dozen or so of his armed retainers to keep safe his hold on his new manor house.

He had addressed Hawisa but once. "See to your mistress; it's high time she was awake. I do not like a slugabed. Tell her to rise up and look to her household." Then he was gone, scattering the chickens in the yard with his hasty horses.

"I've brought you a herb posset, my duck," said the nurse tenderly, ignoring the stained and rumpled sheets. She clucked concernedly when Eden turned her head from the pillow. "Oh, whatever has come to your sweet mouth, my lamb? Has he hurt you so? I'll have the liver of him, see if I don't!"

Slowly, as her body discovered its bruises, Eden sat up, covering herself with one of the furs that lay on the bed. She took the warm, sweet-smelling milk and drank it slowly. Her hands shook as she held the cup.

Hawisa shook her head. "Just you lie there and let the good herbs do their work," she ordered, ignoring the commands of her self-styled new master. "There's camomile and sage in it; poppy, too, to make you drowse awhile."

Eden blushed. The first mentioned were to prevent conception and ensure that she underwent her next woman's courses. Hawisa was skilled in the use and application of all herbs and knew how to doctor most of the ills that troubled the domain. What she could not accomplish, the ancient witch-woman who inhabited a mud cell in the nearby forest could do; all else, such as chills to the lungs, the sudden altering of the rhythms of the heart and the various forms of plague that attacked in due season, were left to God. Hawisa left her and Eden sank back upon her pillow again, trying, despite the nurse's admonitions to sleep, to find her way to an acceptance of what had taken place in her life, so that she might then go on to discover how she might live with it. But all she could feel was a stark hatred. She would kill Hugo de Malfors. She would take a knife and carry it to this chamber, place it in this very bed; then, the next time he forced his loathsome presence on her . . . And what would come to her if she should kill her overlord, the man who was said to be in King Richard's good favor? There could be but one answer.

"And I am not ready, yet, to die," she decided.

Not immediate death, then, for Sir Hugo. But there must be some way of seeking redress; there was justice in the world, surely, and Sir Hugo had flown in its face. He had broken the sacred contract between a lord and his liegeman or woman. If she were to go to the courts, surely it would not go unpunished? She got up and began to dress, fired with the idea that she could, and would, have redress in her weakness.

And then, as she braided her golden hair to fall before her shoulders down the gray wool folds of her dress, she remembered again what Sir Hugo had planned for her. He would have her marriage annulled and would force her to wed him instead; it would be considered an excellent match for her; none would pity her; there would be no interest in her case. As for the matter of rape . . . it took place far too frequently to attract any stir; a Crusader's wife was fair game. If she wished to keep her virtue, her house and her person should be impenetrable. If they were not . . . she had only herself to blame; besides, the man was her over-lord.

Eden felt the beginnings of panic rise within her as she saw her position with an awful clarity. She clutched her hands to her hurt mouth, the pain unnoticed in her fear. There must be a way out!

She would run away! Take her jewels and the money from the Jew and ride away; she would go to her rela-tives north of the River Thames; they would take her in and care for her when they heard her story.

And what would become of Hawkhurst then? She was the lady of the domain, its guardian and possessor; she held it in trust from her father and all his noble forbears for her son and his son after him. She had no right to give it over to the power of the wolf; no right and no desire. She would stand fast; there must be an-other way.

She coiled her hair hastily and placed the gold cross Stephen had given her about her neck. She wrapped herself in the crumpled green cloak once more and searched her face for a moment in the polished silver mirror that had been part of Sir Godfrey's booty from Jerusalem. And when, shortly afterwards, the Lady of Hawkhurst appeared in her hall and her kitchen, neither freedman nor serf noted any change in her usual proud and calm demeanor, though he might have thought her somewhat pale and puffed about the lips.

After she had given her quiet, decisive orders for the day's work, she sent Rollo to beg Father Sebastian to come to her. The serf was in an agony of remorse over his unreadiness for last night's attack and was so eager to make good by serving her that he dragged the surprised priest by the sleeve from his blessing of sev-eral fowl who had incomprehensibly ceased to lay. The chaplain was a short, stout man with the face of a constantly surprised child; he was dedicated to God, Hawkhurst and its lady, ale and food, in that order.

He was a tower of strength to Eden about the domain,
terrifying reluctant ploughmen with tales of red-hot
pitchforks wielded by demons, or slow sheep-shearers
with stories of the monstrous knife which the devil kept
to cut off anything that dangled from a man who was
slow enough to let him. He was an inspired preacher
and had his entire fold well shepherded toward heaven,
in their minds at least, if not always in their behavior.
To Eden he was the wonderful teller-of-tales who had
widened the boundaries of her childhood, and a need-
ful resource of comfort in time of trouble.

He took her hand and led her into the chapel. "I
will hear your confession, child . . . and then you will
be free of this terrible thing," he told her pityingly.

When he had blessed her he gave her a penance of
fifty Aves and an offering for the church at Hawkmere,
still his pastoral care, though he lived in his own chamber, snug in the undercroft below the main solar of the
manor house. "Take comfort lady. Be sure that God is
not mocked for long, though it may appear so at first.
Even as we shall prevail through your husband and all
those like him, over the infidel, so shall we prevail
over Satan's wickedness in the person of Baron Hugo."

"I wish I had your certainty, Father," Eden said.
She felt that her faith had not sufficient strength to uphold her now, and she was sorry for it.

Her pale, suffering face touched his heart. He remembered the golden child who had flashed about the
precincts of the domain such a small number of years
ago, and regretted the swift cruelty of time's passage.
She was all but a child, still, in experience, despite her
twenty years.

He pressed the small hand he still held in his. "Let
your mind dwell on life's sweetness . . . for you have
known it, I think. That way, its wound will heal the
faster. Think of Stephen and of your childhood, for I
never saw two children happier together. Think of your
wedding day . . ."

And he slipped away, leaving her to kneel at the
little, tapestry-covered prie-dieu worked by her mother,
where she stared ahead unseeingly, past the small, sim-

ple altar with its white, embroidered cloth and the fresh grasses the girls had found by the river, through the two tall, slender, deep-embrasured windows with their narrow slits to the waving trees, gaunt in their winter nakedness, which clothed the semicircular end wall of the chapel.

She said her penance, dwelling upon every word of each of the fifty Aves, and was rewarded, as she had scarcely hoped to be, by a deep flood of peace which came to her at the end. God had forgiven her this filthiness, as he had forgiven more and less in every man each day. She poured out a joyful prayer of gratitude, and then made a special offering to Saint Mary of Magdala, the patron of all women fallen into carnal sin. From now on, she would take the Magdalen as her own special guardian. The pallor left her face and even she smiled a little. Father Sebastian had tried so hard to bring her comfort; for his sake, and, yes, because it always pleased her, she would dwell a little upon the past.

Her wedding day! What a splendid, golden day that had been! She had felt herself the happiest of maidens, for, unlike most girls, she was truly in love with her husband-to-be and certain of his love for her. It was not, he had laughingly assured her, fashionable to love one's own lady. The strict tenets of the philosophy of Courtly Love, the rage of the courts of Aquitaine and Champagne, and growing in England under the hand of Queen Eleanor, demanded that a knight should pine and sicken for love of another man's wife. Eden had privately thought this a waste of time, although she loved the stories of King Arthur and his knights as well as anyone, and listened, entranced, when a troubadour rehearsed the well-known tales before the fireside in the great hall. She knew herself woman enough, however, at fifteen, to hold fast to her Stephen, for she was aware of the power she possessed to make his blood run faster so that his breath came fiercely and he would suddenly push her away from him, race off and gallop White Edwin unmercifully across the hillside.

Hawisa had sewn the dress in which she was married, lovingly embroidering the fine, white linen with gold thread about the neck and hem and the long points of the sleeves. She had worn a green veil, to catch the color of her eyes; crowned with a gold fillet, it had fallen, mingling with her unbound hair, far below her waist, like a shower of ripening wheat. She had been grave and composed, conscious of the solemnity of the occasion. Her cheeks had been pale, but she had bitten her lips hard, to make them red and swollen. This gave her a provocative air of innocence and experience combined which caused many a grown man to feel his loins tighten as he drank the bride-toast with a will. But Eden had looked only toward her father, whom she loved, and Stephen, whom she was sure she would love forever.

There had been the brief, simple service in this very chapel after the mass, with the holy words that bound them together spoken amid sheaves of spring flowers that the village maidens had brought to honor her. Stephen had looked like Galahad himself, so straight and proud before the altar. He had been tall for his age and slender, narrow of waist and hip. The light from the scarlet wax candles lit his fine, softly waving copper hair to flame, and filled his brilliant blue eyes with a wondering exultation. Dazed, they had sat through the feast that followed, hands twined fast together, eating little, drinking more perhaps, scarcely speaking, so amazed were they that this day had come to them at last.

Suddenly, in her place of honor at the head of the board, Eden had been seized by a small, growing whirlwind of panic. She and Stephen had been happy together with their hawks and horses and dogs, their dreams, and tales and plans for a future that had always seemed like one of the dreams. Had it not been enough to lie beside the brook at the day's end, holding hands and talking softly, whether of the Holy Grail or the loss of a pewter goblet? Must they now lie in the broad bed she had shared with none save Hawisa during some childhood sickness? Must they become a

man and his wife and make heirs for the domain of
Hawkhurst? She knew well enough how this was done;
Hawisa had even insisted that there was pleasure to be
had from it, though it was not to be expected the first
time. But Eden could not picture herself, less than a
year hence, with a baby at her breast. Why, her breasts
were scarce grown! Perhaps, after all, she was not yet a
woman; perhaps she did not even want to be!
Looking up at her new husband through lowered
lashes, she had worried and wondered and drunk far
too much wine, so that soon the guests, who were still
seated modestly before the board, seemed to be dancing before her eyes.

She did not remember when the dancing started in
earnest, nor yet could she have said when it ended.
Her next recollection was of sitting stiffly next to
Stephen in the great bed, as if they were figures newly
carved for a tombstone, with the curtains drawn back
so that all might pass through the solar and offer their
congratulations. Eden wore a new white shift, with a
rose-colored ribbon at its neck, while Stephen, she
was shamingly conscious, wore nothing at all. The
women had filled the bed with quantities of herbs;
there were mint, mustard and dog's mercury, all to
provoke a healthy lust in the young couple, then
motherwort and stinking arrach to ensure that this
would lead to instant conception, and lastly a great deal
of lavender, simply for the sweetness of its scent.
What they did ensure, most certainly, was a great deal
of prickling discomfort to the naked skin. Nevertheless,
they had responded with a good grace to the admonitions, encouragements and lewd jokes showered upon
them by their guests, in their various stages of drunkenness, all of whom had seemed to press into the
chamber at once, so that they were very glad of the
lavender in the stifling atmosphere. In the great hall,
the minstrels played sweet love songs and bawdy
ballads, while the roaring serfs capered and drank
themselves as incapable as their masters. The dancing
would go on well into the night, now that the putting-
to-bed was done. Eden though that she had never in

her life heard such a din, unless it had been at the
spring cattle fair in Canterbury.

At long last they were left alone and she had fallen
back upon the pillows, light-headed with wine and
weariness.

"That was a day and a half!" she had told him,
smiling nervously up at him, her green eyes enormous,
the sheets pulled up tightly beneath her arms.

"And shall we say that, in the morning, love, of the
night that's to come?" he had teased her gently, well
aware of her fears, though he suffered none of a similar
nature; he had been tumbling willing village girls since
the age of fourteen. A man must learn to be a man,
especially if he is soon to be married, but he had not
been intemperate; lechery was not among his vices.
He was aware of the need for an heir and had made
sure of his ability to get one.

He loved the increasingly lovely girl who had been
his companion for so long, and had every intention of
being gentle and considerate with her, awakening her
young body into an awareness of pleasure without
any suddenness to frighten her innocence.

"Why do you hide your breasts from me?" he had
asked, gently pulling away the sheets so that he might
see their rosy tips.

She had felt herself blushing. "Do you like them?
They are very small."

He had smiled. "That is just the way I like them.
A woman with large breasts is ungainly, like a cow in
calf; a girl with tiny, budding ones like these is like a
deer in flight." He had kissed them, tenderly, one by
one.

"Shall you not like me when I am carrying our
children?" she had asked.

His smile was brief. "We need not think of that yet,"
he said. "Now . . . lie down and let yourself relax, and
you will see how good it is to be married."

And he had kissed and caressed her wondering body,
softly at first, his eyes lingering on her trusting, questioning face, and then, as he explored his new-found
territory more eagerly, an urgency came to him, and

he began to employ what he had learned of expertise to arouse her to an answering desire, deepening and teasing her expectation, until at last she was one with him in delight.

Eden came to herself with a sudden shock of self-reproach, recalling where she was and the reason for her presence; the good father's strictures had most certainly not intended her to dwell upon her wedding night as well as the day before it.

In an attempt to concentrate upon holy things, she muttered more Aves and Paters. But, though her lips mechanically formed the syllables, she could not keep her wayward thoughts in order. They circled about the fear at their center like impatient carrion crows, so that at last she was forced to look at it. Despite her present state of grace, the horror would return with Sir Hugo.

"Mary, blessed Mother, protect me! Show me the way!" she begged in agony. Then, in place of an Ave, she was crying aloud to Stephen, lost among the legendary cities of Islam. Was he living, or not? If he lived, did he ever think of the wife who now needed him so desperately? "You should be here!" she cried, "to look to your lands and your duty . . . and to me! You have given two years to the Holy Sepulchre. God will be satisfied! It is long enough. You must come home!"

Mopping at her wet face, Eden gazed stonily in front of her, prayers forgotten in the return of her despair. Her eyes focused upon the admonition carved into the high arch supporting the roof behind the altar. "Honor God and the King." The words danced across her tired mind in meaningless repetition. God had forsaken her, after all, she thought dully; he would permit the terrible thing to happen to her again, and to Hawkhurst. As for the King . . . he was a friend to the very man who had encompassed her destruction. There was no redress, whatever the priest might say, no redress for the weak. And then a new thought came to her. The King might not care for her wrongs, perhaps, but the King was no longer in England; he was on his way to the Holy Land to take back the Sepulchre from Saladin. But there remained, ruling in his place, Eleanor, the Queen Mother. A powerful woman, in her youth she had dared much to have the directing of her own life. Imprisoned by her husband, the old King, Henry II, it was said for stirring up his own sons to sedition against him, she made a court of her prison at Winchester and lived there still, unwilling to move after sixteen long years of her husband's displeasure. She would know much of the wrongs of women. And now, ruling with the aid of the Chancellor and the Justiciars, she would have the power to right such wrongs.

Suddenly, through the tall, attenuated windows beyond the archway, there came two swift, sudden shafts of thin sunlight, striking down toward the white-clothed altar and on to the honey-colored stones before it; the shafts came together to meet where Eden rested her knees upon the prie-dieu; it happened as swiftly as it must have done in that first moment, she thought, when He had cried, "Let there be light!"

She knew she had been blessed with a sign. The shaft of sunlight was a sword put into her hand, a weapon to aid her weakness. She knew, then, that she must rise and make herself ready at once to leave Hawkhurst; she must go now, this very morning.

She would ride to Winchester, to see the Queen.

▼▼▼▼▼▼▼▼▼▼▼▼▼▼▼▼▼▼▼▼▼▼▼▼▼▼▼▼▼▼▼▼▼▼▼▼▼

CHAPTER TWO

Winchester

Eden left Hawkhurst a mere two hours later. During that time, going unruffled about her business beneath the eyes of Sir Hugo's retainers, she had managed to hold a secret interview with her bailiff, spoken to her most trusted serfs and commiserated, somewhat unnecessarily, she gathered from their bright eyes and pert manners, with the three pretty girls who had suffered a similar fate to her own. Rosy, plump Matty had simply shrugged, saying, "When it happens, it happens; a maid can't look out for herself all the time!"

"Well, come to Hawisa with your problem when the need arises," Eden told them sharply. "The Forest Woman has too harsh a way with misbegettings!" She did not even allow herself to think what would be her own plight if Hawisa's way proved too gentle.

While those of Sir Hugo's men who were about the house were entertained to a midday meal of a generosity exceeding all expectation, she collected together every portable article of value she owned; happily, this amounted to a good deal, as Sir Godfrey had constantly given her jewels upon her birthdays and feast days, all of the finest quality and workmanship. When at last she was ready to take her leave, she carried a knight's ransom in her saddlebags. To protect herself and her fortune, she took Rollo and five other serfs, all young and strong. The departure was necessarily a stealthy one; each man stole away separately from the midday ease-time to the forest glade where Eden and Rollo would meet them. There was no danger of encountering Sir Hugo, whose purlieus lay in the opposite direction from that they must take. Rollo was doubtful about the transport of so great a fortune in jewels. "Would you rather I had left them for the Baron's pleasure?" she demanded icily. She did not, since her strong right arm seemed so nervous, tell him about the Jew's gold which she had in a purse beneath her shift.

Father Sebastian had been sorrowful and filled with trepidation at her departure, but had agreed, when Eden put it to him with more truth than modesty, that it was better than staying to warm Sir Hugo's bed. Hawisa, sage woman, had been grimly approving. She had heard nothing but good of Queen Eleanor and could not but think the journey worth the attempt.

"Be sure, the house will look the same when you return," she promised staunchly, "however long it may be. That black-avised miscreant will get no hold on *my* housekeeping, never fear."

The tale they had devised to pacify Sir Hugo, was that Eden, in mortal fear for her soul and distress of spirit, had gone on pilgrimage to Canterbury, to confess and hear mass in the great cathedral. It was likely that he would accept this, since everyone knows that it is far more efficacious to pray in a cathedral than in a mere village church, or one's own chapel.

Hawisa was crowing in her expectations. "He'll be after you, hotfoot, tomorrow, mark my words! And when he returns empty-fisted, be sure we shall all set up such a wail as you never heard since the Tower of Babel! He'll not suspect, my lady, my chuck. He'll know nothing till you ride back with a fine troop of men at your back . . . and the Queen's warrant to arrest the black devil!"

The first part of the plan worked well. By the time she and her small escort reached their first night's resting-place, Eden had ceased to look nervously behind her. They had ridden some miles and were weary enough to care little for the discomforts of the meager inn, just off the pitted road. Her last waking thought, as she lay down in the broad, lumpy bed beside the substantial forms of three burghers' wives traveling to Guildford, was that, unlovely though her companions were in their spreading, guttural slumbers, she would treasure their memory always, for the sake of the one that might have taken their place. Again she thanked the blessed Magdalen for the divine inspiration for her journey.

At dawn she breakfasted on hard bread and sour ale with the serfs, all of whom were scratching heartily and cursing the vermin-infested straw of the stable where they had slept; the fleas, they complained, were of a different breed to those they were accustomed to.

However, they had suffered two more such nights and such breakfasts before, at last, they rode thankfully into the stream of travelers on the highroad into Winchester, and were as accustomed to Sussex fleas as to Kentish ones. The road to the ancient capital was always busy and crowded, and they slowed their pace, willing and eager to exchange news and gossip with any who wished. Eden learned from a much-traveled clerk that the Queen was indeed at home in her palace prison, but that when the latest word came, some five or six weeks back, King Richard had not reached Jerusalem. He was still on the island of Sicily where he had captured the town of Messina after taking exception to the behavior of the Sicilian King, Tancred, on the matter of a dowry belonging to the Lionheart's sister, Joanna. She heard from a butcher's wife how two devils had been cast out of a woman in Gloucester, who had nonetheless given birth to a deformed child, which had, of course, been instantly destroyed. She was told how one Wat, a charcoal-burner of the New Forest, had failed to lose his hands for poaching the King's deer because the King had sold immunity to forest law to the knights of the county for two hundred marks; the Justices of the forest had held that poor folk's punishments should be softened accordingly. The scandalous price of wax candles was bemoaned among the ladies, ambling contentedly upon stout palfreys, as were those of spun linen, blue and scarlet wool and embroidery threads. Eden was glad of their company; their untiring gossip kept her mind from flying ahead to torment her with ways and means to reach the

Queen, or how she might frame her case when she did attain the presence of that august lady.

The inns of Winchester were full to overflowing, as, unfortunately, were the conduits, and it was an hour before Rollo could secure a place for Eden; two of her serfs could use the stable; the others would have to fend for themselves in the yard with the pigs and geese.

Grateful that her quest had begun in earnest, Eden climbed the ricked and uneven stair to the upper chamber which she would share with only two others, both ladies of high birth, as the hostess assured her, casting a shrewd eye over her clothing and person. She asked for water to be brought and washed herself from head to foot as best she could from the basin, shivering in the unheated chamber, but glad to remove the sweat and grime of the journey. The scrawny kitchen slut who brought the water gave her opinion that Eden would surely catch cold and die, it being dangerous to bath all over before the spring, even for a lady such as herself.

The only dress she considered fit to show at court had been rolled behind her saddle with her best cloak and the soft-soled boots of gray, polished leather that Stephen had given her. The dress was of a very fine wool, the color of sapphires; she hoped the creases would hang out of it before she reached the palace. It looked very well on her, she knew, with the broad, gold cincture just beneath her waist and the jeweled medallion of the Virgin on her breast. Her cloak was of heavy, rough-woven material, a darker blue, with sleeves and hood lined with gray coney. She combed and replaced her hair in its bright coils, then freshened her neck and brow with some of the precious gillyflower water she had brought from home. She had no means of seeing the result of her efforts, but the kitchen wench's wistful look, as she made her curtsy when Eden left, told her all she needed to know.

With Rollo riding at a respectful pace behind her, his hair smoothed in honor of the occasion, she set off on her roan horse, Balan, for the palace, kilting her skirts up around her saddle as they moved through the mired and narrow streets. She admired the neat, two-story houses, built of wood, their interstices of wattle and daub, the roofs thatched with reeds or straw or perhaps wooden shingles. A few of the more imposing dwellings were of stone, with slate roofs and jutting gables. Everywhere the stench of excrement and rotting matter was strong enough to make Eden choke at first and think herself lucky to live away from a town.

The royal palace was a prominent and impressive building, all of stone, its roof rearing high above its neighbors, its many entrances guarded by stolid pikemen.

There was a crowd of people of all stations dressed in their best, milling about outside, and Eden found that she must join a long queue of those who wished to petition the Queen. Eleanor saw as many as she could for two to three hours, several mornings in the week, and at no other time. There must already have been nearly one hundred persons before her; it was clear that she would not reach the Queen this way.

"At what time does her Grace stop seeing supplicants?" she inquired of a soberly dressed woman in a clean, white coif, patiently telling her beads as she waited.

"At noon, my lady," the woman answered, ducking into a curtsy. Eden thanked the woman and walked away from the jostling queue, Rollo striding stolidly at her heels.

"What now, my lady?" he asked as she came to an abrupt halt outside a baker's shop.

Sniffing absently at the delicious scent of fresh baked bread, she found she was exceedingly hungry; inn fare was no substitute for her own board. "I'll not slink away and return tomorrow!" she announced. "Time is precious; I must gain my ends before the Baron comes home from Canterbury and starts asking his questions more seriously; I don't want to find my courtyard full of lopped ears and hands when I return!" Rollo looked uncomfortable.

"No," Eden said decisively, "I shall go back to the palace now . . . not as a petitioner, but as a lady of birth and standing who expects to be well received!"

The serf nodded as if it were the most natural thing in the world, although he must have been aware that his mistress was stepping beyond her station. Had she been indeed the wife of Sir Hugo de Malfors, she might have taken an entree to the royal court as her due. As the wife of his liegeman, a young knight, yet to prove himself, she had no such privilege. Nevertheless, she could not bear the idea of simply waiting about in Winchester until she reached the head of that lengthy queue of supplicants. Neither must she waste her store of money and jewels in buying her way to its head as she had seen an impatient cleric doing not ten minutes since, holding his spice box to his nose as he waved away the lowly farm tenant, in his sacking leggings, who complained that he had already waited three days for his place.

"Look to the horses, Rollo. See that they are fed and fit for the journey home. Wait here for me, at four o'clock. If I am not prompt, stay until I come."

The serf made his bow. "May God bless your errand, my Lady Eden!"

She smiled at him and turned resolutely back toward the palace. A plan had occurred to her, simple, but the more like to succeed; all it required was the confidence to carry it out. This time she did not approach the door whence the long queue still stretched, but walked round the high walls until she came to another, smaller, door, guarded by two men-at-arms.

"My Lady?" said one inquiringly, his eyes frankly assessing her beauty.

"I am a relative of Lady de Burgh," she answered haughtily, without lessening her stride. This was one of the most prestigious names in the kingdom and belonged to a woman whose nobility was only matched by her uncertain temper. The guards sprang to an immediate salute.

"God forgive me the lie!" Eden thought as she swept into the palace, her head high, mien icy.

She found herself in a broad hallway where a small knot of guards fended off boredom by throwing dice. They ignored her as she stalked past them into the first chamber she reached.

This was a large anteroom, of similar proportions to those of the great hall at Hawkhurst, with the same lofty, raftered ceiling and a wonderfully solid wooden floor; there were several tall windows along one wall and a glowing hearth at the far end of the chamber. Various people, most of them courtiers or clerks, sat about in low-back seats, engaged in conversation, while others were hunched over the backgammon tables or busily deciphering a closely penned roll of parchment. At a table near the fire, a graybearded man wrote laboriously in a great book. His bearing and his richly furred gown proclaimed him some kind of court official, so Eden took her courage in both hands and approached him at once.

"Pray, sir, will you be good enough to tell me where I might find the chamber where the Queen's ladies take their recreation? I am visiting a relative and am not familiar with the palace."

The man looked up and subjected her to a deep considering scrutiny. Apparently reassured by what he saw, he signaled to a yellow-haired boy who lounged against the wall. "Sir Squire, you are to take this lady to the solar of the dames-in-waiting to the Queen!"

The boy grinned at her. "Glad to be of service to such unparalleled beauty! Do you stay long in Winchester?" he asked as he led her through two more chambers and up a twisting stairway.

"I trust not," replied Eden, teasing his curiosity; she did not object to his obvious admiration; it bolstered her confidence at a time when she needed it all.

"You do not enjoy the life at court?" he said incredulously. Eden only smiled.

They entered the ladies' solar; this was a spacious chamber with an attractive semicircle of slender, decorated windows to one side of it; the walls were hung with brightly colored tapestries depicting the life and martyrdom of Saint Ursula. Some half dozen very young ladies reclined upon upholstered benches along the walls or upon one of the two wide, heavily curtained beds. One idled softly over her lute; others worked at embroidery; one consumed sweetmeats as if she had been starved for a month. All looked up as they entered.

"Is there ought else I may do for you, lady?" inquired the tow-haired squire.

Eden thought. "Yes," she said then, as though she ordered one of her own household. "You may bring me something to eat, for I am famished!"

The boy grinned crookedly and disappeared.

Without betraying any of the uncertainty she felt, Eden stepped forward and introduced herself to the assembled ladies; all murmured back names of exalted and irreproachable lineage; she kept her head high, thankful that her father had served the old King well in his time and that her name, too, was respected by all who knew of it.

Three of the girls were from Aquitaine, with the dark, glossy head and snapping eyes of the Duchy; two were English heiresses and the last, a small, black-haired girl with kind, soft eyes and a dreaming look, spoke so low that she did not catch her words. The plump blonde who was eating the sweetmeats held the dish generously toward her. "Gilles will take an age! He has to stop before every attractive lady in the palace . . . so that he may admire his own reflection in their eyes!" Eden laughed, accepting a comfit. "Tell me," she begged the plump girl, whose name was Mathilde, "does Lady de Burgh stay within the palace at this time?"

The girl gave a mock shudder of horror. "No, by my faith! She has taken herself off on pilgrimage to Canterbury for the good of her wicked old soul!" A barely suppressed giggle ran round the small circle. "Forgive me," Mathilde went on, "you have some interest in my Lady de Burgh?"

Eden, relaxing into her now wholly comfortable fiction, took her lead, wrinkling her mouth in distaste as she said apologetically, "Alas, she is a cousin of ours, and I have been summoned to court to visit her; she does not like the family to be remiss in its duty."

The giggle became an outright laugh. "I know precisely what you mean, *ma chère!* But you may forget the old harridan and enjoy yourself for a week at least. The lady's sins lay heavily enough upon her soul for a month!" Mathilde was only faintly contrite. "I should not speak thus of your kin . . . but the dame has not been kind; we suffered greatly under her tongue while she was Mistress of the Queen's robes. But sit you down and let us forget her."

"I do not love the lady," Eden said quietly, doing as she was bid and sinking into a vast pile of soft cushions that lay upon the bed. Mathilde pushed the comfits close to her hand and one of the French girls brought a goblet of sweet wine. "Tell me," said Eden, addressing the small, black-haired girl who had smiled so sweetly and spoken so softly, "will it be possible for me to speak with Queen Eleanor today? There is a matter on which I would take her good council."

The dark girl, whose eyes were gray and quiet, looked surprised. "But of course, she comes to us very soon, for the music hour. Do you know her Grace?"

Eden shook her head. Her pretext suddenly seemed to her very thin.

The dark girl's eyes became soft. "Then you will love her; she is a most excellent lady . . . and I do not think she has any fondness for your cousin!"

Curiosity chased away any discomfort as Eden asked, "Is her Grace very old? I have heard it said that she must have reached seventy. It is a great age."

The dark head shook itself forcefully. "She has no age," the girl said.

Plump Mathilde took up the strain, her hand hovering above the near empty dish of sweetmeats. "She is still very beautiful; you will see. And the most gifted woman in Christendom. She does everything exquisitely; her embroidery is a work of consummate artistry; she has written countless ballads and lays of love and chivalry. She plays the lute like King David himself! She has the mind of Solomon . . . and a tongue like the sword of Saladin when she pleases!"

"She is no longer young . . . but she loves to have young people about her," tall, cool Lady Alys continued, her blue-gray gaze considering Eden as she spoke. "She has taught each one of us to read, who could not, and insists that we all play an instrument and must write good Latin. She makes us care as much for our minds as we do for our bodies, even though we are women. And she has promised she will not give us in marriage to any knight who does not value us as much for our accomplishments as for our fortunes!"

Something in Lady Alys's look made Eden very glad that she could read and write.

The little, dark girl smiled in sudden reminiscence. "She said to me once, when we sported together, 'Let your wits go hawking too.' She is magnificent."

Eden did not know whether to be reassured or apprehensive at the prospect of encountering this paragon among women.

"It is well you came to us today," Mathilde told her, pouring more wine, "for soon her Grace will leave England for a time; she goes within the fortnight."

Eden thanked the Blessed Magdalen for her foresight. "Leave England? She journeys to France?"

"Further than that!" Mathilde looked slyly at her dark, contained companion. "As far as : . . the heart's desire! Is that not so, Berengaria?"

The gray-eyed girl blushed and Eden's eyes grew wide. Surely she could not be . . . And yet Berengaria was no common name. But this quiet girl seemed neither to expect nor to receive any different treatment from the others.

"Then where is that?" she pursued gently.

The girl's blush deepened. "The Queen is escorting me to Sicily . . . where I shall soon be married to the King." Her eyes, no longer quiet, held a deep glow of pride.

So it was true. This was Berengaria of Navarre, the Princess who would wed the Lionheart. It was too late for her to fall on one knee; Eden was simply thankful that these high-born girls had so easily accepted her as one of them.

"Allow me to add my congratulations to the hundreds you will have received," she offered softly. "He is the most perfect knight in Christendom."

The Princess looked down, her expression diffident. "To be sure, but . . . I have never met him," she said breathlessly.

"It can't be true!"

"Oh yes," the Lady Alys took over her tale. "The Queen has been trying to get King Richard safely married for months, ever since the old King died. He was never still long enough, rushing hither and yon to take in money for the Crusade; she could not get him to see that England needs its next heir soon . . . saving your presence, Berengaria. Or Prince John or Prince Arthur of Brittany will whistle away his throne while he goes gadding off to Outremer."

Eden nodded sagely; she had already heard something of this; court rumor ever rode swift horses in the home shires. But she had hardly expected to find herself discussing the King's marriage on intimate terms with the lady whom it most concerned. She began to feel a little unreal. Only Lady Alys's calm, considering stare held her back from the sudden wild euphoria that threatened her.

"I only hope that he will . . . like me," whispered Berengaria worriedly.

"Of course he will," said Lady Mathilde affectionately. "You have only to smile at him and he will be bewitched."

At that point the chamber doors were flung apart and a tall woman entered, sword-straight and walking briskly. The high, noble head, with the sharp, clear bones defined beneath the tautened skin needed no coronet to denote its majesty. Fine eyes, blue as thin ice by moonlight, lit immediately upon the stranger in the solar, even as she swept across to the one seat left empty. Eleanor, "by the Wrath of God, Queen of the English," as she was wont to style herself, did not look seventy years old. She had, as Berengaria had said, no age; she was simply a rare and accomplished fact, as certain and as vibrant as the deep chord upon the lute with which the lady Mathilde inadvertently greeted her arrival.

"Thank you my dear! Remind me to find you a trumpet, if you have an inclination to become a herald! You would resemble one of the cherubim!" There was a general smile as they contemplated the irresistible picture of Mathilde's pink cheeks, even plumper as she blew the fanfare.

But the intensely clear eyes were upon Eden. The Queen waited.

The Princess Berengaria swiftly stepped forward. "May I present the Lady Eden of Hawkhurst, of the Honor of Stukesey, your Grace. She has come to visit her cousin, Lady de Burgh, who . . . unhappily . . . is not here."

"A cousin, you say?" Eden suffered the most searching scrutiny of her adventure. The Queen sniffed. "I see no resemblance. Just as well. You are welcome, my Lady Eden. I am sure you have been made to feel so?"

A long hand was extended and Eden kissed it, grateful for Berengaria's championship.

"And now, *mes enfants* . . . what shall we have to cheer us today? I have a new tune for the '*Lancan vei la folha*' of my good old Bernart de Ventadorn. Ah, there was a troubadour! There was fire in his veins and the persuasion of Orpheus in his strain!" The Queen snapped impatient fingers to the page who, unnoticed, had followed in her wake; he handed her the small, full-bellied viol which he carried and stepped back to his place beside the wall. Eleanor's voice was still rich and full, without a quaver, filled with emotional light and shade; the sweet, lighter girls' voices soon took up the melody and the room was golden with the music of love and the coming of the spring.

"And now . . . shall we make a wedding song for Berengaria?" suggested Mathilde when they had finished.

"An excellent idea; it should contain the rhythms of

her native Spain," the Queen began, tuning a few strings that had become discordant. At this point the door opened once more.

It was the yellow-haired Gilles, bearing a pewter tray on which reposed a plate of meats, fruit, a jug of wine, a bowl of water and a napkin.

"What's this?" Eleanor lifted elegant brows.

The squire bent a respectful knee. "The lady with the golden hair requested food, your Grace!"

It was Eden's turn, now, to blush. The Queen put down her viol, waving to the boy to put down his burden and leave them.

"Have you not yet broken your fast, Lady Eden?" The tone was kindly but curious.

Eden knew that this was the time to reveal herself: she could not continue to accept such gladly given hospitality and trust, knowing herself to be an imposter. She must tell the truth and hope that Eleanor would not be too harsh with her. "I have forgotten whether I did or not," she began frankly, "it was some time since." She saw the stern jaw quiver slightly and, encouraged, plunged into her tale. "I am not quite what I seem, your Grace," she started.

"Few of us are!" remarked Eleanor dryly.

"I mean . . . I am here under somewhat false pretences . . ."

"Somewhat?" The tone was formidable.

Aware of the hushed and amazed curiosity about her, Eden was greatly assisted by Berengaria's reassuring smile, as she swiftly outlined the events that had brought her to Winchester.

When she had finished she bowed her head. She had forgotten her shame during this last, unlooked-for, gilded hour; she had even forgotten that she was a married woman, and responsible for a rich and large domain; she had been a girl again, at ease with carefree companions. Now, her trouble hung over her again in all its sordid heaviness and she could no longer meet the gentle, wondering eyes around her.

There was one gaze, however, which held the power to force her to meet it. Almost unaware that she did so, Eden lifted her chin and looked squarely into a face that had seen and recognised and forgiven far greater wrongs than those within her own small compass.

"You did right in coming to me, child," the Queen said, and her smile was an absolution. "You shall have your redress. And at once. We must give your baron no time to make further mischief. Robert!" The fingers snapped like whiphide. "Seek out William de Longchamps and ask him if he will come to me at once in the green chamber." The page was gone.

Longchamps, Chancellor of Aquitaine in the old King's day, was now the great Chancellor of England and the only man who could be truly said to rule in King Richard's place, though his base blood disqualified him from the more honorable title of Justiciar. The Count of Essex and the Bishop of Durham divided that spoil between them, but while enjoying richly the appurtenances of their office, neither interfered much with William where work was concerned.

"I will send a troop of horsemen, with six knights, carrying my great seal, to turn de Malfors from your doors. I shall fine him several hundred marks for the coffers of Outremer, and one of the knights and his menie shall remain to keep the peace for as long as you may wish it." The noble features expressed grave distaste. "If the Baron of Stukesey were a mere serf, I'd have his manhood for what he has done. And we'll make him dance a little to my tune, for all his blue blood. I remember the man; I have seen him about the court when my son was here; a drunkard and a quarreler, black-avised. I did not like him."

Eden bowed low in acknowledgement of all she would receive. She kissed the slender fingers again in fierce gratitude.

But Eleanor had not finished. "You do not find yourself unhappy amongst us, I think, Lady Eden? And your voice lends depth to the music of my singing birds. Why then, do you not remain with us awhile . . . at least, until we go to Sicily. I am sure you would prefer to find your household just as it was when you left it . . . and, for a few days, there may be some slight affray."

Eleanor saw the girl's remarkable green eyes fill with light. She nodded and rose. "I shall give William de Longchamps most detailed instructions," she assured Eden. Then, with the seven girls bowing like slender, blown birches behind her, she was gone, her long veil looped over her arm, lest it impede her swift and certain step.

The next few days were an idyll for Eden; she had not enjoyed herself so greatly since she was first married and discovering what it was like to be in love. There was the same light-headed, open-hearted atmosphere about the Queen's young waiting-women. Eleanor spent a great deal of time consulting grayer and wiser heads than theirs, but it was amongst them that she came for renewal and enjoyment, drinking in their youth and happy expectation of life and giving them her wry wisdom, heavily laced with humor, in return. Eden was grateful for the easy friendship that was offered her. If the Lady Alys was occasionally reluctant to sing a duet or to play at draughts with her, Mathilde more than compensated for this slight frigidity with her unfailing, uncomplicated warmth.

Of the three girls Eden found herself more and more drawn to Berengaria, whose gentle, hesitant and trusting nature complemented her own more aggressive spirit. She saw how, had they but met, they might have been friends from childhood, each one providing what the other lacked. It had been so, she recognized, between her and Stephen. He had always been the dreamer and she the one to realize all possible dreams; he the flint and she the spark. Until he had heard the archbishop preach and had been fired to take the Cross.

Not for the first time, the little Princess sighed that she would miss her new friend beyond bearing when the Queen's menie left for Sicily.

"If only you might come with us!" she mused, as she and Eden rehearsed the contents of her dower chest, discarding and exchanging gowns, cloaks, belts, veils and gloves, until the solar resembled the unruly marketplace in the nearby city square. Her words, only half serious, hung in the air, unanswered.

Then Eden suddenly sat back on her heels, the embroidered linen shifts she held in danger of being crushed between newly tense fingers. "Why not?" she said.

"Why not what?" Berengaria was not looking at her, being in doubt over the usefulness of knitted leggings beneath the Syrian sun; her mother had knitted them before she came to England; they were scarlet and green and very fine.

"Why should I not come with you?" Eden stared at her, green eyes brilliant with inspiration. "You will need many waiting-women. A tiring-maid for your wedding! You have said three times that none can dress your hair as I do. I must come! And then, after you are married, and the Lionheart sails on to take Jerusalem . . ." she breathed deeply and almost shouted her wonderful revelation, "Then I shall take leave of you and go to Stephen!" She was amazed that she had been already a week in Winchester and had not thought of it.

Berengaria's eyes were glazed with admiration. "Why not, indeed?" she whispered.

Eden raced ahead. "I shall find the information I need—of that I am certain. Stephen rode under the command of Sir Walter of Langford; he is well-known and much esteemed and I shall find him without difficulty. Then I shall ask him to release Stephen from his Crusader's oath—so that when I have discovered where he is I may bring him safe home to Hawkhurst." Tears stood in her eyes now. Impatiently she dashed them away.

"Will you speak to the Queen on my behalf?" she begged urgently. "She loves you well, I think, and will not refuse you."

Berengaria smiled. "I do not think she would refuse if you were to make the request yourself; you have touched some deep chord in her. But yes, I will ask her; I would like to do something to help you. I don't

know how your Stephen could leave you so much
alone," she added passionately. Then her face saddened
a little. "I hope that the Crusade will not keep Richard,
also, too much from my side." She sighed softly.

Eden spoke slowly. "It is the King's duty, as leader
of all Christian knights, to drive the infidel from our
Holy Sepulchre; it is Stephen's duty, I know, to follow
his cause. But Richard has good men to govern in his
stead; Stephen has only one weak woman who cannot
hold his fief—and the Queen's justice cannot hold it
forever. If—the Baron—took up arms against us, that
quarrel should be between him and Stephen. At all
events, there is much work for my husband to do at
Hawkhurst—and he must come home to it. And to me,
for in truth I miss him as a father and a brother
and a companion in all things—as much as I need him
as a husband," she finished looking straight before her
and trying to concentrate upon the intricate pattern
traced upon the silver goblet she held in her hand.
It swam before her and instead, she saw Stephen's
sweet, serious face as he had bidden her farewell, its
lines fading even as she atttempted to catch at them.
It had been too long.

"Oh Berengaria!" she cried in sudden distress, "I
can hardly remember his face!"

The Princess squeezed her trembling hand in sympathy. "I will speak to the Queen," she promised,
"today."

She was as good as her word and Eden soon found
herself following the admiring Gilles, his hair a positive haystack, along yards of cold corridor to the room
where Eleanor did the work she liked least, the balancing, by sleight of mind and *legerdemain* of time and
money, of the accounts of the royal household. The blue
veins stood out upon the broad forehead as the Queen
scowled over a monstrous ledger open upon the table
before her, a roll of parchment beside it. "You have
a request to make," the husky voice declared. "Make
it."

More than apprehensive before this unjoyful mood,

Eden did so. She was brief. Then there was a silence
while Eleanor glared and stabbed at the document beside the ledger, her pen dipped in scarlet ink.

"My son," she drawled, without looking up, "has decreed that the only women who are to be permitted
to accompany his Crusaders are bathwomen and what
he hopefully designates as 'washerwomen of good
character.' I am unable, try as I will, to conceive of
you, dear Lady Eden, as either of these."

Eden clenched her hands at her side. "I have
bathed my husband before the fire like many other
women," she said stubbornly, "and I can launder lin-
en as well as any, aye, and use a flatiron without burning a hole. As to my character, your Grace is the best
judge of that, for I think you know it, by now, for
whatever it may be." She saw no change in the fine-
boned face, and added, trying not to allow desperation into her tone. "I have become greatly attached to
the Princess Berengaria—and would count it a privilege
to serve as her waiting-woman."

Eleanor gave a grunt of disgust. "Twenty marks for
robes with squirrel fur for the knight dispensers! Do
these monsters of avarice take me for a fool? I'll manage my household myself if that's to be the way of it."
Her brows disappeared into her crisp wimple and a
shower of ink crimsoned the page. Then she looked up,
her expression less severe. "My dear, have you thought
all this through quite thoroughly? What if there should
be no news to be had of your husband?"

"Then I shall seek until I find some trace of him,"
declared Eden. "No man can disappear from the face of
the earth."

"I shall stay with my son for a very brief time, a
matter of days perhaps. And if this is not long enough
for you to accomplish your mission, will you rest content to stay with my daughter-in-law in Outremer? It
is far from your home and your duty; it may also be
extremely uncomfortable. It is, after all, a land at war."

"I shall be content. I cannot rest until I have found
Stephen."

The Queen looked up and met her eyes. "How if he be dead?"

"Then I shall come home; doubtless there will be many returning who will be my escort."

Eleanor nodded, satisfied. Lightening the mood, she asked brightly, "And shall you like to see the Holy Land, my lady? I swear you will, for it is very fair."

Eden recalled how the Queen herself had taken the cross, when, as a girl, she had accompanied her first husband, King Louis of France, upon the Second Crusade.

"It is a land of blue and gold," the slightly grating voice reminisced. "The lands are endless beaten gold beneath the hammer of the sun; the seas and skies are ever changing blue upon blue; sapphire, turquoise, amethyst, azure . . . a country jeweled in splendor. I was young when I saw it first, and while others drooped and fainted I drank in my strength from that fierce, noble sun. Even the skies of Aquitaine were not so bright." The hawk's eyes gleamed with private recollection and Eden wondered if the Queen thought of her uncle, Raymond of Antioch. They had been two of a kind, it was said, the young Queen of France and the Christian Prince of Outremer, reckless, gay, confident, and much of an age. Their relationship of uncle and niece must have amused them. King Louis, so much older than his lovely and capricious wife, had been much preoccupied with the business of the Crusade; but then, he had always been preoccupied with some dry matter; a busy man, and a saintly one, but no match for the fiery Eleanor. "I have married a monk!" she had once forthrightly declared to the world. And Raymond of Antioch had been no monk. The scandal they had created so joyously between them had reverberated across a dozen lands and down several decades. And, watching that dark gleam in the Queen's fine eyes, Eden believed every word of it.

She smiled. "I want nothing more than to see the Holy Land, your Grace."

Eleanor thrust the offending sumpter list at Gilles, who was still standing alert at Eden's shoulder. "Take this to Master William and ask him how much we must really pay." Then, "Very well, my lady! You will be excellent company for Berengaria. You have a head on your shoulders and do not give in to adversity. You will do her good; she has been bred in a nest lined with silk, it is time she learned to fly."

Eden was so weakened by relief that her thanks were almost strangled in her throat. She hardly dared ask her next question. "And Hawkhurst," she began timidly, "my steward is loyal, but he's no soldier. If the Baron should attempt entry . . ."

"He won't! He will not be able to afford it!" Eleanor laughed dryly. "I don't suppose you can have the least conception of what it costs to raise and equip a Crusading army . . . let alone to run the country in its absence? My son has been heard to make the unfortunate remark that he would sell London if he could find a man rich enough to buy it. You will easily realize, therefore, that his mother will not scruple to sell, very dearly, the pardon of a Baron who has disgraced the name of Chivalry. Indeed, I should not wonder if Sir Hugo de Malfors finds himself forced to take the cross . . . if he wishes to recoup his fortunes after my little excursion into his domain. Have no fear for your lands, *ma chère;* they will be held safe and well husbanded until your return. My steward will be strongly armed as well as loyal."

Eden dropped to one knee in homage to her benefactor. Her face was alight with joy and Eleanor saw that she was even more beautiful than she had thought.

"When do we set sail?" the girl asked eagerly.

"In seven days," the Queen replied; adding with a reminiscent smile, "Get yourself a suit of mail. I did!"

Eden was curious. "And did you wear it, my Queen?"

"Constantly," the dry voice told her, "and it was frequently stuck with arrows so that I resembled a porcupine."

Before she could ask any more questions, Eden found herself summarily dismissed by an impatient wave of the elegant hand. The Queen was already frowning over the next item on her sumpter account.

As she hurried off to tell the good news to Berengaria, the Lady of Hawkhurst wondered whether her Queen was serious about the suit of mail.

"But of course! You will look magnificent!" Berengaria told her later in the warm tones of one who truly admires. "You should have it all of gold, naturally, to match your beautiful hair, but I daresay that will be too expensive."

"A little," Eden agreed gently. "We have already had to mortgage one of the farms to buy Stephen's hauberk and the gear for his squires and horses, and arms for his men. Besides, gold is too soft a metal to clothe a soldier. I should not fare long beneath the walls of Acre, dressed in gold mail; they say the arrows fall all day there, like Lincolnshire rain."

The Princess looked worried. "Will it really be like that? Shall we have to go there?"

Eden shook her head. "Not you, lady . . . but I may indeed do so; I intend to find Stephen, even though the search takes me into the middle of a battle."

"Then you had certainly better clothe yourself in mail. I shall make you a present of it." As Eden opened her mouth to protest, the dark girl stamped her foot and her friend was, for the first time, reminded of her Spanish blood.

"I will not refuse," she smiled. "I am grateful; you may save my life with your gift."

Berengaria clapped her hands. "Excellent! Then I shall ask where we must go for the best suit of mail in England!"

They must go, it seemed, for all were unanimous upon the subject, to the house of one Hugh the Armorer, not half a mile away from the palace.

Accordingly, the next morning, with much giggling and pulling down of hoods over brows, so that none should be able to name the two high-born damsels who occupied themselves with men's business, they muffled themselves extravagantly against the cold and sallied forth, Berengaria's purse filled to bursting point with gold marks. They would have been much cast down had they known that they had been observed and followed as they left the palace . . . and by no court diplomatist, seasoned in espionage, but merely by a certain tow-headed young esquire who had conceived an attachment of the most romantic sort for the fair Lady of Hawkhurst. Gilles was at present engaged upon a series of verses to extol her beauty, and it was just such nuances as he might expect that morning, the tossing of a cascade of gold over one shoulder as she turned a street corner, or the exposure of a dainty foot as she stepped across a puddle, that awakened the most exquisite imagery in the heart of a poet. The squire was also, it must be said, consumed with a burning curiosity about their destination.

Master Hugh's handsome house stood well back from the main concourse of a busy street adjoining the marketplace, his workshop the major part of it. The thoroughfare around his doors had degenerated into a veritable quagmire and sturdy boards had been thoughtfully placed across it for the convenience of his customers. Several horses stood outside, held by patient serfs while their masters sought Hugh's services for themselves or their mounts. The armorer had started in life as a blacksmith and his apprentices would still beat out a shoe or a bit for a regular visitor.

Eden led the Princess firmly across the tremulous planks that led up to the open door and, blinking once, stepped into the sultry gloom of the interior. "It's as hot and black here as in a crypt at a funeral!" she declared, holding out her hand to steady her friend's hesitant steps.

"And the noise! And the stench!" Berengaria wrinkled her short nose. "Are you sure we should not, perhaps, simply send some man about this matter?"

"Certainly not!" Eden was determined. "We've not ploughed through all that mud for nothing! Your ears and nose will soon accustom themselves!"

Hugh the Armorer's workshop was a deep cavern lit by two small, roaring, orange furnaces, orchestrated by the tenor clanging of several hammers in strenuous competition. Its limits were not immediately discernible but the glimmer of brass here and there suggested the walls were hung with harness for man and beast. There was the raw stench of newly tanned leather, hot coals and hotter metal, combined with the mixture of human and equine sweat that always hangs about a smithy.

"Why," murmured Eden, taking a firm grip on Berengaria's hand, "it's like a merry little hell!" Berengaria agreed more fervently than she wished to express.

Eden threw back her cloak in the dense heat and looked about her. At the forges, several brawny men and boys, half naked but for leather aprons, did incomprehensible things with sheets and strips of metal and long pairs of tongs. On an iron table, two men punched rings from a thinly beaten sheet of steel. Another drew out a slender rod of wire to an exact fineness and then passed it to one who coiled it around a rod with the diameter of a link of mail; when cooled, these coils would be slit up one side to form the rings which would make the mail.

Behind a trestle table covered in horse harness and shapeless meshes of mail sat a splendidly muscled giant of a man in late middle-age, a clean dark shirt beneath his apron. He frowned in concentration over the hauberk on which he worked; using a small but densely heavy hammer, he was engaged in riveting a row of the wire rings so that they were linked both to the previous rows of plain, unriveted ones and to each other. His movements were rhythmic and spare and it was clear that he did not relish the interruption when, satisfied at last with a once weak link, he looked up and met Eden's fascinated gaze.

"My ladies!" The man rose hastily, brushing the sweat from his glistening brow with a sweep of his sleeve. "Forgive me! I was unaware that I had such . . . unexpected company! I am Hugh the Armorer;

how may I serve your Graces? Is it a purse to be netted, perhaps? I have some very fine silver put by . . ."

"I would not demean your excellent reputation by demanding a mere purse, Master Hugh," declared Eden stoutly. "I have come . . . that is, this lady wishes to commission your skill in fashioning a suit of mail."

She stood aside so that Berengaria had perforce to come forward, despite her obvious desire to seek the familiarity of cold daylight again. Reluctantly she dropped her hood and spoke to the armorer, her soft, sweet voice all but extinguished by the ringing of the hammers.

"I do indeed," she agreed, "and it must be the very best you can make, for I value the life of its wearer most dearly."

Eden impulsively squeezed her hand.

"My forges have never let down the man who has come in the way of any mortal arrow!" declared the armorer proudly. "Your husband may rely on my steel."

Berengaria smiled, beginning to enjoy the occasion. This large and forthright man inspired her confidence. "I have no husband as yet, Master Hugh," she said clearly. "The suit is for this lady here."

Master Hugh had gone Crusading himself, in his youth, and was beyond surprise. He merely subjected his customers to closer scrutiny; that they were ladies of some degree was clear from their clothing and deportment. Suddenly he smiled and twenty years fell away from his lined and grimed features.

"I made a suit for Queen Eleanor once," he said softly. "So if you'll slip off your cloak, my lady, I'll see to your measurements."

Eden did as she was bid while Berengaria blushed. Master did the measuring himself, using a strip of the wire he coiled for his rings of mail. He noted that his customer was excellently well-formed, her body slender and supple, that the shoulders were straight enough for an hauberk to hang perfectly, that the waist would

have to be smaller than any he had yet fashioned, that
the legs were as long as a man's, and that the breasts
though full enough to fill a man's hand, would not
spoil the shape of his handiwork. If it occurred to him
to wonder why one so obviously fallen from the mould
of Venus should wish to take on the accoutrements of
Mars, it was not for him, a mere Hephaestus, to
quibble, he only hoped it would not start a fashion
among the ladies of the court, as Queen Eleanor had.
He had enough to do these days to equip fighting men,
let alone masquerading ladies.

Eden learned that, in addition to the long, hooded
shirt of mail that reached to her knees, she must wear
mail leggings called chausses, and undersleeves to protect her forearms; these ended in a short mitten, known
as a muffler.

"And will you have a helm, my lady? With a gold
fillet about it . . . or perhaps even a crest? I made a
fine, crested helm for King Richard himself, a season
back, with the figure of a lion upon it." Eden shook her
head hastily. She saw the trembling of Berengaria's lip
and could not keep from smiling too.

"May God keep the King and bring him to victory!"
she murmured.

"And now," said Berengaria in a businesslike tone,
when all seemed concluded between Eden and the armorer, "how much will you ask for your work? And we
will want it finished within five days," she added innocently. Master Hugh checked for a second, then
quietly named a sum that would have kept a freedman
and his family of five in mediocre comfort for a year.
The Princess paid it over without a qualm, counting
the gold pieces into the broad palm in her soft, Navarre-
accented French.

The armorer, who had heard such accents in his ex-
tensive travels, but who had rarely been paid in ad-
vance for any of his work, began to have his suspicions.
A royal gesture . . . or mere female foolishness? No
matter; if the future Queen of England wished to buy a
suit of mail for her waiting woman without undue ad-

vertisement, he was not the man to spread it abroad. He merely bowed very low as he escorted his visitors across his smoky threshold and resolved to provide the golden-haired knight-errant with his most painstaking work. Outside, the cold clarity of the February air was as welcome as a draught of cool ale. The two ladies turned to each other in high satisfaction with their errand and rippled into laughter, like children half their ages, as they picked their unsteady way across the boards.

"A merry little hell, indeed!" giggled Berengaria, hanging on to Eden's cloak. "But Master Hugh was none so fiendish, once he stopped frowning. I nearly gave our game away when he spoke of Richard; I felt so proud."

Carried along on the wave of her own happiness, the Princess did not realize, until she had all but overtaken her, that her friend had suddenly stopped, stock-still in the midst of the board, staring before her like one turned to stone.

"Why, Eden," she murmured wonderingly, following the direction of that petrified gaze. And then, without any manner of doubt she knew what was wrong; knew from their shared nights of confidences and tears, regrets and recriminations that the man who stood before them in the street, dark brows lowering in a face taut with fury, could be none other than Sir Hugo de Malfors.

"Well met, my lady! I have sought you far and wide. But I did not think to look so high, I confess, as the place where I might have found you."

Eden was still standing, silent and frozen to the head of the long plank, her course barred by the Baron's threatening bulk. She did not speak. Revulsion clamored in her throat. For a blind moment she forgot that she was safe, protected by the Queen's justice; she could only remember anew that dark, drowning time when those hot, triumphant eyes had hung close above hers and declared their mastery. The board shook a little as she trembled. Then there was the lightest of movements as someone slipped past her and she heard Berengaria's gentle, courteous tones addressing Sir Hugo.

"Baron . . . will you not let us pass? The Queen expects our company and we do not wish to show ill manners."

Sir Hugo surveyed the small figure with amusement. "I note that my fame has reached the court, lady," he said tartly, stung by her soft reminder of Eden's guardian. Then, sweeping the Princess's presence aside as if she were a mere serf, he turned on Eden, his look smouldering with unsuppressed resentment. "And it is through your good offices, is it not, my Lady Hawkhurst, that I find myself near stripped of all I possess, driven from the gates of the manor which is rightly mine and rendered dishonorable in the eyes of my peers?" He strode up the plank and caught her cruelly by the wrist, bending her backwards as he hissed his words in her face. "They have taken from me what is mine, the long-nosed Chancellor and the old she-wolf. But think on, my lady, to the time when the whelp shall rule and his dam be displaced. For that will be my time, Eden. Richard owes me a favor . . . and he will know how to repay it." His look willed her to speak, to cry out against him, but his words came to her as from a dream, from far off, and she had not the power to reply, even had she wished. She sensed that somewhere there was pain as Hugo relentlessly twisted the wrist he held tight at her back, but that was all; the words could not touch her. "I hear you are to go on a journey, lady . . . running after that impotent husband of yours like any bitch in heat. Well, get him to service you if you can, but when you return, be it one or both of you . . . I shall be waiting . . . and I will have my way with you and yours, just as it has been before."

"No," said Eden dreamily, still distanced, her voice unmoved by emotion, "that is not the way of it."

"No indeed!" Berengaria was turned by indignation into a little fury. She flew at the Baron's large figure like a swallow at a tall tower. "Loose your hold on the lady! By God you go too far! Have you not felt the Queen's wrath enough? I promise you that you will feel it in stripes across your miserable back if you continue thus."

The sheer energy of her friend's anger reached Eden in the almost tranced state into which she had retreated. She shook her head a little, tugging on her wrist. Then, facing at last full recognition of the Baron's hateful proximity, she drew her head back a space and spat, as foully as she could, into the vengeful, gloating features.

She must have known what to expect as she found herself reeling back to clutch at Master Hugh's reeking doorway, but neither she, nor the irate Princess, and least of all Sir Hugo himself could have expected the next event, as a human whirlwind, all flailing arms and kicking feet, swinging a yard of bright-buckled leather about an enraged and roaring head, encompassed the Baron in a battery of violence.

Gone was the drooping lover, the exquisite poet, as Master Gilles exercised everything he had learned in the palace tiltyard of hand-to-hand combat, less fair than foul. It could not have been expected to last for long. Sir Hugo was a large and powerful man, a veteran of too many campaigns to be much affected by a green boy; but Gilles had the element of surprise on his side and gave a good account of himself before the last swinging blow that sent him sprawling in the mud. In a second, Eden was beside him, taking his head in her lap and wiping the blood from his bruised but smiling mouth.

"This is surely what it is like to be in heaven. You are as beautiful as the Blessed Damozel herself!" he managed, very creditably, before falling gracefully into insensibility, the beatific smile fading slowly before the eyes of his amused and distressed idol.

The incident had brought Eden back to her wits. She turned a savage eye upon the panting Baron. "Boys and women! We are both your worthy opponents," she sneered. She was well pleased to observe that Gilles's buckle had done its work and that a long, jagged tear lay open down Sir Hugo's cheek.

He took a step toward her, his hand flying to his sword. "I have a mind to give you the hiding you deserve, lady!" he began, pulling the weapon from its scabbard.

A voice rang out behind them; there was authority in it. "Is ought amiss!" Hugh the Armorer towered outside his doorway, bronzed arms glistening, his hammer still in his hand. "I heard a commotion . . . and that's hard to do in the babel I work amongst!" Sir Hugo met his eye. There was a pause.

"This boy here needs attention!" declared Berengaria, indicating the fallen champion.

Master Hugh nodded. "He shall have it. And you, Baron . . . is there anything I may do for you?" The tone was courteous, but there was enough of a hint in it to let de Malfors know that the armorer was king in his own country and would allow no further breach of the peace.

His sword dropped back in its scabbard. "Indeed there is. I was coming to you on a matter of much torn harness, when this insolent varlet attacked me."

Master Hugh shook his head, clicking his tongue mournfully. "There's no accounting for the young nowadays; he should take the Cross. That'd cool his ardor. Still, sir, you appear to have taught him a lesson." Since the gash on the baron's cheek was at least as salient as Gilles's bruises, there was some doubt of that; but it would be a while yet before Gilles commissioned a suit of mail, and Sir Hugo was an excellent customer. Smiling, he ushered him into the depths.

"I wonder now," observed Berengaria with infinite satisfaction, as two stalwarts heaved the recumbent Gilles onto a litter, "in what little struggle the great, brute beast could have had the misfortune to tear his harness?" They both thought of the Queen's soldier-steward and smiled.

"Gilles is a likely lad, it seems. I had no idea he

could be such a lion roused. He wants to come with us to Outremer. Shall we take him?" Eden felt that she owed something to the boy who was so willing to bear scars . . . and give them . . . for her sake.

"It were better!" Berengaria agreed, "otherwise we shall come across him stowed away with the provisions, and there'll not be enough to go round."

▼▼

CHAPTER THREE

Ship to Sicily

March 1191

The great, painted galley ploughed through the gray, inhospitable seas in a constant hum of noise and color. Soldiers and sailors manned the bright, blue castles at stern and prow and rowdy boys nested at the masthead, beneath the leopard and lily banners, above the striped red and white sail with its great cross. On deck, the pennants flew from spears like heads of waving colored wheat. The horses expressed their disapproval of their situation in their stalls to the fore, while the sinewy oarsmen kept up their pace, when the sail fell limp, with hymns and chants of love and war. They were not slaves, but freedmen who had volunteered for the Crusade and they were blithe at their back-breaking task. Round about them, the Queen and her ladies made the deck a little court, a-flutter with veils and laughter and incessant talk. The world swung gently up and down; now and again it swayed a little sideways. Eden found the motion most soothing and pleasant. It was as though the swing her father had hung for her from the boughs of their stoutest apple tree, had taken on the immense dimensions of the galley in which they sailed. Lulled and drowsy with the movement, she made herself a bed of rugs and skins behind the side of the sterncastle where she daydreamed often of that early time, of her mother's soft hands and frequent laughter, of her father, proud, impatient, ever in motion, most often on horseback . . . and of Stephen, as he was when he first came to them, tall, slender, nervous and glossy as a colt. At night, pressed close to the Princess in the broad wooden bed down in the dark, creaking hollow of the hold, she did not dream, but slept fast like the child of her memories, to wake on each successive day with an increasing sense of the approach of destiny. She felt happy and positive, filled with hope. For Berengaria, alas, there was no such pleasure in the voyage. Almost as soon as the ancient and lovely white cliffs had receded and the vessel was under way, the haze and nausea of seasickness had descended on her and kept her prisoner in its debilitating clutches throughout the journey. Eden was full of pity for her; as she comforted the Princess, smoothing the lifeless dark hair from the hot, clammy brow; she thought there could be nothing worse than nausea, unless it were the toothache.

It was only after three nightmare weeks that the galley rode her way more gently into Mediterranean waters. The hold, filled to capacity with the royal train, its sacks of provisions, barrels of wine and water, and chests of clothing, money and arms, had by now a rank and sour smell not to be alleviated by the occasional swabbing of its tarred and creaking planks. The Queen, with Eden and most of her other ladies, took to sleeping on deck, well wrapped in hides and woollen rugs. At last the reluctant Berengaria was persuaded to do the same. She had not, much to her own amazement, died of her discomfort, but was progressing splendidly from hour to hour, the color returning gradually to her cheeks. The vomiting had ceased completely and she was able to digest small portions of the freshly killed fowl brought along for the purpose, and to wash it down with the rough, strong red wine they had taken aboard at the great port of Lisbon.

As they lay beneath the black canopy of the heavens while the stars moved imperceptibly above them, the two girls conversed nose to nose, their hoods pulled up over their heads, breathing lustily to combat the cold. Nearby, Lady Alys slept fitfully, murmuring and tossing a little. For what must have been the hundredth time, Berengaria said, "If only he will like me a little! I do not ask for love. It cannot be expected. But life will be so much pleasanter for me if he can like me and think me his friend."

"You are too modest and too stuffed with foolish doubts," declared Eden, whispering to avoid waking any of the other ladies, or, God forbid it, Queen Eleanor herself. "Yet I think he will be drawn to you, because you are so unlike to him; it is often so, in love, they say. His power will protect your weakness; your softness will temper his strength; his energy will renew itself in your serenity. You will be well-matched. I am sure of it."

The Princess found this very comforting. "Was it thus," she asked hesitantly, "between you and Stephen? I have seen your strength; I cannot imagine him to be even stronger. And yet I know that you have respect for him, as well as love."

Eden sighed. Her face was hidden in the folds of her cowl, but the Princess sensed her smile as she replied. "In a manner, yes, we are well-matched, though not as I see you and the King to be matched. Stephen was ever wiser than I. He was a dreamer of perfect dreams; he had before him a constant vision of how the world should be—and of how he himself should be—and I and all about us. He envisaged the world as Christ intended it to be, and he worked toward it, not sparing himself. It is no easy road. And it has taken him to Jerusalem."

Was there a faint tinge of bitterness beneath the soft, husky whisper? Berengaria was not sure. Certainly it was gone when Eden spoke again. "I know that he could not have taken the Cross unless its true meaning and beauty were shown to him so that they transcended all else. That is as it should be," she added, but the Princess was aware of an unexpressed doubt. Stephen had wished to go; would he also wish to return?

"If God willed that he should go to Jerusalem—surely he has also willed your own journey? You have told me of your experience in the chapel at Hawkhurst; I am sure that all will be well with you; you will find Stephen and he will know that he must return home."

"I hope so!" The whisper was taut. "But what would I do if he should refuse?" Until this moment she had not allowed herself to doubt; that would have blunted her purpose. But now, floating between the sea and the stars, far out in the Middle Sea, for the first time came the tremor of realization; how greatly she had dared.

"He will not refuse; how could he?" asked Berengaria warmly. "And if he does—I shall order him home as his Queen!"

"Holy Saint Loy!" came a suffering voice behind them. "Have you any conception of how late it is? Will your flow of confidences not wait till it be light?" The Lady Alys had been awakened by their murmurings. Her tone indicated that she was beyond all patience.

"I'm so sorry," whispered Berengaria. "Truly we thought we whispered."

"Whispered! It would not surprise me if the Chevalier de la Falaise himself were to be waiting on the quay in Messina—so far does his lady's voice fly toward him!" It was unforgivable but so was their ceaseless babble.

Eden rose up on her elbow, glaring into the dark. "If our confidences disturbed you so, lady, I wonder you troubled to listen to them so carefully!"

Alys's heavily tolerant sigh was clearly audible. "I did not listen, Eden, any more than I do to the slapping of the waves or the creaking of this abominable tub. However, your voices are more insistent than either of these."

"I am sorry we awoke you, Lady Alys. We will be quiet now," said Berengaria serenely. "Won't we, Eden?"

It was obvious that she, too, must apologize. She didn't want to. "Indeed yes. There is no more to say," was all she could manage. It crossed her mind to wonder if Alys might be suffering as much from pique as from sleeplessness. Had she herself not found her way to the very heart of Berengaria's little group of friends, would it be the other girl who would have lain here in her place? Had she usurped Alys's position in the Princess's affections? Surely this was unlikely. Berengaria had been in England for only a brief period and Alys had served the Queen first and foremost. Besides, Eden could not imagine that proud head bent close to another's in exchange of deepest joys and sorrows.

She smiled to herself as she settled down once more. She was glad she had lived through her moment of doubt about Stephen. It would have had to come to her. Better sooner than late. She snuggled deep into her cloak, closing her great, green eyes. Berengaria, knowing her friend at peace, lay still and allowed herself to enter her own particular private dream—of Richard, the golden, the Lionheart, who would soon lie as close, even closer, to her than did Eden now.

And now, at last, the voyage was ended. They had reached Messina. The world bounded by increasingly blue water had given way to a horizon filled with the reassuring symbols of a civilized land. The rocky coastline was tamed into a town, its flags flying bravely from rooftops and hillside fortresses, and the magnificent harbor choc-a-bloc with what must surely be the most splendid and intimidating sight that Outremer had ever seen—the two hundred war galleys of England, the Lion and the Cross billowing on their full-bellied sails as they came out to welcome the old and the young queens she had brought to them. A hundred times a hundred bright pennants streamed in the light wind; the painted castles were perilously overmanned, tight little forests of waving, welcoming hands; trumpets sounded; kettledrums thundered; ten thousand voices roared and sang. The royal ship moved at a measured and stately pace through the midst of the fleet, so that all might see the two gorgeously clad figures who stood on her forecastle; the taller, all in dark crimson, wore a veil of gold tissue, held by a fillet of gold with a great ruby at its center; the lesser stood at her side, slender in cloth of silver, midnight hair veiled in blue, with the glint of silver about the tautened shoulders and the small, seductive waist.

Such a shout went up as Berengaria had never heard. To the King of England's army, wearied of the long winter's waiting in Sicily, the advent of the royal bride seemed a good omen; surely, after the Lionheart was wed, they would leave at last for the mainland and Jerusalem? To the Princess, swaying gently on her high platform above the waves, it was also a good omen; she was delighted that their presence brought so much obvious pleasure to Richard's men. She began to smile and wave to them; she was enjoying herself, the hideous voyage already a thing of the distant past. Eden, close by, in the new gown of amber cloth-of-Damascus that had mysteriously found its way into her sea-chest along with Master Hugh's handiwork and several other articles of fine apparel, found it hard to preserve the graceful and contained posture that the occasion required. She knew that to spin about and cry out at every ravishing new sight was demeaning in a noblewoman, but everything was so strange and stimulating and wondrously new to one who had not traveled further than Canterbury or Winchester in all her days. One who now found herself in Sicily in the company of the past and future Queens of England, and would shortly bow her knee before the King himself.

Queen Eleanor, who was not averse to a little public appreciation after her long years of imprisonment by her husband, graciously inclined her head and gave the practiced half-salute that she had perfected, long ago, before her own crusade with Louis the monk. She smiled at Eden with more gentleness than usual. She hoped that this courageous and hopeful girl would not find bitterness and disillusion among the lands designated as Holy. It had come to many, herself among them. She had ridden into that burning landscape, a proud and wayward child, masquerading in her silver armor. She had come home a grown woman, scarred by fortune's arrows, strong enough to cast off the King of France and seek the mate of her choice, and carrying within her the knowledge of many men's deaths, not the least that of her gallant young uncle, friend and lover, the Prince of Antioch, who had been murdered because he had not come to terms with the Infidel. There had been bravery and cowardice, intrigue and mendacity, weariness, much disease and the soul's sickness. Few had seen the vision they had sought; in the end all that most men sought was booty, cruelly taken. Eleanor, despite her quicksilver wit and brave exterior, had left her girlhood beneath the bright sun of Syria that she so loved; she did not want the young Lady of Hawkhurst to do the same.

For Berengaria, she had no such fears; once the girl had conquered her excessive modesty—and Richard was the man to help her to do that—she would grow in good sense and wifely attributes and become the soothing influence her unruly son needed. She would also, what was more, give England its next king; and that could not happen too soon; she must see to it that they were wed as soon as Lent was over. She would have Richard's promise on it. He had never been in a hurry to marry; no doubt there were companions enough for his bed; indeed one heard the most unlikely tales upon that subject; wasn't there something said once about his relationship to one of his young squires? The Queen did not wish to know about such matters, but she kept her ears open by force of habit, and occasionally heard things she would have preferred not to. She had no fears for the marriage; she would have his promise and, whatever his vices, Richard was one who always kept his word.

A sudden excited cry from Eden interrupted her thoughts. "Madame! Surely that is he! The King! Oh, he is all golden and shining in the sun! See how it strikes fire from his bright head! And so tall; I had not thought a man could stand so tall! Only think, Berengaria—*that* is to be your husband!"

The Princess became mouse-quiet in response to the outcry. Her composed face lost a little of its color but she kept her head high and looked steadfastly where Eden pointed.

Richard the Lionheart stood on the quayside to welcome his beloved mother and his bride. He was tall indeed, outstripping all about him, his broad shoulders massive beneath the golden cloak with its scarlet stars and its azure, snarling leopards. Like his womenfolk, he stood stock-still while others surged and clamored. And when at last the sturdy ship churned against the harbor walls and their long journey was, in truth, ended, they saw that his face was wet with tears. They coursed freely down the fine, bronzed cheekbones and were dashed away as the King, unable to wait for the disembarking, strode up the hastily thrown gangway and clasped Queen Eleanor in his arms.

"*Ma belle mère!* It has been too long!" He held her at arm's length, surveying the familiar dignity of bone and breeding. "You look wonderful. You age less than I do."

Eleanor regarded him wryly; her son was in his thirty-third year, at the zenith of his strength and powers. He lived to the hilt and would have no regrets for it.

"I," said his mother delicately, "have lived a somewhat quiet life these last sixteen years; it has not been an aging experience so much as a long sleep, somewhat resembling death—if Heaven is to be imagined as a place where one reads many books, plays a little music and gives one's deepest attention to the laundry list."

Richard looked as if he might weep further for a second; then on a sudden he roared with laughter, picked up the elegant figure and whirled her once around. "So you say! But the whole world knows how you schemed and planned behind my father's back; I swear it was you who harassed the old devil into his grave. Unless it was I!"

There was an answering roar to this and Eden, fascinated, again found herself reminded that it was better to be a friend than an enemy to the Plantagenets.

The laughter fading to a chuckle deep in the broad column of his throat, Richard's bright blue eye now fell upon the quiet figure who stood at his mother's side. She raised her chin a little and a long look passed between them. At last the burnished features bloomed into a new, softer smile.

"You are Berengaria," he said, and with consummate grace, he fell swiftly to his knees before her on the deck.

Eleanor was well pleased. He had declared to the whole world that he recognized her as his bride. Again the great, full-throated roar went up from the assembled army. Their leader was the very flower of chivalry.

Gravely, the King took Berengaria's small hand in his and carried it to his lips; he noted that it trembled slightly and smiled once more to reassure her. He looked attentively into her grave, heart-shaped face and saw the peace in the depths of the large, gray eyes, peace for him in the midst of his life's heritage of war upon war.

"I knew," he told her simply, "that you would be beautiful."

Berengaria, who was not, in fact, strictly beautiful, though indeed very comely and pleasant to behold, knew when she read the truth in a pair of eyes. Richard's eyes were so candid, it seemed to her, as to be incapable of lies and she opened her heart to her great, gilded giant of a husband there and then, once and forever. She would not have believed it could have been so simple.

Eden, watching in quiet delight, shook tears from her cheeks like all present and thought fleetingly of Stephen. She sighed. Then she picked up her skirts and hurried, amid the crowd, along the deck; they were to ride to Richard's great wooden castle of Mategriffon, which he had raised on the hillside, overlooking the splendid city and the sea. Here, his sister, Joanna, the widowed Queen of Sicily, on whose behalf Richard had waged his brief, successful war upon her husband's successor, King Tancred, waited to welcome the royal party.

"Mategriffon!" mused Eden, peering up at the winding, hillside streets with their pretty, white-painted houses and glimpses of shady courtyards, "What can it mean?"

"It means 'a curb for the Greeks,' my lady!" young Gilles was at her side, his face alight with excitement. "The King built it to demonstrate to all here that he, and he only, is master in Messina! 'Griffon' is the term the Crusaders have for the Greeks: it is one of their emblems."

"And was such a demonstration necessary?" Eden wondered, accepting the squire's arm as they crossed the bobbing gangplank to the quay.

"Certainly! There's been the devil to pay in Sicily since the King landed here last September. Philip of France was with him then. They say he slunk away only yesterday with his fleet and made for Acre."

"Slunk?" Eden was puzzled. "I thought France our ally?"

"Ah, yes! That was while Richard was still set to marry Philip's sister, the Princess Alais, and before the quarrels over the Sicilian booty and the French King's slimy intrigues with Tancred . . ."

"You appear to be remarkably well informed, Master Gilles, for one who has but this moment set foot on Sicilian soil."

The boy grinned cheerfully. "I keep my eyes and ears skinned! The truth is I was talking to one of our seamen; he jumped aboard when his vessel skimmed our side as we sailed in. Now—let us try to find your palfrey. By Saint Eustace, how I have pitied the horses on this voyage! The poor creatures are stark mad for exercise: I hope Balan will not throw you."

"Not he. He knows me too well. And I have given him a great deal of attention during the journey. I led him three times around the deck in the pouring rain —the only time there was room enough to do so—and I hope he will show his gratitude by good behavior."

This proved to be the case, and Eden, graceful on the finely bred roan that she had broken herself at Hawkhurst, with Gilles trotting happily beside her on his cob, was one of the few travelers to arrive at the wooden gates of the castle with some dignity. Many others limped uneasily up to the vast, iron-barred doors, cursing their recalcitrant mounts while several luckless serfs were dispatched to catch the runaways.

The castle of Mategriffon was a wondrous, exceptional edifice, born of King Richard's own whimsical imagination. Made entirely out of wooden sections, it could be erected or dismantled in a day, given a corps of suitably industrious engineers. Its building had kept a great number of men out of mischief for several weeks, being a more fitting and infinitely more challenging task than that of harrying the local population, which was all that most of the army could find to do.

When Eden dismounted, Gilles disappeared confidently into a nearby stockade, leading Balan and his own beast. Eden followed the eager crowd inside the castle, where a wide gallery gave at once on to the great hall. Here the royal voyagers and their menie mingled in a babel of talk and laughter, with the King's own household. Everywhere she looked, Eden saw Knight Crusaders, the silken cross stitched proudly on the right shoulder or blazoned across the breast of their long, rough tunics. Her throat tightened as she looked about her; almost, she expected Stephen to be amongst them, so closely did she connect that bright symbol with himself. She remembered how her hand had shaken as she had sewn the pale scrap of ribbon close to his slender neck. Her eyes misted.

It was as she stood there that a young squire approached and offered to lead her to the room set aside for the Queen's ladies. This proved to be a bare, sparse chamber, its wooden walls noticeably undecorated and chillingly slit at regular intervals to allow the expulsion of arrows upon less gentle occasions. Several of the young women were gathered there already, busily unpacking their sea chests as they were brought in, one by one, by many willing hands.

"Ma foi!" exclaimed plump Mathilde, munching an apple she had somehow managed to obtain. "This is not much like home, is it?"

"It is a fortress, not a palace," reproved Alys cooly. "And I expect we have turned several unfortunate knights out of their beds."

"Well, indeed!" declared Mathilde, throwing down her healthy young weight upon the leaking, misshapen straw palliasse, "I'm not at all sure I wouldn't prefer to sleep standing up, with my horse."

"Don't worry, *chèrie!* You'll be tired enough to sleep anywhere, after the feast!" comforted dark-skinned Arnoul, the Queen's countrywoman from Poitiers.

"A feast! Tonight?" Eden was delighted. This explained the haste to open the chests. And, locating her own battered box, embellished with the falcon of Hawkhurst, she began, like her companions, to see what could be done to salvage the creased gowns and veils before it was time to appear before their King and the assembled flower of his chivalry.

When, some two hours later, the sound of a trumpet heralded the commencement of the feast, the carefully unwrapped and tenderly handled silver mirrors told all that they were indeed a credit to their country and their Queen.

Eden wore a gown of deep rose, in the heavy, figured cotton found only in Damascus; it had trailing sleeves of apple green and a light veil that caught its tone. This was held by a little chaplet of roses, cleverly fashioned from the stuff of the gown. The cross that Stephen had given her nestled between her breasts, which were clearly defined and a little revealed by the new, V-shaped neckline which was meant to echo the stiffened folds of the veil.

Already the sounds of music enticed them as they made their way back into the great hall, now candlelit and mysterious, with shadows flickering up and down the walls and across the high, wooden rafters. Some two hundred knights and squires and perhaps twenty women sat there. It was good to sense the breath caught in the throats of so many noblemen as they moved demurely to the places provided for them at the King's table which crossed the back of the room forming the

spine of a great "E" which filled the hall. First came
Lady Alys, head high in her faultless blue, then
Mathilde, warm in apricot. Arnoul in saffron and
Marie in deep emerald; then Ysabeau in dove gray
and lastly, because she could not find the ribbon for
her soft slipper, Eden in her garden of roses. For a moment there was silence as every eye followed their
graceful progress. Then a cheer went up as the six
girls took their seats, each one ushered by a smiling
knight wearing his own feast-day finery, and glad of
the opportunity to cast off the ringmail that had become his second, saurian skin.

The trumpet sounded once more and the King entered with Queen Eleanor beside him. Behind them
walked Berengaria, showing no trace of the apprehension Eden knew she must feel in the presence of such
a large and interested company. She was deep in conversation with a tall, dark and stately woman who
could only be Joanna of Sicily. On closer inspection,
she bore a strong resemblance to her mother, far
more so than did Richard, whose russet-gold coloring
was all inherited from his late, unlamented father.
Today he was more than usually resplendent in a
scarlet tunic and a robe of deep turquoise, edged with
gold. He wore his crown, a finely wrought coronet of
deep red-gold, studded with rubies and aquamarines.
Berengaria, as befitted a bride-to-be, wore a simple
white gown, robed in soft blue, her fall of thick, black
hair loose upon her shoulders beneath a thin silver
circlet. She looked about the hall as she was led to her
seat on Richard's left hand, Eleanor taking precedence
while she was still Queen of England.

The feast was generous and more than welcome after three weeks of ship's provender. There were several kinds of meat and fowl and delicious stews with
fruit and spices, all mouth-wateringly new to Eden's
palate. Even the bread was of a lighter and more
pleasant consistency than she was used to, but best of
all were the Sicilian fruits, great, glowing globes of
oranges, deep red apples and bitter lemons served with
succulent sugar-cane to take away their sourness or

whipped into a syllabub with a rich, heavy cream, the most exquisite dish of all. The wine was red, round and full in the mouth and had the taste of the grape still upon it.

Eden addressed herself courteously to the young knight on her left, who had introduced himself as Sir William de Barret. "Is it known how it goes in Acre? The siege has been overlong."

Will Barret's tanned and pleasant face crinkled into a grin. "Alas, I was enjoying my companion's unusual beauty, and did not think to talk to her of war! The siege, lady, is two years old—but all will soon be well; it needs but Richard's hand to set it right. By my troth, madame, you are fair!"

Eden crimsoned, unaccustomed to such frankness. "I thank you sir. Will you not try one of these sugared fruits? They are excellent."

"His tongue is sugared enough already, my lady!" said a deep voice from her other side. The speaker, she learned, was Sir John de Wulfran, a large young man with a wealth of carroty hair, who was paying dedicated attention to his food and drink. "But, for once, his words are no flattery. Tell me, lady, do you return to England with the Queen, or shall we have the pleasure of your company in Syria, with the Princess?"

"I hope most dearly that I may sail with you," she began, watching with admiration as Sir John neatly unseamed, boned, stabbed and devoured an entire baked fish in one fluent action. "I hope to find news of my husband, Sir Stephen de la Falaise; I suppose you will not have heard his name in any matter?" she added, without real hope. These men had not yet reached the Holy Land themselves. Yet, she must ask of all she encountered—or truly, none could answer her.

The broad young knight shook his head. "We've cooled our heels and our steel a winter long now, stuck here, at halfway house. We know nothing of England, and not much more of Syria. We are in a veritable limbo." He spat out an overlooked fish-eye in disgust.

The King had left his tall, carved and padded seat and roamed the hall, clapping his hand to a shoulder here and there or bending to murmur into an ear, even, when he could find a subject for it, kissing a white hand.

"He makes himself an equal with his vassals," Eden observed, watching the feline smile deepen the fine lines about his eyes and the corner of his mouth, until he resembled nothing so much as Tyb, the great orange tomcat that commanded the farmyard at Hawk-hurst.

"He is a friend to each and every one of us," agreed Will solemnly, "which is why we will follow him willingly to the gates of Hades—or to Jerusalem, which will probably be much the same thing, as far as comfort goes! Aye, he's a good lad, our Richard. Christ's bones! Even the French love him!"

Eden was interested. "Tell me—why are the French no longer here? I had thought to see King Philip." She recalled the gossip of Gilles on the quay.

There was a chuckle from both her attendants. "He could not look your little Princess in the face," growled Sir John. "He wanted Richard for his sister Alais."

"But surely, she was . . ." Eden did not know how to continue; she did not want to add fire to the fuel of rumor, if that were all it was.

Will finished for her. "Aye. It was said, and rightly, that she's already been bedded by old King Henry, while she stayed in the royal palace—even that she's been brought to bed of a child by him. Naturally, Richard would have none of her. And Philip pretends to take it as an insult. Faugh! As if any man would take his father's cast-off whore!"

"But surely—Richard and Philip must fight side by side in the Holy Land," Eden said. "How shall mere poor soldiers manage, if their leaders cannot agree?"

Again the laughter rose about her. Sir John lavishly refilled their three goblets before replying cheerfully. "My sweet simplicity, you do not know half the tale. The two are natural enemies. You only have to look at

them! Our fierce, proud Lion and that skulking, un-
dersized one-eyed . . . Listen, as to the men, why,
Philip cannot keep control over his own, let alone
lead them into battle. His fractious Frenchmen have
been brawling and bleeding among the Griffons ever
since they came here and he took not a blindman's
reck. Whereas Richard, when we got a bit out of hand
he raised a gibbet high enough for the whole city to
see and swore he'd hang up all looters, rioters and
troublemakers, no matter what their race or creed. We
came to heel after a while. Or almost; there weren't so
many of us hung. It's hard to have a bastard Griffon or
Saracen call you a malodorous dog and turn the other
cheek, Christian or not. And their women—some of
them are very friendly and persuasive, saving your innocence, lady. And not bad looking, if you like them
big and swarthy."

As Eden hid her smiles in her cup she saw that now
the King was holding his golden goblet high. There
was a call for silence and the almost childishly blue
eye traveled the length and breadth of the hall, gathering them all to him so that each seemed closer to his
neighbor than before, all of them bent upon one bright,
commanding figure.

"Friends!" The tone was light but sultry, the voice
curling about the hall like unseen smoke. "You have
been very patient through this wearisome waiting. I
thank you for it. I too have known impatience—" He
put up his hand but could not stem the cheer that rose
then. The Lionheart longed to be at the gates of
Jerusalem. How well they knew it!

"It is not only for the sweet fruits of conquest that
I have waited." Richard went on, pausing then for a
teasing second, "but for the even sweeter meat my
gracious mother has brought to grace my table!"
And he swept round in a broad, flamboyant gesture,
first bowing deeply to Queen Eleanor, who watched
him with her customary faintly ironic smile, then
stretching both hands toward Berengaria, who rose in
a crimson tide of blushes to take them in her own. The
King pressed his lips to each one separately before

releasing them to hand his betrothed her cup, and taking up his own again, he cried out joyously, "Dear friends, I give you—the future Queen of England. You will not drink to her as I do?"

And as Eden joined her voice in the great cry that reached out to them as they stood, outlined in the candlelight like figures from a fable, her eyes fell again upon that spare, straight woman on the King's right hand. Berengaria would be Queen of England, yes, but never "by the wrath of God." Silently, Eden dedicated her own pledge.

The feast became more unruly as the night wore on. Many left their seats to greet and talk with friends; the musicians played with increasing vigor, bringing forth strange melodies and fierce rhythms unknown to the English visitors, passionate, dark-beating love songs and wild, uncivilized laments, the age-old peasant music of Sicily.

Eden found her foot tapping them out unrealized and her whole body cried out for motion as the warm notes mingled with the wine in her blood. The untamed, insistent measures released in her an echoing restlessness, in aching response to some deeper and more intense experience than she had ever known—though she had sometimes felt its potentiality within her, waiting, dormant. There was a darkness in it, but also, she sensed, a great joy.

As she sat, enchanted, her head thrown back so that the pulse was clear at the base of the long column of her throat, her golden head lit to dancing flame by the rushlight that stood in its tripot behind her, her hand loosely holding the last of her wine, she was suddenly aware of a face, one that she had not seen before, bent questioningly over her own. It was a dark, burnished face, with the intense, speculative look that can belong to man or hawk; a swathe of dark, curling hair hung about it. She caught the scent of sandalwood. Still half held prisoner by the music, she stared upwards insentiently and saw herself reflected, slumberous and wondering, in the dark, autumn-colored eyes.

"Tristan Damartin, Chevalier de Jarnac, my lady. The King sends me to say he longs to meet one who has been so good a friend to the Princess."

Slowly she straightened, conscious now of the wildness of her hair, her high color. "The King is most gracious," she returned. She longed to smooth the wayward hair but would not do so beneath the cool surveillance of the impeccable knight who stood before her. Tristan de Jarnac bore himself with as much pride as any prince of the earth; that he was waiting for her to accompany him was clear, though not quite clear enough to be discourteous. He stood relaxed, his hands quiet at his sides, the suggestion of a smile abut his lips. She gathered her wits and rose swiftly, tossing her hair behind her shoulders. The young knight led her along before the high table opposite to where the King sat, his ear bent to catch Berengaria's soft tones.

"My Lord King—it is the Lady Eden," the Princess said at once, seeing her friend's approach.

"By the True Cross, she is comely!" murmured Richard, rather louder than he had intended.

Eden, with lowered eyes, sank deep onto one knee. The King signed her to rise.

"The Lady Eden of Hawkhurst, of the Honor of Stukesey," proclaimed the tall knight at her side, his voice low but resonant as a herald's.

"It is a pleasure to welcome you," said the King simply. "Your beauty will give joy to many eyes that have looked upon little save ringmail and rough faces for a sixmonth. At least, officially!" he added with expansive good humor. Those who knew him, Tristan de Jarnac among them, made mental notes to be on the *qui vive* tomorrow; when the Lion purred at night, his claws were ever the sharper in the morning.

Her presentation over, Eden followed the swinging dark blue cloak of de Jarnac back to her seat at the end of the board. Here, Sir John was waking blearily from his brief, post-prandial stupor and Will de Barret had reappeared from roaming the room. Both made it clear by the alert manner of their greetings that her escort was a man they greatly respected.

De Jarnac returned their acknowledgements, saying easily. "I leave you in excellent company, my lady. Believe all Will tells you; and discount more than half John says, and you may learn much . . . if you can persuade John to allow Will to speak!" To her surprise, neither knight took this amiss but both fell cheerfully into laughter.

"I give you thanks for your courtesy, Chevalier," she said politely, offering him a hesitant smile. There was something in his contained and confidently attractive presence that disturbed her, though for no reason of which she was aware.

"It was a most pleasant duty, my lady," he replied, his own brilliant smile dazzling her with its suddenness. "We shall meet again, very soon."

He made her an unhurried, fluent obeisance, nodded companionably to her table-fellows and turned to go back to his own seat. This she saw, for she could not help following his tall, graceful figure with her eyes, was very near the King's.

"Sir Tristan . . . is he highly regarded at court?" she ventured curiously.

Sir John chuckled. "You'd best sing the Chevalier's praises, Will . . . for I swear to keep mum for a sennight!"

"Tristan de Jarnac," began Will obediently, "is as close to the King's heart as any man . . . and deservedly, for he has the wit of Alexander in strategy and a sword-arm to dispatch it. Why, he and Richard, fighting back to back, took Messina well nigh between the two of them and glorious it was to see! All men speak well of him and seek his good graces. Even the French King accorded him respect! His lineage is ancient and honorable, his fiefs being chiefly in England and Brittany. His nature is noble above many higher born than he . . ."

"And damn it, the man can drink you under the table and still stand as solid as a keep! He can sing you a good, tuneful ballad over your wine and over-reach you, sword for sword or wit for wit . . . aye, and woman for woman too, more's the pity, any time you care to hazard it!" Sir John exploded, unable to keep his vow for more than a single minute. He grinned widely, revealing several gold-filled teeth of which he was justly proud. "One thing must be added, lady . . . in case you should think us partial. Tristan is our commander. We think him the best a man could follow . . . and by the Rood, we are proud to do so."

"John speaks nothing but the truth . . . with a slight exaggeration as to the drinking," Will agreed. "I don't believe de Jarnac has ever challenged any of his knights in alcoholic combat."

"Another thing," continued Sir John lustily, swinging his own goblet, now he was minded of it, approximately in the direction of his mouth. "He isn't yet wed. 'Tis a mortal pity you have a husband, lady, for I dare swear I have never seen as likely matched pair as you and he walking side by side. Our Tristan should have his Iseult, should he not, Will?"

"Fie sir, for shame!" Eden was angered beyond all reason and, almost as much, surprised by her own anger. Will saw it and took his companion to task.

"John! You have drunk too deeply. Ask pardon of the lady. I make his excuses for him, Lady Eden; he put down a rabble of restless Griffons today; they had been stealing our food. It was a bloody business and not much honor in it. He is weary, that is all, and the wine has reached him quickly." He sighed, drawing his seat next to Sir John's and supporting his heavy, drooping form. "Wine is an aid to oblivion, when it is craved. And at all events, it is all we have."

Sir John looked up once, tried to speak, then the ruddy head eluded Will's hand and cracked down upon the board before him.

Eden was at once all concern. "How will he fare?" she asked, dismayed, her spark of anger dead. "Should we not send for an esquire and have him taken to his bed?"

Will shook his head. "I'll sit with him; he will soon recover; I have seen it often. But do you leave us if you would; you must be very weary after the journey and this night's revels."

She looked toward the center of the table, where she saw that Queen Eleanor still conversed as energetically as if it were noon and not midnight. Berengaria had swayed a little toward Richard and leaned sleepily upon her hand. "I must not leave before the Queen," she told Will.

But it was another hour before that indefatigable lady was ready to retire, by which time Eden was deeply asleep, laid back in the depths of her tall chair. She was only half aware, then, of the strong arms that carried her upstairs to her place in the solar, strong, protective arms—and a trace of the scent of sandalwood.

▼▼▼

CHAPTER FOUR

From Sicily in Ships

The next morning, Richard was in roaring form; he had three men flogged before the gates of Mategriffon for gambling, against his edict, without their superior officers, and seen another hung up on his mighty gibbets for the rape of a Sicilian girl. Also, he had a headache; he was not sure whether this were the mere legacy of the night's carousing or the herald of a bout of the debilitating ague to which he was thrall. He had sought recent remedies for this, en route in Italy, in the great medical schools of Salerno, but none had brought him lasting relief. He watched his hands for the involuntary trembling which was the infuriating sign of the onset of the fever.

Seated before one of the several braziers in his small private chamber behind the great hall, he listened irritably while his mother tried to persuade him to send messages of goodwill to the Pope. He loathed Clement III; he had carefully avoided him in his own travels in Italy and saw no reason to send flourishes to him now. But Eleanor insisted that popes and monarchs frequently had their uses for one another, and it was best to be the Pope's friend, on the whole, rather than his enemy. "After all, he is the leader of the Christian Church."

"Then why doesn't he come Crusading?" demanded Richard, reasonably enough, he thought. "Then he could lead from the van instead of the rearguard."

The entry of Berengaria and two of her ladies put an end to this likely line of argument, which Richard thought a pity because he had just been about to expound his latest theory that the present Pope was in fact the long-awaited Antichrist, due to wreak havoc in the world in the next decade or so.

"There is a matter of some Church land in dispute—your land, or it soon will be," Eleanor said, waving the ladies to seats and cushions around the fires.

"Why didn't you say so? I shall send most tender letters to his Holiness." Richard smiled derisively. "And now, shall we discuss something a little more pleasant than the she-wolf of Rome?"

There was, after all, no trembling in his hands and his good humor had returned. He turned his most luminous smile upon his betrothed and bade her come and sit near him. "You look rested; I hope our soldiers' beds are not too hard for you, even though they are not what you are used to. There will be better quarters when we reach Syria. Mategriffon was never built to house ladies."

"We have slept most excellently well, your Grace— have we not, ladies?" Berengaria's confidence blossomed beneath his appreciative look.

"I am very glad to hear it; now may we begin to talk of what has brought us here?" Queen Eleanor felt time pressing upon her. She turned a fearless face to Richard and asked him the question everyone had been asking him since he had attained manhood. "When, fair son, do you intend to wed?"

Richard threw back his head and laughed while Berengaria looked studiously at her slippers. Still laughing, he held out his hand to her. "Lady, I give you my pledge. In ten days we leave for the Holy Land. As soon as we arrive, you and I will marry. How say you? Shall you be ready?"

"I shall be ready," said Berengaria with her shy smile.

Eleanor nodded, satisfied. He had given his word. "Very well. It is good. Treasure her well; she is better than you deserve."

"Did you then think Alais of France to be my just

deserts?" cried Richard, stung. If he had hoped to
score a point in the continual Plantagenet game of
strike at the family, he was disappointed.

"No indeed," said Eleanor laconically, "the King of
France was our ally already, but the King of Navarre's
land marches close to Aquitaine. I like to think that
your father-in-law will watch out for your southern
borders. And then, my dear, I don't like to say so, but
little Alais *was* rather—used." No one dared to mention the name of the man who had used her.

"Ah, a family gathering! How nice." Joanna of Sicily
entered upon the arm of Tristan de Jarnac, whose good
looks, resplendent in mulberry velvet, commanded
every female eye to the disparagement of the several
other ladies and knights in her train.

There was a general commotion until all had found
places, giving Richard time to recover his urbanity
and Eleanor to remember that, much though she loved
him, Richard had always brought out the cat in her.
Here and now there could only be an echo of what it
had once been like; she had always been able to set
them at each other's throats, her husband and her
sons. Well, she had been in prison for it and perhaps
it served her right. There should be no more strug-
gles between them, not even in jest. She did not think
she had very much time left—and there was a great
deal still to do to guard Richard's throne for the future.

She had begun with Berengaria. It seemed, as she
looked at the two of them now, sitting close in shared
laughter, that she had begun well. And yet the child
was inexperienced in the ways of the world. War would
be a rude shock to her. It was as well the other girl
would be with her; she would need a true friend,
especially if there should be an early pregnancy . . .

"Eden!" She beckoned.

"Yes, your Grace?" Eden sank upon a cushion at
her feet.

"I intend to leave in two days' time. There is nothing further for me to accomplish here. You will wish
to stay, I know; you can have learned nothing. Mathilde
and Lady Alys have asked to remain also. I have

granted them permission. The Princess will welcome you all into her permanent household."

Eden gave her a warm look of gratitude. "My Queen, my heart is in your hands for what you have done for me; I thank you with all of it."

"Nonsense, child. You did all yourself; you always will. When we meet again, you shall tell me how you fared. I hope it will not be long."

"And that Stephen will be with me!" cried Eden. Then, greatly daring, not liking to travel under false pretences, she asked hesitantly. "Should I not tell the King's Grace my true reason for journeying to Outremer?"

"Very well." Eleanor approved so far as to speak for her, claiming Richard's attention and swiftly and succinctly putting Eden's case.

"Soul of Saint Peter!" exclaimed the King, much diverted. "Are we all to be pursued across the seas in ships by our wives?" He enjoyed Berengaria's blush. Eden found her eye uncomfortably caught by the Chevalier de Jarnac, who, unlike the grinning Richard, was regarding her with a certain wary surprise.

"Well, my lady," said the Lionheart cheerily, "as far as it touches me, you may question whom you will, when we reach our destination—as long as you keep out of the way of the arrows and the Saracens. I have no objection to it, but how if you find no trace of him? It is not always possible to know the fate of a knight taken in battle. While some are lucky enough to be held for ransom, others are simply enslaved or sold by their captors, and, though they may live, there is no means to know how or where . . ."

The voice and look were softer than she had known them and Eden saw that the King cared for his Crusaders; they were his brothers and he loved them in true Christian charity.

"I shall go on searching," she told him, feeling that he would, in some measure, understand and applaud her intention, "until I *know* what has become of Stephen de la Falaise."

"By your leave, my King?" Tristan de Jarnac spoke

from the bench where he lounged at ease against the wall. Richard turned toward him.

"When this lady leaves Sicily with us, we are entirely responsible for her welfare. If she were simply to serve the Princess and occupy herself, as might be expected, with domestic matters, all would be simple enough, but if she is to put herself at risk, in her search for her missing husband, outside the confines of the usual security limits for civilians, then how are we to guarantee her safety?" He turned to Eden, who faced him, wide-eyed and intent. "The cities of the Holy Land are cities at war: there is disease and danger in them and death stalks at every street corner. If you were to stray from your proper province, without sufficient guard, I would not give a fig for your safety—even among our own Christian soldiers; some of them haven't had a decent-looking woman for a year." There was a gasp of protest from the ladies, excepting Queen Eleanor, who smiled to herself. De Jarnac continued, unaffected. "It is even possible that, by some mischance, you might fall into Saracen hands —you may easily imagine what would then be your fate . . ."

"More easily than you have knowledge to conjecture!" cried Eden bitterly.

"My own safety is not my main objective, or, as must be clear, I should not be here. It is not my intention, either, to make myself an added burden to your Christian knights—only to ask questions of them. Do you not think that might be accomplished without my falling a prey to these evils you are too chivalrous to mention?" Stung by the calm certainty of his manner, she was too angry to bother to choose her words.

De Jarnac checked, obviously amazed at her outburst. Then, slowly, he smiled. "Alas, my lady—I can give you but one answer to that, which is that I do not think so." There was genuine regret in his tone.

"Let the others ask your questions for you, those who can go where you cannot. It may be a slow progress, but it will be as sure a one as any." He turned back, in appeal, to King Richard, who nodded energetically. De Jarnac was usually right.

"I have something to say in this matter!" Before the King could speak Queen Eleanor commanded the room. "It is this. I brought this lady with me on the understanding that she should be assisted to make all possible inquiries concerning her husband. There are reasons for this which I shall make clear to you when we are alone, my son. Suffice it to say that I have given her my word. Would you have me foresworn?"

The King waved an irritated hand, suddenly sick of the business. "Very well, very well! It shall be seen to. My lady Eden, let you wait upon the Princess while you may. We shall see what progress we may make in your other matter when we are better informed as to how we might begin. Now, *madame mère,* there are several problems pressing our attention; de Jarnac—stay with us. I want to look over the map with you."

For the rest, it was dismissal and they dispersed, the knights to their business and the ladies to their leisure. Berengaria joined her ladies for the first time since they had landed in Messina.

As they made their way to the solar, seeking their cloaks before taking a stroll outside the walls of Mategriffon, Mathilde observed wistfully, "I think I have never seen a man so handsome as the Chevalier de Jarnac. What a fire is in his eyes! And yet, his mouth! It is like . . . iron." she finished admiringly.

"And yet not so," murmured Alys surprisingly. "There is a softness also . . ." Her pale cheek suffused with faint color.

"I think you would like to find out for yourself how soft his lips might be," teased Berengaria, who wanted everyone to be in love.

"You must not say such things! I did but note the look of the man . . ." But her blush now deepened into a glowing rose.

"For myself, I can see no such beauty in the Chevalier," was Eden's comment. This was not strictly true, but she had no desire toward the truth at present.

She still smarted under the knight's unwarranted interference in matters which were none of his concern.

"*Eh bien, ma chère* . . . you must be blind," decided Berengaria.

"He was only thinking of your safety, Eden," suggested Alys, coldly sensing, out of turn, what troubled Eden. Then slowly, "I think there was much good sense in what he said; perhaps you should listen to him . . ."

"You are plainly moonstruck . . . all of you!" replied Eden angrily. With a glare for the traitor, Alys, she snatched up her cloak as soon as she reached the solar and fled again down the steep, wooden stair. She would take her walk alone. The air would be much sweeter to her if praise of Tristan de Jarnac did not float upon every indiscriminate breeze.

He had made her think upon things she had not wished to remember. She would not forgive him, either for that or for his damnable intrusion between her and the King.

After three days of intense, concentrated discussion and wrangling with her son and his advisors, during which she had satisfied herself of his good intentions toward government, Eleanor the Queen was ready to go home. The crowd that watched her set sail was smaller than that which had welcomed her; no one would have believed a woman of her age would undertake another voyage so swiftly. Lacking in bulk, the crowd made up for it in vociferous appreciation, crying "Noel" with all their might, waving arms, spears, caps and scarves energetically to signify that she was much loved.

Eden, who stood close beside her on the quay with Berengaria, found herself fighting back tears of regret as the scarlet and blue galley broke out its striped sail. It came to her just how mighty a bulwark that remarkable nature had been to them all, even to her, who had relied, and proudly, upon her own resources for two years—and looked to continue so. How would they fare each day, without the wry humor, the unimpassioned criticism, the discerning praise, and, what she now recognized as the unabating affection in which the Queen had held her small troupe of neophytes.

Eleanor, dry-eyed and in perfect command of her emotions as always, did not wish her last sight of Sicily to include a group of weeping damsels. She ignored the rising sentiment amongst them, addressing herself to King Richard who was towering uneasily among his attendant knights, himself none so fond of leave-takings, unless they were his own.

"May God's hand guide your sword, fair son—and grant you a swift victory, that you may come home to England the sooner." There were some to whose amused ears her words had more the timbre of a command than a pious hope; the Queen, it was known, was out of temper with Richard's many delays in reaching the Holy Land; whether or not they were his fault did not affect her attitude.

"I thank you, my lady mother and my Queen," Richard responded gravely, giving her, with conscious dignity, this title for the last time, "we shall all offer up our prayers for your own safe passage home."

He strode forward and wrapped Eleanor in his arms and Eden was astonished to see how slight a figure she was, enfolded in that strong embrace.

Now it was Berengaria's turn to say farewell and to whisper her thanks as she was held close. Then the ex-Queen of Sicily took her leave of her mother. And then, although she had only half expected it, the Queen held out her arms to Eden. As the smooth, finely lined cheek was pressed against her own and the firm hands took her by the shoulders, she heard the dry voice bidding her, "Take courage, *ma fille*. Accomplish your quest—and seek me out when you shall come home. *Adieu*, until we meet in England."

"*Dieu vous garde*, your Grace. I shall hold fast," Eden whispered. All thought of tears had left her now; Eleanor had known how to call out sterner qualities than sentiment; she would be alone now, she knew, and must learn to call upon them for herself.

As she stood with the rest and watched the bold little vessel recede until it was a mere speck whose color was hard to determine amid the blue immensity, she felt that at last she had attained the true beginning of her task. Perhaps it was not Stephen alone for whom she must search; she must also look inward and discover the unknown landscape of her true self. She had felt a change in that self in the days since she had known the Queen. The change would continue, she knew, but how and where it would lead her she could not tell. She felt, however, that Eleanor had given her a thin layer of unseen armor that would stand her in as good a stead in the world as Berengaria's ringmail.

Resolutely, she turned away from the sea. Then, suddenly and incongruously, she found her undirected glance caught and held by that of Tristan de Jarnac; she had taken no note of his presence among those who attended the King. He gave her his abrupt, bright smile and made as if to approach her. Instantly she looked away, her face cold and unmoving. He could have nothing to say to her that she could wish to hear.

The feasting that night was somewhat lacking in the ceremonious restraint that had characterized the few previous nights; Eleanor's absence was felt in other ways than those of simple regret.

Sir John de Wulfran had sunk from grace beneath his seat by half-past-nine and Will Barret had, with apologies she was coming to regard as habitual, excused himself to Eden and, assisted by his squire, had hefted the comatose knight off to bed. Eden, weary of the commotion and horseplay within the hall, slipped from her place and, taking her old green cloak from the back of her chair, made her way up to the lofty battlements of Mategriffon.

The night was starless, the skies low, dark and enfolding; the air was warm, its touch on her skin almost intimate. She leaned upon the rampart and looked out over the city. Its black, unexplained shapes were intermittently lit by the glow of a candle through shutters of the steady swing of a lantern as someone picked his way through the narrow streets. Beyond lay the sea. She could not make it out but the night was filled with its presence. There were still lights in the harbor where Richard's fleet lay at anchor, and now and then the sounds of the sailors' carousal was carried faintly toward her with the soft washing of the waves.

She stared out over the limitless blue-black expanse. For the first time since they had taken ship in England, she found herself completely alone, her thoughts all her own. How far she had traveled, across that daunting immensity of water out there—and how far there was still to go. The fancy came to her, as she stood upon the quiet ramparts, that she was also poised upon some intangible promontory between past and future. Behind her, in time as in distance, stretched the long familiarity of the past, where in her childhood, her marriage and her peaceful life with Stephen all seemed part of a gentle, protracted sleep, banished forever by the terrible shock of sin and violence that had been its awakening. She could not become that dulcet sleeper again. Instead, she must use her newly opened eyes to look forward, into the unknown future that waited for her across those unseen, whispering seas. Her whole being was possessed by a restless impatience. It seemed to her that, no matter how many miles of wonders were revealed to her receptive sense, she had scarcely begun to make progress upon her quest. Not all the novelty of wooden decks beneath her feet, the daily, careless magnificence of court life, this charmed island of sunlight upon ripening fruit, the mixing and mingling with all manner of men, from tanned Byzantine oarsmen to the King of England himself, could begin to make their full impression upon her until she had found the course which would lead her to Stephen. She gazed, sightlessly, into the warm darkness and felt that her mind and heart had become like an arrow, forged from strong steel, aimed for a single flight, but the hand that held the bow delayed. Whose hand was it, she wondered; was it the King's? She did not feel that

Richard had cared greatly for her presence and her purpose; how should he? Her cause was not his; indeed, she wished to deprive him of one of his brave Crusaders. And certainly the Queen had done all in her power to aid her; so had Berengaria—and would do more. Why then was she oppressed with this sense of urgency, of waiting, of marking time, needless time? Perhaps she had caught it from the knights who surrounded them, some of them driven almost to accidie by the long months of winter quarters and the blunting of their holy cause in the greedy quarrels of petty princes.

She drummed her fingers upon the wooden battlement realizing the extent of her own impatience. And yet, she thought wonderingly, she had lived and worked daily at Hawkhurst for near two years without this restlessness. Smiling somewhat grimly into the darkness, she saw that, by an outrageous twist of fate, Sir Hugo's had been the hand to forge the arrow's steel. Without him, she would now be snug abed in her chill solar, dreamless after too many chores.

Repentant, she muttered a swift Ave; "I will not ask for more, when so much is already given. Sweet Magdalen, teach me patience; I will try to learn." She sighed, her body still now, and let the peace of the calm night invade her. All would be well; the arrow would find its flight.

A step behind her, swift and light, broke her solitude; sudden torchlight threw a tall shadow upon the rampart beside her own.

"Well found, Lady Hawkhurst."

She stiffened. She knew those cool, dark tones.

"I wished to speak with you. If you will favor me for one moment?"

She did not wish to speak, to lose her hard-won peace. She did not turn. "Chevalier?" Her voice was detached, betraying no interest in his presence.

There was a brief silence. Perhaps he had sighed, perhaps merely smiled. He said softly, "It seemed that you were angered by my words to the King con-

cerning your—personal matter. I wished only to tell
you that they were spoken, not from any desire to
hinder your interests—how could that be?—but from
the wish to ensure your safety among us."

His voice warmed, despite the imperturbable silence
of the figure beside him. "Truly, my lady, I would
count it an honor if you would allow me to be of use
to you in your search. We shall doubtless meet often
—and it would be a pity if my presence were to put
you into a continual rage."

She turned toward him, her face a luminous challenge in the torchlight. Once again he had come upon
her as an interloper, breaking in upon her thoughts
tonight as he had broken in upon her words to the
King in the day. He was irrelevant, an unnecessary
irritation given her by some malicious imp of fate.
He was also powerful, persuasive, and had the King's
ear. Why could he not address his insolent interest to
Lady Alys, who would have the excellent bad taste to
appreciate it?

"I shall hope to avoid excessive anger as I shall hope
to avoid your presence, Chevalier," she told him even-
ly, her lips severely set.

He regarded her without any visible sign of regret,
indeed with lazy amusement. "So you refuse my offer of
protection? Your husband will not, I fear, thank you
for it!"

"And will you offer with one hand what you would
keep back with the other, then, Sir Tristan, as you did
before? You wish to be of use to me, you say. How
far, then, are you prepared to take your magnanimous offer? As far as Jerusalem, or Damascus, if need
be? Or into the distant lands of the Turks, the strong-
holds of Saladin?" Her voice was fiercely mocking. "Oh,
I am very ready to believe that you are most willing to
question any you might happen to meet, on my behalf!
But how many marks will you spend, how many
leagues will you ride, how much of your precious
time will you give? How far would you put yourself
in danger in my cause?" She finished on a note of angry

determination. "I have come to make my own search, sir knight, and fully intend to do so; and I will not brook your further interference in my path."

"I am sorry that you see it so," he answered quietly, with no trace of his previous humor.

"I shall do very well without your aid," Eden said dismissively. "I am accustomed to being my own mistress."

Then, certainly, she heard him sigh; whether this was prompted by a proper dejection or mere irritation was hard to distinguish.

"You are very certain, lady, of what you have not yet met and very sure of dealing with circumstances you cannot yet conceive." He hesitated. She made no reply. "And when I offer you my help," he continued quietly, "I offer it entirely. I impose no limits; what the King and my duty permit, I will do. But you must not expect me to countenance your putting yourself in danger needlessly; that I will not do."

"So!" her voice was strung with contempt. "You will courteously allow me to give over my business into your capable hands—but you will not move an inch to help me if I should in any way attempt to help myself. Sir, you are ridiculous!" Spinning round, she would have left him had he not caught swiftly at her hand.

"Lady, my business here is with God and the King, as it is with all of us. If I offer you aid, it must detract from that dedication; it is no small thing, therefore, that I offer you."

"If it goes so hard against the grain, then why do you offer it?" she demanded, pulling away the hand he held, lightly now, in his.

His voice came levelly. She could not see his face in the shadows, but she sensed some kind of pain in its taut cadences.

"Perhaps because there was, once in my life, a time when my help came too late," he said.

A small flame of curiosity lit in her for a second, then she turned away from him. "I would not take you for one instant from your Christian duty, Chevalier," she said lightly over her shoulder as she left him standing alone on the battlements. She felt in herself the desire to hurt him.

For a moment Sir Tristan stood staring out into the warm darkness, remembering. Then he shook the long-dead dreams from his mind and his heart and swung round in the wake of the angry and disconcertingly lovely Lady of Hawkhurst.

During the next few days the castle of Mategriffon was systematically dismantled and stowed away, in sections, aboard ship; it too, was going to the Kingdom of Jerusalem. The more august of its inhabitants, therefore, repaired to a spacious and elegant house in the city that belonged to the ex-queen, Joanna, the King's sister. This lady had been appointed as Berengaria's official chaperone until she should be married and went about the business with a true Plantagenet's sense of hospitality. Whenever anything lacked she would simply send out her men-at-arms to requisition it from the household of some hapless citizen of Messina.

"Will such things not breed discontent?" Eden was bold enough to ask her, as the tuns of wine, the bales of figured cotton, and the intricate silver jewelery began to find their way, not only into the palace, but aboard the waiting galleys and roundships in which they would shortly sail.

Joanna shrugged, reminding Eden of her mother in her coolest and most practical mood. "Sicily owes me nearly two years of freedom; therefore the island may pay me in kind for its unkindness. I am willing. Besides, Eden—you do not know these Griffons as I do —they would slit your throat for the joy of it if they dared. And then, never think that they, many of them, have not done well enough out of Richard's presence here, especially their women—foul harlots!"

Eden was puzzled. "But were they not your people? Were you not their Queen? Have you no love for them?"

Joanna smiled, considering. "As much as one may come to love a monkey—or a cat," she allowed, trying the effect of a jeweled silver necklet against her deeply tanned skin.

Eden was aware of a certain amount of guilt when some of the spoils came her own way, in the form of a very pretty emerald necklace and bracelet worth some poor Greek's fortune. However she held her peace, save to say her thanks convincingly enough. She would be much in Joanna's company in the coming weeks; it would not be well to be the cause of dissent. Also, she should not frown on fortune's increase, from whatever quarter; she had need of all that came her way.

They left Messina discerningly stripped on 10 April, in Richard's finest roundship, a great deal more comfortable than the galley which had brought them from England. There were partitioned sleeping quarters below, soft seats and a cook who understood the sensitivity of the seaborne palate.

Richard himself traveled in his magnificent war galley, *Trenchemer* . . . the Sea Slicer, in the van of his two hundred strong fleet. He wished to think about the coming campaign and did not want the clamor of women around him.

Sometimes, during the first days, he would ride the roundship companionably close in the high galley, and the ladies, walking the wintry decks for the good of their digestions, would catch a glimpse of the Lionheart doing likewise, his broad arm thrown carelessly about the shoulders of a tall knight in a blue cloak. Lady Alys would lean langorously upon the rail, pretending a sudden all-consuming interest in the species of the seabirds that followed in their foaming wake.

"How stands your acquaintance with Sir Tristan, Alys?" asked Berengaria on the third day, as they gazed across the ill-colored, sullen reach of water, dull as old pewter, that stretched limitlessly about them.

Alys sighed. She had found it impossible to hide her growing interest in the alarmingly handsome Chevalier. "It was kind of you, Madam, to contrive that he should be my companion at the feast on the last night," she conceded gratefully. "He spoke with me a great deal, telling me much of his sojourn in the Holy

Land before his present service with the King; of his hideous strife that was there . . . the sieges and the terrible battle at Hattin." Eden saw unaccustomed softness in her eyes as she continued. "There was, it seems, a lady somehow lost to him on that dreadful day. I cannot tell how, for, though he started to speak of it, he fell suddenly silent and would go no further. I fear that, whoever she was, she meant much to him . . . and does so still . . . for though he spoke to me gently and with the greatest courtesy . . . I could not feel his words were meant for me . . ."

Berengaria was encouraging. "Then for whom? You are too modest . . . isn't she, Eden?"

Eden, who had felt a swift reawakening of the spark of curiosity she had known on the battlements of Mategriffon, did not see fit to reveal this.

"I know nothing of the Chevalier's mind or heart; how should I?" she said without emphasis, carefully examining the freshening of the white-tipped waves. Conscious of Alys's faintly calculating gaze, she added, to change the subject, "I believe we shall soon have a storm."

Berengaria, who had been excellently well thus far, saw the specter of the dreaded *mal-de-mer* arise before her. She too stared into the grim waters. "Surely not," she hoped. "It is only the little white horses. A pretty effect, don't you think?" Eden did not reply.

A mere hour later, seasickness was the least of anyone's troubles. There was indeed a storm. The ship which had seemed so mighty in its security was swept up, shaken, rent and crushed in the grip of what must surely be the hand of Satan. All about her the waters churned and groaned and chasmed, while the wind kept up a terrible skirling that sounded to the terrified ears of her passengers like the laughter of attendant devils as they welcomed a myriad Christian souls, unshriven, to the deep. No man could hold the tiller. It had been lashed down in an attempt to steady it, but the strong rope broke like a strand of soft silk as the vessel plunged into abyss after abyss. The sound of desperate prayers mingled with the hellish windsong.

Somewhere, out in the deepening blackness to the
west of them, the King had set a light burning at his
masthead, to guide whoever might see it; others followed suit. In this manner, the greatest part of the immense fleet was, by the grace of God, kept together.
The captain of the roundship saw the faint glimmer
come and go in the murky turbulence and made a man-
ful attempt to steer by it, but the storm had chosen
them as the plaything of its vortex and there was no
way to hold the pitching vessel on a course.

And then, as suddenly as it had arisen, the demonic
wind dropped, leaving them in the midst of a silent and
terrifying calm. Truly there could be no better proof
that the storm had been the work of the Devil and all
his imps. The captain fell to the deck in prayer, the
sailors following suit. Eden, clinging to Berengaria,
both of them lashed by their precious veils and scarves
to the uprights of their sleeping partitions, was as-
tounded by the instantaneous change. She held her
breath for the next cataclysm, which would surely be
the last and greatest. It did not come.

"Are we alive?" breathed Berengaria doubtfully.

"So it would seem!" replied Eden, smiling shakily.
"It is over. At last!"

So she untied herself and the Princess and set about
helping the other ladies, all placed in similar bondage
by the despairing captain, more, had they known it, to
keep them from shrieking and wailing in his preoccupied ears than for their own safety. As she did so,
she reflected that she had not, in fact, expected to die;
it was clear that God had a further purpose for her; he
had indicated as much in the chapel, at home in Hawkhurst. Accordingly, she too fell to her knees to thank
him for the grace given to her to know it. Hardly had
the soused and battered crew and their bruised, thankful passengers risen from their knees, however, than
they sank down again in renewed supplication. The
end of the storm was by no means the end of their
troubles. They now found themselves, at nightfall, in
total darkness with no friendly mast-light in sight.
Their course was irrevocably lost and there was not

a single star in the black void above by which they might recover it.

This time their prayers, it seemed, were not well received. As the night wore on, the accursed wind rose again, and though its force was far from tempestuous, it bowled them along at a boisterous pace in what the Captain asserted, in tones of well-enacted nonchalance, to be a southeasterly direction.

For a day and a half they scudded before the stormy wind. For much of this time Eden paced the deck, tormented by the fear that they might be traveling in an entirely different direction and would shortly find themselves cast upon the coast of Africa—at the hideous mercy of those black Saracens whose legends had haunted her pillow as a child. It was while she was brooding frustratedly over the heartless playfulness of the ocean that the lookout's wavering cry of "A sail!" broke her black mood. Two more of the King's ships had been sighted. Both had been blown off-course, as they had, by the storm. Their spirits rose; they were no longer alone.

In the merry convoy of three they continued to run before the wind, keeping together by the exchange of lights when darkness fell. At last the stars reappeared and informed the captains that their involuntary course was set for the island of Cyprus.

This, Eden was surprised to learn from Joanna Plantagenet, was not altogether a welcome piece of news.

"Isaac Comnenus, who styles himself Emperor of Cyprus, is a member of the imperial family of Constantinople; he seized his power by a trick—arriving on the island some five years ago with forged papers, claiming to be its newly appointed governor, sent from Byzantium. No one suspected him; his lineage is impeccable. All the Cypriot fortresses were given over to him; the government was his. Then the insolent masquerader threw off his deception and declared himself Emperor and independent ruler of Cyprus. The Byzantine government was—naturally—more than a little displeased; its nose had been well pulled. In order to hold their revenge at bay, this amazing man allied himself at once with Saladin. It has even been said that they drank each other's blood to seal the pact!"

"But surely—Isaac Comnenus is a Christian prince?" said Berengaria, bewildered.

"Certainly! Of the Greek persuasion, but a Christian sure enough."

"Mother of God! What perfidy! To ally himself with the infidel!"

"Many do it," replied Joanna laconically, "to protect their lands and commerce. The Christian settlers in the Three Kingdoms of the Holy Land are in their second generation. How else should they survive?"

"Yes—but this man is little better than a bandit!" declared Berengaria firmly. "I hope we shall have little to do with him!"

"The length and breadth of the matter is," interrupted Eden, seeing the shores of Jerusalem recede once more in her mind's eye, "that we are being driven, without choice, toward a land where we are uncertain of our welcome. This 'Emperor' may offer us his hospitality as Christians like himself—or he may give us a hostile welcome as being the enemies of Saladin, his sworn blood-brother."

"Perfect, Lady Hawkhurst." Joanna was dry. "But fate does not hold us entirely within its balance. The Princess is, after all, to be England's Queen—and I am the Lionheart's sister. By now, Isaac will know of Richard's approach. He will also know of Tancred's fate and Sicily's! I doubt," she finished, with a curl of satisfaction to her lip, "if a mere renegade Comnenus princeling will risk being similarly disadvantaged."

Eden began to relax. "As long as he will allow us to speed on our way once this fiendish wind has blown itself out."

Joanna shrugged and suggested a game of backgammon. She had seen much of the world and had learned to avoid anxiety where possible.

"Do not worry, *mes enfants!* It accomplishes nothing—and is aging to a woman."

Again, it might have been her mother who spoke

and Eden was cheered. Her optimistic mood was not to last, however, for as the three ships neared the equivocal Cypriot coast, a strong current conspired with the still restless wind to drive them on at an increasingly headlong and dangerous pace.

It was night. The passengers stood huddled in their cloaks, peering uneasily into the darkness, trying to make out the shapes of the approaching shoreline. There were stars above but also clouds, while a pale moon threw deceptive shadows across the water and the landfall, making them difficult to tell apart. Eden stood with her companions at the rail. They shivered as the seas lashed over them in sudden unpredictable gusts, almost sweeping their feet from under them. On all sides there was the rushing and swirling of water and a confusion of cries and orders from their own ship and the other two galleys, speeding somewhere to the east of them. The most terrible part of it, for Eden, was the terrified screaming of the horses, penned in their stalls in front of the forecastle.

"I must go to Balan. If he breaks his ropes he'll be taken overboard!" She was gone before the Princess or Joanna could protest; she heard their cries, torn into single, ragged notes behind her as she forged slowly, hand over hand, along the groaning rail, toward the pitching fore of the vessel.

The fear among the horses was pitiful to see. They stamped and squealed and pulled desperately to be free of the very bonds that held them safe. Eden could see Balan, his head tossing in mindless terror, his hooves beating the air as he strove to keep his feet and break his ropes at one and the same time. As she made her way along the outer limit of the pens, Eden was suddenly aware of a great, dark, heaving shape that seemed to rise up out of the water beside her own vessel; for a moment it hung over them, like some unrecognized phantom; there were sounds, somewhere within its black center, which she half thought she should recognize; then both sound and shape were gone, plunging headlong past them in a rush of churning water, leaving the ship dancing madly among the

hurrying waves. And then there came a sickening
sound, a grazing and a grating, no, a shock and a
rending, as the sister ship that had outrun them fetched
up and foundered, every voice and every timber crying out in its extremity, fast in the teeth of the cruel
rocks ahead.

"Merciful Heaven! We must save them!" was the cry
washed with the waters along the deck to Eden's
anguished ear.

"If we can save ourselves, it'll be a miracle!" bel-
lowed an oarsman, rowing with the desperate movement of one who cannot swim but tries to keep afloat.

"We cannot hold her off the rocks! We must jump,
or we're done for!" cried a hideously tempting voice
somewhere to the left.

The confusion from the other ship was appalling
as in pain and terror the unshriven voyagers cursed
and prayed amid the unearthly screeching of their
horses. Eden stood uncertainly at the rail still. She did
not know if this was her own overstressed body that
shook so that she could not control its movement, or
if the ship itself were trembling so hideously in every
timber. She made a motion toward Balan, but found
that her step had taken her backwards. The deck was
slippery beneath her feet. There was a sudden tre-
mendous lurch and she had lost her foothold, the rail
sliding through her clutching fingers. For a moment
she saw the black depths of the water, swirling and
leaping beneath her; then it was as if she had amazingly discovered the power of human flight. For one half
of a delirious, surprising second she lay upon the
winds over the waters—and then they rose with a
swift, terrifying solidity; there was a brief, scarcely
experienced shock of meeting and then all was black
falling, endless, soft and merciful.

CHAPTER FIVE

Cyprus: Isaac

There was no longer the turbulent movement, nor the terrible cries. She was still and she was cold, dreadfully cold. Her whole body shivered convulsively. She lay upon her face, the surface beneath her painfully hard and strangely shifting. There was water everywhere. She tried to move and found herself vomiting weakly, the taste of salt strong in her throat. This was no longer the ship, but the shore. Pushing with her hands against the unfriendly shingle, she attempted to rise, but sank down again with a swift cry of pain. She felt as though every part of her body had been kicked by horses. She tried again, slowly this time. Her clothing clung about her, weighty and unfamiliar; she was sodden to her very bones.

Even as she began to realize what had happened to her, Eden became aware that the air was filled with unintelligible cries. Men's voices, sharp with command, peopled the darkness, together with answering shouts, excited, triumphant. Instinctively she knew she must move, but as she lifted her hands to push the soaking strands of hair from her eyes, she heard the crunch of boots among the pebbles behind her and a hand descended heavily upon her shoulder.

The Cypriot soldier was delighted. This was the best prize yet. Most of the shipwrecked Franks were only soldiers like themselves, carrying little worth the picking, now that the sea had taken first choice. And, since most of them were dead anyway, there'd be few left to ransom. There'd be better things to do with this one, however, than to strip her for her riches—though stripping her would certainly have a great deal to do with it, from what he could see by the thin light of this accursed moon.

"Hey! D'mitrios!" he called to his sergeant. "Come over here and see what I've got!"

Eden made out a sturdy shape, legs asplay, hands planted firmly on broad hips. The face seemed to be bearded and she caught the gleam of teeth as he smiled, well pleased with his booty.

"What is it? Gold?" the sergeant enquired hopefully, plunging toward them. He reached them, panting, and stood beside the other. His words meant nothing to Eden as he pronounced, after a brief survey: "My, you have done well, young Akis. But she's no common soldier's trollop, this one!" He grinned.

"She'll do for an officer when she's cleaned up a bit! Come on, my little half-drowned kitten. Let's see if we can't make a nice, plump pussy out of you."

Between them they pulled her, none too roughly, to her feet, and, thankful that at least she wasn't to die on the spot, she staggered willingly enough, with their aid, to the more hospitable part of the sands. As she went, Eden saw that the beach was full of moving shapes as the Cypriots went about their salvage work.

Turning to look out to sea, she saw the dark bulk of one of the galleys, riding at anchor just beyond the jagged rocks that filled the small bay. She prayed that it would be the one which carried Berengaria and Joanna, and they were still safe aboard her. The stricken forms of the other two ships, their shapes made even more unnatural by the cold moonlight, protruded brokenly above the line of the rocks like the fractured bones of some poor skeletons, long since without flesh. She saw a light flicker and grow strong upon the deck of the one which was afloat and hope grew within her. Perhaps her friends would be safe, and Gilles and the terrified Balan with them. Hope was all she had.

Prodded by her captors, she turned away from the desecration on the beach. Behind it rose the dark bulk of an immense cliff, which stretched unevenly as far as her eye could make out. From the great number of lights at its head, it was obvious that they had been wrecked near some large city, and, if the galley captain's last hopeful computation had been correct, it would be the port of Limassol; how nearly they must have missed gaining the safety of its harbor!

Eden spoke the name clearly as her escort hurried her along.

"Eh? Yes, that's right, beauty. Limassol, home of the brave," the sergeant agreed cheerfully. "You'll like it here—if you're a good girl and give us no trouble. Though like as not we'll soon be giving you some. All of them little ones!" Eden needed no Greek or Cypriot to recognize the note in the guffaw that followed. A shiver, entirely unconnected with her sodden state, ran through her. Then she pulled herself up with sudden resolution. She had not escaped the attentions of the Baron of Stukesey merely to become the plaything of common pikemen or archers. With as much dignity as was possible in the circumstances, she came to a halt and drew herself to what she hoped was a commanding height.

"I am the Lady of Hawkhurst," she declared firmly, addressing the sergeant and looking him severely in the eye. "I am a personal friend of the future Queen of England, and of Queen Eleanor, regnant of Aquitaine!"

The two stalwarts came to a halt also, and looked at each other in perplexity.

She drew breath and tried a simpler message. "Richard Plantagenet," she announced, "the Lionheart."

The dark brows cleared as if by magic. "Ah!" They nodded. "Lionheart!" repeated one, with execrable but recognizable pronunciation. Then he spat, copiously.

Eden thought it unadvisable to continue the conversation. She contented herself with holding her head as regally as she could, despite her aching bones, and, shaking off the hands of her guard, she paced ahead of them grimly.

By now they had left the beach, a stark, chill scene of death and despolation, and were climbing the

twisting path which scaled the vast outcrop of rock.
She saw that other prisoners walked, similarly guarded,
before them, and doubtless others would follow behind. She gazed upward and saw, in the flaring light
of the myriad torches that crowned the heights, that
they were approaching the squat and forbidding outline of a great fortress.

"Limassol!" the sergeant repeated triumphantly,
pointing at it.

Eden suddenly remembered what Queen Joanna
had told them of Cyprus.

"Isaac Comnenus!" she cried confidently. This time
the reaction was all that she had hoped for; respect
opened the sergeant's lascivious eyes and fear darted
in those of his inferior.

"Take me to Isaac Comnenus," she continued forcefully, pointing first to herself and then to the castle on
the heights.

There was a swift altercation between her captors.
This continued, growing in volume, until they reached
the top of the rockpath and entered, beneath an iron
grille which was raised for them, the precincts of the
fortress itself.

If she had hoped for an immediate interview with
the self-styled Emperor of Cyprus, Eden was swiftly
disillusioned. Within moments of her entry into the
fortress of Limassol, she found herself cast into a
large, ill-lit and vile-smelling dungeon, in company
with some two dozen of her fellow captives, who had, it
seemed, been swept ashore from all three of the King's
luckless ships. There were none she knew well, though
she recognized several faces. No one was able to tell her
what had been the fate of the Princess, though it was
generally thought that there had been far fewer cast-
aways from the royal vessel.

When all the prisoners were assembled they were
subjected to a thorough search of their persons. This,
Eden found very humiliating and her two guards extremely pleasant.

"Here's a fine, gold cross," cried the sergeant in delight, fumbling about her breasts. "T'would be sacri-

lege not to kiss it." And grinning, he pulled the wet cloth of her gown from the chilled globes beneath, so that they, together with the rest of her body, were instantly warmed into a deep blush of mortification. With what little strength she had, she swept her fist into the side of his head. He frowned and was about to take further liberties when another soldier, evidently his superior, cuffed him impatiently away from her, himself snatching at the cross. They left her trembling with fury and disgust, the memory of Hugo Malfors a living presence in the dank cell.

There was an angry murmur among the prisoners and someone cried out, "For shame!" The officer disregarded this show of solidarity and gave curt instructions to the caftaned clerk who now appeared in the chamber, burdened with a small, portable writing desk, inkstand and quill pen. The clerk, a bowed, scurrying individual with a worried, short-sighted look, moved toward the nearest prisoner and dug him interrogatively in the chest with his pen. The captain stood by, idly swinging Eden's cross between his fingers, while the names of the captives were listed on heavy, greenish paper.

"We had best make as much, or more, of our lands and titles as we may," suggested a thickset knight whose deeply tanned and scarred features betrayed enough experience for his words to be heeded. "The more it seems we may be worth in ransom—the longer we shall live. If you have little in land or fortune, let it grow on the paper. Richard will have us haled out of this before we can be found out, I'd stake my name on it."

Eden thought that, by now, her friendships might stand her in better stead than her lands when it came to bargaining, but she added the Barony of Stukesey to her titles, just for the peculiar private pleasure of it.

It seemed that they were to be left alone after this. The guards turned about smartly at the captain's command and marched away, the sergeant casting one last look of self-denying lust in Eden's direction as he went. A pile of blankets was thrown in at the iron door before it was locked; a single torch was left to light the gloomy, airless cell.

"Are we not to be fed, or given to drink?" many demanded, angrily.

"Apparently not," murmured the knight of the many scars, casting off his wet cloak and wrapping himself tightly in one of the blankets. "But then neither, it seems, are we to be killed, or put to the torture. For which mercy I recommend we thank God—and then address ourselves to sleep."

Once again, the old Crusader's advice seemed sound, and, accepting the blanket that one of the younger knights held out to her with a shy smile, Eden too, wrapped it as closely about her as she could and lay down upon the hard stone floor. It was uncomfortable, but it was not, as it might have been, damp; and although it was cold, there were nearly thirty of them in the dungeon and they would give each other their warmth as animals do. If they could but forget their aching, bruised limbs and the nagging in their empty bellies, they would do well by several hours sleep. Before she closed her eyes, Eden offered up a brief prayer of thanks to her patron, the Magdalen; she was the only woman among the prisoners, and an unusually comely one, but, apart from a few minor indignities, she had come to no harm by reason of her sex. She prayed, too, that this acceptable state of affairs might be allowed to continue. In mid-prayer, she slept.

In the morning, much to her surprise, she was awoken neither by the complaints of her fellows nor the rough hands of the fortress guards, but by a plump and smiling girl of about her own age, dark-skinned, bright-eyed and evidently pleased with her errand.

"Xanthe," she whispered, pointing to herself. Then she indicated that Eden was to get up and follow her, without waking her still slumbering companions. Eden rubbed the sleep from her eyes. Apprehensive but much intrigued, she stumbled after the Cypriot girl, her stiff joints and muscles beginning to complain; she was conscious that her face was dirty, that her hair hung matted about her shoulders and her clothing was reduced to mere misshapen rags.

They made their way along passages and up a stairway, passing out of the cold level of the dungeons and storehouses into the warmer regions where the life of the fortress went on. Eden had enticing glimpses of sunlit, agreeable rooms before they halted outside a wooden door from which she was astonished to see steam escaping at every possible aperture. The door was swiftly opened and shut at her companion's knock and she found herself suddenly in a white world of shifting vapors filled with the scents of a hundred woods and flowers.

Queen Eleanor had built herself a bathhouse in her palace at Winchester, horrified by the English determination to live and die as what she called virgins of the bath. The Cypriot variety was even larger and more splendidly sybaritic. There was hot water, steaming perpetually, gushing at intervals through vast sunken pipes into the wide, shallow baths where several glossily naked women lay cushioned against the tiled sides. There were three or four of them, their skin the color of polished oak, gleaming in the fragrant water. They all had the dark, heavy hair and wide, deeply lashed round eyes of the true Mediterranean woman. They lay back langorously as half a dozen dusky hand maidens gave them a vigorous scrubbing. These girls, slender and also naked except for a small strip of striped cloth about their lions, attracted Eden's interest even more than their mistresses—for they were completely black.

If the bathing beauties had skins of golden oak, theirs were surely like ebony. Eden had never seen a black-skinned person before, and found it impossible not to stare. She thought them beautiful, but in the manner in which a carving or a picture might be beautiful, by its own intrinsic standard. Their hair was tightly curled and cut close to their heads, much shorter even than a man's; their bodies were longer and more slender than any she had seen, their hips no wider than their thin, straight thighs. Their lips were very fine, proud and curling beneath fine, flaring nostrils. She knew that they must be of Moorish blood, brought from the north coast of the dark continent of Africa. They seemed happy enough at their work, however, trilling and babbling in their own, barbarous tongue while they scraped and pummeled their mistresses with gray, perforated stones and with strange, evenly-shaped objects resembling some pale, wholly unlikely flower which expanded as it absorbed the perfumed water.

She looked at Xanthe and pointed to her ill-smelling dress. The girl nodded energetically and within seconds Eden, too, lay blissfully in the huge basin. Its first occupants immediately set up a shrill, questioning babel, turning from Xanthe to her ward with rolling eyes and demanding tongues. Eden supposed it must be Greek they were speaking, though the accent was unlike that she had heard in Sicily. Laughing, she shook her head, trying to show, also, that she was disposed to be friendly. The noise abated a little, but the swift stream of questions continued, most of which Xanthe tried to answer, though with little success, as was clear by the shaking of the shining heads.

Eden had bathed naked among other women before and this, in itself, did not trouble her modesty; she soon found, however, that these women, both black and golden, were apt to gaze at her body as though it were that of a rare and spectacular animal. Their look was curious but not unfriendly as they stared at the peach-gold of her skin and the delicate modeling of her bones. The color of her eyes, in particular, intrigued them and that of her hair, especially her maidenhair, a bright, gilded triangle, almost as fair as her head. One of the Moorish slave girls lavished this with attention, rubbing oil of cedarwood into it and grinning widely as she made some remark to her fellows. The sensation was very pleasant and Eden relaxed under the gently caressing fingers, though she felt herself blushing when later, two of the black girls gently parted her thighs and began their massage in earnest, their long, sensitive fingers shamelessly provoking responses she had all but forgotten. Her heart pumping, she moved to dissuade them, but they only laughed and pressed her back in the warm soft water. Another one slipped in beside her and, putting her arms about Eden's body from behind, half supported her as she delicately stroked the pink tips of her nipples until they stood proudly erect.

She lay helplessly floating between embarrassment and pleasure, the impulse to leap from the bath and run, naked as she was, away from her own sinfulness and the desire to stay where she was and let these extraordinary women do as they wished with her. She drifted, thinking of Stephen . . .

The dragging aches of the early morning dissolved in the silken waters. There was a sudden commotion about the door and the slaves became still.

Paralyzed by fear and modesty, Eden raised her apprehensive eyes. There was no doubt of the identity of the man who had just entered. He wore, as elegantly as his sleekly padded form would permit, a silk toga dyed with the imperial purple from the shellfish of Tyre and richly bordered with gold thread. A circlet of gold leaves crowned his heavy, oiled black hair. The flat sandals laced about his plump calf were also of gold. The Emperor was accompanied by a small boy who stood close to him, a very pretty boy with vine leaves in his hair. He wore a very brief tunic and carried a lyre. Isaac Comnenus was lightly caressing his neck.

Eden remained quite still while the bizarre figure subjected her to a total examination. He lifted a negligent finger. The woman pulled her gently up so that she stood in the shallow water, facing a dozen pairs of unequivocal male eyes.

Isaac smiled. His captain had not lied. The woman was tall, stately and lissome as linden. Her breasts were pure poetry and her thighs invited his loins, making them throb delightfully. Her face was proud and cool amid a cloud of hair that had taken all the sunlight into itself. He looked at her eyes and lips and the sweet curves of her body and promised himself a most delectable morning.

Eden forced herself to relax her frozen attitude and reached out her hand toward a girl who stood holding a length of fleecy white cloth. The slave looked toward her master who nodded briefly. Eden was wrapped in the long robe which she noted abstractedly to absorb water very quickly. Then the Emperor clapped his hands and her dark body-slaves disappeared, giggling mightily, through another door at the back of the chamber. Xanthe, nodding and smiling encouragingly, was the last to go.

The Emperor sat down upon one of the numerous couches disported in the Roman style about the bath, indicating that she should sit beside him. There was no alternative. She was enveloped in a heavy floreate perfume that was almost tangible.

"My Lady . . . Hawkhurst is it not?" He addressed her, to her amazement, in a throatily accented French.

She nodded, not trusting her voice to be steady.

"Come closer to me." He reached for her hand and pulled her toward him. The soft white cloth brought her sliding to him.

"Do not hide your body; it is very beautiful." He gestured impatiently at the wrap. "You stood like Aphrodite among the waves. Did you know that she was once the Queen of Cyprus?"

She made no reply. He had taken her other hand; the robe fell around her on the bench. Suddenly he crushed her body to him, bruising her breasts against his chest. She heard herself whimper as his hands made themselves master of her nakedness. She had not felt so desperately helpless since . . .

With a shuddering effort she tore herself from him as he sank his warm, moist mouth upon hers. It was somehow more intimately unbearable than the firm, exploratory fingers that searched thigh and buttock, breast and belly as though discovering the virtues of a blood mare or a fine bitch. He laughed from sheer enjoyment as he retrieved her easily and held her lightly before him, gazing into her distraught features with an expression that was something between malice and mischief. She saw that he was a man given to the immediate indulgence of his lightest wish. His eyes were heavily lidded and glistened as though perpetually filled with tears. This gave him an aspect both soulful and peculiarly untrustworthy. His black-thicketed head was large, the nose fleshy and the lips very full, their deep red color putting his prisoner in mind of raw, dark meat. His body was heavy but held an elastic quality, its rolling muscle not yet turned to fat. He held her easily with only the lightest pressure. His liquid eyes fed upon her body. She tried hopelessly to pull away from him. Isaac frowned. He had told the women to make her ready for him. There should not be this resistance. It was tiresome.

"If you continue to struggle," he told her softly, "I shall have the women come back and hold you for me. How would you like that, eh? Or would you prefer it to be several of the guard? It is something they enjoy."

Shocked, she shook her head, her eyes filling with tears of fright and shame. Somehow, she had not believed, until this moment, that the terrible thing could happen to her again. She prayed as she had never prayed.

Isaac made her lie down upon the couch. He placed a cushion beneath her buttocks. He knelt beside her and sucked at her breasts. She lay quite still. As he ran his questing tongue about the more delightful parts of her exquisite body, Isaac began to experience some difficulty. It was an old enemy and, these days, a more and more frequent one. When he first had seen the girl, standing there so magnificently with the water dripping from her long, smooth flanks and off the engorged tips of those wonderfully full, tight breasts, he had become instantly aroused; he could not wait to have her. Indeed, by now he was beginning to realize that he should not have waited, for, by the most damnable and unamusing trick of his over-indulged flesh, he was very much afraid that, just at the moment, he could not take her. Too late, he cursed that Syrian wench he had had for the night, not to mention that grubby little urchin he had sampled first to whet his appetite. He had often told himself he should not bother with such very young boys; they were never worth it in terms of energy expended. And the woman had possessed the unparalleled sexual prowess of the true Saracen whore. He looked regretfully at Eden's body, outstretched for sacrifice. Sensing her surprise, he covered it up with the bathrobe.

She would keep. Meanwhile there was something else she could do for him. With the unabashed zeal of the dedicated sensualist, he raised her hand and kissed it. "You are truly beautiful, but . . . later!" he announced without any obvious shame for his unwilling manhood.

Dazed. Eden sat up, pulling the robe around her.

"I will send the women to you; you must have suitable clothing."

Then, with a last lamenting sweep of his dark lashes across her relieved and shaking body, he clapped his hands and left the chamber, with the smiling Xanthe at his heels.

As he had promised, the women returned. Their giggling had died down somewhat by now. Eden wondered whether they could tell that she was as yet undefiled by the imperial lust. So great was her relief that she found herself smiling at them, despite their earlier complicity. Perhaps "later" would never come; perhaps Richard would come sailing in long before Isaac thought of her again. He evidently had numerous other diversions at hand.

In an attempt to put this last experience firmly behind her, she threw off the robe and plunged once more into the bath. At once the willing hands were there, though this time she discouraged their more intimate attentions, washing herself instead with the soft, flowerlike object there for the purpose.

Soon she was wholly cleansed, oiled and scented, and the slaves offered her a dark, sweet liquid in tiny enameled cups. At first she was suspicious of it, but she saw that they all drank it. It was fiery and stimulating after the bath and much to her taste. She tried

to ask Xanthe its name, but could not catch the girl's
unintelligible answer.

When she pointed to the admirable tangle of her
hair, however, her guard and guide's bright eyes lit
up. She snapped her fingers and a slave fetched her a
broad comb made from some dark bone, its handle
covered with silver. Xanthe was tirelessly patient but it
took nearly an hour to undo the snarl that the sea had
made of the yard-long tress. Eden sat and dreamed
beneath her efficient fingers. Whatever was next to
be faced, she would feel more capable of it in this
pristine state. She hoped they would give her something
other than her old, sea-torn gown, as Isaac had indicated. She was entirely grateful for the pampering of
her body, even though it had not been mainly for her
own benefit.

At last the tangled web of her hair was reduced
to a manageable swathe and Xanthe coiled it admiringly round her fingers, watching it spring away with
its own ebullient life when she let it go. Now she took
away Eden's bathrobe and brought in its place a floating, insubstantial garment of thin cotton, in a singing
cerulean blue; there was a small slit between the
breasts, bound in gold braiding and a sleeveless coat
of cloth-of-gold tissue to cover it. Its lightness and delicacy delighted her, and yet, when she had put it on,
over the white shift which went with it, she did not
feel cold.

Her previous companions had returned while she was
dressing and now nodded and smiled their approval.
Eden wondered about their status in the Emperor's
household; it was all too evident what it might be, and
yet they were clearly not peasant women or brothel girls.
As they arranged themselves at length upon the
couches and nibbled at sweetmeats in tiny, bright
dishes, their brown eyes wide with interest as they
smiled upon her, they reminded Eden of the basking
seals she had once seen upon the coast of England
during one of her few journeys from Hawkhurst. She
knew that Isaac Comnenus had a wife. It surprised her
to realize that she, whoever she was, must be aware of

his bathhouse full of basking seals. She felt a sudden sense of foreignness.

Xanthe had now produced a long, flat box which she opened with care. In it were many squares of colored pigment, of every conceivable shade. She selected a rosy tint which she proceeded to apply, with a tiny, hairsbreadth brush, to Eden's lips and cheeks. Eden, who knew that certain court ladies were accustomed to paint their faces, Queen Eleanor herself among them, held her peace, curious to see the result. She even managed to keep quite still when Xanthe attacked her eyes with another scarcely existent brush, this time holding a pigment of a green so dark as to be almost black.

When the girl held up a mirror, Eden hardly recognized herself. Never had her skin seemed so translucent or gleamed so softly; never were her eyes as large or as dramatically slanting as this Cypriot sorcery had made them. She could not help but be delighted with this new image of herself; she looked bolder, less abstracted . . . a little dangerous. She smiled; she looked like a woman who knew how to deal with the world; suddenly, for no reason at all, certainly no good one, she found that Tristan de Jarnac had crept into her mind, with that maddening look of his that said she knew nothing, and he? Why, everything! Frowning, she shook her head.

Xanthe, hoping the frown was nothing to do with her handiwork, for she was proud of her skill, applied a last, generous amount of perfumed oil of roses upon each of Eden's pulses and between her breasts; then she walked seriously round her, twitched several times at the gold coat and at last made small crooning sounds that pronounced her satisfied. After a perfunctory and unnecessary tidying of her own neat little person, she indicated that it was time to leave the chamber.

As she left the warm, vaporous chamber she felt a sudden rush of apprehension. Where was she being taken? Perhaps Isaac had already recovered his potency. As she followed Xanthe's comfortably rolling hips down steep passages hewn from the cliffside, she wondered what would become of her and of her companions below in the dungeon; she had eaten nothing since before the shipwreck. Had they been fed? How far was the Emperor their enemy? And how long before Richard would find his missing bride? And, having found her, would he sail away, satisfied, or would he employ more valuable time in recovering her friend and waiting-woman?

They climbed a steep stairway and came suddenly into a broad hall whose bright spaciousness gave a shock of pleasure after the confinement of the dungeon and the closeness of the bathhouse. It was a long room with a tall, vaulted ceiling. On one side, a row of fluted pillars and onion-shaped archways gave on to a broad battlement. The walls were hung with amber cloth and there were several finely carved settles, some of them occupied by swarthy men dressed in rich, loose robes. Others stood and talked together in groups or drank wine and watched the sea, for the splendid apartment faced the bay which had proved so tragically inhospitable to the English ships. Numerous guards stood about the walls, wearing the short toga and leather breastplate of Roman soldiers. Eden, to her chagrin, recognized the insolent grin of the sergeant of last night. He did not look her way and she turned her face resolutely toward the sea as she followed Xanthe down the long room.

It was now a smooth sheet of glistening innocence, sweetly blue as a baby's eye. The royal galley rode at anchor well out in the bay, while further round, beyond the jaws of the rocks to the southwest, the stricken vessels reared their sad skeletons. With all her will, Eden prayed for the safety of her friends. At the far end of the room, Isaac Comnenus now presided over his court. He reclined upon a wide, purple throne raised on a dais. Behind him his pretty boy played upon his lyre; there were vine leaves in his hair. Several of the courtiers or councillors whom Eden had already seen were clustered about him, seated or standing according to age and rank. She avoided their prurient eyes. Isaac observed the approach of his prisoner.

"You may be seated in my presence." He was magnanimous.

A servant brought her a low stool and she sat, straight-backed, clasping her hands loosely in her lap and giving the Emperor look for look, unsmiling. The courtiers, interested, ceased their chattering.

"There is something I wish you to do for me," Isaac told her without preamble.

"Indeed?" She tried to read the affable, close features.

"The graceful galley that is riding in my waters . . . this belongs to Richard of England. It carries his bride and his sister, the ex-Queen of Sicily. I have sent messages to these royal ladies, requesting that they leave the doubtful comfort of their damaged vessel and become my honored guests. The Lady Joanna, however, sees fit to refuse; she asks only for water for her vessels and claims to do very well where she is." Isaac frowned. Here in Cyprus he had created the perfect empire. It was rich, beautiful and impregnable, protected by the great Sultan Saladin himself; and he, Isaac Comnenus, was its absolute ruler.

It did not, therefore, please him to be told of the appearance of a vast fleet of Frankish war galleys in Middle Sea waters. But his anxiety was much tempered by the felicitous arrival of the ship that carried Joanna and Berengaria. Isaac loved a bargain, and there was no bargaining power as strong as that of a hostage in the hand. He wanted these royal fish trapped in his bay to be landed.

"You will send to Queen Joanna. Tell her you are safe and content here, that she should take confidence and come ashore at once."

Eden could not forbear a brief smile of irony. Did this thieving, whoring despot intend to have her betray her friends to him one moment and become his concubine at the next?

He continued. "Have you, perhaps, some small trinket still in your possession that she might recognize? Something not taken by the storm?"

Her smile became grim. "There was something of that nature . . . a small cross of gold; it was not however, the storm which took it . . . but the captain of your guard."

The bland features expressed immediate shocked concern, the pink tongue clicking softly behind the sensual mouth. "I am sorry to hear it. I shall have it recovered at once."

"There is no need for such a token to be sent," she murmured quietly, "I can write; the Princess will know my hand."

Isaac was impressed. "Can you so? An unusual accomplishment in an Englishman—and in a woman, unheard of. I congratulate you. I will have sheets of writing material brought to you," he said, looking at her bosom and thinking of a different kind of sheet, entirely.

Eden waited, demurely; she was conscious, as she had been in the bathhouse, of being the center of a circle of curious eyes. The little lyre-player touched a wrong note and the Emperor turned to clout him severely. He dissolved into tears and was sent away. Then the small, scurrying clerk, of the dungeon, made another appearance, burdened as before by his little portable desk, which he set before her, together with parchment, ink and sand.

She was uncomfortably conscious of her dilemma as she prepared to write. When the letter was sent, was it truly likely that the wily and cautious Joanna would come ashore on the strength of it? And if she should refuse to write it, what would be her own fate at the hands of an angry Isaac? If only there were some way to warn the galley that they should not trust him. She took as much time as she dared in shaking out her skirts, folding back the gold coat, well out of the way of any errant inkspots, and pushing her hair behind her ears. "What shall I write, Imperial Highness?" she inquired biddably, allowing a little warmth to touch her eyes for the first time.

"I will leave the exact phrasing to you, my lady. If you will perhaps permit me to cast my eye over it when you have finished? I am," he added delicately, "a most fervent student of the Frankish language and take every opportunity to see it written."

Eden smiled in recognition of his diplomacy. Her smile broadened as she began, slowly, to write. She had conceived of a stratagem; a poor one, but it might rouse the suspicions of Queen Joanna, or even Berengaria.

She bent over the desk, unconscious of the tempting picture she made as her breasts fell forward against the open neck of her gown. It was all Isaac could do to restrain himself from sending his court packing and falling upon her there and then.

Eden concentrated deeply on her task; it was several weeks since she had cause to hold a pen, but she was confident of her calligraphy; Stephen and Father Benedict had taught her well.

"To my beloved liegewoman, the Princess Berengaria of Navarre," she wrote. "It grieves me deeply to learn, gracious lady, that while I and many others sojourn here in comfort, as the guests of his Magnanimity, the Emperor of Cyprus, yourself and the honored lady, my Lord King's sister, the Queen of Sicily, should suffer the discomforts and difficulties of remaining on shipboard. I beg, therefore, that you will alter your mind upon this matter, and join us here, at our ease. For you shall have a right royal welcome, as I dare swear by all the saints and upon the bones of my beloved father, Sir Hugo de Malfors, Baron of the estate of Stukesey in Kent."

It was customary to add some such exaggerated flourish at the close of a letter and there was no way in which the Emperor might tell, when he sought Eden's name among the list of titles upon the green parchment, that she was not truly the daughter of the Baron of Stukesey; she had, after all, claimed it as part of her patrimony and was very glad now of the tiny impulse of mischief which had made her do so. Certainly, it would give the royal ladies great cause to ponder. She sanded the letter and handed it to Isaac, smiling gently.

He took and read it swiftly. "You write a fair hand, lady, and have said most fairly. You have my thanks. And now—you will be shown the chamber you are to occupy while you are my guest. Food will be sent to you there."

"There is one thing, your Imperial Highness—"

Isaac beamed. "You have a wish? Express it."

"It is the matter of fresh water for the Queen of Sicily's galley. It comes to me that you might well gain her complete confidence if you were to be so generous as to supply it."

The Emperor's face was again closed, the liquid eyes expressionless. "I'm sure you are perfectly in the right, my Lady Hawkhurst," he said flatly.

"Then you will . . ."

His smile returned, less expansively than before. "You will find your chamber to your liking, I am certain. It is furnished, I believe, most agreeably. Xanthe is yours to command should you lack the slightest comfort."

She was clearly dismissed. There was nothing to do but to follow the ever smiling Xanthe with a good grace. Isaac would send no water to Joanna, she was sure; his intention was to drive the passengers of the galley to the shore, where they would become his prisoners, as she was.

The room assigned to Eden lay at the top of one of the towers of the fortress. Xanthe ushered her within and left her; the door was gently locked behind her. She stemmed the useless anger that the small sound aroused in her and looked about. The spacious room was, as Isaac had said, very comfortable; she had an impression of much purple and gold and of soft rugs beneath her feet. The main feature was the vast and magnificent bed, carved with a rollicking saturnalia of Roman deities in all manner of erotic pursuits. The heavy silk hangings were Tyrian purple; the deep mattress was filled with soft wool and spread with cushions and coverlets glowing with jewel-colored embroidery; a

bed to be shared . . . and there was no doubt who
intended to share it with her. Throughout the day she
simply waited. He did not come.

Toward the end of the afternoon she relaxed a little.
She curled upon an upholstered window seat and gazed
through the trelliswork that covered the aperture,
finding that to her great pleasure she faced the sea. She
could just make out the royal galley on the headland.
She told herself that, however terrible her prospects
appeared, as long as she could keep that sturdy little
ship in sight, she could keep up both hope and spirit.

When Xanthe appeared, bearing a loaded tray, even
the expected advances of the Emperor were forgotten
as Eden fell upon its contents. She had never been so
hungry. There was a dish of yellow rice mixed with
fruits and spices and succulent meats that melted on
the tongue; several piquant sauces complemented it,
and there were small loaves of bread, hollow in the
middle and almost white; these were light and delicious. The wine was strong, a rich, dark ruby which
played havoc with her emptiness. By the time she had
eaten all she could, and a wonderful fresh orange besides, her head was gently swimming and all she could
think of was sleep.

She climbed drowsily on to the great bed, and her
last waking thought concerned the sudden realization
that, amid the crowd of gods and goddesses who
frolicked and trolloped about the painted wooden canopy, was set a very large, well-polished mirror. She
stared, startled, into her own surprised eyes and fell
almost instantly asleep.

Her dreams that night were fractured and elusive.
Strangely, Isaac Comnenus did not figure in them.
They were filled instead with images of Stephen, and of
herself with him as they had been in the early days of
their marriage; languorous and expectant, she saw his
dear face swimming above her, beautiful in his delight
in her. He was just about to take her; every inch of
her starved and unused body rose up toward him . . .
when he was gone. There was no longer Stephen, but
another face had taken his place; sardonic and aloof,

its coldly sculptured lines denying pleasure to her . . . and yet, she saw that there was also a promise for her in the clear eyes, a promise which she knew was desperately important to her and yet one which she could not read. She must know what it meant! She must! But alas, like Stephen's, the visitation was fleeting and the face was gone before she could recognize either its features or its deep intent.

When, with the early dawn, she awoke, refreshed, she was greatly amazed to realize where she was; there had been such swift changes in her fortune that at first she hardly knew whether she was on ship or shore or even the hard cold floor of the dungeon. Then she looked up at her reflection and knew at once.

So he had not come. Passionately, she gave thanks to the Magdalen. Soon the ever-smiling Xanthe appeared with her breakfast. Beside the bread and wine and cold meat there was a small cedarwood box. At Xanthe's excited nod, she opened it. She gasped! There, upon a little white silk cushion reposed the emeralds that Joanna had given her in Messina. Isaac must have recovered them from his looters of the shore. She could not help but be amused at the quirk of fortune that had brought them back to her. She saw that there was a tiny roll of parchment beside them and broke the seal at once.

"My lady, it saddens me that, for the moment, we shall not meet again. I leave to make ready my island for the visit of your King. You will receive every comfort until my return, which I hope may be swift." Isaac's flourishing signature was appended.

While the admiring Xanthe fastened the jewels about her neck and wrist, Eden assimilated the Emperor's meaning. To make Cyprus ready for Richard could only mean to make it ready for war. She felt a stab of fear. With the sword of Islam to assist him, Isaac might conceivably win such a war. He would certainly receive such help; it would be of great benefit to Saladin to have Richard's fleet destroyed before it even reached the Holy Land.

She rose from the bed and crossed to the window,

to stare out into the blue bay. The galley reared reassuringly behind the unfriendly rocks. Her eyes narrowed; something had changed. What was it? Then she realized with a little cry of joy. Joanna had run her personal flag up the mainmast. It was a sign that she was present on the vessel . . . and that as long as the flag remained, so would the Queen of Sicily.

As her eyes traveled back to the shore, she saw that here, too, something had changed. The beach was no longer a deserted stretch of wreck-strewn shingle; it was covered in busy figures, each one working frantically. They were Isaac's ubiquitous guards . . . and they were building what appeared to be walls of timber and stone. Looking more closely she saw that they were, in fact, using the wreckage from the English ships together with blocks of stone fallen from the cliffs. They were putting them together to form a bastion. Against what? Certainly not the sea.

It seemed that Isaac intended to be well prepared for his visitors. During the next few days, with increasing sensations of fear and frustration, Eden watched the sea wall grow. It became for her the threatening symbol of her own hopeless situation. Day by day it grew, keeping her more securely on the island . . . and Richard more certainly off it.

It was at the beginning of her third week of imprisonment that she began, idly, to consider the possibilities of escape. They were apparently non-existent. She was locked in her chamber at all times. Even the relief of nature was cunningly disposed of by a narrow oubliette behind a thick curtain in the corner of the room. And, even supposing she should overpower the sturdy Xanthe there were two or three guards outside the room at all hours. If she were to jump from the window, she would undoubtedly die upon the jagged cliffside. If she were to insert herself into the oubliette she would stay there until she rotted; it was very narrow.

There was only the door. She would stare at it fixedly for minutes at a time as if expecting the wooden panels to come alive and speak words of wisdom to her.

Gloomily, she stared out at the still rising bulwark on the beach. Now the soldiers were adding anything that could be moved, justifiably or otherwise. Chests, chairs, doors, bedsteads, flooring, statuary and the abandoned hulks of ancient vessels were fitted together with eager satisfaction and hammered with iron mallets until they were inseparable.

Eden felt as though they hammered the nails of her coffin. Xanthe, who now served her mistress-prisoner with something akin to the dedication of Hawisa herself, and had been whiling away the weeks by teaching her Greek, could not comprehend her unending distress. She thought her the luckiest, as well as the loveliest, of ladies to be so singled out by the Emperor. She tried constantly to wean Eden away from the window to the more satisfactory view to be found in the mirror. She was a little hurt at her charge's lack of interest in her skill with the array of lotions, potions, paints and ornaments she brought to tempt her.

And then, at last, the long watch was ended. Eden awoke on the morning of 6th May to see the Lion flag dancing in joyous welcome at the masthead of Joanna's galley. There could be no doubt. King Richard was coming.

Down on the beach the usual activity had increased to fever point. Behind the bulwark the Cypriot troops were drilling, bristling impressively with swords and spears, menacingly adult now. Several of them wielded the terrifying curved blade of the Saracens, the deadly scimitar whose edge must be keen enough to take off a man's beard . . . or his entire head at a single slice. In the midst of the melee rode a thickset, purposeful figure on a remarkably fine bay stallion; his purple cloak flying, his voice ringing with proud command, Isaac Comnenus had returned to lead the welcoming party. He lined up his men, behind the bastion, now higher than a man and ten times as solid. The sunlight glanced flatteringly off weapons and harness.

A movement on the eastern horizon caught her eye. There was the first of the English ships, a vast carrack with oars ploughing her decks and castles overflowing with men whose bright shields blinded the bay. Eden caught her breath and gave a great, glad, involuntary cry. Xanthe, intrigued, hurried to her side. The sea was filling with ships; galleys, carracks, roundships, all gay with flags and pennoncels and filled to overflowing with fighting infantry and bowmen.

"Aieee!" cried Xanthe, making the sign of the cross with one hand and throwing her veil over her head with the other.

"It is not the devil, girl; it is only King Richard, come to take back what is his." *If he can,* she added silently, eyeing the still rows of Cypriots, Moors, Turks and Greeks on the beach.

Xanthe, who would have preferred the devil, whose ways she knew, moaned and sat upon the floor, rocking herself to and fro and muttering prayers and charms against evil.

Watching her with amused sympathy, Eden was visited by the first, tentative, doubtful possibility of an idea. Judging from the excitement outside, and Xanthe's entire collapse inside her prison, no one was going to be thinking very much about her or her welfare this day.

She stared at the weeping girl, her resolution crystalizing. "Get up," she said. "Take off your gown and cloak!"

Xanthe stopped crying, puzzled. Eden was stripping off her blue gown. She threw it at the sniffing girl and crossed to the cedarwood chest which held the box of face paints and the bronze mirror. It also held the emeralds. Xanthe, accustomed to obey and quite undone by her fear of the Lionheart, with whom her mother had threatened her not many years before, took off her clothes in a daze of incomprehension. Eden was rubbing the walnut pigment into her face, neck and bosom, also her hands and arms and feet. She applied a generous amount of the greenish-black substance around her eyes and on her lashes and a deep red-brown to her lips. The result was startling. She fastened the emeralds about her neck, low down near her breasts. She picked up Xanthe's discarded robe and struggled swiftly into it. She wound the veil tightly over all her hair as she had seen the girl do sometimes, and pulled the hood of the dark djellaba up over it.

She gazed into the mirror. She would not have known herself. She did not think she looked much like Xanthe either, but she hoped she would pass in all the excitement. She laid two fingers on her lips, picked up her used breakfast tray, and marched toward the door before she came to her senses and changed her mind.

Xanthe moaned behind her. She had not yet dressed. Eden went back and shook her. "You *must* keep quiet. You *must!*" She could not bear to think how Isaac might punish the girl . . . but who knew which of them would be alive to be punished by which other . . . at the end of the day?

She threw the blue robe at the quivering girl, flashing her brief, encouraging smile, then tapped smartly upon the door, as Xanthe did when she wished to be let out. The key seemed to turn endlessly, its grating tearing at her nerves. The door opened. She pushed, not too quickly, past the guard who held it open, her head down, the tray balanced near her chest. He could not have seen her face. Another guard stood at the head of the stair. He was doing his best to get some view of the proceedings on the beach through a narrow crenel in the wall. He called excitedly to his companion, who slammed the door again, locked it swiftly and joined him in the hopeless exercise. Eden was halfway down the stair.

One turn. Two. And she had reached the bottom. There was a low door behind her. She must be at ground level. Surely it would lead to the beach.

But no, that was not where she wished to be. She did not want to find herself in the thick of whatever fray took place. She would leave by the side of the castle and hope to find herself a hiding place somewhere nearby until all was over one way or the other. Perhaps she might even somehow make her way out to an English ship. One step at a time; she had only this one chance; she must not mar it for lack of thought.

She started off down a long passageway. Too late, she caught the sound of rough, masculine voices round the corner at the other end. She turned and went back the way she had come. Behind her, the cheerful soldiers called after her by name. They must have recognized Xanthe's dark blue djellaba. They were not near as yet; she turned and risked a saucy wave. There were four of them. One waved in return. She continued on her way, her heart dinning in her ears. There were no more shouts. She had gained the small door behind the stair. She had no choice. She opened it and went out into the daylight.

She found herself on a broad pathway; the castle reared behind her and before her there was a small troop of Cypriot soldiers on horseback. Their backs were toward her and they were staring out to sea.

They were about halfway down the cliff path and the way narrowed immediately after the broad, jutting space where the men and horses stood. For a moment she was paralyzed. The soldiers who had followed her down the passageway would appear at once. Her only way was forward. She could not simply run to her left, down the cliff path; she would be seen or heard. If she ran to the right, she would have to pass in front of the fortress and risk meeting other troops.

She raced diagonally across behind the lookout soldiers. If she could gain the edge of the cliff before the others came out of the door ... Scarcely stopping to determine whether she faced a gentle roll or a headlong drop, she let herself over the edge of the cliff, dragging at the folds of the djellaba. She hung for half a second by her hands, then, finding a firm foothold, wide enough to give her confidence, she put all her weight upon it and released her handhold.

She was on a narrow shelf just below the road edge. She could not see any soldiers but she could hear their voices. She heard the men from inside the castle come out and shout a greeting to their mounted companions before they tramped off down the path to the beach. She looked down. The cliff was perhaps sixty feet deep, and quite steep. It would be a difficult climb. Clearly, however, she could not remain here. Sooner or later someone on the beach below would look up and see her; they might even, she thought ironically, decide to rescue her from this perilous perch. And if she managed to climb down to the shingle, what then? Isaac's troops would hardly welcome a woman.

She almost wished she had stayed where she was and taken the fortunes of war as they came. She was as much a prisoner, here on her exposed and dangerous outcrop, as she had been in the gold and purple chamber.

She gazed at the soldiers, some fifty feet below. All of them, standing well back from their bastion, were staring out to sea, Isaac among them, statuesque on his fine horse. Many of them murmured and shuffled in their ranks; they were becoming restless, despite their leader's attempt to imbue them with the Roman virtue of perfect discipline.

But the pattern of movement had changed on the painted galleys. The Lionheart, too, had given his battle orders. Little silvery-gray figures in conical helmets piled into dozens of boats and rowed lustily for the shore. As they grew larger in her eyes, Eden saw that the foremost among them were equipped with crossbows, the deadly and merciless weapon that the Pope himself had placed under his interdict as being unfit for Christians to use.

Almost as soon as she took in this fact, she saw the first of Isaac's men go down, screaming in hideous agony as their breastbones were smashed into their spines by the terrible, barbed bolt. The English bowmen had opened fire as soon as they came within their range. This was considerably longer, Eden realized, than that of the light bows of Isaac's archers . . . a stark and simple fact that gave her more hope than she had ever expected to have. Feverishly, she started to make her way down the jagged and precipitous cliff. If the English could win the engagement—and the foul crossbows gave them every chance—if she could gain the beach at the right moment . . . then there was a slender possibility that she could reach one of those small boats and get out to the royal galley.

It was far more likely that she would be picked off the cliffside by an arrow, whether Cypriot or English, but she would not think of that. She concentrated on her climb, slowly down, feeling for every foothold and keeping a terrified eye on events below.

The attackers had leaped from their boats and charged up the shingle, swords in hand. Richard himself, his face translated by fury, was their leader. They made pitifully short work of the brave bastion, swarming over it in dozens while the crossbowmen reloaded behind their long shields. The Cypriots who had attempted to defend their handiwork soon lay dead behind it, their throats cut by the efficient invaders.

It was only a skirmish, as battles went, but it was the first Eden had ever seen and the horror of it was so great that she could not, at that juncture, afford to let it reach her. If she were to give way to fear and pity, she knew she would undoubtedly die.

She clung to her rock and did not even think to pray while she watched others die beneath her. The Cypriots were demoralized and their defense was crumbling despite Isaac's desperate howls of encouragement and rage.

She was only some thirty feet above them now, and would go no closer yet. She began to pick out faces she knew amid the fracas; Richard himself, of course, hacking and slicing with his yard-long, fearful sword, his face split by a grin of concentration and vivid joy; she saw him kill four men in as many minutes. Three died by the sword, two taking it in the breast and one, poor devil, in the bowels; the last lost his head in a single second of pure surprise as the Lionheart swung his mighty battle-ax. Eden would look at him no longer. Although she knew that this, this very carnage that she was now unwillingly and half-incredulously witnessing, was the aim and cause of all their beings, something had gone for her from this hour out of all the childhood legends of the heroes. She was watching the heroes now . . . and they were not what she had thought.

And then she heard a sudden almighty roar. Turning, she saw that Richard, his helm struck off, had been brought to his knees by one of Isaac's fierce Turkish captains. His sword, drawn back to strike, would never make contact before the swift silver curve of the Turk's scimitar descended.

There was a flash like lightning! A swinging figure started out of the sand beneath their feet; the King fell back unhurt as a dagger took the Turk in the throat. The scimitar came down, its arc deflected, the weakened blow striking into the savior's shoulder. Eden cried out in shock as Tristan de Jarnac cursed and clapped his hand to the gushing wound.

Instantly his lieutenants surrounded him, materializing from nowhere after the manner of their master. Will Barret guarded one flank, an unknown knight the other, while burly John de Wulfran covered his back. At least ten men had rushed toward the King, who was now roaring even more ferociously; he hated to be bested; it happened rarely. She heard him cry his thanks to de Jarnac before he whirled the dreadful ax about his head once more and plunged further up the beach.

Will Barret had strapped Tristan's left arm to his body; he fought on; his sword arm was unimpaired. It did not look as though he was conscious of pain. Nevertheless Eden could not bear to watch his grim face. The agony was much worse when she knew the man who suffered. She wished she had been more courteous to him in the past. She prayed that he would not die as a result of his foolhardy bravery. She had a foolish wish to touch him.

But the dying, or most of it, was done. Isaac's men were in retreat, their confidence broken. They released one last fusillade of arrows from a position near the foot of the cliff, but the English mail was thick and the Crusaders plucked them out of their hauberks like briars. There was still a little hand-to-hand fighting, the brutal and crippling sword-cuts aimed most often at the sword arm so that the man lost both livelihood and lust for life. For the most part the beach was a bloody arena of dead men and men with gaping wounds, bruised bones and torn flesh. Blood. Blood upon the sand in the sunlight, seeping away life after life, was a sight that Eden knew she would never, at some deep level of her being, cease to see. Dreamily, she noted a crossbow quarrel, plunged deep into the rock at her elbow. She had almost forgotten her own danger. It was as if she were unseen, up here, clutching the sharp stone and waiting for the end. But now she had been seen. To her horror, several of Isaac's soldiers were gazing up at her. They waved their hands and shouted incomprehensibly. It was clear that they meant well. Two of them started to climb the cliff from below. The others joined the general retreat that was ascending to the city by all possible paths. Those who had gone round by the road reached the top of the cliff a little before the two who climbed toward her. There was no hope for it; she was about to be rescued.

She closed her eyes and groaned. She thought of calling for de Jarnac, or for Will Barret, but what would be the use amid the clamor of the disengaging troops? She had left it too late. She let them take her, refusing to speak. She did not react even when they had pulled her efficiently back to the cliff road and one of them pushed back her hood and veil, curious about the rivulets of sepia upon her cheeks. She simply bowed her head and wept. She had never been so weary, so hopeless or so abandoned by all belief as she was now. They could do what they liked with her.

As she stood there in the road, surrounded by puzzled Cypriot soldiers, a fresh troop came running up the hill, crying Isaac's name in urgent tones. Hard on their heels came the Emperor himself, his magnificence as tarnished as his bloody sword. He saw the little group at the turn of the road and immediately drew rein. He looked at Eden once, then gave curt orders to a cavalryman. The man dropped from his horse, then picked up Eden unceremoniously and dumped her on its back. He remounted, behind her in the saddle. There were a few more hasty orders and the small troop spurred away. Isaac was in retreat and he was taking his prisoner with him . . . as she had been so thoughtful as to meet him on the road.

There was no pursuit by the victorious Crusaders; they were still held back on the beach for the moment, by the last of the Cypriot garrison, acting under orders to give the Emperor time to escape.

They clattered through the streets of Limassol so swiftly that Eden, even had she cared, would have gained little impression of the capital. Their journey was swift and short; its objective was Kilani, a village on the vine-clad slopes of Mount Troodos, five miles out of the town.

It seemed that Isaac had been prepared for retreat, for his troops were already setting up camp among the vineyards when their party arrived. The soldiers sent up a cheer for the Emperor. The inhabitants of Kilani, who had stood by impassively, while the troops ravished their food supplies and their daughters and trampled their carefully tended vines, did not join in.

There was a gentle, dreaming warmth upon the hillside that seemed to belie any possibility of blood and battle. Eden, as numbed and uncaring as if she had not been present, was taken to the Emperor's personal tent. Had she been in the mood to think of it, this was somewhat impressive. It was designed as a field of golden silk, richly sewn with flowers and fluttering with birds, embroidered in lustrous, gem-like colors. She was led into it with as much ceremony as if it had been a palace, and indeed, if interior furnishing were the criterion, it might have served as one. There were three separate apartments, the main section being a jewel-bright cavern of glowing carpets and cushions. Eden found herself left alone here, although she knew there to be guards posted at intervals outside. She sank down upon a pile of cushions and stared unseeingly before her, the sights and sounds of the battle still foremost in her consciousness.

Suddenly she was aware that she had company. Over

in the corner, from behind a table, two bright eyes regarded her solemnly from under a tumble of black-cherry curls. It was Isaac's lyre-boy. He smiled at her hesitantly. A little shakily, she returned the child's smile and held out her hand to him. He would be about ten years old. She was glad he had been safe from the battle. While she slowly allowed herself to return from the distance where she, too, had been safe, from the terror at least, if not the danger, she let the boy bring her water to wash away the last of her ill-fated disguise. She learned that his name was Spiridion.

An exchange of names was all that could be managed by way of conversation between them; he did not seem to understand Eden's few words of Greek. He could, however, play his lyre to comfort her, and this he did. She found his gentle singing welcome amid the continual, unexplained commotion outside the tent as Isaac made his preparations to do battle in earnest with the Lionheart tomorrow. He had sent the English King a message to that effect, in case he should think his small victory on landing any larger than the infinitesimal event it had been.

Spiridion sang a series of languorous Cypriot love songs, to which Eden responded, accompanying herself more and more surely upon his instrument, with some of the ballads of Chretien de Troyes, whose popularity was spreading wherever there were Crusaders. It was a pleasant, softly waiting time, and all too soon it was over. Only the fear remained.

As the sun sank with flamboyant bad taste behind the mountain, the flanks of the tent were deepened to a rich blood-orange, a tint which suited Isaac Comnenus extremely well when he strode into it looking amazingly pleased with himself.

He caressed Spiro's head then touched the soft skin of the boy's cheek. The child smiled up at him with all the soulfulness he had put into his love songs. Eden was aware of a certain distaste.

"You may continue to play for us, Spiro, while we eat," the Emperor allowed, smiling upon his recaptured prisoner. She had expected anger, and was surprised.

A succession of servants, both black and white, brought a selection of the spiced and savory dishes of the island. Eden did not wish to eat, but Isaac displayed a healthy appetite. He did not seem like a defeated man. His liquid eyes glistened at her across his wine-cup. When he had satisfied one appetite, he would begin to consider another . . . and a payment overdue for his emeralds. He had hoped to engage her gratitude, at least, by his gift. If he could have her before the battle, he would fight like a wolf. He moved across the tent to lower himself gracefully beside her on the cushions. He motioned to Spiro to pour more wine.

His purple robe touched the corner of her gown; his eyes devoured her. Warily, Eden sat up very straight, drawing her legs beneath her. So the reckoning had come, after all. She wished wearily that she had a weapon of some kind, a dagger, perhaps, or a sharp knife. She sipped at her wine while Isaac drank deeply and with enjoyment. She eyed the wine jug hopefully. Was it possible that salvation lay in its depths? Isaac smiled at her. She was too quiet; he did not like his women silent.

"Talk with me, lady," he demanded. "Tell me of your cold, northern land, where the men are said to go barefoot and dress in skins, traveling on foot like so many pilgrims."

She attempted to comply. While they talked he might think less of how he wished to take his pleasure of her.

"Not so, Highness," she said, with some semblance of interest. "We wear skins, true, but they are fine furs and well-tanned. Our boots are of excellent leather and we ride upon good horses, as you do."

"Horses!" She had hit upon Isaac's pride. "You have seen my bay destrier? He is magnificent, is he not? He came originally from France, though his sire was an Arab. He is named Fauvel, because he was wild and difficult to break. I enjoyed that challenge. It is always more satisfying if a horse holds out against a man at first . . ." He did not make the obvious comparison but it gleamed in his eye. He was warning her, but there was humor there too, and as yet, thank God, no real impatience.

She filled his empty cup; he drank frequently, appreciatively, sniffing delicately to savor the heavy fruitiness of a wine that had come from France in much the same left-handed fashion as Fauvel.

The Emperor moved closer and pledged her with his gold cup. "To your perfect beauty," he declared, draining it.

She was half amused at his determined courtesy.

"Drink, my lady; you have taken no sustenance." He had filled his cup again and held one out to her. She took it, her mind circling feverishly in search of some miraculous deterrent to the increasing amorousness she read in him. She had sipped once from the silver cup when it was dashed from her hand; the Emperor was upon her, his thick lips fastened to hers, his hands warmly discovering for themselves the soft whereabouts of his emeralds. She saw, through shocked and irrelevant eyes, the dark wine seep away into the rich carpet . . . like blood into sand, she thought hazily. Her head seemed to be spinning. She did not know whether to be glad or sorry that she was probably about to lose consciousness.

Isaac was just starting the voluptuous process of undressing her, when he noticed a certain inertia. "My lady," he shook her. The world reeled; the sun-struck tent became an inferno, a womb, the inside of some exotic, flesh and blood fruit . . . Eden moaned.

The Emperor laid her gently down amid the cushions. "You have courage, lady. Your attempt to escape was a bold venture; do not sorrow too much at its failure . . ." He considered. She was exquisite, but he knew himself better than to imagine he would want her company forever.

"Perhaps," he began, tantalizingly, "after the next battle . . . after the *last* battle . . . perhaps I will offer you for ransom, with the rest."

A great surge of hope arose in her, so strongly that she almost felt sick with it. He saw the change in her face.

He bent over her, his body brooding with lust. He lowered himself upon her. Beneath his weight, they sank into the soft cushions. She was no longer afraid. He would not kill her, neither would he cause her pain. She could not prevent him from doing what he wanted to do; but she would not respond in any way. She loathed him, his full flesh, his sensuality, his slobbering mouth, his plump and thrusting fingers . . . but Isaac was no Hugo de Malfors. He did not seek her destruction, her defeat, the utter subjugation of all that she was and cared for. She could and would endure.

She became a doll, maumet, a creature without sensation, willing herself into a kind of limbo of the flesh. To his more intimate caresses she closed her mind. It seemed that every moment she would find herself trying to rise, to scream, to vomit up the vileness that was happening to her . . . but it did not happen. She lay as if she were a dead thing . . . let him take joy of her if he could.

To his overwhelming dissatisfaction, Isaac could not. It was not that he was impotent this time; far from it; his lust moved in him like a caged dog. He had been a dedicated sensualist all his life. It rasped against his fine sensibilities to take a woman who had turned herself into an inanimate object. A woman who struggled, yes; one who kicked and bit and tore, yes; one who was proud and cold and held herself rigid, who could be ridden until she was broken like Fauvel, yes, yes. But not this. Never this.

He was nothing if not a most patient man. He rose. He would take a breathing space. He reached for the wine jug once more and refilled her cup. She smiled and raised it to her lips. While he refilled his own he turned away from her slightly; she poured the Burgundian into the Persian rug behind the pile of cushions. They continued in a similar fashion for what seemed to Eden a very long time. Between draughts she suffered his caresses. If Isaac did not fill the cups, she did so herself.

It was beginning to take effect. With a slowness that racked her nerves, Isaac was succumbing to the wine.

Pushing back her distaste, Eden began a pretense at
drunkenness, leaning upon Isaac a little, then moving
away. It was she who had command of the wine jar
now. He drank like a greedy child. Behind them, the
carpet swam.

With a little flurry of laughter, she let herself fall
back onto the cushions. When Isaac followed her movement, his eyes shining wetly, she rolled swiftly sideways, immediately stemming any annoyance on his
part by crooning softly, "This is much more comfortable," and pushing back the thick, dark hair from the
imperial brow. The too-red lips opened; they smiled
waveringly. He reached for her breast as she leaned
beside him, pulling down her gown to take it to his
open mouth. His mouth was still open when he sank
back, murmuring fretfully and frowning slightly. Eden
crooned something indecipherable, inching herself
away from his still seeking grasp.

"Later, Highness; let it be later; we have the whole
night ahead of us—" she whispered, feeling a little like
Delilah. Then she took up Spiro's discarded harp from
where it lay and softly gave Isaac the entire benefit
of her new repertoire as the drowsy monarch drifted
slowly and inexorably into oblivion. Elated, and a little surprised at her success, she covered the sleeping Isaac with one of his rugs and considered her own
next step. It was unlikely that she could elude the
imperial guards, or, should she do so, find her way
through unknown territory to the English camp. The
only sensible alternative to escape was to follow Isaac
into sleep, although she did not look forward to his
mood in the morning. And so, not without a sensation
of amused amazement at her extraordinary situation,
she settled herself among the cushions a little removed
from her would-be lover and closed her eyes.

The night was silent, dreamless and very brief. Just
before daybreak it was brutally cut short by the realization that one of the guards was shaking her urgently
by the shoulder and babbling in high-pitched Greek.
Beside her, Isaac was in hasty conversation with another, his expression one of deep alarm mixed with

anger and self-disgust. He sprang up and clapped a hand to his head with a swift imprecation.

"What has happened?" asked Eden, conscious of some great commotion outside the tent. Isaac's eyes snapped. "Your King has arrived, that's what! Early— as it happens! It is both unchivalrous and unprecedented to take such advantage of an opponent who intends to offer battle in good time."

Eden wanted to laugh; the Emperor so clearly believed his own preposterous words. The man who had unmercifully scavenged and harried the unfortunate victims of disaster upon his shores was offended when his enemy appeared a little earlier than expected.

Isaac was screaming commands. His mail was brought and she heard the stamping of horses outside, mingled with shouting—in Greek, in Cypriot, in heathenish Moor's babel—and praise the Lord, at last in God's own tongue.

Ignoring Eden's presence, the furious Emperor dragged off the loose purple caftan he was wearing, his curses muffled in its folds. A squire held out a knee-length silken shirt and Isaac fumbled it on. At that moment a sweating courier thrust his way into the tent and fell on his knees, jabbering with excitement and haste. Eden distinguished the words *"Coeur de Lion."* Richard must be very near. Quite how near she was to discover when Isaac, his eyes bulging with mortification and, it must be said, with fear, took one longing look at the rest of his clothing and his harness, then, yelling a desperate order, bolted out of the tent.

Following with the courier and the guards, Eden was rewarded by the unusual sight of the Emperor leaping unceremoniously onto the back of the waiting Fauvel and galloping hell for leather out of the camp, his naked rump bumping helplessly beneath the brief gambeson, against the hardened tapestry of his saddle. Her face crimson, she gave way at last to the laughter that had been growing within her, scarcely even known to herself, ever since she had begun to know Isaac Comnenus.

The Emperor's personal guard looked severely for a

moment at his personal prisoner and then, joyously, their stern faces too collapsed into merriment. "He must not be take prison," explained the anxious courier who was proud of his French.

"No. No, indeed not," agreed Eden, composing her features. "That would never do."

There was little time for laughter after that. Nor was there much matter for it, as, close upon the heels of the departing Isaac, Richard Plantagenet came roaring through the tents of his enemy. Retribution was what he sought, and he took it where he found it on every side, hacking out of the flesh and bone of Isaac's army the insult and the suffering sustained by his sister and his betrothed wife.

Isaac had underestimated Richard; also he had overestimated the weight carried by his own imperial authority in Cyprus. He had been an avaricious and oppressive ruler and the islanders had no cause to die for him. Instead, they had willingly informed Richard's scouts of their tyrant's movements and the exact location of his tents. Thus, while Isaac had gently succumbed to Eden's lullaby and the guard nodded at their posts, the camp was silently surrounded by the Crusading army.

Those of Isaac's leaders who had not fled after him made a token resistance for the sake of appearances and many bemused men died in this unheroic cause before the brief engagement was over. Eden, who had watched the bloody skirmish on Limassol beach almost in its entirety, went behind the golden pavilion and was violently sick. It was the senselessness of it all rather than the bloody deeds that turned her stomach.

Suddenly, the small figure of Spiro caught her eye, trying to wield a great longsword he must have picked up, and running shakily toward a large mailed figure who had engaged one of the imperial guards.

Careless of safety Eden raced forward crying his name and grabbed roughly at his tunic, dragging him toppling toward the silken tent. "Little fool! It's not your quarrel!" she told him sharply, smacking the

sword out of his hand so that it fell harmlessly on the
threshold. There was a step behind her.

"A rare sight—a lady rescues courage in distress.
Good morrow, Lady Eden. I am right glad to find you
safe and whole."

She whirled, knowing at once whom she would face.
Only one voice could sound so damnably unsurprised.
She was disconcerted to find her heart racing. She tried
to match him with her own cool tones. "Sieur de Jarnac! I give you greeting. But pray do not immediately
damage my attempt to teach this urchin the difference
between courage and stupidity. A child who wields the
sword of a man can expect only death—not glory."
She fought to keep her tone detached; she was damned
if she would demonstrate any manner of relief at
his appearance.

And yet, this above all, was what she felt. She also
wanted, crazily, to laugh. She pulled Spiro after her
into the tent, indicating that he was to sit down and
stay sitting down. Pouting, but curious about the new-
comer with such an air of hard authority, he did so,
eyes wide and intelligent. De Jarnac stood in the sunlight at the opening of the tent, the dawn light glim-
mering on his silvered steel hauberk and mellowing
his bloodstained white tabard to rose-beige. Instinctively, Eden looked at his shoulder where the tunic
was dark with blood.

Seeing the direction of her eyes, he smiled faintly.
"A flesh wound only. It will heal cleanly. As for the
rest . . . it is Cypriot blood . . ."

"I know . . . I saw it," she said, impelled by an urge
she did not quite understand. It was as if she sought
some equality with him; she too, had been a part of
that battle, that wound.

He clearly did not comprehend. He frowned, impatient.

"I had—escaped from the fortress at Limassol," she
began. There was some satisfaction in watching his
frown deepen, then dissolve into incredulity. Hastily,
she told him her story, without, since it was not his

business, mentioning the proclivities of the Emperor of Cyprus.

"Blood of Christ, my Lady Hawkhurst, you have a mightily independent spirit!" he told her at last, inspecting her as though she were some newly discovered form of life. "And a happy facility for survival against the odds."

The impossible knight then turned away from her and addressed himself to the interested Spiro. He spoke in the child's native Greek and Eden felt a swift pang of envy as she listened, watching the boy's eyes grow large and solemn.

"I bid him not to take foolish risks . . . as you would have me do, no doubt. Though you do not take such advice to heart yourself." There was no warmth in his voice. If she had expected any sort of congratulation, either for her luck, or her enterprise, she wasn't going to get it from Tristan de Jarnac.

"A bright boy," he continued, ignoring her sultry looks. "A pity he was fated to become the Emperor's little catamite; I hope it hasn't spoiled him for the less luxurious life!"

He began, as he had been asked, to take a swift mental inventory of the contents of the pavilion. Richard loved booty.

Eden watched Spiro give Tristan his too-ingratiating, sweet smile and realized the sad truth of his words. She remembered Isaac's sensual caressing of the boy. This was a part of human experience that had so far been removed from her. She knew of the existence of love between man and man, knew even that several of the great Greek masters of learning had accounted it the highest form of love, but this was the first time it had touched her, however obliquely, and it cast a shadow on her mind.

"We must take him away from here . . . He could take a place in the King's menie . . . He is a pretty boy and my Lord Richard loves music . . ."

Tristan, gauging the value of one of Isaac's jewel caskets, laughed curtly. "I think not. He would only become . . ." He broke off, smiling. "But certainly we must leave. You must be escorted to Limassol . . . where you will find the fortress in more friendly hands."

"The Princess Berengaria, and the Queen of Sicily . . . they are safe?" She was ashamed not to have asked sooner.

"Quite safe, though very glad to rest on solid land again. I think the Princess will have to grow wings if we are to get her to Jerusalem, for she has sworn never to set foot on shipboard again."

"I could almost do the same," said Eden, remembering her introduction to Cyprus.

His face darkened. "Indeed yes, my lady. You have had a heavy time of it. I wonder it leaves you so sprightly." He looked at her closely. "Tell, my lady . . . during your imprisonment . . . did this self-styled Emperor attempt to . . . harm you in any way?"

She gave him stare for stare. "On the contrary; he treated me well. He did not . . . force me, sir knight, if that is what you would know."

He nodded expressionlessly, apparently satisfied. What Eden did not know was that Tristan had learned, since their last encounter, a great deal about her, including her appalling treatment at the hands of Sir Hugo de Malfors. The Princess had recounted the tale to the King and Richard had handed it on to his favorite commander one night off Rhodes, to take his mind off his own accursed seasickness, a lifelong penance which he shared with his betrothed. Tristan had been saddened at the thought of so much beauty delivered to the wolf. Later, as he turned the tale over in his mind, he had come to feel a certain amount of admiration for the girl who had so resourcefully put her misfortune behind her and set out to put her small world to rights. This did not mean, however, that he approved of the fact that she had been permitted, even encouraged to do so by those who should have known their responsibility somewhat better than they did.

Now, finding her composed and placid, seemingly, at the heart of a battlefield, however undistinguished, his blood failed in its pulse. There had been another, once,

who had braved a battlefield . . . She saw his eyes widen
for a second, as though a forgotten wound pained him,
and then the shuttered look closed his face to her
again.

"It seems that the Comnenus left in somewhat of a
hurry," he said brusquely, plunging among the cushions to emerge with Isaac's imperial standard, bravely
embroidered in cloth-of-gold which had lain drunkenly among the furnishings much in the manner of its
late owner. "Richard will be pleased with this."

"He will be pleased with all Cyprus. Isaac is very
rich," Eden remarked dryly, still unaccustomed to the
ancient, and by now doubtless honorable, tradition of
pillage. She had conveniently forgotten the origin of
her emeralds.

"And will he take it—all Cyprus?" she continued.
And if he did, how long would he take to conquer it?
And when would they leave, at last, for Jerusalem?

"I imagine so," nodded Tristan, "and what of it?
He cannot prove a worse ruler than the Emperor. Richard takes all he may get, yes—but he only asks for
money, not blood. The Comnenus has sucked the population well-nigh dry, from what we have heard. We'll
take what was his, but we'll not take their livelihood."

Eden thought of Eleanor, who had said her son
would sell London if he could get a buyer, and held
her peace.

She is right to be impatient, he thought. God knows
we all long to be at the walls of the Holy City. And yet
he knew that if they could take Cyprus, they would
hold the golden key to the Mediterranean, an un-
matched strategical base which could be used both as a
vital supply depot and as the departure point for future
attacks on the mainland. Cyprus was worth the conquest, though perhaps they would find it hard at first
to justify the time it would take, and not only to this
green-eyed adventuress before him. He smiled at her
then, wishing he knew her well enough to ask her what
she was thinking, for her gaze was dreaming far into
the distance.

"Come, my lady. I'll take you home—or to what

must stand in its place." He strode out of the tent and she heard him issue orders outside.

Eden hung back, biting her lip as she looked helplessly at Spiro, who now crept out of his corner and timidly took her hand. She hesitated briefly, then, smiling encouragingly at the boy, she led him determinedly out into the morning.

"The boy comes with us," she announced coldly. "It will be a little difficult to accomodate the three of us upon one horse."

His own destrier stood quietly ravaging the nearby bushes. He was a huge animal, deep-chested and strongly muscled with long, slender legs. He was white and his flanks were dabbled with blood.

"That, too, is Cypriot blood, not equine," remarked Tristan maddeningly before she had opened her mouth. "We will leave the boy in Sir Will Barret's charge. I trust you will consider him a sufficiently capable nursemaid?"

Eden nodded, inwardly fuming. Why did he set himself against her at every least turn?

But when Will Barret rode up, horse and man covered in the gray dust of the hillside, streaked with sweat, she was so glad to see him that she almost wept.

"Aye Lady Eden—we are all fit and thriving," he said in answer to her swift question, "though Sir John has a gash in his leg that makes him look drunken, even when he's sober. So he reckons little worth in being sober, for the present."

"Sober enough to lead our detachment until noon, I hope?" De Jarnac's voice held a steely courtesy. "For I have a commission for you, Will—or rather Lady Eden has. You are to become guardian to the engaging young imp you see hanging on her arm. I assure you he would just as well hang upon yours. See that he comes to no harm. Find an interpreter and see if you can discover his village, his home. If you can, see he gets back to it. Richard has sent for me to Limassol."

Eden silently admitted this to be a better solution to Spiro's problem than her own had been. She made no remark, only waved cheerfully to the child as Will clapped him on the shoulder and ruffled his hair. She also noted that de Jarnac did not travel merely to suit her convenience.

Tristan helped her on to his saddle where she sat demurely, sideways as was proper, holding tightly to the beast's harness while he sprang lightly up behind her. He reached round her to take the reins and to give the horse an encouraging pat on its graceful neck.

"Go gently, Gorvenal; it is long since we carried a lady."

"Gorvenal!" Eden was intrigued. "The friend and companion of Tristan; so you, too, read the legends?" She was conscious of a softening toward him.

"I was raised first in Brittany on my father's lands, then in Cornwall on my mother's domain," de Jarnac replied. "How could it be otherwise? The very stones speak of Arthur and of Guinevere, of Tristan and Iseult."

You have your companion in arms, your Gorvenal, she wanted to say, but no Iseult. For the first time she allowed herself that she was curious on that score. She would never admit it to the moonstruck Alys, not even to Berengaria, but she could not to herself deny the evidence of her eyes; Tristan de Jarnac was an exceptionally handsome man. He was also very well-born and the King's friend. Why, then, had he no wife, no sweetheart even? And what of the mysterious lady, even more mysteriously "lost" at Hattin? Her own curiosity annoyed her.

She was very conscious of the steadiness of his arms as they guided the reins behind and before her. She had to lean back a little sometimes to prevent his left arm brushing against her breast. She noticed, too, the depth and clarity of his eyes as they watched the way. She had never encountered such a color before: a deep, glowing chestnut, with a light at the center that held a hint of pure red. She would not like to witness the anger of such eyes.

And then there were his lips, which to her embarrassment set traps for errant tendrils of her hair. She could feel that she was blushing as they rode through the tents, where the soldiers were engaged in the mopping-up operations that follow every battle. Several called out to their commander as he rode by, and there were many uncalled-for familiarities touching upon Eden's bodily attributes and Tristan's good luck.

The unaccountable man was actually smiling. She could not imagine why. His men were behaving like the lowest rabble before his very face; and since he had made it abundantly clear that he had no time for attributes, whether physical or spiritual, why pretend to a pride in her company that he did not feel? Surely he was not susceptible to mere masculine conceit in the display of a pretty woman upon his saddle.

"You must forgive them," the dry voice interrupted. "They have fought and won two engagements in as many days; no doubt they feel their victories have earned them a little license."

Since it was clear that he was entirely in agreement with this feeling, she shifted her position a little and said nothing. The shell of courtesy, if not the meat, should be preserved between them; it was near an hour's ride. It was only when they reached the perimeter of the camp that she saw how fierce the brief battle must have been. Isaac's pavilion had been pitched for his safety at the center, surrounded by circle upon circle of the close-drawn tents of his knights. Most of the fighting had taken place upon three main flanks, leaving a quarter of the circle free as an escape route for Isaac's undignified retreat. The greater part of his knight-cavalry had followed him, leaving the struggle, as was common in a hopeless cause such as this, to the infantry. These were mostly mercenaries of mixed races who had no desire to lose their lives and were inclined, if possible, to continue instead to earn their living on the other side. Those who had the misfortune to be in the path of the Crusader's first charge died willy-nilly, but nevertheless King Richard's recruiting officers were kept busy for the rest of the day and both sides found satisfaction in it.

Those of Isaac's infantry, however, who had been

badly wounded, were swiftly put out of their misery by the English knights; men who were not whole were of no use to a victor, unless, of course, they could be ransomed for a sum that justified their keep.

"It pains me that you should have to witness such sights," declared Tristan, his tone hard as a man grinned cheerfully up at them, wiping on his thigh the knife that had just slit the throat of a Cypriot with an arrow through his lungs. "But this is the truth of war," he continued, gazing about him, "as much the truth of it as is the glory and the honor."

"Indeed it is," agreed Eden vigorously, "and as for glory and honor—though I have already seen enough of this for me to know and hate its nature—I have, as yet, seen neither of these. Perhaps I would not recognize them if I did, beneath their bloodstains."

Tristan looked into her face in surprise. Their eyes met and he saw the challenge in her.

He sighed then, searching for words to meet her with. "Perhaps you may not, lady," he began gently, his face somber, "for they are masks made by men to cover what they cannot understand in themselves and what they cannot bear to see; what you have seen today—and will perhaps see again. But do not be too swift with your contempt, Lady Eden. If the ugly face of war went unmasked, none would follow him. If I were asked to risk death simply in order that I myself might be the death of a number of Saracens, with no greater cause given me—I would not do it. But when I am asked to do it to rescue the land where my God walked in my image for the salvation of my soul, then I do it, for the honor. The glory I can safely leave to my King. It follows him like a saint's nimbus—and make no mistake; it does much to aid our cause. A hero's reputation is a wonderful inspiration to lesser men."

Silent, she stared at the face whose purity of line had seemed almost illumined a moment ago. She thought of Stephen who had also spoken of God and his cause; but he had been untried, his only battles fought out at the quintain in the Hawkhurst tiltyard.

This man had already seen a lifetime's hard fighting in his brief span and yet he still held fast to the same young ideals.

"Saladin has sworn to drive the Christians into the sea," Tristan continued, since she had no answer for him, "and we have sworn to drive him from Jerusalem and back to his mountains and deserts. We will do it. God will aid us." Then his voice recovered its customary tinge of irony. "I only hope that he will continue to do so even when we do not aid each other. There are three Christian Kings and a parcel of Princes on his side. Allah has only Saladin, who is single of mind and purpose."

Eden nodded, smiling briefly. "I've heard of the quarrels of King Richard and Philip Augustus. But I can't believe that they will continue to allow their petty disputes to prejudice the common cause."

"I wish I were as sure," Tristan said curtly.

His superiority was irritating, chiefly because it was justified. "Grant me the wit, sir knight, to know that you surmise from experience, and are therefore more likely to be right."

He grinned at her sardonically and she wondered that, only seconds ago, she had found nobility in that insolent countenance.

They scarcely spoke again until they reached the outskirts of Limassol. The city was the scene of energetic bustle as the English helped themselves in an organized manner to the welcome abundance of wine, meat and corn they found there. The citizens wrung their hands, but not, alas, the hearts of their liberators. This was the price they must pay for their timely delivery from the tyrant, Isaac. They wondered and grumbled. Had they but known, this was only the beginning of their ordeal by extraction.

"You may leave me here, if you will, Sir Tristan," said Eden thankfully when the fortress reared ahead of them, utterly unforbidding in the bright sunlight. This, he told her, was where they would find the royal ladies. The knight grimaced impolitely. "I shall deliver you personally into the presence of the Lady Berengaria, so that if you should choose to go adventuring again, none can lay it at my door."

Eden gasped, furious. "Adventuring! Is that how you would describe the experience of being helplessly shipwrecked, beached and flung into a stinking dungeon, then besieged by the dishonorable proposals of a dissolute prince? I assure you, Sieur de Jarnac, had I as swift a claim on God's holy ear as you appear to have, there would have been no damnable storm and no deplorable wrecks. We should now be in Jerusalem where we ought to be, instead of setting out to play William the Conqueror all about this accursed island."

Tristan then did entirely the wrong thing. He laughed. With a rich curse, gleaned from her recent experience of the English fighting man, Eden dragged at the reins and brought Gorvenal to a sudden, surprised halt. Then she slid from the saddle and marched toward the fortress without a backward glance.

In a wide embrasure, many stories high in the castle, three ladies looked at each other doubtfully then burst into helpless giggling.

"He looks so dreadfully offended! What *could* she have said to him? And whatever could he have done to deserve it?" the Princess Berengaria was round-eyed with curiosity.

"They were sitting very close, almost touching! Perhaps he—well, you know—took liberties?" Mathilde crunched a stolen sugared almond excitedly.

"He couldn't. He isn't that kind of man." Lady Alys was icy in de Jarnac's defense.

"I'm sorry, Alys! I didn't mean to imply that—I don't suppose Sir Tristan has any real interest in Eden. Besides, she's married, probably—" her breathless voice trailed away, dismayed and unconvincing.

Alys longed to slap her, but confined herself to remarking coldly, "You'll soon be as fat as a Cypriot bourgeoise if you keep on eating those things at that rate." She swept out of the chamber, hooking her gray gown over her arm in a regal manner that Berengaria envied from the bottom of her heart. And then, suddenly, she realized. Eden had come back to her! Not

drowned, nor put to the sword, not murdered by rav-
ening Griffons, but safe and well enough to be enor-
mously angry with the handsome Sieur de Jarnac.

Picking up her own crimson skirts in both hands
like any washerwoman, whether of good or bad character, she grabbed Mathilde by one plump, white hand
and rushed her out of the room, then whirled her down
stair after spiraling stair until they arrived, breathless
and ludicrously giddy, before the door through which
Eden must come and flung it open in laughing, tear-
stained welcome.

"Eden—my dear! *Mi corazon!*" Berengaria lapsed
into Spanish as she clasped her friend in a warm and
loving embrace.

Eden returned it, crying incoherently, "Princess!
My sweet friend! Oh I am so glad to see you. I can't
begin to tell you—everything has been so, so—senseless!" And, released at last from all need to be brave,
or seem nonchalant, or argue with anyone, she put
her head on Berengaria's shoulder and wept with relief.

In half an hour it was as though they had never
been parted. And for the next few hours their tongues
flew like weavers' shuttles as they told each other every
minute of their adventures, although Eden was unerringly careful never to employ just that particular word
in her descriptions. All thought of past hardships was
forgotten when, that evening, word was brought to
Berengaria from King Richard, encamped amidst his
army just outside the city. The messenger was someone Eden recognized with a glad cry.

"Gilles! No one knew what had happened to you!
I feared you must be dead or else a prisoner."

The squire grinned, flattered to be the subject of so
much interest on the part of his lady, and more than
pleased to see her safe and sound. "I feared the same
of you—but here we are, snug in the Emperor's palace."

"I was very angry with you when you disappeared
this morning," scolded the Princess.

Gilles looked unrepentant. "I wanted to be in the

fight," he admitted, "and besides—I thought I might find the Lady Eden. Trust the Sieur de Jarnac to have all the luck." Gilles had heard of the manner of Eden's return and was quite put out, for he had planned to be the one who bore her in triumph upon his saddle; still, at least his dream had come true in essence. "But you'll want to hear about Balan?" he offered, conveniently changing the subject.

"Oh please! Is he—did you—?" Eden was breathless with hope.

Gilles smiled proudly. "He's safe, mistress. He damaged his leg during the storm, but it was not broken and I soon patched him up."

"Oh Gilles, how am I to thank you?" she was delighted with him.

The squire eyed her brazenly, squaring his shoulders. "Well—I could think of a way!"

"Shame on you, you wanton boy!" But she kissed him all the same, and was a little taken aback at the enthusiasm of his response. Gilles was becoming a man.

Berengaria was tapping her foot in impatience. "You have news of my Lord Richard; how does he? He has sustained no wound, I hope, from today's business?"

Gilles beamed and shook his shock of yellow hair. Then he cleared his throat importantly and stood back a little from the Princess, looking around until he had assured himself that all attention was riveted upon his slight figure. Having thus charged the room with expectancy, he fell upon his knees and proudly addressed Berengaria.

"It has fallen to my happy duty to demand of you, Princess, on behalf of my liege Lord, Richard Plantagenet, by the grace of God King of England, Duke of Aquitaine and of Normandy, whether you be ready and willing to wed with him upon the twelfth day of this month at the Chapel of Saint George in this city?"

There was a satisfying chorus of feminine gasps and sighs and Berengaria's hand flew to her breast.

A little silence and then, with a calm composure

that she did not feel, the tiny Princess said softly, her face glowing like a rose, "Go, thank my Lord King for his message, sir squire, and tell him that his wish is also my heart's best desire. I am—more than willing."

Gilles, smiling, executed his very best flourish and at once took leave to do her bidding.

"And I shall attempt to be ready," the bride continued doubtfully, "though as to what we can achieve in four brief days, *Demoiselles*—" They all fell upon her at once and hugged and kissed her halfway to suffocation.

"Four whole days! The good Lord only took six to fashion the entire disk we live on. Surely we can furnish forth a wedding, and a right royal one, in four!"

The Lady Alys spoke in the ringing tones of her conquering ancestors and Eden noticed a slight squareness to her noble jaw that she had not seen before. She approved her spirit, however, and they all set to work to find ways and means. Happily the Princess had at least managed to preserve her wedding gown from the depredations of the deep. Alys, too, was the lucky possessor of a full leaden coffer of clothing. But most of Mathilde's gowns, when examined, proved to be stained beyond salvation by the salt waters of the Mediterranean; some of the cloth, indeed, was already quite rotted away and smelled most fouly. As for Eden, her stout wooden coffer had disappeared from the ship as untraceably as she herself had done.

"But you can wear your beautiful blue gown and mantle; it becomes you so," said Mathilde, pulling a wry lip at her own old dun-colored dress, "though I certainly can't be seen in *this* hideous thing!"

"You may have one of my gowns, Mathilde," offered Alys, conscious of her magnanimity, "if it can be altered to fit you—"

"Eh bien! We can take a little off the hem to let into the bodice," began Berengaria helpfully. Mathilde looked miserable, vowing silently never to touch her secret hoard of sugared almonds again.

Eden cast about for a better solution, gazing ab-

stractedly around the chamber as if for inspiration; and
found it right in front of her.

"Mathilde! You shall have a new gown—and a very
splendid one, too. Now then, which should you prefer?
A cranberry velvet? A silvered blue cloth-of-Damascus? Or perhaps an apple-green silk, embroidered
exquisitely in white?"

Puzzled, they followed the direction of her dancing
eyes. They were in what must have been one of Isaac's
more private reception chambers. It contained a good
deal of comfortable seating, arranged to favor the intimate tete-a-tete of which the Emperor was so fond;
there was also a prodigious wealth of fine fabric displayed; the fine length of cranberry velvet at present
obscured the narrow, arched doorway; the silver-veined
damask hung sumptuously along a wall, so that one
might imagine a blue sky in place of the gray stone;
the apple-green silk was in fact a magnificent table-
cloth which none of them had dared to endanger by
actually resting anything so coarse as meat or drink
upon it. Smiles broke out as the ladies took her drift.

Mathilde was immediately decisive. "The green, assuredly!" she cried, "then we may eat at the table!"

Although Eden stoutly averred that she never wished
to see her erstwhile prison-chamber again, the other
ladies declared that they wished to watch the sea while
they sewed, and since the chamber light proved excellent for their purpose, she complained in vain. Every
female in the castle who could ply a needle was pressed
into instant service and the airy chamber sang with
ravished toiles and tapisseries. One of their number
who counted herself overjoyed to be of service was
Xanthe, whom Eden had concernedly sought out soon
after her arrival. It had at first been difficult to persuade
the delighted girl that she now owed her chief allegiance to Berengaria, for she showed a touching attachment to Eden and would not leave her side. Once she
understood that the Princess was to be a bride, however, she revealed a swiftness and delicacy with her
needle that none of the other ladies could match.

"We cannot afford to lose such a treasure, Eden!

How would it be if she were to join our number—
as your tiring-maid? You should have one; we all have
except you."

And so Xanthe's future was decided upon. It would
not have occurred, even to Eden herself, to ask the
girl for her own opinion on the subject. She was, after
all, part of the spoils of war. Luckily she was content.

▼▼▼

CHAPTER SIX

Cyprus: Princes of the Earth

Richard and Berengaria were married on the morning of 12th May, 1191 by God's grace and the Bishop of Evreux. The wedding procession was brief and joyously uproarious as his loyal pride turned out in their festive array to see the Lion take his mate. The cheers and "Noels" of the Crusaders were prolonged and vociferous enough to make it difficult for Bishop Jean to catch the responses of the tiny, coruscating bride, whose dazzle was more the work of her sensationally happy smile than of the diamonds which had been her father's parting gift. Richard's answers rumbled like thunder, starting the echoes among the mellow stones of the Chapel of St. George, pattern and patron of all Crusaders. After the marriage, with due sanctity and more simplicity than pomp, Berengaria was crowned as his consort. So that thus, in this Cypriot city, a Queen of England was crowned by the Bishop of a Norman see; and if Berengaria found among her fragmented thoughts on that momentous day, the hope that England might one day prove a kind home to her Queen, her husband nursed no such sanguine desire. England, to Richard, meant little more than a damp and dreary prison which his father had rendered even more unpleasant by the tournaments, the only honorable recreation of any knight not engaged in actual war. True, the land was prosperous and becoming more so; the thriving wool trade saw to that; but there was nothing in England to catch at an Angevin's heart nor would there ever be. It was no secret that Richard preferred his golden duchies of Aquitaine and Normandy to his dun-colored kingdom across the tempestuous Sleeve.

So long as the lacklustre land continued to produce a satisfactory level of taxes, its King didn't care if he never saw it again. He didn't suppose that little Berengaria would greatly care for it, either, hailing as she did from warm-blooded Navarre. He looked at her covertly as she knelt before the Bishop. Demure and contained, she would cut exactly the right figure at his side. She could never aspire to be the sort of woman his beloved Eleanor was; no woman could. But then, women were generally of precious little use. His blue eyes roamed the packed church. That self-conscious young squire with the scarlet feather in his cap, now. There would be a very pleasant hour or so. What was his name? The one he'd sent to Berengaria the other evening.

Catching the gleam of the Lion's gaze, Gilles, proud and flattered, broke into a wonderful smile. The King had looked at him.

After the wedding came the feast. It took place in the expansive reception chamber where Eden had first set eyes upon the unlamented Emperor of Cyprus. The superlative meal was not, to the bride's sorrow, accompanied by dancing; there were relatively few ladies of a degree allowing them entry to the hall, and, although many knights had been known to trip it together in the privacy of their own encampments, they were not about to do it in public. However, there was music enough, provided enthusiastically by the King's consort of viols and citterns, drums and tabors. Ships from Acre had brought Bohemund of Antioch and his son Raymond, Guy de Lusignan who was King of Jerusalem, Humphrey of Toron, Leo of Roupenia and upwards of fifty knights and templars to welcome Richard's arrival.

The Queen and her ladies were hard-pressed to prevent the high table devolving into a mere board for a council of war as Richard, with Guy of Jerusalem beside him, and Tristan de Jarnac at his shoulder, called to himself one after another the knights who for two years had laid siege to the city of Acre. He wished, ostensibly, to present them to Berengaria who glowed next to him in the golden gown and veil she had preserved from the waters of the bay. In truth, he was greedy to hear all that they could tell him of their unhappy situation. Eden, honored by a place at the royal board, was seated on the right hand of Humphrey of Toron. Pale, slender, the young Frankish lord reminded her fleetingly of Stephen, and as they exchanged their first courteous remarks upon the joy of the occasion and the largesse of the feast, she found herself watching him closely to discover just where the likeness lay. She found him an attentive companion, if a little diffident and soft-spoken. He had a nervous habit of pushing back his fine, pale hair with his left hand and then immediately shaking it back again over his brow. Although Stephen was not given to such mannerisms there was something in the elegant flick of the narrow wrist which she recognized. Perhaps they simply shared a slender frame and a certain unstudied grace of movement. Whatever it was, she felt drawn to the hesitant young knight and did her best to set him at his ease.

For his part, the young Lord of Toron was pleased enough with the company of this splendid golden creature with her candid and intelligent green gaze; but one beauty was much like another to him and had been ever since the cold November of last year; before that, his life had been so different . . . The girl was certainly looking at him closely. Curiously? Of course, she must know. Who didn't?

The King of Jerusalem called for a toast to the bride. They rose and drank with a will.

Then, "Are you wed, my lord?" Eden asked casually as they sank down again. She had some idea of drawing him out a little, reminding him of happier matters, perhaps, than those that seemed to sit so heavily on his brow.

The effect of her innocent question was like that of Greek Fire. Humphrey of Toron struck the board with his right hand, knocking over his hanap and sending a shudder down the polished board. His look was murderous.

"What's amiss, sir? Are you in some pain?" Eden was alarmed, as were their immediate neighbors and some beyond. She signaled to a varlet to wipe away the wine then turned back to Humphrey's bowed figure, repeating gently, "Something is wrong; what is it?"

He groaned and turned upon her such pain-filled eyes that she gasped and laid her hand on his, thinking she understood.

"I'm sorry. I spoke in ignorance, my lord. If I had known of your lady's death . . ."

"Not dead!" He shook his head vehemently. "Is it possible you don't know? Is there anyone who doesn't know my shame?

"I had a wife, lady, until last winter. She was beautiful, rich in spirit and joyously young. We loved each other dearly. And then," he pushed back the hair distractedly, "she was taken away from me. No, not by death; that I could have been reconciled to, as we all must be. We were parted by the forced annulment of our marriage."

Eden was shocked. Scandalous indeed, and exactly what her marauding overlord had planned for her.

"Who performed such a ceremony, against your will?" she asked, scorn in her tone for the shamed churchman.

"The Archbishop of Pisa. He was doubtless well rewarded. He wanted your Archbishop of Canterbury at first, but he would have no part in it. Baldwin was a good man, a true Prince of the Church. God rest his soul."

Eden had heard how the old prelate had died, worn out with the tasks of a younger man. "He?" she queried tentatively.

He drew in a long, shuddering breath. "Conrad, Marquess of Montferrat!" Humphrey almost choked on the name.

She frowned, trying to remember. "Wasn't he the man who held Tyre against Saladin's siege? I heard—"

"Oh, yes! The Hero of Tyre. The man of the hour. Or if you like, a common thief! Tyre belongs to Jerusalem but Conrad has refused to allow King Guy to enter his own city. He has made it impregnable against him." He smiled. "Indeed, it was because he could not regain Tyre that he decided to march away and besiege Saladin's garrison in Acre. We all thought he had left his few wits behind. But, ludicrously, it worked. Guy set up on the hill of Turon outside the city, ringed with his troops, and though he could not take Saladin's garrison, neither could Saladin dislodge him from his hill. Stalemate. It has been thus, more or less, give or take a few hundred men, living and dead, for two years. We need your King, lady. We need him badly!"

"But Conrad . . . your wife," she prompted gently.

"Ah, the Tyrant of Tyre!" he sniggered, the wine beginning to tell on his clarity. "Conrad was a success —and he made sure it spoiled him! He'd proved himself a worthy commander, I won't deny that. And there are many who think that Jerusalem needs a worthy commander to lead her. Guy—he is, well, you've only got to look at him. He didn't even want to be King. The throne came to him through his wife, Sybilla. He wasn't the only one who didn't want him to rule; there were dozens of them, all leading men in the Christian Kingdoms; some of them even asked me to take the throne!"

"You?" Humphrey did not, at this precise moment, appear to be any more fit to govern than Guy, whom Eden had already judged to be weak and lacklustre.

"Guy married Sybilla. I married Isabella," he said simply. "Sisters! Isabella's claim and Guy's fumbling inefficiency were enough to make to a likely risk to depose him in my favor; but *I* didn't want to be King either." He drank again.

"I still don't understand how . . ." The trouble was still there inside him. He waggled a reproving finger at her. "Wait! It's obvious. Sybilla died, and her two daughters with her. Epidemic."

"I'm sorry. How terrible for . . . Guy."

Humphrey nodded solemnly. He was near enough

now to the root of his own pain to afford a little sympathy for his King, for whom he had never felt either affection or respect. "So then," he continued, enunciating carefully, "the only true heir to the throne of Jerusalem was Isabella, my wife."

"And they asked you again to be King, when Guy's claim died with Sybilla?"

He laughed, irony dismissing alcohol in his next words. "No. 'They' have now become the panders of Conrad of Montferrat. Both he and they see him as the only possible king. They still want Guy deposed. And, truth to tell, Conrad would make a better job of it. Especially now that he has legalized his claim by marrying Isabella."

"Christ's wounds!" Eden saw it all now. "But that is inhuman. To take her from you and marry her to him —merely to give him a claim on another's throne!"

He shrugged. His movements, though less well coordinated, were still graceful, though he no longer brought Stephen to her mind.

"They have not been—kind. It was suggested, rumored, spread about that I am incapable of satisfying a woman, that my pleasures are—other. It has not helped me that Isabella and I have had no children."

He sighed and stared unseeingly across the heads of the assembled revelers, his eyes gentle and sad. Eden put her hand upon his arm, with a soft pressure.

"Those who know you will not believe it," she told him firmly, thinking of Stephen.

He smiled, covering her hand with his. "You are very kind."

She shook her head. "It isn't merely common kindness. I feel a great sympathy with you because I, too, know what it is to lose a loved one. Though in my case, perhaps all is not yet certain . . ."

"Indeed?" Weary of his own inescapable problem he welcomed hers.

Concisely, Eden explained the reason for her presence upon the Crusade, ending with the fact that Stephen was last heard of in Acre, serving under his commander, Walter of Langford.

Humphrey's reaction was practical and immediate. Snapping his fingers to waylay a passing servant, he ordered him across to a table against the wall where he was to find one Pierre de St. Omer and request the favor of his company as soon as he wished.

"I know him for a friend of your Sir Walter," he explained, all trace of the slur gone from his voice. "They have lands that march in Brittany. He may be able to give you some useful information."

Eden felt a growing constriction about her breastbone as she waited out the seconds while the servant delivered his message and the knight shoved his way to them through the close-packed throng of diners.

A heavy, beetle-browed man in his fifties, his movements and manner were agonizingly slow.

"My Lady of Hawkhurst. My Lord of Toron. How may I serve you?" he asked courteously with a hampered attempt at a bow.

"We seek news of Walter of Langford. The Lady's husband is among his knights."

"Alas, poor Walter," the man sighed and shook his head. "He is like to leave this life. He led a reconnaissance party up into the hills—a foolhardy errand but he wouldn't be gainsaid. His troop was ambushed and savagely slaughtered. Out of thirty men only three came back to tell the tale."

Eden gave a brief, gasping cry. "Stephen de la Falaise—was he with him? Did he come back?"

Again the burly knight shook his head. "As to that, I can't say, my lady. I remember the boy—that blond head of his—but I know the names of neither those who rode out nor those who returned, saving Walter himself, and I met him in the care of the Hospitalers. His wound was very sore and he could not speak. I fear—I am sorry, my lady."

Eden's face was ashen and her eyes tormented. The knight nodded and left them.

"I too am very sorry," Toron said gently, supporting her with his arm as she stared, rigid, into nothingness. "But you must not give up hope. There are a thousand circumstances to be discovered. Hope is the one thing you have to sustain you." He turned her chin, forcing her to look into his sad, brown eyes. "You can only begin to calculate the value of that hope, my lady, when you know with all certainty that it is irretrievably lost to you."

She nodded in swift, anguished agreement. Then, touching his hair for a moment in tenderness and gratitude, she rose from her seat and wordlessly fled from the feast.

Hardly aware of the direction she was taking, Eden ran through the anteroom where contented guardsmen were enjoying their share of the feast and along the passage to the twisting stairway. She swirled swiftly up the uneven steps and it was only after she had sunk, panting and weeping, upon the embrasured window seat that she realized she had found her way to her one-time prison, now the ladies' favorite solar.

At first she let her sobs take her, wracking her body almost as unmercifully as the raw ocean had done on the night that she had come here. Soon, she forced control upon herself. Weeping was an indulgence that would do no good at all; not to her and certainly not to Stephen—if he lived. She knew that the tragic and abused young Lord of Toron was right; there must be room in her heart only for hope, none for self-pity.

She gazed out through the familiar casement. The royal galleys still lifted and sank in the shelter of the harbor, and with them rode at least a hundred more. Others joined them daily. Richard's war fleet was growing fast. If only they could pull up their anchors and set sail now, today! The impatience which she had learned to hold in check like a well-trained hound strained upon the taut cords of her mind until she felt that their rupture must become a physical fact, endangering both her reason and her future. She ground her nails into the sculptured sill as though she would wear her way through the insensate stone. Several of them broke, raggedly, and brought her to herself with sharp discomfort. She took a deep breath and relaxed consciously, scorning her lack of control.

Suddenly she was weary to the bone, drained of all

emotion. Isaac's great bed was still in the chamber, pushed against the wall to be used as a daybed by the Queen's ladies. It was covered in lengths and scraps of silks and velvet, the residue from their ravishment of the castle's furnishings. Yawning, she lay down gratefully in their midst, and their brightness hummed softly beside her until the colors mingled with those of troubled and intangible dreams.

A burly knight with a meat-knife in his hand gestured into a misty distance where there stood a tall, younger knight with his back toward her. It was Stephen: she knew this. She swam toward him as if through an obscene swamp that sought to suck her down; only in dreams do we move thus dreadfully. At last, the knight turned. He had the face of Humphrey of Toron. Infuriated, she woke up. Or perhaps it was the sound of feet upon the stairs that had woken her? She wondered idly who it would be. Mathilde, possibly, overcome by the size of her eyes in relation to that of her rotund little stomach?

But the curtain across the open doorway was pulled back to reveal none of the Queen's ladies. It was the Sieur de Jarnac, arrayed in festive black and silver and an expression of polite concern. Eden groaned.

Unmoved by his reception Tristan examined her closely. He assured himself during this enjoyable process that, although she had undoubtedly been weeping, she was doing so no longer and had evidently had the good sense to sleep it off.

"I saw you leave; you seemed distressed." There was a faint unsteadiness in his tone. De Jarnac, whom his lieutenant had praised for his ability to drink any man under the table, had for once underestimated the quality of the wine. This was not immediately obvious to Eden whose eyes were blurred by sleep and tears. She stared at him, bewildered and silent.

He leaned upon the archway in an elegant pose. Not long ago it had seemed imperative to him to come here; now he could not quite decide why he had done so. "I was concerned for you," he told her slowly, his eyes slitting like a cat's. "I feared lest you had taken flight and bribed one of the King's sea-dogs to ferry you across to Acre; I hear you've word of your husband?" The lightness of his tone was unbearable to her. Her eyes snapped like naphtha. She very plainly loathed him at this moment. He felt vaguely that she was unfair.

"I once offered you help," he said then, simply, the raillery discarded like a cloak. "I offer it once more. Truly, your happiness is my concern."

"Take your concern to the devil," she grated between clenched teeth. "I want none of your interest. If you know I've had news, you'll know what news. Have the decency to leave me in peace."

She sounded as though she'd given up. She mustn't give up; she mustn't be allowed to give up. He would goad her beyond the reach of tears.

He smiled, somewhat crookedly. "I'm afraid I can't do that. You see, Richard, our King, now below making the best of being a married man, Richard feels that I should keep an eye on you. He asked me particularly to discourage any . . . eccentric behavior on your part. The Queen, too, thinks you need looking after."

She answered his bland smile with a glare of unconcealed shrewishness. He noted the sewing shears, close to her hand on the bed and calculated her chances of hitting a moving target. Eden sniffed and drew a fist across her tear-stained features. She felt flushed and her hair had fallen from its elaborate, marriage-day coils; she must look a mess. De Jarnac, on the other hand, looked as if he had never stepped further into the daily disarray of life than the Queen's presence chamber at Winchester.

"Please go away," she said with controlled fury.

He sauntered further into the room and stood looking down at her. She began to feel at a disadvantage. Why did he stare so? Because she suddenly felt she had to talk, she asked, in a tone she tried hard to keep neutral, "Since you will not do as I ask, you may give me some information concerning yesterday's council of Kings. Sir Humphrey's conversation did not take that direction and I'm curious to know what brings this pride of princes to our camp." He seemed, she thought, a little dazed by her question. "And," she added, for this was what had made her ask, "whether their presence means we shall leave Cyprus the sooner?"

He nodded, sobered by the longing he sensed in her. "Guy of Jerusalem comes to seek Richard's support against Conrad of Montferrat. Philip Augustus has aligned himself with the Marquess and this means there'll be a strong move to put Conrad on Guy's throne. If Richard backs Guy, he'll have help in Cyprus and the conquest will be swift. Not a bad bargain. Richard has accepted it. He wants Cyprus. He also wants to see Acre, just as much as you do; so you may look with favor upon Guy de Lusignan. If not on me," he finished, grinning.

"Can I so?" She was contemptuous. "Even the Lord of Toron gave the opinion that Conrad is probably the better man. And that is the man who has stolen his wife."

Tristan sighed. How badly the unfortunate Guy needed Richard; at least the Lionheart would lend some glamour to his flagging cause. "It may be so. It may even be so proved. But until that time comes, we are Guy's men as we are Richard's. And God save us . . . on top of that, we are all, Montferrat, Lusignan, Plantagenet and Capet, sworn to the same cross and the same end." There was a slightly hectic note she had not heard in him before.

"How it must delight the Saracen," she murmured, noting that his sartorial perfection was, in fact, marred by several straying locks and that the brow beneath them had a distinctly higher color than usual; she was charitable enough to hope he was not taking a fever.

"Saladin?" he muttered, seeing the softening of her face. "He thrives on it, uses it, certainly, how not? It must be painful for a man of such subtle intellect to watch the shameful antics of an unworthy enemy."

"Curse Saladin!" Her eyes were again ablaze with scorn. "You have a very great admiration for the scourge of Christendom," she challenged. He was close to her now; she did not know how it had come about.

"No, I have not. But for Saladin, yes. I have," he said softly, leaving her to catch at his meaning. His whole world had somehow become bounded by her bright-eyed, suspicious little face and he wanted to hear no more words, nor to speak any more. In fact, he wanted . . . he laughed as he discovered what he wanted. He bent and pulled her to him. He had not intended this, but he felt an unholy joy as he kissed her. It was both longing and longing satisfied. For a moment her lips were soft, opening beneath his own and he felt the softness of her breasts against his chest. Then his head was ringing to the resonance of her stinging blow on his cheek.

"Dear God, Sir Tristan! Are you mad?"

She was so white; he hoped she would not faint. He rubbed his cheek, without regret. "Not mad, my lady. Possibly just the slightest bit drunk." He smiled gracelessly. "That, at any rate, is what you may tell yourself . . . if you need a suitable excuse . . ."

"I?" Her voice soared with indignation, the naphtha snapping once more. "What need have I of excuse?"

He trapped her gaze before she could rail at him further and she slowly lowered it, inch by inch. He knew that she, too, would have to remember that sweet flowering of her open mouth under his . . . whether she wanted to, or not. He favored her with a smile that would have reduced Lady Alys to swooning ecstasy and turned, then, to leave her, his silver cloak swinging in a glittering arc behind his shoulder.

She stared balefully after him, belatedly considering the sewing shears. She found her tongue. "Why?" she cried, her voice tuned with resentment.

The light reply floated back through the velvet curtain. "Why not?" as he clattered, laughing, down the spiraling stair.

It had been a merry wedding. He wished the King joy of his little brown bird of a bride. But he hardly knew whether or not to wish the same joy to Stephen de la Falaise of his angry-eyed, free-flying falcon.

In the tower, Eden rose from the disarrayed bed and started to disentangle the web of her hair with her fingers; the mesh of her thoughts and confused and sorry emotions she would not tackle now. There flashed across her mind one memory her senses would not spare her . . . of another feast day, much like this one, when Sir John de Wolfran had been the one to succumb to the wine . . . while she herself had given in, much later, to sleep. There had been the scent of sandalwood about her chamber when she awoke . . . just as there was at this moment.

It was subtle, sweet, disturbing . . . just as his lips had been. With an oath that would have shocked the most inebriated knight in the hall, she seized the innocent shears and hurled them through the archway of the door.

When Tristan reached the foot of the stairs his head continued to spiral though his feet had done with it. He stood still and shook it. That was better. He couldn't understand it; he had always been able to hold his liquor; he had won many an argument with his so-called superiors merely by his ability to drink them under tables and into beds. He had occasionally used the same methods with coy ladies, though he left out the table in these cases. They had, of course, been ladies of pleasure, though some of them had come to it by leaping down the branches of astonishingly tall family trees. The ravishing Lady of Hawkhurst, whom he seemed just to have kissed, was not, alas, one of these. She was a woman with a mission, a quest. There was nothing more tiresome in the world. He was glad he had kissed her, though. He had enjoyed it. He touched his cheek tenderly; it stung. He smiled. She had fetched him a crack worthy of an alewife. Suddenly there came to him the memory of Sir Hugo de Malfors and his pleasant smugness dropped from him like a cloak. Oh God! No wonder she was so swift with her blows! And yet he did not wish to regret the last few moments; indeed he found it impossible to do so.

"Why, Sir Tristan! What are you doing here? Are you quite well?"

He blinked and focused properly. "Lady Alys! Well enough, thank you. Perhaps I liked the wine better than it liked my stomach. It seems to have attacked my head ferociously." He gave her the disarming smile that had awoken hope in numerous breasts, only to dash it at last when the sorrowful ladies realized that it was all he would give.

Like everyone else, from King to cook's scullion, Alys had drunk a little more than was her custom. Her pale features glowed, the calm-sea eyes were unusually turbulent, the lips parted and rosy. She was on her way to the solar to lie down, having tired of Will Barret's attempts at a sensible conversation which he was in no state to conduct.

"Perhaps some air . . ." she suggested. There was a door behind the stairwell. "We could walk a little; it is cool now . . ." She so much wanted his company. She wondered how she dared, knowing it was more than half the wine talking.

Tristan was amused. The frozen Lady Alys asking him to take her for a walk. He was aware of her interest; it had sat behind the cool detachment of her daily face throughout a dozen dinnertime exchanges. He had come to accept that she should partner him on these occasions. Perhaps they wanted him to wed her. She was an heiress, a considerable one; her lands were nearly as broad as his own, her family as high-born. It would, he knew, be a suitable match. And he must marry, sooner or later. If they would give him time, he would come to it, as a sensible man must. It was just that he still remembered Claire and how she had died . . . and he could think of no woman in that way, not just yet. Not even for the sake of Jarnac.

So he smiled with a piercing gentleness at the Lady Alys and shook his head. "I thank you, no, my lady. I have business with some of my men . . ." He bowed to her with perfect gallantry and swung off toward the confusion of music and laughter in the hall.

Alys bit her lips to stem the quick tears and leaned her hot brow upon the cool stone wall. She had never wanted any man before. Nothing else that she had

wanted had been refused her. She was rich and beautiful and her father wielded power among his peers.
She straightened. There was time, a great deal of time.
The Crusade had not yet begun. She picked up her
trailing skirts and climbed the stairs to the solar. It
struck her then that Tristan must have come down
from there; he had been standing at the foot of the
stairway. She quickened her pace, her heart thudding
suddenly. Just before the threshold of the solar, the
sewing shears lay upon the floor. Automatically she
picked them up.

In the darkening room Eden of Hawkhurst was sitting on the edge of the daybed, surrounded by silks.
There was an expression on her face that Alys could
find no means to interpret. It was gone instantly, however, and, as always, they spoke softly and courteously
to each other. They discussed the strength of the
wine, the success of the wedding, the happiness of
Berengaria. There was no discord between. There was
no reason for it. Only beneath their discourse, there
stole across their senses a faint echo of some unname-
able perfume.

CHAPTER SEVEN

The High Seas

The taming of Cyprus was, in the event, as brief as even Eden had any right to wish. The island was a mountain-covered, sea-girt stronghold. Its army was assisted by the mountains and its navy by the Saracens. It was no easy conquest, yet Richard and Guy de Lusignan accomplished it in just three weeks. The Emperor, blockaded in his northern fortress of Kantara, surrendered unconditionally and his people acknowledged the Lionheart as their sovereign lord. A great surge of happiness and hope swept through the Crusading army. Cyprus was theirs. They were free to leave.

The only person reluctant to embark was the Queen. The King had already set sail from Famagusta where he had marshaled his army, while Berengaria and her entourage were to leave from Limassol. They had been separated once before. She could not help dwelling fearfully upon the dreadful train of events that had followed that parting. In vain they assured her that the sea was calm as a baby's bath and that Cyprus was so close to the mainland of Palestine that a man who stood upon the highest hill in the district of Stavrovouni would see the cedars of Lebanon upon his horizon.

At last, because she must, she consented to go aboard, gripping Eden's hand firmly to give herself courage and praying heartily that the next time she saw her husband he would not be in heaven.

The galley sat heavily in the blue-green water. The conqueror of Cyprus had reaped rich and relentless rewards and she was loaded to the limit of her capacity with the spoils. The depredation of Messina had been a mere exercise in comparison with this. Isaac Comnenus had been a far more efficient and enthusiastic robber than Tancred of Sicily, or even than Joanna Plantagenet in the acquisitive mood. The Queen herself and each of her gratified ladies had received a generous portion of the booty, recompensing them many times over for anything they might have lost to the ocean or to Isaac's soldiery.

Stephen's ransom, if it were needed, would be rich indeed. In addition to what he could carry away, Richard had imposed a levy of fifty percent on the goods of every Cypriot citizen. He had further deprived them by demanding that they shave off their long beards, as a somewhat whimsical earnest of their faithful adherence to the liberation. As for the erstwhile Emperor, his destination was to be the grim fortress of Marquab, above Tyre, which belonged to the Templars. His little daughter, who had not as yet had time to be corrupted by her father's decadent ways, was to be attached to Joanna's court, there to learn to behave like an Angevin and be a credit to her conqueror. "Not Lionheart but Lionshare!" the King of England was heard to remark, neither for the first nor the last time, as he watched the rocky coastline recede. He had forgotten nothing—not even Fauvel.

Contrary to Berengaria's expectation the crossing was smooth and uneventful and the galleys put off Limassol scudded to rejoin those sent down from Famagusta on a favoring wind, so that the whole mighty fleet appeared together off the coast of Syria at twilight on the sixth of June.

Their first landfall was the city of Tyre, the stronghold of the redoubtable Marquess of Montferrat. A detachment of men-at-arms was despatched with their unhappy imperial prisoner to Marquab, twenty miles back in the hills, while Richard himself sought entry to the city, strangely quiet behind its impenetrable walls.

The Queen's galley, much to her personal disgust,

did not put into shore, but dropped anchor a tantal-
izing sea bird's view away from the coastline, so that
their only visual impression of the long-awaited Holy
Land and of their King's first fortunes therein was that
of a hundred bobbing lanterns as Richard's landing
party marched toward the gates of Tyre. A smaller
circle of illumination, decreased steadily to that of a
single candle as the prison-detail wound across the
plain behind the city and up into the hills that loomed
over it, their shapes alien and black against the lighter
darkness of the sky. The air was intimate and warm
even around their off-shore anchorage and the women
padded the deck, prey to a restlessness that was part
impatience and in part a heightening of the senses,
every nerve awake and softly expectant in the deep
velvet night.

The Queen did not take her eyes off the torches,
convinced that she had managed to pick out the one
that Richard must be carrying in the van. "See, it leaps
above the others. It can only be the King's."

Where the King was, Tristan de Jarnac would not
be far off. Eden did not invite the thought; it came, unwelcome, and she sent it away into the dark. She
smiled. "He makes you happy, your King?" It was the
nearest she had come to asking how it had gone between them.

Berengaria reached for her hand where it lay along
the deckrail. "Very happy. I had no notion—I mean,
no one could tell me it would be . . ."

Eden nodded, reassured and returned the light pressure of fingers. "It is good to be able to remember one's
wedding night like that." She gripped the rail a little
tighter beneath the Queen's hand. "It is a talisman to
hold against the future. Against lighthearted kisses and
too much wine . . . and uninvited thoughts on heavy,
alien evenings."

Berengaria was surprised by the faint suggestion of
a chill in the tone. "What do you mean? Do you fore-
see evil, then, for me and for Richard?"

"Oh no!" Eden turned quickly to forestall her alarm.
"It was not of you I thought. Forgive me. I don't know

why I spoke so. It was just some random vapor of the mind. Don't think of it. I beg you."

"Perhaps you meant to say that the memory of one happy hour can light us through many dark ones," the Queen said softly. "That is often the way it must be. We should not sorrow over it; only be glad for what we have had."

Had that been her meaning? She did not know. It had been an unrecognized instinct, even a prescience, that had ambushed her here in the soft Syrian night. A presentiment of unhappiness, but for whom? For herself, for the Queen, for the whole land of England? She could not say. It was gone now, that swift apprehension of a single heartbeat, but she could not cast its shadow from her spirit and she turned away from the shoreline with its moving human candles. They were singing now, as they often did when they marched. It was the well-loved song of Guiot de Dijon which told tenderly of the loneliness of the woman whose lover has taken the Cross and sends her the shirt he has been wearing so that she may crush it in her arms at night as she weeps for an absence that she does not expect to end.

The bittersweet words, softened by distance, caught suddenly at Eden's heart and she strained to hear them better.

> *De ce sui molt decüe*
> *Quant ne fui au convoier*

"What saddens me most of all is that I did not leave with him—"

She stared out to sea, her chin lifting. She had not left with him—but she had journeyed to seek him and now she was near the end of it, please God.

In the morning the ladies were awakened by the now familiar sounds of the galley preparing to be underway. They were set for Acre and would reach it well before noon. They were all but away when the King's flagship passed by, coming close enough for delighted good-days to be exchanged. The ladies learned that Richard and his disgruntled troops had bedded down, many of them, in nothing but their cloaks, outside the gates of Tyre. The loyal garrison of Conrad of Montferrat had orders to admit no one, not even the King of England.

If the son of the easily offended Henry Plantagenet had hesitated as to the choosing of his candidate, in the struggle that would one day have to be settled between Conrad de Montferrat and Guy de Lusignan for the city of Jerusalem, his last doubts were done with.

His greeting to his wife was somewhat tempered by his brooding thoughts along these lines. She might, indeed, have been privileged to a display of the famous Plantagenet rage, known as the Angevin sickness, had not an extraordinary incident temporarily distracted everyone from the subject of the Hero of Tyre.

The flagship, sailing closest to the shore, flanked the smaller galley which was guarded on her other side by a fast bireme commandeered in Cyprus. This was under the command, over her captain, of Tristan de Jarnac. The three ships easily outstripped the heavily loaded busses, the transport vessels, which followed behind with their convoy of galleys and old-fashioned English roundships which carried the horses and equipment of those fighting men who were not knights. A fair, slightly fractious wind took them clear ahead without the use of their oars, then dropped them again, leaving them very close to their destination. They could see Acre, perched on her promontory, rear from the cerulean waters with the proud invulnerability of the natural fortress, her golden seaboard about her feet.

Eden gazed and thought of Eleanor. "Blue and gold; you would like it well." Then, ahead of them, they suddenly descried a large vessel, under the flag of France. It showed every evidence of running for port before them, and, despite the signed alliance between England and France, did not offer the courtesy of any greeting or welcome.

On the deck of the *Sainte Cecile* Tristan de Jarnac screwed up his eyes against the sun. It was hotter, getting hourly hotter, and he had stripped off his tabard and rolled up the sleeves of his gambeson. Frowning suddenly, he called for his hauberk and his sword.

"What's amiss, Sir Tristan?" the captain asked him.

"I don't believe she's a French transport," Tristan replied, pleasant anticipation in his voice, "but I do believe we should take a closer look at her."

The captain grinned. It had taken him very little time to discover why the Chevalier had been given command of his ship. His primary resentment had soon turned to respect. The man was near as good a sailor as he was said to be a soldier. He knew that Richard had put him aboard to assess the condition and discipline of the crew as much as those of his army passengers. The slow, disrupted journey from England had taken its toll; there had been wounds sustained in Cyprus. Sleep had been intermittent; tempers were short. Only last night a fight had broken out between a sailor and a sergeant of archers. The latter had felled his man with an almighty blow from the hand that constantly rewound his crossbow; the sailor had fallen back against the bulwark and his head had split open. He was dead before they reached him. Despite the sergeant's plea of accident the captain had been the first to uphold de Jarnac in the carrying-out of the King's ordinance in such circumstances.

"Any man who slays another on board ship shall be thrown into the sea lashed to the corpse."

The man had shamed himself by screaming as they hurled him over the side. When the Chevalier ordered him to catch up with the suspicious transport, therefore, the *Sainte Cecile* cut through the water like a sword through butter. Soon, despite the evident shyness of their supposed brothers-in-war, they had put but the flight of a crossbow between them. As the *Cecile* closed in curiously upon her prey, it became obvious that the only thing that was French upon the heavy vessel was the flag, which even now, was being hauled from the masthead.

"A blockade-runner! We're in luck!" De Jarnac gave his order to the ranked bowmen. Their arrows, many of them tipped with burning pitch, sped to their home, the sturdy ship following them as fast as her rowers could take her. Just before they had to bend their heads beneath their shields to receive the return volley, the archers had the satisfaction of seeing the Saracen's stern afire and the little half-mailed, turban-clad figures scurrying to hurl sand and vinegar on the flames. Next time, *Cecile*'s aim was even surer and the enemy's vast rudder burst into flame.

Under cover of her own hail of arrows, the *Cecile* moved in inexorably until she was close enough to grapple with the burning transport. Tristan de Jarnac was first over the side as they boarded the rocking vessel, his sword slicing the air in front of him in a broad, dancing pattern that no man dared to challenge. Soldiers and sailors alike swarmed after him.

The hand-to-hand combat was fast, ferocious and to the death, no quarter given or wished for on either side. Tristan hacked his way to the Saracen's captain, thrusting into one man's heart and slitting another's throat with his dagger in order to do so. He fought almost automatically. He had fought many battles and his experience told him that this one would be brief. The face of the enemy was universally dark; eyes lighted coals of loathing for the Cruciati, eaters of unclean meat; nose thin and curved like the unholy crescent sword; an enemy who gave out the terrifying ululation of *"La ilaha il Allah!"* while carving a Christian's way to eternal damnation. An enemy dedicated, not to war, but to God, and fighting with the strength of this knowledge. Not the sword alone, but the man who wielded it were forged together into a weapon.

Among the best of the Christians this was also true, but they were not many. Thus, those for whom this was the first battle with the Infidel were much surprised. Others, already experienced, had tried to tell them how it would be, but could not find the right words to describe the man who does not fight for his own gain or his leader's glory but for his Truth.

Tristan, his sword all but smoking in his hand, had lost sight of the infidel captain in the thick of the

fray. He cursed and killed others, but the disappearance worried him. Moments later he knew why, as
there came the sound of axes splintering toughened
wood. The Muslim captain, having nothing more to
lose, was determined that the Christian devils should
make no gain. He was unemotionally scuttling his
ship and destroying her precious cargo. His carpen-
ters had all but finished their work when de Jarnac,
roaring the name of his accursed son-of-God, stopped
the captain's hand by severing it at the wrist. Disre-
garding the spurting stump, the son-of-Allah spat
copiously in de Jarnac's face and ordered his men to
continue their destruction. But it was over and he
knew it. With one last, curiously flat look at Tristan,
the captain jumped through the hole he had caused
to be made in the side of his ship.

What remained of the cargo was hurriedly brought
on board the *Cecile,* where the weary victors lined
the rail to watch the last moments of the ruined transport as she sank smouldering, into the innocent blue
waters.

From the deck of the flagship came the triumphant
brass laughter of trumpets as Richard saluted his in-
trepid commander. Tristan, in return, offered the spoils
to his leader. Besides wine, grain and siege equipment
there was a good selection of jewelry and unset gem-
stones, whose value would increase with the length of
the siege. There were also several chests of clothing
and materials of a superlative quality. Richard magnanimously indicated that half of these be given to
the Queen and her ladies. There was an excited flurry
as the chests were fetched aboard and set down before
the mainmast, the boarding party led by Sir Tristan
himself.

Only two of the chests had been opened before every lady present began to wonder how she could best
dispose of the garments made from Isaac's old curtains.

They had soon marked out several articles by eye.
Lady Alys favored a silver-blue gown in the loose
style of Muslim ladies. Mathilde fancied a chemise of

palest pink gauze; it made her think of weddings and
her cheek bloomed to match it. Eden had discovered
a pair of finely netted mail gauntlets, decorated with
embroidered leather, for hawking which was ever her
favorite sport. She was careful to avoid de Jarnac's
merry eye. The Queen had already draped about herself a light, stripped cloak of the cloth known as cotton and rarely seen in western lands, when they bent
expectantly over the third chest. The iron clasps were
broken and the lid flung back.

A good half of the English fleet must have heard
the ladies scream. The chest was filled to the brim
with convulsed and sibilant snakes, their reared heads
dead-eyed and malevolent.

Several dozen of the reptiles had already escaped
before de Jarnac had the presence of mind to close the
lid with the point of his sword. "I know the breed,"
he snapped, "a kind of viper, and deadly. Kill them
all. And for our sweet Savior's sake—and our own,
Messires, someone stop those women screeching!"

The pandemonium that followed rivaled even that
of the preceding battle. The writhing, green-black
bodies of the serpents seemed to be everywhere, their
smooth, gliding motion almost hypnotic in its effect.
The knights and seamen lay about them with all available weapons; the prudent chose oars and battered
the venomous heads into the boards, some with daggers only. Two of these last were bitten and their cries
of pain and terror were added to the screaming of the
terrified women. The Queen stood at bay behind the
sterncastle where a demonic obsidian eye threatened
from a leveled, hissing head. Will Barret trod swiftly
and precisely upon its tail and it turned its attention
obediently toward him. He cut off its head with a certain finesse, using a whistling sideswipe of his shortsword, then wiped the blade carefully upon the under-
side of his surcoat lest the ladies be offended by the
dark, unwholesome blood. At least, he thought somewhat shamefacedly, he had taken a life for one of
his sovereigns today, albeit only a snake's.

Eden, thinking it good sense, had remained beside

the chest when de Jarnac had closed the lid and, though at first she had screamed as lustily as any, felt herself safe as the vipers sought to put distance between themselves and their prison. Leaning against the mast, she watched the energetic chase that followed. She did not notice the pair of vipers that writhed their sinuous way from beneath the sea-chest —not until it was almost too late.

With a shriek that curdled the blood of all on board except the snakes, she turned, impelled by blind, insensate instinct, and began to claw and clutch her way up the slippery rope footholds of the mast. The snakes, following the helpful flourish of movement slid, as if bidden, after her and, looking down in horror, she saw that they too were beginning to smooth their silent path up the ropes. Incoherent sounds tangled in her throat and her body chilled with fear. Her limbs were overwhelmed by a dreadful lassitude; she could not move further. She looked down again and despaired as the first flat head reared toward her ankle.

During the seconds since her scream had rung out, de Jarnac, having dispatched several of the creatures, was on the point of sheathing his sword. It was in his hand again as he cleared the deck toward her and then dropped carelessly at his feet as he saw how close the danger was. He seized the topmost serpent in his left hand as it drew back its head to strike, then grabbed the hissing mask with his right as it turned its flickering tongue toward himself.

"Christ! Tristan!" De Wulfran, who still held his slimed sword unsheathed, ceased to lean upon it and was across the boards in an instant, so that de Jarnac now held the two halves of the snake, one in each hand.

"There's another!" he cried suddenly, slamming his shoulder against the mast. This time he used his dagger as the dark coil unwound toward him. He threw the body on top of its companion and looked obliquely upwards, smiling faintly.

"You can come down now, Lady Eden."

Her thin voice was almost extinguished. "I . . . can't."

Tristan raised both eyes to heaven. Sir John made a forward motion but his commander stayed him. Quickly and lightly, with practiced ease, de Jarnac used the sailors' ropes to gain her side.

Eden was frozen to the mast, a little over halfway aloft. She could no longer feel either her feet or her fingers and did not understand how they could be supporting her. She closed her eyes, unable to bear the vertigo induced by the sway of the ship. She gave a brief gasp as she felt his arm come around her. Opening her eyes, she found herself staring at a masculine chest, covered in blood and blue velvet. Her voice little more than a sob, she muttered foolishly, "You have spoiled your beautiful surcoat, Sir Tristan."

He bent his head until it was very near to hers. "And you," he murmured, "have ruined your exquisite gown."

For once, Eden was in no doubt of his motives. She smiled shakily. "Rather my gown lost than my life," she said, her voice nearly her own again.

"By the mercy of God, yes," said Tristan somberly. It came to him then just what a matter of fractions of seconds it had been: he found himself, to his great amazement, shaking a little. He stared into the flooded green eyes, so close to his own and there was a moment of silence between them when both acknowledged the intimacy of their rather ridiculous predicament. He opened his lips, but then did not speak, though she felt his breath touch her cheek as a long exhalation escaped him. She moved her head so that she should not look into his puzzled eyes, and her hair brushed his skin. She felt him flinch as if it caused him pain. She wondered if he would kiss her again. She almost felt as if he had.

His nearness was now a more disturbing threat than her fear of height and she swallowed and whispered unsteadily. "I think I can go down now."

They descended slowly and carefully. He kept his

left arm about her until they reached the deck, then abruptly let her go. Eden stood for a second, absorbing the fact of her safety, and then, stunned, the extent of the danger she had passed through, and the extent of that he had taken on himself for her sake.

She turned instinctively, her face alight with gratitude. "There are no words or ways to thank you, Sir Tristan," she told him softly, her eyes swimming and warmly gold as he remembered them first. "You will ever have my prayers for this."

He nodded, his smile more curt than she could understand. Perhaps he did not care to be thanked. Men were often so, and to rescue a foolish lady from an even more foolish situation was hardly an act of glory to be sought by the King's commander, even a lady whom one had once, even more foolishly, kissed. She wondered if he regretted it. He had, after all, been a little drunk. And yet, as de Jarnac marshalled his men and descended into the *Cecile*'s waiting boat, her smile for him lingered after he had gone from her sight. She too had been a little drunk. Surely . . . it had not been important enough to regret?

A gentle voice spoke at her elbow. "Amen to your prayers, Eden. That is a brave and excellent man." Berengaria took her arm, tears of relief standing in her clear eyes. "And so excellently well-favored," sighed Mathilde, breathless after the energetic squealing that had provided more than her share of the recent alarms. The Lady Alys rested her cool stare upon Eden and did not speak. Neither did she see the understanding look Will Barret gave her before following his commander over the side.

Across on the flagship, Richard Plantagenet rocked with delighted laughter. He had mightily enjoyed his morning's entertainment. He didn't know whether he had laughed most when the vipers were first discovered or when my Lady Hawkhurst ran screeching up the rigging like a bo'sun's monkey. The amazing woman had a penchant for finding herself in out-of-the-way situations. Such was the stuff of which good fireside tales were made and there was nothing Richard loved so much as a story.

And thus, high in spirit and counting himself rich indeed in his army, his navy, his assorted booty and his new-wedded wife, the Lionheart sailed with the sun into Acre.

CHAPTER EIGHT

▼▼

Acre

A shimmering mist lay upon the water, irradiated by the hot, golden disk of the sun. The great ships moved through it like the shapes of dreams into daylight, agonizingly glimpsed through veils of obscuring vapor by the hungry watchers on the shore. And like dreams, they were not at first credited with reality. It seemed impossible that their savior had come to them at last, after so long a delay. And yet the tall ships with their crossed sails and their blood-red hulls appeared more corporeal, more tangible, more numerous with every stretch-eyed second. What had at first seemed the mere scintilla of sunlight upon the volatile air now contained the marvelous possibility of a thousand spearheads glittering in mailed fists; the likelihood of a multitude of shining helmets; the near certainty of sunstruck bucklers, swords and flashing daggers; the sure security of the brightness after the long dark of the soul. The Golden Warrior was with them.

If Richard had been angered by his churlish welcome in Tyre, that slate was wiped clean in Acre. Every man who could be spared from his post, and many who had not been, wrapped a white cloth about his head, Saracen-style, and hurried down to the burning strand beneath the rising heat. They cheered themselves hoarse as they counted the brave ships that swam before their weeping eyes, twenty-five in the van, more following on the horizon. Men from Champagne and Burgundy, from Flanders, from Swabia and Brabant mingled their disparate accents and forgot their nagging disputes as they pummeled the skies with their shouting for the First Knight in Christendom. Upon the crowded decks their roar was caught and echoed and the ships came thundering in to shore like the wrath of God himself.

The triumph redoubled as Richard left the flagship for the broad-beamed barge they had sent for him. Towering under the crimson canopy, he gave himself up to his worshippers. He had left his head bare save for a golden circlet so that all might recognize the red-gold birthmark of the Plantagenet. He wore a scarlet tunic over his hauberk, embroidered in gold and bearing the great white cross upon the breast. With his right arm he held his sword uplifted, dedicating himself to them and to their shared purpose in full view of all. It was Richard's day. Perhaps the best he was ever to know.

On the shore a well-built but slightly stooping figure of middle height awaited him, the one sighted eye glistening with a tear of welcome beneath a shock of disarrayed brown hair. Philippe Auguste had come to meet his friend and enemy. Richard landed. The two Kings embraced. The crowded beach was one long wave of hysteria as each man embraced and kissed his neighbor, just as if the row of gibbets swinging above the plain were not loaded with the results of frequent international murder.

Acre, like Tyre some twenty miles up the coast, was built upon a promontory above a natural harbor. It had been one of King Solomon's famed "Chariot cities," where he had imported the noblest Arabian horses. It had been a center of trade and pilgrimage since the dawn of navigation; it had also been occupied by innumerable armies, of fair and foul intent, since the dawn of warfare. Therefore, great walls extended into the sea on both sides of the harbor, each culminating in a sturdy tower. Between the two walls stretched a great chain that could be raised to keep out unwelcome vessels. There was a double line of fortifications guarding the city, embellished with thirty strong towers. The huge, impregnable keep on the northeast corner of the fortifications was known

as the Accursed Tower. Legend had it that this was
the striking place of Judas's dreadful bargain. The
Crusaders cursed it because they could not destroy
it. Another tower, one that faced the harbor, was
once the scene of fearful rites and bloody sacrifice; on
the latter account it was known realistically as the
Tower of Flies. Neither this nor any one of its twenty-
eight neighbors had yet fallen decisively to the Franks.

Behind the city lay a plain that became a quagmire
when the rains came and a breeding ground for the
much feared swamp fever which decimated the troops
at certain times of the year. Here the majority of the
Crusaders were encamped, perhaps thirty thousand
of them spreading from the base of the low hill of
Turon where Guy of Lusignan had established his
first base. Behind and beyond them, across the plain
and swarming up the hillsides and valleys into the
mountains, were the numberless cohorts of the Infidel.

The new arrivals made a ceremonial entry into the
Christian camp. Richard rode at the head of his army
on a white destrier equipped with fine purple harness.
He was flanked by the Dukes of Bedford and Leices-
ter. Behind him rode his chief commanders, Tristan
de Jarnac among them. Then the martial theme of the
day was minutely relieved by the Queen's small party,
dressed to stun and delight, a flutter of veils and eye-
lashes, and for once, silent, as they acknowledged the
cheers and tears of the Crusaders who lined the route.
There had been nothing to compare with them since
the death of Sybilla of Jerusalem. The delicacy of the
women's flesh and dress and manners took the breath
of those seasoned warriors and knocked them sideways so that they didn't know whether to roar or whisper. Many of them knelt in the sand as they passed
in tribute to forgotten beauty.

Eden, dazed at first with the sun and the welcome,
both beating about her ears like Master Hugh's anvil
chorus, pushed back her veil from a damp forehead
to look more widely about her. She saw that the men
were, for the most part, thin and strained beneath
their fierce tan, that they bore many scars and lacked

many limbs. She realized suddenly that amongst the
men there were a few scattered women, equally worn
and thin, their breasts drooping, some even bright-
eyed with fever. They made no sound or movement
as she passed, only eyed her bright clothing and her
clean, healthy body with a weary hatred. Two were
pregnant. Almost none were pretty though all of them
might once have been. These, then, were the camp-
followers that Richard was so determined to avoid.
From the avid way they gazed upon new arrivals it
seemed unlikely that there was much he could do
about them now. The Englishmen were hale, well-
fed and might even have a little food or money about
them to pay for their pleasure.

It was a long time since anyone had taken much
in the way of pleasure in Acre. The Christians had
just come through the leanest Lenten-time of their
lives. With the price of an egg or a dozen beans at one
whole silver penny, there were no honest men left with
energy to expend on a whore. Indeed the whores fell
to with the common soldiers when they fought with
the dogs for the bones . . . *what* bones none dared
guess. After the bones they ate the dogs. The knights
feasted more fully, but an infinite sadness sat at their
board, for they ate their splendid, uncomplaining
horses and left themselves bereft and insecure. When
there was nothing else left, many ate grasses, sickened
and died. Many simply died. They filled the moats
about the besieged city with their dead, and the sickly
scent hung in the heat together with the increasing
savor of desolation. They did not expect to live. They
did not expect to be saved. And then, in March, a single cornship broke the winter's deep blockade. Within
its limits they were indeed saved. It was regarded
as a miracle.

Up the hills, meanwhile, the colored ranks of Saladin's tents increased daily as Islam's reinforcements
came in; Syrians, Egyptians, Persians, Kurds, Armen-
ians, Seljuk Turks. Merchants arrived and set up in
business; great kitchens were established which could
feed a thousand at a sitting; the hills abounded with

the nomadic flocks and herds that supplied them. Physicians and barbers, musicians and blacksmiths, washerwomen and chroniclers brought the ways of a great city to the gigantic, sprawling encampment. And with them came the women, clean, beautiful, flashing-eyed and raven-haired, fat and fulfilling and filled with laughter. Was it not, after all, springtime?

And now it was summer and things were better for the Crusaders. The supply ships, held up by winter, indolence and a cruel eye for the main chance, had arrived and so had Philippe Auguste. There were fresh horses and the dogs reappeared from God knew where. But the beauty of the women was gone forever, unless they were very young or very lucky.

The military situation had vastly improved, first with the arrival of Henri, Count of Champagne, with ten thousand troops and then of the French King with his army, his senior authority and his respected reputation. Saladin, as he beheld the tide of ships, men, arms and war-engines lapping at the walls of the stubborn, brave city, must have regretted daily his failure to take it from the mere rabble led by Guy de Lusignan, two unspeakable years and perhaps twenty thousand deaths ago.

At present, fighting was reduced to skirmishing and waiting; waiting for the Lionheart so that the walls might be breached at last. Philippe Auguste thought privately, and some stated publicly, that he could do it without Richard . . . but this was not the way that war was waged. It behooved them to await their golden warrior as it behooved him, eventually, to come to them. To the triumphant mass of the common soldiery his arrival was like the second coming of Christ himself, and Philippe knew that as well as Richard himself knew it. A hero was imperative at this hour. Philippe was a good king, but a less than attractive man and on no account a hero. He commanded respect but not adulation. Only half of his men would recognize him if they met head-on. The whole civilized world knew what Richard Coeur de Lion looked like.

Philippe knew he was accused of jealousy but he did not feel it. He was eight years younger than Richard and had already been king for ten years. The experience had taught him wisdom, cunning, disloyalty and patience. He had come Crusading because of the political necessity of keeping the goodwill of the Church and of the landed aristocracy of half Europe, who owed him homage. He would deal with Richard, for whom he had a certain amount of personal affection, and whose boundaries in France he longed to push into the sea, after the Crusade. Meanwhile, let this be Richard's day.

Day became night; a night that resounded, echoing, into the astonished hills; one which, in later days, would echo still in the memory of all who shared it. The castle of Mategriffon had been raised in an impossibly brief time by several hundred willing hands. Alight from head to foot with flares and candles, it acted as a beacon drawing all who saw it to Richard. Along the plain, bonfires were lit among the thousands of tents and their myriad colors stained the darkness, glowing like the windows in a great cathedral. Each man, knight and squire, lit his own torch in honor of the man and the occasion and there was such a coming and going amongst them, such an excited milling and turning that the only way to tell the light-strewn immensity of the plain from that of the star-filled sky was by the constant motion of every tiny luminary.

From their home in the hills, Saladin's armies, having gloomily noted the large numbers of horses and equipment already unloaded from the English ships, were now diverted by a necessarily public entertainment, even though it was not for their benefit. Everywhere the Franks drank King Richard's wine and praised his prowess to the heavens. When their blood became too heated to allow them to sit still and drink, they danced, each cavorting and carousing in the manner of his own town or village. Those who could no longer stand were content to sing, to the accompaniment of drums and tabors, lutes and rebecs, the songs they had learned as children, songs of God and love and wine. Later, as the night wore cold and the last candles burned low, they turned to the songs they sang when they marched together, the great Crusading songs of the troubadors with their strong, relentless rhythm and their noble, Latin words. Few men knew their meaning, though every man felt in his blood the exalted, the martial, the holy intent.

It was past three in the morning when Eden, drowsing in contented half sleep beneath warm furs in the dormitory of Mategriffon, lulled by the harsh sweetness of the night's music, awoke fully to a gently insistent shaking of her outflung arm.

"Eden, please. I am so unhappy!"

It was Berengaria, shivering in her shift, her hair casting wild shadows in the light of her candle. Eden whispered, to avoid waking Mathilde and Alys who shared her bed, "What is it? Here . . . cover yourself. The night is so chill. I wonder they don't cease their celebration out there and seek their beds!"

Berengaria crept miserably beneath the skins beside Eden. "You may well say so. Say it to my Lord the King if you will. I became so weary and so lonely with waiting for him to come to me that I . . ." She hung her head at her own temerity, "I sent to his tent where he carouses with Guy of Jerusalem and the French King, to ask him when he would come to bed. I thought he had forgotten me."

"And he is not yet come?"

"No. But it isn't just that which makes me wretched. It is that he sent Gilles to say that he would not come to my couch this night . . . nor did he know when he might. 'A soldier must snatch his sleep when he can,' he said, and that he didn't wish to incommode me and therefore it is better I sleep alone or with one of my waiting-women, as I please. He will visit me when he can. Oh, what can he mean, Eden? I cannot think that he can love me and treat me so!"

Eden took the weeping Queen in her arms, trying to find words to comfort her. "Don't distress yourself so much. The King loves you, certainly he does. Think of that first night . . . and think, too, of the

next night you will share. Do not trouble about what
lies between. Men are often thus. The King must
deal in warfare and leadership now; he knows best how
he must use his time and his energies. War is a more
demanding mistress, lady, than any mere woman
can be . . . even a queen!"

Berengaria looked at her doubtfully, weighing her
whispered words.

"There is wisdom in what you say, but surely . . .
after that first night . . . surely he must want . . ."

"He will wish to repeat it, yes. Of course he will,
especially if it was as sweet as you have said."

"It was . . . for me; but for him? How can I know? I
only know what he tells me. I do not yet know *him,*
Richard the man." Slowly she tried to piece together
what was disturbing her. "He is always the *same,* Eden,
always fair-spoken, confident, humorous. He is with me
as he is with the world. He says wonderful things, but
in some strange way, they are always less than intimate. He is not *private* with me. I don't feel that he
sees me, feels my presence as I would wish, as I feel
his, so that my breath quickens at his very step. Oh,
it is as Alys once said of the Sieur de Jarnac, do
you remember? That his words were not meant for
her. That is how it is with Richard. His words are
for the world, not for Berengaria."

"You must not think so!" Eden could have wept
for her distress. "These are early days. You will
learn to know each other."

"Yes. I suppose so. I will try to be patient." The
Queen's eyes filled with tears to belie her words and
a deep anxiety choked her speech as she said, "I
love him, Eden. He is everything to me."

After this she blew out her candle and sat staring
into the dark. It was a long time before Eden could
persuade her to take what little sleep the dawn would
leave to her.

Had Richard changed, or was his wife suffering needlessly? Why was it that love so often went hand in
hand with pain? It had never been true for her and
Stephen. But then they had been brought up together

and were, in part perhaps, brother and sister as much as man and wife. It was not the great adventure that Berengaria's marriage had been, but at least that way a woman knew who it was that she married. A longing for Stephen washed over her and she mingled her sighs with Berengaria's in the darkness. Tomorrow . . .

In the morning the Queen appeared as blithe and carefree as she had ever been and Eden, tired-eyed, found it hard to believe that their nighttime conversation had ever taken place. As for herself, she found that she now felt too sick with apprehension to break her fast. Even the luscious Syrian oranges did not tempt her. For now she must set out upon the most momentous part of her quest; today she must find Sir Walter of Langford and put her question to him. God permit that his answer be the one she had traveled so far to hear. She did not think she had strength to bear any other. That Stephen be alive was all she asked, a prisoner if it must be, but alive.

"Must it be today?" asked Berengaria wistfully. She had arranged to spend the day with Joanna. They would do what they could to civilize the somewhat masculine domestic organization of Mategriffon.

"Today." Eden was firm.

"And you will go alone?"

"That is what I want." If there were to be any risk in her search, today or any other day, she would make certain she shared it with no one. Tristan de Jarnac had taught her that. She thought briefly of the stern young commander, a momentary embarrassment taking her as she recalled the unexpected kiss that had ended . . . not quite soon enough, as she saw again his disturbing, indecipherable gaze while she stood trapped ridiculously high up on the galley's mast.

Then she shook him determinedly from her mind where he had no right to be, and prepared herself for her immediate task. Cloaked lightly and veiled against the sun, she took a fond leave of the Queen.

The tents of the Hospitalers, where Walter of Lang-

ford lay wounded, were some distance northward from
Mategriffon, near to the walls of the city. Eden would
have enjoyed walking through the vast bivouac of
conical tents, each with its gaudy banner proclaiming
its owner, but she remembered the glances she had
received from the soldiers, even when she had shared
de Jarnac's saddle, and she sought Balan in the stable-
tents.

As the horse took his first ambling steps Eden
looked about her and realized with a shock the unnerving immensity of the Christian camp. Mategriffon
was drawn up opposite the ramparts of the city on
fairly high ground. Behind it, to east and west, as far as
she could see, the colored tents stretched away across
the plain like the tiny houses of a vast city, over to
the hill of Turon with the great golden tent of Guy
de Lusignan at its summit. She would not have believed that an encampment, an army, could be so
mighty. Surely Saladin, even with all Islam at his
back, could not hope to prevail over it. And that
sore-pressed little garrison within the white, many-
towered walls, what godlike manner of men were they
that they had held out for so long? Saracens or not,
she felt they were brave beyond the ordinary.

As she rode slowly between the red and white
striped tents she became aware of a heavy, revolting
odor which assailed her in waves and made her gasp.
It came from the latrines. Although the morning heat
was still more or less pleasant, with a breeze blowing off
the sea, the soldiers were finding it hard to dig their
trenches deep and fast enough in the baked and arid
soil. There were a great number of flies about; they
clung about Balan's eyes and nostrils and made him
switch his tail in irritation. They buzzed about the
openings of certain tents like a midsummer midden;
there would be wounded men within.

Eden asked the way of a young squire who was
cleaning a destrier's hooves outside his lord's tent. He
directed her northward, skirting the beach and passing
the Accursed Tower, spitting as he named it.

"Don't venture too near, my lady. They'll likely tip a cauldron of pitch on you, or hot oil." It was coffin humor and she knew it.

Down on the beach the English ships were still coming in, and more from Genoa and Pisa. They were expensive, but carrying some of the best fighting men in Europe. Richard could afford it. The business of unloading was in progress with harassed sergeants giving orders in a dozen languages to soldiers, sailors and squires, sweating and grunting as they landed struggling horses, bent under chests of arms and great boxes of wheat and salted meat. The engineers jealously attended to the siege machines and the towers and catapults, mangonels and trebuchets were trundled as gently over the sand and stones as if they were babes taken out to the sun in their cradles.

No one stopped Eden as she rode slowly by, though many called greetings to her, decent for the most part. She drew near the notorious Accursed Tower and reined in toward it. It reared in the angle of the great wall which held the city in its outstretched arms. Its once white walls were streaked with earth and pitch and it was pitted with holes where the mangonels had discharged their rocks. Breached and cracked in several places, it had cost the besiegers dearly in blood and sweat. It was surrounded by siege machines, notably Philippe Auguste's monstrous catapult, Malvoisin, the Bad Neighbor, and the communally owned machine known as "God's Own Slingshot." The complex mechanisms of wood and iron looked to Eden much like the underpinnings of some vast bridge.

It came to her that here the stench of excrement was overpowered by something more stringently noisome. It came from the direction of the walls. Moving forward she saw that the moat had been used as a charnel house for the countless bloated, fly-ridden corpses of men and horses. Swollen and blackened, in some cases their bones were half picked clean by the huge, dark-winged carrion birds that constantly circled overhead. Gagging, horrified, Eden turned away from the mass of corruption. She was not a second too soon in doing so, for even as she kicked Balan into a trot in the direction of the hospital, a hail of slender, black-feathered arrows scattered about the spot she had left. For the first time she became aware of the Saracens within those rusty, crenellated walls as living beings and her enemies. She would not let curiosity take her so close to the walls again.

"My lady, that was a fool's trick! I am sorry I did not catch you up before this."

Gilles, riding hard with four men-at-arms behind him, was clearly in a tearing fury. He had planned to spend the morning close to the King, not chasing after a careless woman, who, however dear to him, was behaving in an unforgivably foolish fashion.

"You don't see anyone else ride up to the god-damned walls, do you?" he demanded angrily, pulling at her bridle as if she were incapable of guiding Balan herself. "That, lady, is because there are dangers . . . as you may have observed."

"That tone does not suit you, Gilles. You are discourteous. Anyway, they missed."

Gilles raised driven eyes to sweet heaven. "That was because they wished to miss. We are not attacking at present. We are waiting. So are they. That was a warning . . . and anyway, you should avoid that foul pit; there are diseases enough in the camp without you adding to the burden."

Eden looked at him thoughtfully. She had detected another mentor than the King behind Gilles's social conscience.

"I need not ask why you are here," she said curtly, "but I tell you now to turn back to Mategriffon and tell the Queen that I do very well without you. My business is my own."

"I have my orders," the boy replied stubbornly.

"I liked you better when you played the court poet!" she flashed at him, angry. "Are you now studying to match the Chevalier de Jarnac in your wet-nursing of me?"

Gilles glared, his patience gone. "Were it not for

Sir Tristan's good offices, you'd be a corpse yourself
by now, and laid to rest at sea for the fishes to feast
upon."

Eden cursed herself for having mentioned Tristan.
Dashing Gilles's hand from her rein, she urged Balan
into a sudden canter.

She rode swiftly away from the sinister vicinity of
the aptly-named tower, trying to quell the nausea
that had turned her belly at the sight she had seen in
the moat. She had consciously tried, since leaving England, to accustom herself to the uglier faces of death,
knowing that she had chosen to walk in their path,
but this was too much for her stomach. Once more
she was struck by the sheer unreason of it; why did
they not bury their dead? Those putrid bodies must
have lain there since the last attack on the walls. It
occurred to her then that all that foulness was, in
truth, much closer to the nostrils of the Infidel garrison than it was to the Christian camp, and that the
enemy, therefore, would be the ones to suffer any ill
effects from it. It was, as Gilles had suggested, a
breeding ground for disease, crawling with flies and
maggots. But to wage war with stinking corpses! It was
beneath contempt. It could not find favor with God.

The red cross upon the white banner of the Order
of the Knights of Saint John of Jerusalem was an
emblem of cleanliness and decency that did something
to raise her failing spirits. She made her way to the
most imposing of their tents, circular and blood-red,
to the fore of the long rows of white, rectangular
ones. An esquire in a long black tunic, girdled in
white, hurried to take Balan's bridle and help her
down. He would be a lay brother still, his vows in-
complete.

Inside the tent, amid furnishings of practical economy, some half dozen knights were occupied with
pen and parchment or long lists upon pieces of slate,
while one of them carefully tied some message to the
leg of a patient, bright-eyed carrier pigeon. All wore
the stark uniform of the order, the long black tunic
with its skeletal white cross on the breast. All eyes

turned inquiringly to Eden when she entered. They were accustomed to female visitors to their hospital beds; a man's whore might visit his bedside for one of two reasons; to keep his favor if he recovered; to be remembered in his will if he did not. Eden was obviously no whore, not unless she belonged to one of the Kings or princes.

"I wish to speak with Sir Walter of Langford," she said as soon as she had introduced herself and her errand. "He is the only man who may be able to help me." They saw her impatience clearly.

The knight who held the alert-eyed dove smiled and signaled her to follow him. Outside, he held up his arms and released the bird into the limitless, unclouded blue.

"Is it not too hot for her?" Eden wondered, uncaring but needing to quiet her clamoring nerves with small talk.

"She'll take no harm. She goes only as far as Tyre, to our Brothers there. We have great need of opium." He guided her between the rows of tents.

"Do you not fear that she may fall into the wrong hands?"

"The enemy? I think not. She's well-trained and trusty. It would go ill with us if she did. The Sultan has declared a personal *jihad* upon Hospitalers, Templars too. He would spike our opium with a different poison."

"Why does he hate you? Because of your valor in battle?" The reputation of the two fighting orders was second only to that of the Lionheart himself. He shook his head. "All of us have valor, when it comes to it. No . . . it is because we hold fast as strongly to our God as he does to Allah, and his prophet."

"Don't all Christians do likewise?" murmured Eden, impressed by the fervor of his look and tone.

"Not quite all," the knight returned drily, with a shade of irony that was strangely familiar to her. She thought of the stripping of Sicily and of Cyprus and held her peace, ashamed. Not unto God only . . . by no means. The Hospitaler stopped, drawing back the tent flap in front of them that had been closed against the heightening sun.

"I must warn you. Sir Walter does very ill. He may not be capable of conversation."

Eden bit into her lip to stop its trembling and followed him into the tent, walking swiftly between the rows of camp beds made of wooden slats and wool-stuffed mattresses. She had no eyes for the wounded or fevered men on either side of them, no care either for their ills or their curiosity. If they groaned she did not notice. Her heart hammered at her ribs. The black knight stopped. A strong reek of herbs assailed them.

The long figure lay as quiet upon the bed as in a grave. The eyes were closed and the cheeks and brow as bloodless as the lips. The head was completely bald, so that altogether it resembled a skull. Sir Walter was breathing, but only just. The knight surgeon who stood at his side lifted the skinny wrist and shook his head. Eden noticed that the hand was completely without fingernails.

"What is his hurt?" she whispered. "Will he . . . ?"

"It was a swordthrust at first. We mended that. But then he took the fever, the Arnaldia. We have done all we can. He'll not recover."

Eden saw in her mind's eye a comely, middle-aged woman in a neat coif, surrounded in her hall by an unruly brood of young men; Sir Walter's wife and his six sturdy sons. She wondered how many of them had taken the Cross with him, how many were dead. Then the truth that she had pushed away broke upon her. Sir Walter could not speak to her.

"Please! I *must* ask him . . . Can you not . . . ?" The surgeon caught the green, despairing gaze. He sighed. She was lovely.

"I cannot wake him. It is not a natural sleep; it is the stupor of the fever. He comes out of this only into senseless fits of broken speech. It is kinder to leave him as he is. Arnaldia gives great suffering."

She nodded, trying to control her fears. She had

heard many sad tales of the hideous fever that was known as Arnaldia, or Leonardie to the French. Recovery was swift . . . or it was not likely to occur.

She turned away from the old man, almost hating him for his uselessness to her. "If there is anything, if he should speak . . . you'll send to me? You will ask him what became of Stephen de la Falaise of Hawkhurst?"

The surgeon nodded, repeating the name. "It's a slender chance, my lady." Then he frowned slightly. "Stephen of Hawkhurst? There was a knight came here before you, inquiring after him. A dark fellow . . ."

"I know him." She cut him off warmly. She might have known de Jarnac would have made it his business to map out her path for her, just in case it should be filled with snakes. She thought of the hail of arrows that had missed her; she wished he could have seen it.

Then another question occurred to her. Perhaps there was still one last chance. "There were three knights who escaped from Sir Walter's last engagement. Can you tell me who were the other two?"

The surgeon hated to disappoint her. "They weren't brought here. You'll have to ask among Sir Walter's confreres."

"And where do I find them?" The surgeon shrugged, the white cross lifting on his breast. "There are perhaps forty thousand men out there, my lady. I regret . . ."

A great weariness overtook Eden suddenly. Had she come so far . . . for this? The younger knight guided her gently away. He saw that she was weeping and sought desperately for words of comfort. "You may yet find them, my lady. Be sure that many will wish to aid you . . . I will make inquiries . . ."

She sighed and let him lead her back to the administration tent. It would be like looking for a single blade of grass upon a mountainside. Sadly she accepted Balan from the lay brother and said her farewells, turning the glossy head back toward Mategriffon. It was as she reentered the neighborhood of the Accursed Tower that she heard the shout behind her.

"Lady Eden! Wait!"

"Gilles!" She was furious, her bitter disappointment turned to hissing anger.

"No, wait! You don't understand . . ." he gestured toward his left-hand side.

It was only then that she noticed the younger rider beside him. He was a dark-complexioned boy with a girlish face; he wore a white turban wound expertly round his head. He could almost have been a Saracen.

"This is John of Cobden. He was . . . is . . . Sir Walter's esquire."

Eden's eyes blazed. She didn't know what to say to him. "Gilles, I . . ."

"I know. Don't think of it. I simply took pleasure in asking a few relevant questions of my own. I don't suppose it occurred to any of those high-born Hospitalers that anything so low as an esquire has ears and a tongue . . . even if they recognized his existence."

Impatient, she had to allow him his triumph. He enjoyed it so.

"Tell her, John," he commanded, lordly.

The boy cleared a nervous throat. He would not look at her directly. "It was almost a year ago, now . . . but I remember it well because . . . Well, they had gone up into the hills. Saladin had sent for reinforcements. We needed to know the numbers. I was left behind. Sir Walter thought me still too young to go with them." The memory of shame was in his voice. "Sir Walter led the reconnoitre; Stephen was his second-in-command." The boy blushed as she stared at him. "I'm sorry. I always called him Stephen. He . . . I . . . he showed friendship to me."

Aye, for the sake of the frightened boy he once was himself, she thought, smiling.

"Anyway . . . they left me at twilight. They were back before midnight. Most of them were unhurt but . . . Stephen had brought up the rear with two others. They left it too late and were seen and taken.

The next day the pigeon came down with the ransom demand . . ."

"Ransom! Then he lives!" Her voice almost failed her.

"Aye, lady. At least . . . he did a year back." The boy looked at her dully.

"But why did I never hear of this? Why has the ransom not been paid? I should have been told. I could have raised it. I *have* raised it!"

John shook his head. "I know nothing of that. I asked Sir Walter about it once. He said it was in the hands of the King's Treasurer."

"The king? What king?"

"Guy of Jerusalem, lady. He was the only king we had, a year ago."

"You have spoken with this treasurer?"

The boy crimsoned. "Not I, my lady. He is a great lord. But I did ask again of Sir Walter." He hesitated.

"Yes?"

His eyes clouded; he bit his lip. "Sir Walter was . . . is not a man of much sentiment, my lady. He said . . . he said it was best I should forget Stephen." He gazed at the gray sand.

Gently, Eden thanked him. He had done what he could. He was only a boy; a child still, a year ago. He had given her back hope, however slender, and for that she was more than grateful.

Later, as she helped Joanna and the determinedly bustling Berengaria with their domestic rearrangements, Eden was taken aback by the arrival of Tristan de Jarnac, unannounced and unsmiling, dressed in the full accoutrement of war.

"Your pardon, ladies!" His bow to the Queen lacked all ceremony. "It has come to my ears that the Lady of Hawkhurst has taken it upon herself to go jaunting for her pleasure about the camp and the walls of Acre." He turned on Eden, his eye cold as slate. "I wonder, my lady, that you are still so stubborn in your blindness to all circumstances save those confined within your own narrow, self-interested vision." Before she could do more than gasp he had swung round upon Berengaria. "And I am surprised that you, Madame, are so unthinking as to allow such junketing. This is a field of war, ladies; you will very soon need no reminder of that stern fact. My Lord King has bidden me, in addition to my other burdens, to keep a watch over this lady. I wish that he had not." Eden lowered her eyes before his hawk's gaze. "However, unless I have your assurance, and yours, my Queen, that she will keep within the safety of these walls unless guarded by my own men-at-arms . . . I regret that she is to be kept under lock and key."

"But I did *not* allow . . ." began Berengaria.

Her soft voice was drowned in the hot torrent of Eden's rage. "You need not make others responsible for my actions. I am no child! As for your trouble . . . *I* did not ask for your shepherding. You know why I am here . . . yes, perhaps indeed I am blind to all save my sworn task. I am proud to be so; this way I may have some small hope of accomplishing it. Leave me to it, why can't you? Must I trumpet my message for you to comprehend it, knight? Hear me then, for the last time! I am none of your concern!" Her voice was high, resonant and very loud. Berengaria, embarrassed, found a sudden interest in one of the tapestries; Joanna, behind them, paused in her chivvying of a reluctant squire in the matter of laundry, and chuckled rudely.

Tristan coldly surveyed the obstinate figure before him. Eden knew she was behaving like an alewife; she gloried in it. She longed for the satisfaction of striking that sculptured, superior countenance as she had once before. It did not aid her cause that, beneath the flood of anger which carried her with it, there flowed a quiet current of common-sense, reminding her that she owed a great deal to this man; that at present he was merely carrying out the King's commands; that he would much have preferred not to; that he had left the proper scene of his command in order to do so . . . and that he did it for her safety, however hard were his words.

The floodtide abated a little; but only a little. "I shall be safe enough in Mategriffon, my lord," she told him icily, meeting his narrowed eye. "And you have my word . . ." she phrased it very carefully, "that I will not knowingly move into danger." A green glint warned him. "However, I do not think I shall require deliverance from any vipers in this castle. Seemingly, I am more like to be tormented by a species of gadfly. Its bite is irritating . . . but it leaves no impression. My skin is very thick, Chevalier, had you not noted it?"

Tristan smiled with something of Gilles's insolence. "I had not," he said with glacial courtesy. "Indeed I would have said your hide was a remarkably soft and delicate one . . ." He raised a single brow in an attitude of pleasant private reminiscence. She hated him!

"It is, however, in rare need of tanning," he finished with grim decisiveness, then strode, stone-faced to the door, where he paused with one hand on the arras to repeat his threat. "Make only one transgression, my lady, and you will find yourself an instant prisoner. I have not the time to shepherd you. You are not worth the lives you may put in danger by your foolishness."

They stood, silenced, and heard the clatter of his spurs upon stone as he left. Eden balled her fists and brought them together with a crack that bruised her knuckles and didn't aid her ravaged temper.

"God's Holy death! How I wish a whirlwind may take that man and set him down without succor at the opposite end of the world!"

Joanna laughed, quite without sympathy. "You should be flattered. The handsome Chevalier is torn by the pangs of courtly love. He bears it well . . . and it would behoove you to do the same."

"Nonsense!" Eden spat, careless of Joanna's rank. "He offers me the thorn, not the rose. Continually pricking at my side! If only God would send him some wound . . . not to kill him; I know we need our knights . . . just enough to keep him, even for a blessed sennight, out of my business."

Berengaria disapproved of such arrant loss of control. "You are not to speak so, Eden. It is unworthy in you. Sir Tristan has the right of it where you are concerned; my lord Richard has decreed it." She added somewhat snappishly, "And it gives me no pleasure to note that he thinks me fool enough to let you roam the camp without an escort. From now on you will do as he has said. I myself will see that you do."

Eden stared at the Queen's set little face, her anger draining like water through sand as she listened to her one true ally speak so.

"Oh . . . don't show me such a woeful face." Berengaria softened. "If there is a way to Stephen, you know we will find it. Only it must be a safe way. I do not want to lose you to a Saracen arrow. *Ma chère* . . . you must not spoil all for the sake of a little more patience."

Eden bowed her head, knowing she was right. Tristan de Jarnac was, she supposed, equally right, but his expression of it had been crude and painful. But though she acquiesced, she did not mean to let them talk her into resting here while Stephen languished in some godforsaken outpost of Islam. If she must dupe her friends, then she must. Meanwhile her head was bowed.

"I'm sorry. I caused you discomfort before the Chevalier," she murmured, kissing Berengaria's warm cheek. "This heat has taken hold of my temper. It won't happen again. And I'll stay quiet at home, I swear . . . if you will only do one thing for me. Send, I beg of you, to King Guy's treasurer, if you can discover his whereabouts; and ask him what news he has of Stephen's ransom." Her eyes implored. The Queen was quick to reassure her.

"Send de Jarnac about the business," drawled the laconic Joanna. "He'll be delighted with the task."

Eden scowled at her. Joanna said sweetly, "You are not gracious, my lady! You deserve a penance. Go and seek out the Comnenus infant in the kitchen. The cook was making her sweetmeats. See if you can teach her a few words of honest French, or English if you must. I'm tired of her heathen prattle. Has she your leave, sister?"

Berengaria shrugged. It would perhaps keep Eden from brooding on de Jarnac's ultimatum. "As you will," she agreed.

Eden curtsied briefly and left to do as she was bid. She knew they meant kindly by her. Everyone did. If only they would be less thorough about it. She found Isaac's little daughter in the kitchen as Joanna had said. The child was amusingly reminiscent of her father, with his soft skin and large, liquid eyes, as well as a certain engaging charm which caused her would-be tutor to smile more often than she meant to do. Her wide, slanting gaze and the fluffy dark hair that surrounded her pretty face were those of an inquiring kitten and accordingly Eden christened her Minou, so that her first word of French was her own new name.

Eden was putting her small charge to bed at the foot of the broad couch she shared in the small solar when Gilles burst in, breathless, his look important. Across his shoulder was a bulging sack which he threw excitedly at her feet.

"My lady! Behold, I give you back that which was lost!" His eyes sparkled.

"What *is* it, Gilles?" Eden stared at the sack, now a mysterious shape on the floor.

"Open it!"

More than curious, Eden fumbled for the opening of the sack. Not finding it, she picked it up by a corner and tipped its contents impatiently on to the floor. "Gilles! How wonderful! How did you come by it?" Her cry was delighted for there, glinting silver-gray in the rushlight, was the hauberk that Berengaria had given her. Around it lay her gambeson, her tunic and her toughened leather boots. All had come back to her, even as her emerald booty had done. She gazed, speechless, at Gilles, who took on his most lordly tone to answer her question.

"It was a matter of chance entirely. I was returning from an errand for the King; I happened upon two young esquires playing backgammon. I was about to cuff them for wasting the morning so while Richard's mail was in need of mending, when I saw the hauberk lying between them. It wasn't likely either of them could have afforded it; they were base-born, both. I had only to look at it clearly to know it for yours. I soon had it out of the young devil who reckoned he owned it. He'd stolen it aboard the galley after the storm died down off Cyprus.

Eden's eyes blazed with pleasure. "You shame me by your kindness, Gilles. I don't know how to thank you enough. I value these above anything I own."

His smile was as radiant as her own. "I am ever yours, my lady." He hesitated. "One more thing, Lady Eden . . ."

"Yes?"

He seemed reluctant to continue. Then the words fell over each other in a sudden rush. "The Chevalier de Jarnac . . . he bids me tell you that the treasurer to the King of Jerusalem has been informed of your inquiries about your husband. He will send to you on the subject as soon as may be."

Her gathering frown turned to blank surprise. She shook her head and could think of nothing to say. "Thank you, Gilles. And . . . please convey my thanks to the Chevalier . . ." Her tone was wondering, lost. She seemed stunned.

He bowed solemnly, but Eden scarcely noted his departure, nor his words of farewell, so bemused was she by Tristan de Jarnac's message. How was she to understand the mind and heart of the man? Only hours since, he had hauled her over hot coals in front of the two Queens and openly accused her of a well-nigh treasonable selfishness and stupidity. And now, with a swiftness that had defeated even her own impatience, he had calmly sent her what she most desired.

Why should he do it? She had condemned and derided him, shown herself lacking in all gratitude and grace; while he, for his part, had not concealed his anger and contempt for her behavior. They now stood as far apart as it was possible for two people to be . . .

and yet he had done this for her. Even as he had saved her life aboard the galley. Even despite the fact that he now found her as much a thorn in his flesh as she had claimed to find him.

A wave of uncertainty flooded over her. She felt suddenly vulnerable. She stared unseeingly across the dark head of the drowsing child. She was miserable. She wished she had not lost her temper that afternoon.

She sighed. What *was* it in the dark knight that drove her to such unacceptable extremes? She sensed that she had never, from the first time of their meeting, been able to be simply *herself* in his company . . . as she could not help but be with any other man, from Gilles to the King himself. What was it about him that rubbed so sorely against her grain? And now, as she wrapped herself close in the warm knowledge he had given her, why was she unreasonably filled with a gentle melancholy, outweighing her joy and causing thin tears to trace her cheeks?

Heavily she rose and took up the restored hauberk, lying with its arms outflung, embracing empty air, and stored it away at the bottom of the chest which held her fine new gowns and mantles. She locked it and replaced its key about her neck, next to the little gold cross which was now all that remained to her, save memories, of Hawkhurst.

That night she prayed fervently that Tristan de Jarnac be spared from all harm and that, truly repenting her cursed temperament, she might find her way back to grace.

▼▼▼▼▼▼▼▼▼▼▼▼▼▼▼▼▼▼▼▼▼▼▼▼▼▼▼▼▼▼▼▼

CHAPTER NINE

Siege

For the next few days, penned up in Mategriffon, Eden waited, her hope taut as a bowstring. The days became a week and still she had heard nothing from Guy of Jerusalem's treasurer. She roamed the wooden castle like a caged yellow tigress, as Joanna was pleased to remark, with the captivated Minou gamboling, cub-like, at her side.

Berengaria also waited, in vain and in increasing distress, for King Richard to come to her. He did not do so, either by day or by night, for he had thrown himself into action with an exhilaration and a determination to crush the exhausted defenders of Acre that infected all who came near him.

At a careful distance from the thousand times Accursed Tower, he and Philippe Auguste walked about in close conference, directing the closing operation of their massive siege engines. To the Lionheart's secret chagrin, the French King had devised a machine that looked as though it might prove the answer to the terrible naphtha-based mixture known as Greek Fire, which the infidel garrison hurled in pots from their battlements. A vast wooden tower, it was covered from head to foot in lustrous copper plates. Since the infidel fire-pots were made of copper, Philippe reasoned that the metal must be resistant to the lethal contents.

As the French wheeled their tower to the walls of Acre under Richard's envious gaze, the bowmen crowding its upper platform began to fire at the Saracens. Pot after fire-pot fell harmlessly against the tower. Richard sulked; the French archers cheered and intensified their fire, paying no heed to the once terrifying liquid that adhered so insistently to their clothes.

Suddenly a huge tree trunk, ablaze from end to end, was catapulted over the wall in a hail of flying sparks. It hit the tower and fell, flaming beside it. It crackled; all were paralyzed. Then an encompassing, hellish white flame leaped up about the base of the tower and in seconds it was a consuming conflagration. Every man in it was burned alive; others covered their ears. Richard turned away; he felt sick. Beside him, Philippe, shivering unaccountably in the melting heat, muttered prayers for the unshriven dead.

When Eden heard of the tragedy, her chief reaction, after the initial horror, was an irrational fear that Tristan de Jarnac might, in some inexplicable way, have been directing the fire beside the archers who had died. Gilles was able to put her mind at rest, if not her conscience. But he brought no word of the ransom. She tried to accept that all men's minds were occupied by duty and prayed studiously for patience.

Berengaria also prayed for a sudden and miraculous end to the siege so that Richard might remember that he had married a wife.

Joanna declared that Mategriffon had degenerated into one vast wooden privy and scolded the infant pages and Cypriot girls, all the servants now left to them bar the cook, into scouring its fouled and smeared boards.

A few days after the failure of his attempt at chemical science, Philippe Auguste took to his bed. His shivering had become a raging fever. He sweated and shook alternately, recognizing the symptoms of the loathed Leonardie and praying to Saint Luke that he might keep his fingernails. He was already losing much of his hair.

He was very ill. From now on every day would be Richard's, for whom the Accursed Tower had taken on the lure of a superstitious charm by which to judge his fate. If the tower fell, he told himself, Acre would fall after it.

In his domed pavilion, amid a forest of yellow banners upon the summit of Mount Keisan, five miles southeast of Turon, the grave ruler himself, el-Melik en-Nasir al Sultan Salah-ed-Din, Yusuf Ibn Ayub, Commander over all the armies of Islam, lay in the grip of the debilitating fever that was the scourge of Frank and Saracen, king and commoner alike. It was an old enemy and a strong one and came like an unwanted houri to sap his strength when it was most needed.

He had heard that now the Lionheart too had succumbed to the epidemic fever, and must keep to his bed. Richard, however, had had himself carried on his campbed to the fighting line amid the frenetic cheering of his troops. Too sick to ride about or even to stand for long, he managed to find the strength to operate a crossbow, with which damnable weapon he was said to be excellently skilled, and was accounting for enough Muslim lives to rend from the fevered Sultan an unaccustomed curse upon his own fragile body.

Allah would prevail . . . but Lord, it must be *now!* The numbers of the enemy had increased in their thousands, but where were the new armies promised to him? From Egypt, from Sinjar, from the Lord of Mosul? Time after time the assault on the walls had been driven back, but the constant pressure was beginning to tell upon the courageous garrison. They needed supplies. The English and French galleys rode in the bay and only the very occasional blockade runner could break through. The gallant defenders of Acre looked to their Sultan for salvation; surely, in the name of Allah, the Compassionate, the All-Merciful, the city had suffered enough.

The waiting had long since become unbearable, as had the sights and sounds of the bombardments and the tension of the intermittent Saracen attacks, before Tristan de Jarnac strode into the hall of Mategriffon and demanded the Lady of Hawkhurst.

He looked weary, his eyes heavy-lidded, lacking lustre. His tunic was spattered with mud and blood, his hauberk laced with rust. He spoke abruptly as if conserving words would also save his strength.

"I came as soon as I could. There was a lull . . ." He saw the long waiting hounding her eyes, saw how it played with her strung nerves. He wasted no time. "Your husband is in the hands of one Emir Ayub Ibn Zaydun." He ignored her gasp. "He holds lands among the hills up behind Tripoli. He inhabits his fortress there. The ransom he asks is ten thousand marks of silver."

"I have it!" Her voice, bell-like, blessed the conquest of Cyprus.

He continued. "My Lord the Treasurer regrets that it has not been possible to pay the sum. There have been many noble knights held to ransom—some thousands in all. Coin, as you know, has been scarce—and needed for other purposes. Your husband was not a known leader, for whom there might have been some barter, nor was he a knight of Jerusalem, though he took service with King Guy until his own lord should arrive. Therefore . . ."

"Therefore Stephen has languished in the Emir's fortress for nearly a year for want of being higher-born! It is well, is it not, that his wife cares more for his welfare than the men for whom he was so willing to lay down his poor life?" He knew that this time her scorn was not for him and his smile acknowledged her small triumph.

Eden realized suddenly that they stood alone in the almost empty hall, facing each other across several feet of scoured floor. She relaxed. Clapping her hands twice, she asked him if he would not be seated. A page appeared and was told to bring wine. They sat down at the long board at the top of the room. Resting her chin on her elbows in front of her, Eden drew what seemed her first easy breath since she had left Hawkhurst. The tension flowed from her in a sudden rush that left her weak and close to weeping.

"I cannot believe it!" She stared at him, her eyes luminous. She looked, he thought, as though she had found the Holy Grail itself. "All these interminable

days . . . I have had to tell myself, and others, that I
believed it. I could not have come so far on a diet of
doubt. But now I see how small, how insignificant was
my belief. It was God's will that I should find Stephen
again, and he gave me just enough faith upon which
to travel. And now, with your blessed help, he has
given me an even greater gift . . . that of an end to
all the undermining doubts. At last I have knowledge. Stephen is alive."

Tristan looked steadily into her transported face.
He could not bring himself to say what others would
doubtless say to her; that a year was a long time to
keep alive a prisoner of no political importance whose
ransom is unpaid. Especially long in the wild, moun-
tainous region behind Tripoli, the sovereign territory
of despotic chieftains who were for the most part
little better than successful brigands.

The girl's happiness had transformed her beauty beyond the merely sensible into something rare which he
could not name but suddenly knew he coveted. A
turmoil of questions and unwanted answers afflicted
him. And yet, "I am glad to see you so," he found
himself saying, the words called forth without his
volition.

Her lips caught the sparkle from her tear-misted
eyes. "You have my thanks . . . with all my soul,"
she said, her voice throbbing. He sat there so quietly,
so still, his hands resting empty upon the table. She
wanted to give him something; he had given her so
much. There was only the wine. She poured it carefully and held out the cup.

He took it from her. His fingers touched hers briefly.
And as the unremarkable cup, filled with wine of no
particular quality, passed across the board between
them, Tristan de Jarnac knew beyond any hope of
return, however longed-for, that an irrevocable change
had taken place in his life. He had not wanted it.
Without looking at her he tossed back his head and
drained the cup.

Eden refilled it, pleased by his thirst. "What must
happen now?" she wondered dreamily, her smile at

rest and content. "Will my Lord King send a troop at once for Stephen? Do you think I may go with them? When will he need the ransom? I have it all ready. Some of it is in gems, but that will . . . ?"

Tristan shook his head, hating to dim such incandescent happiness. "I have not yet spoken to my Lord Richard. He is occupied with an assault he plans with the French King. There is some altercation . . . I doubt if . . ."

Her bright voice preceded him. "How far away is Tripoli? I have not seen a map of this land since we left the galley. Please God, not far! We have had enough and to spare of waiting."

He said gently, "It is a hundred miles and more, Lady Eden."

Her smile faltered and he saw the first signs of alarm in her.

"So far! I had not thought . . . Will the King . . . ?"

Reaching across the table she seized his hands in hers. "Will you take me to the King? I must talk to him myself. I can make him see how urgent . . . Will you take me, Sir Tristan, I beg of you?"

He held to his stillness. It was his only protection against the warmth of those demanding little hands. He looked at her and could not refuse. He knew that the exercise was more than likely to be fruitless, but there was always the least amount of hope. So, "I will," he said and smiled to see her brightness restored and heightened.

He wanted to warn her that she could not count upon the King. He had only lately come from Richard and the royal mien was not pretty. Behind the closed doors of a council chamber sat a different man from the Golden Warrior the public was permitted to adore. And this morning things were not going Richard's way. Yet, if they were to wait, events might have swayed even further from the Lion's grasp and lesser kind would suffer all the more for it, regardless of errand or sex. He made up his mind.

"Come," he said. "I'll take you now. Cover your head. There is no breeze today."

The sun, indeed, struck them like the blast from a baker's oven as they went out into the heavy, shimmering heat. A sweat broke out on Balan almost as soon as they started and Eden found the density even of her Cypriot cotton gown oppressive.

"I don't know how you can bear to go mailed at all times," she sympathized with Tristan who had put up the white hood of his gambeson, so that his dark, bronzed features sprang into vivid relief against it.

"One becomes accustomed," he said, wishing it were true.

Once again, as they rode, she thought how much he resembled a hawk, and yet there was a tenderness about his mouth that showed him to be no such predator. It was only in the brightness of his eyes that the likeness lay, those singular, piercing eyes that were the color of chestnuts or of dark, rich Jerez wine. There was nothing of the falcon, either in the well-shaped nose nor in any of the smooth, finely angled planes of his face. And yet the simile persisted. In the midst of wondering why this should be, Eden found she was admitting to herself that the Lady Alys was right, that Tristan was a very comely man. They had even been correct in calling him beautiful. Not with the fine-drawn, elusive quality of Stephen, of course . . .

And did Stephen still look the same? He must be sun-burned like the rest of them. Nearly two years older . . . and not easy years. He would be changed. She must be prepared for that. But not, please God, changed toward her. She resumed her covert glances at Tristan as he rode slightly ahead of her. She did not want to dwell too much on Stephen. A superstitious fear prevented it. For was it not often the case that when one had set one's whole heart on something it was spirited away just when it was within one's grasp? She trusted in God, who had guided her so far . . . but it was also as well not to tempt fate. She wondered if Tristan knew that the Lady Alys wanted him for a husband. Not that she had said as much, but it

was clear enough to all about her. Poor Alys! She had
seen little enough of her idol these last days. For although many knights supped at Mategriffon when they
could, neither he nor the King nor anyone she knew
had been amongst them. The greater number were
those who had slight wounds to coddle. Indeed, unless
a man were wounded it was Richard's contention that
he had no need of the company of women. And then,
if he were sorely wounded he would get the Hospitalers to mend his hurt; women were only good for
scratches and bruises. Berengaria, who had nourished
visions of binding up her hero's wounds herself, was
particularly sensitive to this opinion.

Their ride was taking them a short way from Mategriffon up the sloping sides of Mount Turon, toward
the spacious pavilion that was Guy de Lusignan's
headquarters. Eden was so intent upon deciding what
she would say to the King that she gave scant attention to the sights and sounds around her. There was
no bombardment at present, though the infidel garrison loosed intermittent showers of their unpleasant *per-
riers,* arrows tipped with splinters of bone, happily
with small effect. Occasionally they heard the dull
crash of stone against stone as someone fired off a
French or English trebuchet.

"It's a quiet ride. I'm surprised," she said nervously,
her misgivings building up within. They had been silent most of the way, and comfortably so, but mounting tension made her seek the sound of his voice.

"I should not have brought you, if it were not," he
reminded her.

A flicker crossed her lips. "Ah, so you still count
yourself my guardian? It is a blessing for me that you
do so. I have done little to deserve so well of you."

They were approaching Guy de Lusignan's headquarters, where the morning's conference was underway.
The gilded banners of the pavilion drooped in the
breathless air.

She had a sudden imperative sense that all must be
well between herself and Tristan. Why this should be

so at this moment of all others, she could not have said. "I am sorry for the trouble I have brought you," she said. "I behaved very ill. I wish I had not."

He raised one winged brow, keeping the amusement from his eyes. She was so very much in earnest. "Today you make amends and are gracious," he accepted cheerfully. "And I, too. I need to make amends to myself—for trusting you not to roam alone about the camp!"

His tone kept its lightness, and saved her pride. She eyed him with suspicion.

"I had Gilles and a stout guard behind me," she told him, outrageously.

"*Well* behind . . . from what he tells me."

She smiled as disarmingly as she could, then shrugged faintly. Disarmed, he returned the smile.

They found Richard in a vintner's tent seated in a low-backed camp chair, one foot up on a barrel before him, refreshing himself after the morning's conference with his fellow kings and commanders. He twirled a cup of red wine between his fingers with every evidence of pleasure in its contents. The conference had by no means gone badly. After a fierce dispute with Conrad de Montferrat and Philippe Auguste over the partition of spoils, especially Cyprus, he had made it clear that if de Montferrat and the French King wanted to launch an attack on the Sultan today, they could do so without English support. That, he thought, should prove conclusively whose army was most needed at Acre.

He beamed as Eden and Tristan de Jarnac entered. "De Jarnac. I missed you, lad. And good morrow to you, Lady Hawkhurst. I trust you have been undisturbed by vipers of late?" He wanted no answer. "Will you join me? This is very potable stuff. It's thirsty work, talking."

The vintner, a middle-aged Jew with a light in his eye signifying the likelihood of selling his barrels to the King of England for twice as much as he had been offered by the King of France, served them smoothly.

Richard waved an airy hand, but Eden would not sit.

Tristan, too, remained standing. Seeing her nervousness, he made a start. "The Lady Eden has a request, my Liege."

Richard grunted. "Say on."

"No! I'll speak for myself . . . thank you, Sir Tristan." She placed herself right in front of the King, addressing a swift silent prayer to Saint Jude as she did so.

"You know my history, I believe, my Liege Lord?"

Richard nodded uncomfortably. Berengaria had said the girl had been raped by that old reprobate, his drinking companion of other days, Hugo de Malfors. Instead of making the best of it . . . for Hugo had wanted to wed the dame . . . she had talked his blessed mother into letting her come gallivanting after her Crusader husband, whoever *he* was. He also remembered an irritating interview with her and his mother in Sicily.

"You promised to aid me when the time came."

He didn't remember that. Had he? Perhaps he had. To please Eleanor it must have been. He cleared his throat unintelligibly.

"I have found my husband." Her voice rang strongly. "He is held for ransom near Tripoli . . . by a mountain Emir. Will you be gracious enough to send a troop of men with his ransom which I will give to you? And my Lord King, may I be permitted to go with them? It is long since I have seen my husband."

The King watched the light changing upon the bright blue enamel of his cup as he twisted it between slack fingers. He said nothing for an endless moment. Eden was still as marble, her whole being given up to expectation.

De Jarnac looked at the King's eyes and saw that they were veiled. He cursed inwardly.

"My Lord Richard . . ."

"Oh, come, de Jarnac! You, above all people, must know it is impossible. I wonder you raised the lady's hopes in this irresponsible way. To send a knight's ransom as far as Tripoli—and up into those godforsaken hills! I'd need thirty men, at least! Even then they'd lief as not get their throats slit, every one. More like than return with your husband . . . if he's still alive. And anyway, I can't spare such a number. It can't be done, my lady. You must wait out the siege with the rest of us. There are upwards of three thousand prisoners to be returned by Saladin when the treaty's made. You'll have your husband then, never fear! It won't be long . . ."

Eden cast an imploring glance at Tristan. Was there nothing they could do? Nothing, he knew; nevertheless, again, he tried.

"Please you my Lord Richard, I myself would be willing to . . ."

"Nonsense! Out of the question! How can I do without you? How can your men do without you?" He hoped the handsome knight wasn't going to start mooning after a woman again. He thought that had all come to an end with that business they'd told him of, at Hattin.

Without comment, for he had his answer, Tristan begged their leave and took Eden out of the vintnery. He knew she was trying hard not to weep. He reached out a hand as she walked unsteadily before him, but he did not touch her. He felt wretched; he had done her no good. He had known her hope was vain, but, seeing her feel it so strongly, he had begun foolishly to feel it himself.

When they were well away from the wine tent, she turned to him at last, her face white with disappointment and with anger.

"So the King of the Franks, also is foresworn. No wonder the Sultan felt such joy at finding one honest man! Sir Tristan, he vowed to his mother the Queen that he would give me his help. He is said to love and respect her. He has treated me as he treats his ally, the King of France, like a simpleton or a child of no account . . . to be fobbed off with the first half-conceived notion that comes into his arrogant head. God's teeth, how I pity Berengaria! To give so much and be given so little . . . by *that!*"

Then her bitterness spilled over incontinently. She

wept before him without pride or consciousness of self.

He took her into his arms as if she had been his sister and rested her head against his shoulder. Gently he stroked her hair. Her veil had fallen about her shoulders. He longed to kiss her again but knew that, now, he must not. So uncontrollably was she trembling that she did not know that he too felt a tremor that threatened to displace his whole being. Now was not the time to tell her this. It was not likely that there ever would be such a time. Unless . . . He chased the half-formed thought from him and resolved to pray that night for the safe return of Stephen de la Falaise. And held Stephen's wife in his arms as if she were his sister and quieted her despairing tears.

After some time had elapsed he was able to speak to her. "It is more than a pity there is such littleness in the King," he said reluctantly, "as well as the greatness in which you cannot, just now, believe."

Violently she shook her head, burrowing into his tunic, denying any greatness. Then she raised her tear-stained face. The faint imprint of his linkmail had penetrated the thin silk of his tunic and patterned her cheek. The sight of it loosed a wave of emotion in him that almost lost him his carefully stabilized control. He had to dispel the moment; he sought and found a rational note.

"What the King has said is true, all of it, though he put it roughly enough, in all conscience. It is also true that all prisoners must be returned to us when we have taken Acre. It cannot be long now . . ." He echoed Richard, but, he hoped, a dozen times more kindly. "The hardest thing, I know, will be to go on waiting. But that is what you must do . . . I will not keep you penned up. You may ride out when there's no bombardment. I'll give back Gilles to you, and any men I can spare from time to time; the King need not know."

He would not give her false hope but he had spoken the truth. He could not, however, prevent her from deducing other, darker truths. Even Saladin could not make a mountain Emir give up his prisoner if all

he got for him were empty thanks. Ayub Ibn Zaydun, he of the fortress behind Tripoli, would be more
likely to kill his useless captive. If, indeed, he had
not done so long ago. And there was the other possibility, never admitted; suppose they were to be beat-
en by the Sultan?

Eden, grasping blindly at self-command, had almost attained it. Her frightened eyes told him that
she understood his thoughts but would not speak of
them. "I will try to wait a little longer," she said. "I do
not know if I can."

"There is no alternative," he said, as gently as he
could.

It was after they had silently ridden back to the
wooden castle that Tristan de Jarnac learned of the outcome of the morning's conference. At once he resolved to speak to Philippe Auguste, to persuade him
against making the assault on Saladin without the
strength of the English army behind him.

The King of France laughed, as convincingly as
his condition permitted, at de Jarnac's council.

"What, defect? And give Richard the chance to
call me a coward?" he said bitterly. Then: "I like you,
de Jarnac. You're an honest man. I used to think
that each man got the leader he deserved; now I'm not
so sure. You're an exception. If ever you feel like
joining me I can pay you even more than three
besants a day."

He watched regretfully as the knight departed, his
back reprovingly straight.

In the event, the assault had to be left to Conrad
de Montferrat while Philippe lay sweating and groaning in his tent. It was not a success; neither did any
man on Richard's generous payroll lift a finger to
prevent the immolation of his allies by fire, steel or
stone. They simply took a holiday, playing gambling
games and shouting to make themselves heard above
the din of the carnage, during which de Montferrat
was cruelly repulsed at first from the city walls and then

faced with Saladin's sweeping attack from the hills. The Sultan's reinforcements had started to arrive just in time. It could not be said that either side was the winner, but Conrad, having succeeded at least in making a wide breach in the wall of the Accursed Tower, was accounted the hero of the day.

In the stifling prison of Mategriffon, the heavens were bombarded as incessantly as the city walls with prayers and promises of good behavior. At the same time Minou wonderingly added to her growing vocabulary words that no lady should have known.

"Even when he isn't fighting, he won't come to me!" cried Berengaria, crushed by the unfairness of it. "I have a mind to go to him myself! Perhaps if I remind him how it was between us . . . on that first night."

But Eden would not allow this. "If he had wanted your company, he would have replied as much to your note. Leave him, Berengaria. You wouldn't recognize him in his present mood anyway." She sighed fretfully. "It seems as if the whole world must hold its breath until the end of this accursed siege. Whoever would have thought that just *waiting* would make one so unutterably weary?"

Berengaria was dissuaded. She had been shocked and distressed on her friend's behalf when Tristan had brought her back, pale and stunned, from her interview with Richard. Once more she asked herself who it was that she had married. And yet, when she searched her memory, she could not remember that he had made any promises of a specific nature . . . though he had certainly seemed to be doing so beneath the gaze of the strong-willed Eleanor.

Eden looked at Berengaria's quiet, sweet features, now settling into a permanent sadness, their color all but extinguished, and thought that although she pitied her, at least Berengaria had a clear objective in her life—to make Richard love her; even as Alys wished to make Tristan de Jarnac love her. Eden wondered if she would succeed. She was beautiful, well-born and rich; there was every reason why she should. And yet, for no reason that she could quite pin down, Eden found herself hoping that she would not succeed. Truly, Alys was too cold, too humorless, too much the *grande chatelaine*, to bring happiness to such an unpredictable creature as Tristan de Jarnac. He needed resilience, laughter, and a strength to match his own . . . aye, and a tongue, too.

She, too, of course, had her objective. She was coming closer to it; sometimes she felt that the passage of the days had turned around and she was further from Stephen than she had ever been. One more week of frayed feminine tempers and frantic pacing of wooden floors and she would be too far advanced into madness to be capable of attaining it. And all the time, beneath the petty, heightened level of her daily existence, was the consciousness of the bright hauberk lying at the bottom of the chest in the solar, unused and waiting, even as she was.

In early July Richard planned a little personal reprisal against Philippe Auguste and Conrad de Montferrat. While almost the entire encampment was at its unappreciated dinner of fish and meal, he took a company of English sappers, archers and Pisan pikemen and made a flamboyant assault on the walls about the Accursed Tower. The bowmen, their clothes soaked in vinegar, now reinstated as the only deterrent to Greek Fire, kept the Saracens off the walls with their measured fire, while the miners tunneled their unenviable way beneath the foundations, underpinning them with timber props as they went. They filled their tunnel with brushwood, set it alight and beat a hasty retreat. The props were burned through; the battered masonry above collapsed; the pikemen, covered by the archers, raced through the smoking gap.

They were welcomed by a strong force of defenders whose desperation they could not begin to realize. Karakush himself, the Commander of Acre, formerly

Saladin's chief engineer and city architect, was the first to hurl himself and his flailing scimitar into the breach. But he knew now that they could not prevail. The siege had been too long. The appallingly gallant defenders were exhausted and literally decimated. They had been thirty thousand once; they were now three thousand.

Savagely, with the last of their strength, his garrison drove the Franks back across their lines. On the other side of the plain, the ramieh, Saladin's mounted archers, swooped down to harry the entrenchments, riding easily in their light mail, drawing all fire after their galloping, wheeling figures while the defenders seized the chance to shore up their wounded walls.

There followed at this point a diplomatic dance in several measures. Richard of England, seizing the initiative before Philippe Auguste had turned twice on his bed of pain, sent an ambassador to Saladin's camp with orders to arrange a meeting between himself and the Sultan. The Sultan, curious though he was to meet the feared and respected Lionheart, refused with his customary grace, on the grounds that as long as Richard was still attacking Acre, there could be no basis for talks. If the attacks were to cease, Saladin would be delighted to meet the English King.

Soon after this, the Sultan had word from the despairing Karakush. Acre could hold out no longer. At once, Saladin ordered an overwhelming assault on the Christian camp. The Crusading armies, working together as if they had never exchanged a single hard word, held the Saracen hordes efficiently at bay while the industrious sappers disposed of another section of the crumbling city wall. Karakush, a realist, proposed a truce. He asked for terms and demanded that the two Christian Kings should honor the valor of the garrison by allowing the defenders to march out unmolested, as had been Saladin's humane habit in similar circumstances.

Richard the Lionheart and Conrad de Montferrat for once concurred in demanding unconditional surrender. The order was sent to Karakush. Who spat upon it, cursed long and carefully and ordered his superhuman garrison in holy rage to fight on until they fell. It took another five painful days to accomplish their fall.

▼▼

CHAPTER TEN

Victory

On the morning of 12th July it was as though the world had suddenly come to an end. Its ending was not in cataclysm, in flood or in fire, but in a devastating silence which was more terrifying than any of these.

There were no longer any sounds of bombardment. The cracking collision of stone against stone, the whine of the crossbow quarrels, the hiss of arrows, the ragged clamor of steel and bone and men's curses . . . all were gone. Only the suspended silence strained the ear and struck fear to the soul with its terrible emptiness.

It had once seemed that the noise of battle had augmented the daily onslaught of the onerous heat. Now it seemed otherwise; in the absence of sound the objects of other senses were experienced with an almost surreal sensitivity.

In the yellow, windless air the heat came down like a brass fist and beat about the heads of victors and vanquished as the gaunt, hollow-eyed defenders of Acre marched out through the gates and into the hands of their enemy. The orders were that none should molest them and the Christian soldiers stood silently, their heads bowed, as the proud scarecrows passed, the streaming rags of their clothing a dissonant echo of the gonfalons of Christendom now hanging, motionless, along the ruined battlements.

"They're brave men. 'Tis a pity they're damned to hell—after going through it once already," observed a sympathetic archer behind the canopied dais where the English royal party stood.

Eden stared at the peaceful scene of utter destruction around them. The stained and battered city walls, where they were not mere mountains of rubble and human remains, were seamed with cracks where the battering rams had smashed against them; empty siege towers leered drunkenly over the ramparts, their lowered drawbridges testifying their successful use; scaling ladders leaned where they were left. At a distance the great war engines stood as awkward and unnecessary as the leftover leviathans of an old, discredited tale. A thick, gray pall hung over the city, part smoke, part dust. It seemed like the visible spirit of grief.

"This then," offered Eden softly to anyone who might hear her, "is victory." She did not know why, but she hated herself.

"Oh no!" drawled Joanna with the stunning practicality of her family. "Victory is expressed later, in the terms we make them accept. This unpleasant spectacle is for the troops. It teaches them what to expect if *they* should be so remiss as to allow themselves to be defeated."

Berengaria, who was weeping as the emaciated women and starved, pot-bellied children dragged themselves by on the heels of the garrison, turned on her in sudden spitting fury. "You are hateful, Joanna. You have no heart!"

Joanna sighed, impatient, "Your trouble, *ma chère belle soeur,* is that you have too much. Since, with God's aid, you will assuredly look upon such sights again, I advise you to learn to do so with some attempt at detachment."

"I don't want to be detached," muttered Berengaria furiously. "They are human as we are, even if they are unbelievers. I pity them . . . as I pity all who suffer."

"Blood of the Virgin! I can't bear so much emotion together with so much heat. If you'll forgive me, I'll beg my leave of you ladies." So saying, the ex-Queen put up her small square sunshade and left them to stroll with her own ladies among the tents.

"A good riddance!" Berengaria glared after. "You

know, Eden, I don't think I like Joanna. You'd think
she would be softer, having known so much unhappiness on her own account."

"She has a sharp manner, certainly, but I think it
might conceal a kinder heart than you think. Think
of her mother. She was rarely gentle, but none of us
doubted her goodness."

"I shall never understand these Plantagenets," complained the Queen. "Why can't they say what they
mean and be what they seem, like my own family and
the friends of my heart?"

Eden knew she was thinking of Richard, riding in
triumph at the head of his troops. "Come on, my
lady," she said swiftly, in an attempt to banish the
sadness of the morning. "We'll go through the gates
and ride about the city. We have our freedom, now.
Just think! No more armed escorts as though we
were prisoners like those poor pagan souls." She
nodded after the departing column, each of whom
would now, according to rank on both sides, be appor-
tioned to a captor among the Christian armies.

There was a general movement in the direction of
the open city gates, and now that their spirits were no
longer weighted by the forced observation of other
men's misery the Crusaders began to relish their victory. They marched into Saint Jean d'Acre with drums
and trumpets, the magnificent Marquess of Montferrat narrowly beating the equally magnificent King of
England and riding triumphantly, first through the
gates. Everywhere, upon the walls and towers, in
crenels and castellations, over portals and from embrasures, the banners of Christendom flowered; fleurs-
de-lys, lions and leopards, ermines and eagles, bars and
siltires and above all, the crosses, white for England,
scarlet for France and emerald for Flanders. A light
wind rose and set them waving and cheers of gladness
rang across the town. The sadness was gone and suddenly it was a holiday.

With only a token force of four men-at-arms, the
Queen and Eden plunged into the open city. The
soldiers found it hard to prevent them from being

jostled by the cheerful, curious crowd. Their curses mingled with the occasional "Noel" when someone recognized Berengaria.

"How can they know me?" she pondered. "They can only have seen me at a distance, upon the quay. They must be cheering simply the stuff of my gown . . . or the beauty of my attendant."

"Could it be because our escorts cry 'Make way for the Queen!'?" suggested Eden drily.

"Is that what it is? Their speech is so outlandish, I can't comprehend a word of it."

"It is English, my lady," explained Eden, faintly reproving. "They are of Saxon parentage, from Norfolk, not far north of my own domain."

Berengaria laid a penitent hand on her arm. "Forgive me. I dare swear you'd find the native speech of Navarre every bit as strange to your ear."

At that moment her horse shied and an expression of alarm filled her eyes. *"Ma foi!* Here are more of those terrible beasts! Cannot we go another way?"

A train of loaded camels had entered the city. The end of the siege promised untold gold for merchants both Frankish and Moslem and they were already descending on the crowded harbor from all directions.

"Isn't that the emblem of the Marquess of Montferrat?" murmured Eden as she stared at the oddly-shaped beasts with their delicate step and their contumelious, pontifical faces. They were led by a swarthy Italian who salaamed like any Turk when he caught their eyes upon him.

"What have you there, Signore?" demanded Eden, pointing at the heavy loads beneath the fine Persian saddle-cloths worked with the fleur-de-lys of the marquessate.

"Spices, madonna, of a hundred different kinds, for the quays of Genoa and Pisa. Also dye-stuffs, brocades, baldechino, taffeta . . ."

Berengaria silenced him with a wave of her hand and he bowed again and continued on his way, encouraging his heathen train in what sounded much like its own guttural animal tongue.

"He wastes no time, our proud Marquess," noted Berengaria. "But why does he choose Acre as his port rather than his own city of Tyre?"

Eden shrugged. "Perhaps he already thinks of Acre, too, as his own," she suggested. "It pays homage to Jerusalem and he clearly expects to take the crown from Guy."

"Not if Richard can help it," said Berengaria tartly.

Eden grinned. "Conrad was first through the gate. Let's hope that wasn't a sign for the future."

The Queen kicked sharply at her horse and they moved further into the city. Toward the center the damage seemed less and already, indeed, several houses were being restored to their former dignity by troops of soldiers turned masons. Others were hard at work on the walls and their thirty tall towers. The houses were mostly two or three stories high and gave a blessed, cooling shade to the riders. There was no sign of their inhabitants and it was impossible to say how many still cowered behind their locked and barred doors.

Berengaria followed a fancy to see the harbor. It was easy enough to find on account of the foul stench that left it with every landward breeze, and they could stand for only a few minutes upon the choked and filthy shore in front of the Tower of Flies, now fully worthy of its name. The beach was the only outlet for the drainage and garbage of the city, as well as for the hideous effluent of the slaughter-houses, the tanneries and skinners that stood close by. After the siege, the sights and smells were enough to turn the hardened stomach of a charnel-house dog. Determinedly they averted their gaze to the painted ships that filled the bay, the merchant flags of Saint Mark, Saint Lawrence and Saint Peter now mingling with the lilies and the crosses; Conrad's Italian fleet awaited its cargo. Kerchief to nose, the Queen turned away, not before time, Eden thought.

"Faugh! This isn't to be borne! Come, we'll visit the marketplace in the Italian quarter; they say it's exactly like Venice."

With a white smile and a pointing finger, one of the Marquess's pikemen directed them to the section of the town inhabited by his compatriots. *"Il Fondaco? Par-la! Belle, belle signora!"*

The crowd thinned considerably here. Most of the Christian troops were making for the newly opened hostelries, where, for want of much in the way of wine, the innkeepers, Muslim or Frank, allowed the scrawny harlots of the city and the camps to set about getting fat again. Several of the more adventurous soldiers went to the public baths. Someone had started the unlikely rumor that cleanliness helped to ward off disease. The houses became taller, more ornate, closing in around them as they leaned toward each other across the sandy street.

They could hear the sound of shouting just around the next corner. Not wishing to return via the stinking port, Berengaria urged their escort to investigate following close behind them with Eden. The shouting redoubled. With an impatient click of her tongue, the Queen rounded the corner.

A young Syrian girl, not more than thirteen or fourteen years old, lay spread-eagled on the ground before an open, splintered door, while a grinning soldier knelt at each of her hands and feet. Between her brown thighs, his hose about his knees, their sergeant was going about his vile work. The girl could not move, was far past screaming. Only her eyes stared crazily at the uncaring sky, their terrified, tearless rolling more significant than any howl of pain. A small, pathetic pool of blood soaked her white djellaba beneath the sergeant's heaving buttocks. Behind her, held by three more soldiers, her elderly father stood against the wall of his house, weeping and powerless to help her. He wore the black cap of the Jewish merchant and he was bleeding steadily from a broad gash in his side.

"Mother of God, won't you stop them?"

The Queen's small guard stood shamefaced and uncertain. They were four against seven; and anyway, the men who were raping the girl were English soldiers like themselves. Had they not had the ill luck to be detailed to dog the Queen, they might well have been in their places. They stood grinning awkwardly, their movements random and ineffectual.

The horrified Eden, meanwhile, had slipped from her horse and lifted her whip almost before she knew what she did, slashing it down vehemently across the sergeant's still working back. The whole world turned scarlet before her gaze and she did not know how she cried out as she put all her strength, all her balked and pent-up energy, all her bitter loathing of Hugo de Malfors and his kind behind each wickedly incisive stroke.

Confusion broke loose in the narrow street. The stricken sergeant, swearing fouly, staggered away from the bleeding girl, shielding his head from the furious onslaught of blows. His accomplices let go the girl's arms and legs and while two of them leaped, murder-eyed, toward Eden, the rest laid swords and pikes about their unwilling antagonists of the Queen's guard. Berengaria, driven by panic, sent her horse instinctively toward Eden, so that only one man was left holding her, surprised, as his companion went skidding to perdition down the street with a black-rimmed hole in the side of his head where the frightened mare had kicked him. The old man, left to himself, slid slowly down against the wall of his house. His daughter lay quite still, legs wide, her skirts still bunched around her belly.

Eden, her whip gone, was fighting for her life with the man who held his broad-bladed dagger poised above her breast. Her head rang with the clamor of steel behind her. A hopeless voice cried out, "You b'lady fools! It's the Queen!" half strangled by the necessity to dedicate all drawn breath to survival. None heeded it. The combat was close and to the death, punctuated only by grunts and curses and cries of pain. Berengaria's mare, flailing hopelessly amid the melee, lost the last of her few wits and went plunging back the way she had come, the Queen screaming Eden's name in terror as she clung to the flapping reins.

As Eden pushed at the blade that threatened her throat she felt her angry strength failing. Then suddenly the pressure was released as her tormentor chuckled, holding both her wrists, and cried out to his remaining companions, "Here, lads! We've lost one . . . so what of it? We've got another! Better fare too, and you can't say she hasn't asked for it!"

Hearing this, the Queen's guard arrested their efforts. If the girl was for it anyway, why throw a good life after hers? Avoiding her terrified eyes, they slowly allowed themselves to be overpowered, crying "Peace, friend! We won't quarrel over her; she's yours!" She would not live to reveal their cowardice. One already pressed his hand to a spurting wound across his sword-arm; another would ever walk limping. "Sorry, lady," a third said, ashamed despite his companions' good sense, as he obyed the order to face the wall, hands high against it.

"Keep quiet, and we just might let you live," the raw-backed sergeant told them, moving greedily toward Eden, now held fast between two of his men. They stretched out her arms while he reached to rip her gown open from throat to groin. It fell about her exposed body in limp folds.

"Sweet Saint Ursula!" one blasphemed, whistling. "Isn't she a plum?"

"Aye . . . and she'll be plum-colored before I've finished with her, the bitch! Inside and out." The sergeant loosed his points once more.

He came closer. The reek of sweat was strong on him and the sour odor of expended lust. He grasped one of her breasts and squeezed it cruelly, suggestively fingering the dagger at his belt. "I think I'll leave it there . . . for now, eh, confreres? I like a nice pillow to rest my head on." She did not speak, neither did she pray. It would have been quite pointless.

Conrad, Marquess of Montferrat, had passed a pleasant hour upon the quayside, his nose well-protected by a silk muffler. His Genoese fleet had unloaded and were reloading even now. With a little effort and organization, a few thousand dinar in the right hands, it was amazing what could be done in the way of trade, especially during a blockade. Riding with his plumed and perfumed entourage through the deplorably filthy streets, he was just considering whether or not to go hawking among the hills with his pair of trained cheetahs; he might meet with hindrance from Saladin's troops if he encountered them. It would never do to jeopardize the truce. Like everyone else, he had had enough of this phase of the war.

He had almost determined to challenge his noble prisoner, Emir Tarapesh, to a game of chess instead, when he came upon a most extraordinary scene. In a narrow street, just off the main thoroughfare, a half-naked native girl lay shamelessly in the roadway, while four excited English infantrymen were in the process, obviously much-relished, of laying down another one beside her. This one, who was struggling desperately, was white, astonishingly beautiful and more than half naked. Three more soldiers stood clutching the walls of a looted house, while another lay bleeding from an arterial wound. The Marquess took in the scene in the split second before he had cried "Hold!" in the iron voice which had so often struck terror to the bowels of 30,000 men like these. Then he spurred forward his destrier and kicked their lusty sergeant upon his naked backside.

"You! Get your arse back in your horse and explain yourself! Cover yourself, madam!"

His eyes raked her while she did so. Eden, still not quite crediting escape, was almost as terrified as her molestors as she recognized her rescuer and realized that she was looking closely for the first time at the Tyrant of Tyre. Stern-lipped and frost-eyed, his pride clothed him as palpably as the rich cloak, the new-fashioned German breastplate damascened in gold, the rubies chained around his neck, the gauntlets sewn with pearls. In sculpturesque hauteur upon his perfectly still horse, he surveyed the white-cross soldiers with a devastating coldness.

"Well?" he rasped.

The sergeant was goaded by his striped and smarting back and his throbbing coccyx. "You see for yourself, m'lord Marquess! She's English!" It was known that the terrible Marquess had no liking for the English. What could one whore more or less matter to such as him?

"And so, I can see, are you." His voice was very quiet.

He did not move his hand, but his armed knights dismounted. The sergeant was cut down where he stood, a Florentine blade deep in his chest. His companions, one by one, followed him into death as they had so mistakenly followed him in life; the blood and the sand became indistinguishable, uniformly dark; Eden shook.

"Move those corpses. No, stop. The girl is yet living."

Before the knights could touch her Eden dropped swiftly to her knees beside the barely breathing child. She straightened her torn and bloody skirts, cradled the lolling head on her lap, stroked the damp hair.

"She'll not want to see a man, my lord . . ."

De Montferrat nodded, approving her practicality. She had not thought for herself; there was no sign of the usual hysteria; most women would have thought it their due. He leaned forward.

"Tell me your name, lady?"

As she did so he looked at her thoughtfully. A beautiful face. Fearless. A beautiful woman, by God, though not one to his personal preference. He liked them little and dark and indolent like his Isabella. But he liked this girl because she did not weep and because she wore her dignity with her rags as though she were at the head of her own board.

He gave swift orders and Eden found herself covered in his dark velvet cloak, while the Syrian girl, who had not stirred, was laid upon a makeshift stretcher of swords and tunics; they would bear her to the hospital. There were certain women among the brethren; they would look after her. Balan, excellent animal, stood nervously a little way down the street. He had not left her. Gratefully, the Marquess's cloak fastened tightly about her, she watched as a soldier gentled the animal back to her.

"I will take you back to your lodging," Conrad offered. "I have business in the English camp. I may as well conduct it today as tomorrow."

The business was with Richard Trichard, the maker of treaties and breaker of oaths. He would have preferred tomorrow; he did not like the English King. It would give him little pleasure to reveal how his infantry behaved to his wife's waiting-woman. The English were barbarians; everyone knew that. Because he wished to take her mind off her recent experience and because he had an undying curiosity about everything around him, the Marquess asked a good many questions as they rode. He had learned a substantial amount by the time the Queen of England's rescue party nearly ran them down.

As for Eden, she had learned that Conrad de Montferrat was an enthusiastic champion of the native population of Acre, that he valued them as highly as any Frank, and looked forward, one day, to ruling over a united city, dedicated to healthy trade. He did not, therefore, hold any brief for Richard's crude and selfish terms of treaty which would make a present of the city, and every ship in its harbor, to the Christians alone. He also demanded a ludicrous ransom of 200,000 gold dinars for the lives of the captive garrison.

Eden was less surprised than she would once have been at the rapacity of England's lionhearted leader, and she was only very faintly surprised to find that she had an increasing respect and liking for the single-minded Marquess, not merely as her rescuer from ravishment, but as a man who might, if any could, pull together the disparate strands of the fortunes of the unhappy Kingdom of Jerusalem.

Richard was moving his household into the Royal Palace of Acre. He was in a very bad temper and the sight of Conrad of Montferrat, flaunting the Lady of

Hawkhurst upon his sleeve like a favor at a tournament, did nothing to improve it. He stood, growling, in the exotically blooming courtyard at the heart of the airy, graceful building, his face red as the hibiscus, waving his sword about as though he were still on the battlefield. Soldiers with set faces stolidly moved where he pointed it, as they emptied the contents both of Mategriffon and the royal pavilion into the cool and stately rooms.

Berengaria sat on a camp chair beside the circular fishpond with its playing fountain at the center of the yard, working serenely on the handkerchief she was embroidering for her husband. Her concentration was rather too taut to bear inspection and she looked up with a glad cry of relief when Eden and the Marquess appeared beneath the colonnade of pointed archways that surrounded the garden. When Eden had kissed her she swiftly presented her companion and briefly recounted the details of her rescue.

Rising tremulously, Berengaria took both of Conrad's hands in her own. "I owe you much thanks, Marquess; it is to my shame that my own men would have arrived too late to save her."

Kissing, in turn, the small hands that gripped so warmly, Conrad had the impression that this was a lady of great sweetness; too fine-drawn by far for the Lionheart. His smile, as he assured her that he had done no more than any true knight in his place, was one of genuine appreciation.

From across the court came an interrogative bellow; Richard, sword in hand, was tramping toward his visitor.

"You may put up your sword, sir. I am no Saracen," said Conrad with amusement.

To make Richard aware of his bad manners was no way to ameliorate them. Leaning on the sword, he favored the Marquess with a contemptuous glare. "What brings you outside your Fondaco? I had thought you fully occupied with haggling over merchandise. I heard you had set up your stall in the suk."

Conrad ignored the insult. "I am in no such hurry as are you to set up house in other men's property. It would seem, however, that this is a common trait among your followers."

"What the devil do you mean?"

Berengaria wished Richard would not shout so; it did nothing for his dignity. Conrad had ceased to look amused. "I mean, Sire, that your troops . . . barons and knights as well as common soldiers . . . are helping themselves to the property of the Frankish population of Acre, not content with their rightful Saracen booty. They are forcibly entering private houses, offices of the port, palaces . . . What use to send the Saracens packing if the merchants and churchmen, the ship-owners and commercials come back to find their hab-itations overflowing with brawling English Crusaders, looting and defiling where they will?"

Richard scratched his beard and shrugged.

"King Philippe has set a strong penalty on such be-havior," Conrad continued. "He asks you to do the same. We came to save the city, not to strip it. Your men are scavengers who will even prey upon their own kind . . . witness what occurred with your wife and the Lady Eden!"

"If the damn silly women go looking for trouble, they must expect to find it," he grumbled, glowering at the peaceful figure of his Queen.

"Put it this way," said de Montferrat with dry im-patience, "my Lord Philippe Auguste bids me say to you that, unless you moderate the conduct of your army, you will have little help from him when you move toward Jerusalem! He requires your assurance that this looting be stopped. And so do I."

"You!" Richard's sword clashed to the ground as he stepped forward angrily. "You go too far with your meddling, Marquess! You may have brought your up-start banner first through its gates, but nevertheless this city is none of your concern. It does not lie in your hands but in those of Guy of Jerusalem . . . and so it will remain!"

The hatred between the two stalked openly about the quiet court. The Queen's hands fell still and Eden held her breath.

Conrad held Richard's angry blue stare without expression. Softly he delivered his last words to his enemy. "I have heard that you are a betting man, my lord; if I were you, I would cast no dies against my wearing the crown of Jerusalem . . . for wear it I will . . . despite all the Kings in Christendom!"

He turned to bow briefly to the Queen and to Eden. *"Mesdames* . . . if I may ever do a service for either of you, count it already done!"

He exchanged no farewell with Richard but left at once. Beneath the colonnade he passed Tristan de Jarnac, grim-faced and purposeful. The two saluted each other with mutual respect.

"Damned interfering, Italian viper!" muttered Richard to the approaching knight.

"He hangs on Philippe's coat like a tail on a dog. Much good may it do him; he'll not have Jerusalem! I take my oath on that!"

Tristan ignored the outburst. "My Lord, you are needed in the city. I have just hanged a dozen pike and bowmen for looting the Patriarch's palace. It is imperative you give the order to stop this pillage. While you do not, it will continue. The men see themselves as stealing thunder from the French, who may touch only proven Muslim property."

"By the bleeding heart of Christ!" The Angevin sickness had Richard by the throat. "Did you pick up the Italian's banner as he dragged it in the dust? Am I now to be hounded by my own commanders? It's too much, by God! I will give no such order! Leave them to it, de Jarnac . . . let them take what they find. And as for rape, saving your presence, ladies . . . there'll be enough willing whores queuing up to satisfy them; I doubt there'll be many virgins pierced by their swords."

Eden hated him, thinking of that small, still body in its pool of blood.

"This will do no kindness to your reputation here,

my Lord." Tristan was abrupt. One day the King's sickness would be his downfall.

Richard's eye was malign. De Jarnac was becoming altogether too independent. "Pick up my sword," he commanded.

Tristan saw where it had fallen in the dust. He made no move. Eden knew, with a flash of instinct, that he would not. In an instant she had left her seat and lighted upon the sword; then it was in Richard's hands and she was giving him a smile of interested innocence. "Oh, my Liege, how heavy it is! I didn't believe it when I was told of its mighty weight." She shuddered daintily. "To think of dying beneath such a stroke!"

Richard only growled, balancing the broad blade in his hands. He stared suspiciously at the girl. But no, she was just a woman, with a woman's foolishness. De Jarnac could wait; Richard never forgot an injury he meant to perform. He sheathed the weapon and cried out for his breastplate and horse. He was going sick-visiting. He would see if he could knock some sense into the addled bald pate of that one-eyed vulture, Philippe.

Tristan watched his departure, his eyes narrowed to arrow-slits. "What offense has put him in such a rare temper?" he demanded. When Richard was angry he was apt to make unreasonable demands; this could be dangerous at a time when a treaty was in commission.

"It was Leopold of Austria," Berengaria offered with a sigh. "The Duke of Austria planted his banners upon the ramparts, next to Richard's and King Philippe's, thus claiming to be equal in the victory. Richard was furious because, although Leopold is the German leader, he has few troops to command, and being unequal in resource, has no rights to equal victory. Some of Richard's men tore the banner down and the Duke is leaving Acre in protest."

Eden thought this typical of Richard's quick pride. She was enlightened when Tristan added, "An equal share in the victory means an equal share in the plunder. Neither my Lord Richard nor King Philippe was likely to agree to that." He ran a violent hand through his hair. "But why, by all that's holy, cannot the King settle such differences around the council table? Why does he have to make yet another enemy?"

"Leopold of Austria holds little power outside his own lands," suggested Berengaria peaceably. "He can do no harm to Richard here." Her voice changed, taking on determination. "Tell me, Sir Tristan . . . in the matter of the looting . . ."

"Your Grace?" It was a matter he must find a method of mending, and that quickly, pleasant though it was to watch the sunlight upon Eden's golden hair.

Berengaria still hesitated. Then: "Could I not give you the order to stop it?" she asked. "I would not have Christian blood upon our hands."

Tristan was conscious of a growing respect for the tense little figure. He answered her gently, "If I were to disobey, I should be strung up alongside the men I hanged . . . but there is, perhaps, something I can do . . . I am charged with the overseeing of the rebuilding; I can therefore commandeer as many men as I consider necessary for my purpose. I will give orders that all found looting are to be pressed into my service."

"Excellent, Sir Tristan. Richard himself would thank me, were he at rights with himself today, for being his better nature." Berengaria saw only the sickness, Eden thought. She had not, perhaps did not wish to see, the malice in her husband. But which of us see the faults clear in those we love?

It suddenly occurred to her that she herself had what Tristan might well regard as a fault to confess; she did not want to delay him but she would enjoy her freedom better if he knew of the morning's business.

When she had told him, she saw, as she had feared, the blaze of anger in his eyes. But it was not for her. "You should have taken a larger escort," he said abstractedly. Then savagely, "We owe much to the Marquess of Montferrat. It seems he is the only man who will trouble to control the conducting of this licentious liberation. I am sorry, your Grace," he added to Berengaria, who was biting her lip. "As you say . . . my Lord Richard is not himself."

He allowed his lips to linger fractionally on the smooth, gold-tinted skin of Eden's hand before he left them. She appeared to have taken no hurt from her recent unpleasant experience and he inwardly applauded her courage. She drew back her hand and held it softly enclosed in the other as she looked after him, as though it were a dove she held, a living thing. He did not, she saw, kiss the hand of Lady Alys, whom he had encountered beneath the pointed arches, and who now stepped, bright-eyed across the sunlit stones to join them.

"What a pity you delayed, *ma chère,*" said the Queen innocently. "You too might have talked with the Chevalier." She added thoughtfully, "When next you do . . . you also, Eden . . . I think you would be wise if you were to give him . . . in no way heavily, of course, some slight warning. His future, as it stands, is very bright; his reputation second to none among his peers. He must not be allowed to cast away so much good fortune to feed the pride that will not stoop to pick up a sword."

"If it were a gauntlet, he would pick it up soon enough." Eden sprang to Tristan's defense once more.

The Queen laid a gentling hand upon her arm. "I know, my dearest friend, I know; and that is why I fear for him. One day . . . perhaps Richard will have a gauntlet to hand."

Despite Richard's bullying, Philippe Auguste did, at last, leave Acre. His health was broken and there was work for him at home in France; it meant more to him to secure his part of the Flanders inheritance in Artois than to be acclaimed with the doubtful glory of a successful Crusader.

Philippe marched away toward Tyre, taking with him the Marquess of Montferrat, to whom, to Richard's fury, he had given his share of the plunder of Acre, to aid his cause in Jerusalem. Conrad had no desire to remain in a camp dominated by Richard. He did not care what was the outcome of the Princes' deliberations upon the future of the disputed crown.

If they gave it to Guy, he would simply bide his time and then take it from him. He would be glad to see his own beautiful city again and to spend some time with his highly desirable little wife.

In the pleasant city of Shefar'am, inland from the bay of Haifa, the defeated Saladin took his ease in the divan. His warlike brother Al-Adil shared the masculine retreat with him. They had talked of hunting and of falconry, of the fine horses whose pedigrees they knew in their hundreds. They had not spoken of the siege; it lay too heavily upon their hearts.

At length the deep-chested warrior rose. He looked down with affection at the slight figure on the cushions, the black hair and beard straggling a little with ill-health; he noted a dullness, too, in the dark eyes of the Sultan, and promised himself that he would send personally to the brilliant Jewish physician Moses ben Maimon in Cairo. Now known as Maimonides, this great scholar had been captured and forcibly converted to Islam by Saladin's followers, but far from bearing the Sultan a grudge for this treatment, he had been instantly enchanted with his captor's far-ranging intellect and curiosity. The two had become firm friends and Maimonides often gave Yusuf excellent advice on his health. Few men, reflected Al-Adil, are capable of thus inspiring the love of their enemies. Truly, Allah had given his brother many rich qualities, and Yusuf had given him unswerving service in return.

And yet, now, instead of showing him a victorious countenance, as he deserved, Allah had turned away his face, and the Cruciati had prevailed.

"We are not yet done, brother," he murmured, touching the thin shoulder beneath the white djellaba. It was all the comfort he could find.

Yusuf ibn Ayub el Salah-ed-Din briefly covered his brother's hand with his own. "Allah will inflict on them the supreme chastisement," he quoted, finding his hope, as always, in the words of God to his prophet, Mohammed. But his hope was not strong at that moment. For the first time in his life he was suffering the humiliation of a defeated leader. He, who had not lost a battle in fifteen years, had been bested by a King of England no older than many of his sons.

Unable to be comforted, Saladin bade Al-Adil farewell and sent for his writing implements. He would write to Al-Khatun, the exquisite mistress who reigned in their palace in the garden of the world, Damascus. The knowledge of her love was a talisman to him; it brought him great joy whenever he thought of her. He had not seen her for so long, so very long. If only he could feel her cool arms about him, could hear the soft tones of her voice, he knew he could shake off this foolish illness . . .

It was not possible; he must find what solace he could in their letters.

"Beloved Lady of the Moon," he began, "I am here in Shefar'am because I could no longer remain within sight of that tragic city for which, alas, I can now do no more. Acre has been the chastening of Allah to his servant and even now the pain is not ended; El Malik Rik, the English King, has forced upon us a shameful treaty; I cannot repudiate it as I would wish, for it was sworn to by my servant Karakush in his extremity. 200,000 dinars are demanded of me, a sum I do not possess. They have given me three months in which to gather together this money and the Christian prisoners distributed throughout my lands, some 16,-000 in all. I have made the first payment and already El Malik Rik accuses me of breaking the treaty. It is thus; unable to trace each of the hundred high-ranking noble captives especially demanded of me, I sent those whom we had found, together with several of my brave Emirs who volunteered themselves as hostages for the return of the rest. Now El Rik refuses to release the captive garrison of Acre, saying I am foresworn since he has not yet his hundred knights! I had thought to find greater nobility in the man; truly it is he who is foresworn.

"Yet will he have his way for there is none to dissuade him in the Christian camp. The French King is gone, and the proud Marquess, though the information is that the struggle over Jerusalem continues. Long may it do so, for their contending has ever been our strength.

"Yet I fear all may end at last when this young Marquess comes into his own; he has strength and purpose and his following grows daily. Truly, heart that lies within my heart, it would be well for us if this Conrad of Montferrat were to die young.

"Forgive me, beloved, for sending harsh notes of discord into your tranquil courtyard. In the midst of adversity, I take strength from the sweet thought of you, beauty in you, beauty around you, held safe within the bastion of my love. I long to return to you, light of my eyes. My soul aspires to you; my body remembers you. The days are as dust in the desert until I can come to you ..."

In the royal palace that had once belonged to Guy de Lusignan, Richard of England was giving a feast for that discomforted monarch.

The eating was done and Richard had retired with his Queen and her ladies and a few chosen friends to a more intimate chamber than the dining-hall. They had fallen into little, separate groups; Richard, with Guy beside him, drank wine and strummed melodiously upon his lute, a thing he loved to do when time allowed. Berengaria plied her needle between Joanna and Alys, while the latter cast frequent unquiet looks toward the domed window alcove where Eden sat with Tristan de Jarnac, now restored to Richard's grace by the efficiency of his arrangements for the rebuilding of the city.

As it so often did during this waiting period while Christian and Saracen ambassadors came and went from Acre to Shefar'am, the conversation turned to the vexed problem of Jerusalem. The ladies, bored, had tried to coax Richard to sing to them, a thing which he did with surprising artistry, but he and Guy worried away at Jerusalem like an old bone, long since lacking in either meat or marrow.

In low murmurs, their heads far closer than Lady Alys liked to see, Eden discussed with Tristan the reasons why Stephen had not been one of the first batch of returned prisoners.

"He was too far away; perhaps the message had not yet reached Ibn Zaydun. I warned you not to look for him too soon." He had hated to see her bitter disappointment, as she had counted and questioned each new arrival in the camp. None had seen or even heard of Stephen. He was further away than any of them had been. Since then Tristan had watched her hope grow again; he had neither starved nor fostered it.

"You are *sure* the message will get through?" she demanded as she had done time after time.

He took her hand and held it fast, as though the slight pain he caused her would burn a way for the facts to reach her. "His name was put to Saladin, who is a man of honor and has sworn to return all who were named."

She did not release her hand; her eyes were abstracted and troubled. Her uncertainty tore at him for now his own had increased to join it. Sometimes he longed, shamefully, for the Saracen couriers to bring news of Stephen's death, as they had of others. Perhaps, in view of certain things he now knew about de la Falaise, that might be the best thing that could happen . . . for Eden as much as himself . . .

For he had now admitted to himself that he loved her. The sweet fire of this knowledge filled his veins as he sat now so close to her, her tense little hand in his, and yet so far from her questing thoughts.

He had wondered, after that brief, illuminating conversation with young John of Cobden, whether he should tell her what was spoken of her husband. He had been with her many times since and had not found himself able to hurt her, to dash that glowing expectation from her. There was no need for that; it was enough that she should be safe, among friends, and that he could be with her on occasions such as this. Like her, he would await the outcome. Besides, who was he to play the God in her life, when God himself would bring all to its close?

"You are right, I know, and yet . . . if only I could be sure . . ."

Her eyes entreated him in an agony of not knowing, of endless waiting, of too little faith. An overwhelming longing came to him to speak to her of his own agony, to confess his love and be damned for it, to hear her denigration, call up the anger and disappointment that, perhaps, would give them both their different kinds of relief. Happily, Richard saved him from such folly.

"What do *you* say, de Jarnac? You're a man of opinion. What treatment shall we mete out to the Tyrant of Tyre?" The wine had made him friendly.

Tristan was weary, like many another, of the interminable question. He was even more weary of the infantile and selfish answers that were all he had heard from Richard and his more sycophantic barons. He strode out of the alcove, the candlelight glowing upon the ruby velvet of his surcoat and striking sparks from the decoratively lethal dagger at his slender waist.

Eden, sensing something unaccustomed, caught the Queen's look of apprehension.

"For what it's worth to you, my Liege," Tristan began with brutal flatness, "I would have this unprofitable dissent dissolved into a compromise."

He ignored the fading of Richard's goodwill face and addressed himself now to Guy de Lusignan, nervously pulling at his scanty beard.

"Forgive me, my Lord, if I state that you are no longer young. Your wife and the heirs of your body were lost to you in the plague . . . and we all sorrow for it . . ."

A sick weariness passed across de Lusignan's lined features and Tristan gave him pause before going on. "I make no doubt but that the throne of Jerusalem is yours . . . and should be so until your death. But the heir to that throne . . . equally without doubt . . . is Isabella of Tyre. Therefore, it seems to me, that true justice would be done if you, Sire, were to rule until your death, whereupon the throne would revert to Isabella and her heirs."

He had expected the outcry, Richard's snarl above the rest of the pack. "God rot you, man! What you speak is treason. Or insanity! You would give the throne to Conrad and his brats?"

"I would. It seems to me the only way to put an end to strife; do we want true civil war in Jerusalem? Because that is what will happen if we do *not* compromise."

De Lusignan, whose kingdom had thus neatly been disposed of, raised an excited voice. "One thing is very clear in all this, Sieur de Jarnac. Your plan is an open invitation to Montferrat to take all, crown and revenues, whenever he will . . . by the simple pretext of having me murdered!"

"If you fear that . . . give the Marquess a half share in the revenues while you live," Tristan suggested. Conrad was rich; he would probably be quite happy to wait for Guy to die.

Eden, listening aghast as Tristan, despite all attempts on behalf of the Queen and herself, not to mention Lady Alys, unconcernedly threw the King's renewed friendship in his face, nevertheless found herself much in accord with his argument.

Amazingly, there came the unexpected deep rumble of the Lionheart's laughter. "It is almost infallible that you are right, Guy, *mon chevalier*. And yet, if you only think, there is an answer. Staring you in the face, man!"

Tristan knew a sudden moment of dreadful prediction.

"It seems more than likely that our friend the merchandising Marquess would be only too pleased to accept such terms of tenure . . . they are, after all, exceptionally generous!" Here he grinned unpleasantly at Tristan. "We should therefore have him very much where we want him with regard to the disposition of his troops and the like. As for the matter of murder, why, man . . . two can play at murder, but only one can play first. Bring the assassins down on him; it's said they have never failed . . ."

"Assassins?" queried the Queen, half fascinated by the outlandish name.

It was Tristan who answered her.

"The term is rightly Hashasheen, the eaters of Hashish. They are the members of a fanatical religious sect who inhabit the Ansariyah mountains to the north of Syria. Their leader is Rashid-ed-Din Sinan, known to all Christians as the Old Man of the Mountains; his base is the impregnable fortress of Alamut which even Saladin could not take by storm. Sinan can call upon his followers' absolute obedience in anything he may command. Their religion stands upon the unshakable conviction that they can only achieve the delights of paradise through death in the service of Allah; they go forth, therefore, driven into ecstacy by the drug hashish, which also gives them inhuman courage, to seek out and kill whatever victim their leader has named; secretly, and without trace. The Hashashin have amassed great wealth and power to match their notoriety; they are hated and feared . . . and used . . . by Christian and Muslim alike. They owe allegiance to none and kill where they are paid to kill."

"Exactly so," murmured Richard, impervious to the shudders of the women. He slapped Guy's narrow shoulder. "What say you, King of Jerusalem? Shall we put the word about that we are in business for the assassins?"

Guy swallowed. He moved determinedly away from the companionable hand and turned in his seat to look Richard full in the eye. "Sometimes it is no wonder to me that they call you Richard Trichard," he said dully. "We are no Romans, to stab each other in the back. We are men of honor. A joke's a joke; now let's forget it."

"As you will." Richard shrugged but the look of

crude satisfaction did not leave his face. He noticed suddenly that his wife was staring at him, her expression incalculable. "Cheer up, chuck," he urged her genially. "I am not such a villain as you think."

Berengaria noted absently that his moustache was too long. "It would not matter to me if you were," she said with simple truth.

Richard wondered, as he had since his cradle, at the odd morality of women.

Tristan, watching the King's shifting moods, asked himself if he would seriously consider using such dishonorable ways to gain his ends. He doubted it, but was aware of doubting it less than he might have done a year ago.

But now the Lionheart was bored with sitting still. He rose and stretched his long arms, feeling the pleasurable pull of his muscles.

"I'm for a walk in the streets. Who's with me? Guy? De Jarnac, you traitor? Christ, but my arse is stiff!"

Tristan would rather have stayed, but it was tantamount to a command, and he knew that Richard would keep his shaky favorite beside him until he had satisfied himself that he understood the workings of a mind that could gainsay him. He did not relish a roister in the stews of Acre. Richard's pleasures were not his own.

He looked at Eden, so unconsciously lovely, leaning back in her seat with that slight, parted-lipped smile she had. He felt a sudden stirring in his loins and damned her unreasonably to hell for it. The King could go where he pleased for his perverted pleasures and take Guy with him; as for Tristan de Jarnac, he was going to drink himself oblivious for the first time in his life and then find a nice, plump, lascivious whore and ride her till she came apart at the hilt.

Lady Alys, surprising this intention upon his customarily unmoved countenance, suffered a frisson of something that, had she recognized it, matched his own feeling. She told herself again that she must have him for her husband. No matter that it was Eden who was

in his care, Eden with whom he shared his infrequent
laughter, Eden with whom he now sat at dinner, at
backgammon, at rest. Eden with whom he became
angry, or amused, or tolerant. Eden was wed and her
husband would shortly appear. Alys prayed nightly for
his swift return and could not, would not, conceive
that it might not occur.

"Sir Tristan had an angry look," she murmured
when the men had left. She needed to speak his name.

Eden was surprised. "Perhaps he tires of my constant
harping on Stephen," she surmised.

More than likely, Alys thought bitterly. So, too,
thought Joanna, who had noted the way the wind blew
in more than one direction.

"No . . . it would be Richard," the Queen sighed.
"He is hard to bear just now; with Philippe gone he
has no target for his barbs and we all must suffer."

"You don't appear to be suffering greatly," remarked Joanna with unconcealed curiosity. "How goes
it, then, between you and my big, bold brother?"

Berengaria laid down her embroidery. She hesitated, then, with obvious reluctance, steeled herself to
speak.

"You will forgive me, Joanna, and Eden too. There
is something that troubles me. I should not ask you
this . . . but there is no other I may go to." She
stopped, blushing violently, her hands twisting together in embarrassment.

Joanna threw an irreverent glance at Alys. "Be-
gone, *ma chère!* Here's no matter for virgins."

Alys curled her lip. "I have no intention of remaining
so all my life."

"Go on. Do not mark them," Eden softly encouraged the Queen. She had known there was something
distressing her, but it had not been spoken of, and she
had not liked to ask. She frowned slightly at Joanna.
A little of her brand of sardonic humor would help
to ease Berengaria's discomfort; too much would send
her flying from the room.

"It is this," the breathless voice continued. "As you

know, when I was first wed, Richard . . . he only visited me but once . . . in my bedchamber; it was the night of our marriage. After that he was occupied with the fighting, the siege; there was nothing. And then we came here to the palace . . ." Her face brightened. "Since then the King has . . . become a husband to me. He does not come nightly to my bed, but that's no matter. It is that, when he does, he has lately started to . . . use me unnaturally." She ended on a whisper, her eyes wide with tears.

Alys wondered, with some annoyance, what she could mean.

"But *what*, dear sister, do you consider to be unnatural?" asked Joanna sensibly.

The blushes clamored about Berengaria's cheeks. "He . . . he takes me . . . like an animal," she managed unhappily.

Joanna was suspicious of her sister-in-law's knowledge of anatomy, whether animal or human. "Exactly *how* does he take you?" she insisted gently.

The Queen clearly did not wish to say. Nevertheless, "He does not use my woman's part," she muttered, "but that which the Church has declared it to be sinful to use."

Joanna was taken with a sudden fantasy whereby her brother, huge, naked and hirsute, forced this tiny, delicate creature like a rutting stallion. She sighed. Marriage to an old man made one subject to fantasies. Curiosity dispelled this one. "Doesn't it hurt?" she asked.

Berengaria bit her lip. "Not so much, now," she confessed, "though the first time I thought that I must die. I know I should not submit to such sinful practices," she cried passionately, "but he is my husband, and my King; it is what he requires of me. I love him. How am I to refuse him?"

"You could tell him he'll get no heir to his throne after *that* guise!" declared Joanna forthrightly. "You could also express your own preferences once in a while. Richard always was a selfish pig, his mother spoiled him. If you want something from him you must learn how to take it for yourself . . . for he thinks of none but Richard."

Eden broke in. "It isn't that, Joanna, can't you see? What she wants to know is whether this is some form of depravity, or just a man's normal appetites."

Berengaria nodded. Joanna laughed harshly.

"Normality! What is that? What the Church has decreed? Why, there was a monastery in Sicily, next door to a nunnery . . . but no matter! I could tell a tale or two about normality. William, my husband, was impotent, but he did not lack the desire. Some of the things he wanted of me . . . what he could not perform, he liked to watch. He would have had the very dogs use me if he could." She stopped suddenly, her contorted features relaxing into gentleness. "Richard is a man like other men, my love. Sin with him . . . and ask forgiveness after. It is all you can do, being but a woman, and his wife."

The Queen nodded slowly, her face calmer. "Eden, you have said nothing in this."

"I can say nothing that will aid you," Eden replied, "having no such experience to offer. Perhaps Lady Joanna has the right of it . . . but for myself, I would use all my strength before I would permit a man to use me as I did not wish . . . though perhaps it would avail me little," she added bitterly, thinking of Hugo de Malfors. She had listened to the conversation with great sympathy for Berengaria and a fine contempt for the King, but beneath these feelings came the half-remembered promptings of something else . . . for there had been a time, once, long ago, when she was first married, when Stephen had laughingly attempted such a coupling as this they talked of. It had been impossible; she was too young, too taut; and all had dissolved into laughter . . . but she did not wish to speak of it. What, then, could she say to her troubled friend?

"Surely, all that matters is that you love him? And that he has come to you at last? Say to him that you long for a child. If he loves you, he will listen." Berengaria was grateful to her. She wished now that she had not told Joanna. Her cool sister-in-law seemed so worldly, so experienced, perhaps even a little tarnished, while Eden appeared as fresh and innocent still, beneath her determined practicality, as the virgin who had married her Stephen.

There came a day when innocence, though not of such a kind, became impossible for all of them. Since the siege had ended, Richard had been restless. His commanders were restless; his armies were restless. Tempers were short and time leaden. Even Tristan de Jarnac's rebuilding of the city was coming to an end; there is a limit to the useful employment of 30,000 men, even on a large task.

Richard brooded upon his position. Conqueror of Sicily and of Cyprus, Savior of Acre, Herald of Release to the Holy City, where did he stand? Who and what was he now, the golden warrior, the Lionhearted?

He should have been almost at the zenith of his power, his popularity, his reputation as a warrior and a leader. Instead he sensed that in some subtle, insidious fashion, perhaps it was possible for all of these to slip away and leave him with nothing but the naked reality of Richard Plantagenet. The thought, only half-conceived, frightened him.

The only cure for such sickness was action. He must get out of Acre. He must leave the equivocal city with its miasmic mists and its whispered intrigues. He must take the armies and weld them into a single sword to take Jerusalem. That was his destiny and God had made it clear that he alone was capable of it. He called his commanders to council and informed them that he had sent word to Saladin that his delays had broken the treaty, that the Sultan's three thousand prisoners were now forfeit. The man he chose to take charge of the executions was the only one who had throughout the council looked him steadily in the face and allowed his contempt to blaze in his eyes—Tristan de Jarnac.

De Jarnac thought at first of disobeying. The captive Saracens were unbelievers, certainly, and condemned to eternal damnation. Saint Bernard himself, when he had preached the first crusade of all, had said that Christ was glorified every time a pagan died. But Tristan could find no personal grace from the premature hastening to hell of nearly three thousand souls, even to the greater glory of God. Slaughter was necessary in battle; he had even enjoyed it upon occasion. But this would be an ignoble, meaningless slaughter. No excuses could dignify it to anything better. And by now, the King was not the only one who was full of excuses. They were now called "reasons" and they abounded. Only Tristan and a few others, mostly his own men, held otherwise.

Yet, in the end, he performed his duty. There was no way, he knew, for he had sat up late into the night with Richard, drunk and sober and drunk again, to make the golden warrior see the difference between one killing and another. Killing was killing; Saracens were Saracens; the two went together very satisfactorily. Tristan was beautiful and he was, despite his independence, still beloved; but, over these executions . . . he was also a fool.

Tristan had tried and failed; his failure gnawed at him, for perhaps of all of them, King, Queens, retainers, soldiers, he was the only one who could have articulated the loss to the Crusade of its innocence.

All of them, in some way, were aware of it, however, when in the cruelly clear morning light of August 20th they watched Tristan and his Christian soldiers carry out their orders.

Eden stood with Berengaria at a point carefully chosen by their military escort for its excellent view of the proceedings, which, now that they were unavoidable, the soldiers, if not those they served, intended to enjoy. They had lost both good health and good companions to that stubborn and inventive garrison in this plague-ridden midden of a city; now they would reap their revenge.

Eden had not wished to be present; she was there in some sense because Tristan must be there; because of the friendship that was growing between them and because, though he loathed the task from the depths of his soul, he would carry it out and he would endure. In friendship, she too would endure. Similarly, she knew, Berengaria was here because Richard had ordered this massacre. Because she loved him, she would take upon herself some of his guilt, as Eden, in mere friendship, would take Tristan's sorrow.

There was no wind. The members of the infidel garrison were marched and ranked outside the rebuilt walls as they had been on the day of their defeat.

Above the city, on the lower slopes of the hillsides, several Saracen outposts were still encamped. They would be able to see what took place. The captives were weary, ill-fed and dragging unhealed wounds. Beside the soldiers in their tattered mail crept other, smaller figures.

"Dear God!" Eden cried out. "He cannot kill the children!"

Indeed yes, Richard had agreed in the leaden, early hours while a blood-eyed Tristan still battered at him uselessly . . . the wives and children were innocent, but who would feed them, when their breadwinners were dead?

At first the cries were terrible to hear. Eden did not think she would ever sleep again for the wailing of one particular baby whom she had foolishly singled out in his young mother's arms. He had begun by laughing, playing with some trinket at the girl's neck; his bubbling laughter had caught at her heart so that she had wanted to snatch him from his mother's arms and swear to her that he would be loved and cared for always.

Now it was much later and his laughter had drowned amid the universal tears about him. Irrevocably he and his mother, sheltered in the arm of his proud-eyed, pitifully young father, moved down the long queue which led to the executioners and their doom.

Eden had perhaps hoped, she saw now, to escape the full horror of what was taking place by her concentration on this one pathetic little family; but now that the inevitable moment was about to overtake them, it encompassed her, too, with all its terror and its waste, and although she was quite overwhelmed by grief and pain, she could not look away as the baby was torn from the terrified girl's arms. She stretched them emptily after him, pleading uselessly, but they were pinioned and dragged roughly behind her back. She cried out once but her husband spoke to her clearly with love and pride and she did not do so again. It was Eden who screamed in horror and disbelief when the knife was drawn in a swift silver streak across the baby's throat.

"Why now?" murmured Berengaria uncomprehendingly as, numbed of all sensitivity by the endless repetition of abominations that she had not thought she could have borne, she watched the man and the girl lay their heads upon the bloodied blocks.

There were 2,700 of such deaths that day.

From the hills, Saladin's outposts, maddened by horror and misery, descended in a hopeless dream of defense and prevention. They were very few; most died. When the slaughter was over the ground could not be seen for headless bodies and bloodless heads. The axes and the sabers lay scarlet and indifferent, their duty done, while those who had wielded them ravaged the corpses with the patient companions who had waited to let them have first pickings. There was not much to be had. The young mother's circle of sandalwood beads would doubtless look just as well on the neck of a pikeman's whore as he sunk his bloody memories in wine that night. One day, perhaps, her child would play with it, laughing, in her arms.

But the pikeman, together with his sergeant, his captain, his commander, his Queen, would know no more of innocence; and all, from the least to the highest, were made aware of it as it looked at them out of the eyes of a friend. Only one man did not partake in this common loss, and that was the King.

They carried the news to Saladin at Shefar'am and he laid down his head and wept. He too would take upon himself the guilt of the spilled blood of his people. He cursed himself for failing to see what a demon inhabited El Malik Rik. He had frowned when mothers had frightened their children with tales of how the Lionheart would catch them and cut off their heads . . . He set aside his Qu'ran. For once, it could hold no comfort.

For Eden, the terrible day became a turning point, setting her free from the King and his wishes as surely as those thousands of heathen souls had been set free from their bodies.

She had found a place to be alone in the intricate palace, and she had prayed for many hours. Gradually, as she did so, the turmoil of horror and shock within her abated, and something stronger took its place . . . the dull, calm, certainty of resolution. It was quite clear to her what she must do. Later, she stood with Tristan de Jarnac, high in one of the formal, rooftop gardens of the palace, amid one of the most ruthlessly gorgeous sunsets she had ever seen. The clamoring color beat at her senses; so much rose and crimson and vermilion. It could, after such a day, signify only blood and yet more blood. She turned her back on it, and leaned against the low, white-washed wall to face Tristan, whose pale and strained features disturbed her deeply. She had weathered his anger when it had come her way during the difficult days in which they had known each other; but she could not bear to see his sorrow.

"You could not have prevented it," she said, knowing how insistently he had tried to do so. "Had you not carried out his orders, another would have done."

"Had I not carried out Richard's orders, I would have been first in the line for execution," he replied with grim certainty. "I am not, I think, made of the stuff which makes a martyr. Especially not a martyr for the cause of condemned infidels," he added with an ironic curl to his lip.

"It was they who were the martyrs," Eden saw again, with the same helpless pity, the desperate girl and her baby. "Martyrs to Richard's accursed pride." Her voice rose, filled with hatred.

"Not to his pride; merely to his impatience. Though the pity of it is no less."

She stared stubbornly ahead of her. She did not understand Richard.

"What has changed in him so much that he is able to do this thing?" she demanded.

He heard the wondering hurt in her tone and felt sympathy for it. Richard knew how to hurt.

"When I think of him as I first saw him," she continued passionately, "standing on the quayside at Messina, clothed in the sunlight like the great, golden idol of all our dreams. Kissing Berengaria's hands and telling her she was beautiful . . . embracing his mother with true love and gladness . . . conquering the hearts of thousands who would work and fight and dream for weeks, months . . . upon the strength they took from that one glimpse of their lion-hearted King!" She shook that vision fiercely from her eyes. "And when I see him now . . . a monster of pride and anger who cares nothing for any save himself . . . nothing even for his sworn word, whether to Saladin, or, yes, even to me! A man who commits mass murder for convenience! He is cruel, vainglorious, dishonorable . . . and this the first King in all Christendom. And when I think of my poor, sweet Berengaria . . ." She broke off. There were some things that could never be spoken.

He longed to comfort her anger, calm her hatred, give her back the peace she must once have known, back at home among her woods and fields at Hawkhurst. But the times did not deal in peace. "It is not that Richard has changed, or at any rate not greatly. It is rather you who now see him in the light of experience, rather than that of hero-worship. If you wished him to remain a hero, you should have remained safe on your domain with your hawks and your hounds."

It was brutal reasoning, but she had to admit that there was truth in it; though it could never be the whole truth.

"Philippe Auguste found no need for such cruelty," she began, "nor Guy de Lusignan, nor the Marquess of Montferrat . . . no, nor Saladin himself."

He sighed. He was tired, desperately tired. Death had been infinitely more demanding to witness than to deal. He had drawn no sword during the executions, but had stood by, expressionless and motionless as befitted his state, while his soldiers carried out his orders. He had thanked God, who had permitted this senseless carnage, that he could not see Eden from where he stood.

"Who can say what any man will do, when the time comes to take action?" he demanded wearily. "The King of France is a strategist; Richard's ways are not his; he has the gift of patience . . . and yet a man may wait too long and lose the moment. De Lusignan is a coward . . . and cowards are often cruel. As for Conrad of Montferrat, we have not yet begun to see what he might do. But think of the way he got his wife . . ."

Eden bowed her head; he was right. "And Saladin, they say, is a man of honor above all things. Though Richard would have us think otherwise."

His sternness softened slightly to regret. "Aye, by God. If only he had been able to send us our prisoners."

"Indeed yes," she echoed with a sudden harshness. If only . . . No need, then, for the decision forced upon her by this day of wrath.

Tristan's weariness was turning swiftly into an irritating weakness. He reached out to steady himself against the wall. He must keep talking; the words would chase the foolish moment away.

"The King may be all you have said he is . . . and after his late showing, I am not far from agreement with you . . . but he is still our leader and a great one when he chooses. He never could abide confinement, waiting, stillness; he must have action. You'll see; you'll like him better when we have left this sorry city."

She thought then of what she must say to him, for she might not have another chance to speak to him alone. She was still seeking the words when he swayed suddenly and caught at the parapet.

"Tristan! Sweet Jesu! What ails you?"

He was upright again, supporting himself against the wall. "It's nothing. My shoulder. The wound I had in Cyprus. It opened up when . . ."

"Are you sure? Let me look at it. But it's bleeding badly. I did not mark it under this dark cloak. Oh, you are a fool to stand there on your feet! Come within; I'll bind it properly for you." Her concern was sweet to him. Some of the strain left the fine lines about his eyes.

"No . . . let us stay a while. It's none so bad. I'd rather be here, out in the soft air; it is easier to breathe."

She understood him. Inside, Richard was giving one of his interminable feasts, where any late pangs of conscience were being drowned in wine or strangled in conspicuous good cheer.

She drew Tristan to a wooden seat beneath an arbor of plaited orange trees. Their heavy scent hummed about them as she helped him out of his cloak. The dark blood was seeping slowly through to his white tunic.

"It should be washed and bound. We'll not stay long. How did you do it?"

"It was as we repulsed the attack from the hill camps. I felled one of the Ramieh from his horse. He gave me a strenuous time." The man had fought well and there had been tears of anger in his eyes for the dying garrison; he had not enjoyed killing him.

Eden questioned no further but put up her hands and gently loosened the strings of his bloodsoaked linen shirt. He wore no mail, so it was a simple matter to unfasten both shirt and tunic and lay bare the four-inch-long scarlet wound, that had hacked into his shoulder beneath the bone.

"It is clean and does not mortify; but you must see a physician at once."

He smiled with gentle contempt at her urgency. "No need. My squires are well-skilled in such medicine as I require. I assure you it has come to worse than this with me a hundred times. I have good healing flesh. There's naught here won't keep for half an hour."

Half an hour! How brief a time it was. She longed to tell him what was in her heart, to explain to him now, when the warm night and his wound drew them so close, what tomorrow he would, perhaps find inexplicable. And yet, perhaps he would not, for he was beginning to know her now. And she him.

"Tristan . . ."

Her face swam toward him, her eyes huge with some unrevealed emotion.

Her hand was still warm upon his body. "I'm listening," he prompted gently. He had almost said, "My love!"

"I want to . . ." But what could she say to him, since she could not say the only thing that had any importance? She searched for vaulting, unforgettable words, but could find only poor, broken-backed things of little significance. "I think I will . . . always remember this night. Whenever I catch the scent of oranges, or see the sun sink down in splendor . . . I will think of the day and this night. So much beauty after . . . Oh, my lord, I . . ." She could not go on.

He saw the tears in her eyes. A premonition of great loneliness had come to her. She gazed at him out of a torment of confusion. He had kissed her once, this stern and proud chevalier, in one of his rare and unpredictable moods of lightness. Suddenly she wanted him very much to kiss her now.

He could not believe the pleading in her eyes. Then, with a broken cry she was in his arms, his wound forgotten, his mouth on hers, hers on his. Who knew which was seeking and which response? A fire and a sweetness coursed through her and her lips parted, flowering under his. She pressed against his naked chest and his arms crushed her. She raised her eyes and his face was fierce and pure and beautiful against the dying sun. They kissed again with a desperate, questing urgency and she felt that she had become a part of the sunset, her senses swimming among the burning, swirling colors until she was no longer conscious of herself or her separate will but was joined with him forever in a single, aspiring flame, that surely no power on earth could extinguish.

Moaning, she moved her mouth upon the unimagined, unfamiliar surface of his breast, where the skin was as soft and as vulnerable as her own until her exploring lips met the dark tangle of fine hair below the collarbone. All at once she tasted the blood that still seeped sluggishly from his wound; and tasting it, knew an instant of bitterness of a different kind and was returned, undefended, to her waiting self.

He felt her pull away from him and let her go.

She put up her hand to her lips . . . and they were imprinted upon it in his blood. He took the hand and lingeringly kissed it; the blood was shared between them. Her face luminous with a new and sorrowing beauty, she stared at him with the terrible knowledge that had overtaken her.

There were no words.

He leaned to touch her cheek with a gentleness that was almost painful to her. He longed to kiss her, to hold her again, to make her a part of him, weld her to him so that they could never again be separate. But he must not. Her stillness and her sorrow told him that. He must rest content with the miraculous knowledge that now, for her, the world had changed as it had for him.

He had not the power to prevent the joy from flooding into him as the reality of the miracle touched him. Eden saw his look and gave an incoherent cry; then, rising from the seat, she fled from him and from the garden without once looking back. She did not expect, as she ran, that she would ever see Tristan de Jarnac again.

Behind him the sun went, sorrowing down in its own blood.

▼▼▼▼▼▼▼▼▼▼▼▼▼▼▼▼▼▼▼▼▼▼▼▼▼▼▼▼▼▼▼▼▼▼▼▼

CHAPTER ELEVEN

Cities and Mountains

The feast had reached its height. The clamor, the heat and the stench of a hundred sweating bodies, following upon the hideous exigencies of the day, threatened Berengaria's slender hold on her senses. She had dispatched Alys to her chamber, therefore, to find her smelling-bottle.

When she opened the chest at the foot of the Queen's bed, where the little phial of astringent herbs should be, the tall girl noticed a small roll of parchment lying on top of its contents. It was inscribed, in green ink, to Berengaria and the hand, Alys recognized, was Eden's.

Strange! What could Eden have to say to the Queen, her friend, that she could not convey by word of mouth? Following an impulse she knew to be base, she untied the twist of embroidery silk that held the scroll. Its message was brief.

"To my royal mistress and the friend of my heart, Berengaria, Queen of England: Believe me, I sorrow to take leave of you thus. I long to kiss your hand and beg your blessing in my venture, but I cannot, for I know, alas, you would not give it. But knowing me as you do, you will, I hope understand and forgive me. I go to seek Stephen for myself and I should have done long since. I leave his ransom in your hands; I beg you to give it to any who come to you in my name, bearing Stephen's cross that I always wear about my neck. I do not know how long the journey may be, but be assured, as I love you, that one day I will bring that love and service back to you. Christ be with you, as I hope he is with me. Eden of Hawkhurst."

Alys stared at the swooping, confident signature, a prey to confused and warring reactions. Her breathing was swift and shallow.

"Well, my lady . . . so you have become dishonest."

She spun round. Eden stood in the doorway, her face cold with rage. She appeared unnaturally tall in the light of the branched candlestick which she held above her head.

No use to pretend. Alys stabbed contemptuously at the paper in her hand.

"You *cannot* mean to do this! It would be foolhardy beyond measure."

Eden moved toward her very slowly, her body rigid with anger. Her heart pounded; she must keep her head. There was too much at stake to lose now.

"Put the letter back where you found it," she said quietly, forcing steadiness upon her voice.

Alys, feeling the cutting edge beneath the steadiness, became equally angry. Who was this fly-by-night daughter of a secondary nobleman to give an order to Alys de la Marche de Maury, related in blood to the kings of England and of France? And, planning what she did, could the creature dare to call her guilty? Her face emptied of all save disdain. She held out the paper toward Eden and deliberately tore it across and across.

"You should not have done that." Eden's tone was dangerous. She had very little time; none to spare for this.

"I would have hazarded, my lady," she pronounced with careful contempt, "that you stand to gain much by my absence. You want Tristan de Jarnac for a husband, do you not? Very well, you will never get him for one while *I* am still at court. Stand out of my way . . . and I'll stand out of yours."

Alys had blanched, her features surprised into pain. "It is not for this that I seek to prevent you," she replied fiercely, "though it seems all things are ignoble to the ignoble mind . . ."

Eden's bitter laugh forestalled her. "You say so, who are found with my letter in your thief's hand?"

"I do not dispute my rights in this matter," Alys declared without shame. Her look was proud and cool once more. "I did not trust you; I was right in that. And now that I know your mind I cannot let you go . . . though for myself I'd as lief see the back of you as anyone in Christendom. But you know the Queen, Eden, you know how deep would be her distress to find you gone. By Saint Ursula, has she not enough to bring her sorrow in this uncouth land . . . without the desertion of her dearest friend?"

Eden saw that she spoke the truth according to her lights. She would do her duty to the Queen rather than follow her own desires; Eden accorded her a grudging admiration for this. But nothing must stand in her path.

"I am leaving, Lady Alys," she insisted in a voice like sharpened steel. Her mind raced to discover a means of keeping her unwelcome discoverer silent until she should be well away. Any means, that is, other than the obvious and most unfortunate one . . .

There was none. So be it! Swirling suddenly, she drew back her heavy candlestick and brought it crashing down upon Alys's head; the ice-blue eyes were wide and startled before they fluttered and closed. The girl slid to the ground. The fine skin of her temple was broken and the blood showed bright against its pallor.

"Oh Jesu!" breathed Eden in terror. "Don't let me have killed her!"

Distracted at her own violence, she fell to her knees beside the still figure, cradling the flaxen head in her lap. Alys's eyes were still closed, but she breathed sure enough and her heart beat strongly. With infinite relief, Eden gently laid her head upon a cushion and covered her with a warm rug. She regretted having given in to such a barbarous impulse, but now it was done, and since there was no undoing it, she might as well make the best use of the incident. Alys would not regain her senses for several minutes . . . but

when she did she would certainly give the alarm after
Eden. That being so, it would be best if she were to
be delayed . . .

She rummaged in Berengaria's chest, beneath the
small sack which contained her jewels and the rest of
Stephen's ransom, quickly finding what she sought.
She turned the recumbent Alys upon her side and
bound her arms behind her with a woven girdle of
thick linen; then she secured her feet with another.
There was no need for a gag; the din of the feast
would muffle all cries. Alys stirred and moaned a little, but did not open her eyes. Eden examined the
wound upon her brow. A lump was fast appearing
but there had been little bleeding. She took some linen
clouts from the chest and cleaned the gash with some
of the Queen's water-of-rue.

It was enough; she must go. Then she remembered.
She picked up the pieces of her letter from the floor
and pinned them to Alys's slumbering breast. Let her
explain them if she would; there was no time to write
another.

The next steps must be swiftly executed. She had
thought them over often enough; there was little to go
wrong. She closed the curtain on the unconscious girl
and collected a rolled bundle from her own chamber.
She stole down the stairs and through the courts and
passages to the palace stables.

A sleepy guard challenged her, ale-pot in hand.
She gave her name.

"Saddle Balan for me," she demanded in a tone of
clear command. "Several of the knights and ladies are
taking a night ride up into the foothills; hurry! The
others are all saddled and wait for me."

Her urgency reached him and the roan was soon
ready. Eden walked him softly across the moonlit yard
and out at a postern gate; there was no guard. She led
the horse into the black shadows cast by the colonnade
which led along the side of the hall where the knights
resided. There would be none to hear, even had she
made any sound; every man had been bidden to
rejoice in victory with Richard.

They stopped beneath the deep arches, and Balan stood snuffing gently, flaring at the unaccustomed night air, while Eden, with feverish haste, pulled her rosy gown over her head. Beneath it she wore a hooded white shift and dark blue hose with riding boots. Plunging into her bundle she drew out her thinly padded gambeson and Master Hugh's pristine hauberk.

In less than a minute a slim youth stood there, a fine dagger at his hip and a jaunty velvet cap on his head, taking an inventory of the worldly goods that were all he had to serve him for many a day. The map, yes; she had taken that from the guardroom where it would not be missed; most of the senior knights possessed such a chart of the roads and dangers of the land. The money was sewn into the padding of her gambeson, except for a very little in the flamboyant scarlet purse that hung from her belt, to match the insolent feather in her gray cap. Then there was the little box containing some of Xanthe's colors; she might have to appear as a Saracen at some point and the walnut dye would be the very thing to accomplish the transformation. She placed the box into her saddlebag, rolling it up in her gown and pushing them in beside the cloak and the blanket already there. She wished she might take more, but it was best to travel light; there would, at any rate, be little time for vanity. Ready at last, she mounted. Balan needed no urging but was away like the wind at her first whistle.

Filled with a sudden, heady exultation, she leaned low across his neck and let him have his head. The spirited little thoroughbred gloried in the unexpected exercise. He laid back his ears and flew through the soft night air toward the north. Above him, drunk upon freedom as she had never been upon mere wine, Eden released her voice, her bright singing streaming on the wind in a fierce hymn of thankfulness and joy.

Before dawn they would be at the gates of Tyre.

Behind her, more than an hour afterwards, a dismayed Mathilde discovered the Lady Alys's wretched plight. When it was made known, it was spoken of in hushed, religious tones; none could believe; none wished to believe that they must lay that livid scar at Eden's door.

Alys herself said nothing save to the Queen.

Berengaria, scanning the four quarters of her letter with pale, tightened lips, wept a little and spoke not at all. For a long time she was even more than usually gentle with Alys.

In the knights' residence, Will Barret and John de Wulfran, reeling home from their festive duties with an addled eye toward bed, found themselves wide awake and smarting under the vitriolic tongue of their infuriated commander. They were accustomed to his irony, even to sarcasm upon occasion, but this was purely vicious and they were troubled. What could have ailed him?

The truth was that Tristan too had received a letter. It had been couched even more briefly than the Queen's . . . and it too was torn across and across . . . though this time by its recipient. Nevertheless, a dozen of his reluctant knights were hustled, grumbling, into their harness and hounded, at a pace set by Satan himself in the person of Tristan de Jarnac, northward, along the only road that could have the gall to call itself such . . . along the coast toward Tyre.

Isabella de Montferrat was intrigued. Nothing so entertaining had happened since Conrad had carried her off from poor Humphrey and wedded and bedded her before the night was out . . . the latter with a satisfactory thoroughness that had left a gleam in her eye never since quite extinguished. She was twenty. She was deeply and sensually in love with her energetic and surprising husband, and life was a constant pleasure to her, especially since his recent return from Acre. External events of any nature still had the power to please her, however, and Eden of Hawkhurst was a decided event.

It seemed that her lord, the Marquess, had saved the astonishingly lovely creature from a certain disagreeable fate and that, liking her undaunted mettle upon that occasion, he had professed himself ever her servitor. And today, before they had properly got their eyes open, the exceptional girl had ridden up to their gates, disguised as the prettiest boy in the kingdom, and demanded that he make good his profession. She wanted an armed escort of twenty men, no less, to ride off into the wilds of Syria after a husband who had shown the ill judgment to leave her behind him when he came Crusading.

And even more amazing to Isabella was the fact that her husband, not best known for excessive generosity unless it would bear some tangible fruit, had thrown back his head and laughed heartily for several seconds before giving the redoubtable woman exactly what she'd asked for.

The two ladies sat together in the Marquessa's splendid apartments overlooking the radiant waters of the harbor, discussing men, love and morality. Isabella had already elicited most of the details of Eden's personal life.

"Is he a strong man, your husband?" she wondered further, popping a sugared date between pouting, deep red lips.

Eden, wearing her rose and green gown once more, though regretting its creases, was reclining on a low sofa and sampling delicious spiced prawns in batter. "He has a certain nobility which is very much his own," she said thoughtfully. "It is a quiet strength . . . not of the kind which lets the whole world know of its existence."

"That is Conrad's kind," smiled Isabella, her black eyes sparkling proudly, "and I like it well. But I am glad that Stephen is a proper man . . . he would need to be so to deserve the devotion you show him."

Eden was put in mind of a conversation, similar to this, once held with Berengaria. She did not think, however, that her beloved Queen and this worldly, bright-eyed Marquessa shared a common notion of what might be strength in a man.

Isabella, watching the hidden thoughts fleeting across the faintly tired but exquisite features, wondered if she should tell her what she had lately learned from Conrad; that a certain man of undeniable strength, not to mention unquestionable respect, had just turned away from their doors; a man who had come in search of Eden, and whose interest, Montferrat had intimated, had appeared to be deeper than that demanded by mere duty. Isabella had caught sight of him herself as he left the palace . . . a tall knight with the most excellent figure God ever gave man to torment woman . . . and a face whose beauty looked, at that moment, to have been graven out of stone by a mason who had not determined whether he depicted a devil or the Archangel Michael. If she had been so lucky as to have had such a one so hard on her heels, thought Conrad's besotted wife, she would have turned about before he could say knife . . . although she would rather he'd have said bed.

But Eden had insisted that they throw off all pursuit. It was scarcely to be borne, but Conrad had lied and smiled as efficiently and charmingly as he always did . . . and the beautiful, stern knight had ridden off with his troop to comb the foothills, where wound the only other, very doubtfully marked route for the hardy traveler.

Isabella told herself that Stephen de la Falaise must indeed be possessed of some unique virtue, for his lady to hold so single-mindedly to her quest, if that dark seeker had truly given her his heart.

"Tell me," she began, her eyes innocent as a flower, "have you never found your emotions engaged by . . . any man other than your husband?" She saw Eden's enviable green eyes widen in surprise at the question, and, yes, perhaps wariness. Isabella gabbled on. "I only asked because, when I was married to poor Humphrey, although he was quite beside himself about *me*, I must confess I was constantly turning my head in one direction or another." She tried to look ashamed but did not succeed. Instead she shrugged and said very sweetly, "It is inconvenient, I suppose, especially to one's husband . . . but there is no great sin if our thoughts be pure . . . and very little if not," she added in honest acknowledgement of her own impurities.

Eden gave in to the desire to laugh at this disarm-

ing sinner. But even healing laughter could not keep
the shadow of Tristan from her soul. All night she had
ridden as if to outstrip her own uncontrollable thoughts;
she had formed a wall of muttered prayer about her
mind and would not let him in . . . and now, in the
blue daylight, this lovely, voluptuous child had accomplished her downfall in a single second.

"Yes," she sighed slowly, dragging the words from
the depths of herself in response to a terrible honesty
that she had not been able, in her brief missive, to
show to him who most deserved it, "I have . . . turned
my head . . . and perhaps my heart; but it is nothing. It
shall be nothing. I shall make it so."

Isabella saw that she suffered and pitied her, regretting her curiosity now. "Your determination, my dear,
will have to be stronger, then, than either head or
heart." She was sure now; her instincts had been unerr-
ing, as ever. This girl was not so much flying to find her
husband as to lose her lover. She would not torture her
any further now . . . but later, perhaps, when Eden
had left them, she might reconsider her vow of silence.

"You must come back to us, since you take our men
with you," she said sunnily, "but I should like to
have news of you before that, if I may. Send to me
sometimes; I should be so happy."

"Indeed I will. You and the Marquess have been
more than kind. I shall always be grateful that you
would do for me what my own King and guardian
would not."

She would be sorry to leave that night. She liked
Isabella greatly, despite her curiosity . . . or perhaps,
she considered, on account of it, for it was all a part of
the rich love of life that flowed from the dark-eyed,
sweet-natured girl. She was as vibrant as a well-strung
lute, attuned to all the harmonies and discords about
her. And if she was bold, as befitted her black and passionate eyes and her high, dramatic coloring, Eden
knew instinctively that she was also brave and resolute,
a fit companion for the man who had married her. She
could no longer feel that Humphrey of Toron had

been cheated of anything that had ever, in deepest truth, been his.

It was good to ride out of the gates of a great city at the head of one's own troop of armed men. Although she had followed often in Richard's train, or in Berengaria's, Eden had never before experienced such a powerful delight in her own standing in the world as was conferred upon her by Conrad of Montferrat with the loan of his twenty uniformed soldiers. There were four knights among them and all were splendidly accoutred in black and silver surcoats, quartered with the arms of Montferrat. They were well-mounted and their swords shone as though they had never drawn blood. There were spare horses to act as a baggage train and as substitutes when necessary. They carried money, arms of every kind and generous provisions. They were a passing brave sight. Eden wept shamelessly when she first set eyes on them, not believing they were for her.

"I wish you Godspeed, *ma belle!*" cried Isabella, kissing her heartily on both cheeks. "And I must say, in a way, I rather envy you. Shall I not go with her, Conrad?" she appealed to her husband who was giving last instructions to the knight he had selected as captain, one Robert des Moulins.

"Not you! I want you where I can see you. You'd soon put paid to my hard-won treaties," was the rude retort.

Eden smiled affectionately; she had never expected to see the magnificent Marquess in such a domestic light as she did now.

"If you should encounter a Saracen troop," he told her reassuringly, "especially during the first day or two, it isn't likely you'll be troubled." He helped her lightly into Balan's saddle. "The Sultan and I have . . . certain understandings about the territories near to Tyre."

His eye sparkled with satisfaction at her answering gasp. So it was true! The terrible rumors which had pervaded the Christian camp, saying that Conrad made his own treaties with the Infidel behind the backs of the three Kings. But now, strangely, with Conrad's men at her side and his young wife's kisses still warm on her cheeks, they seemed none so terrible at all.

She kissed her hands to them both in a last salute and resolutely tapped her heels against Balan's sides. Her soldiers fell in behind her, two by two, and she was away once more, without danger of pursuit and with a great deal more protection than she had ever expected.

The journey would be long and physically demanding. They would have to keep to the foothills and the desert scrub, avoiding the coastal cities and their outposts; for Sidon, Beirut and Byblios were all in Saracen hands and their garrisons might not be aware, so far north, of their Sultan's dealings with the Marquess of Montferrat. They would make camp at night and sleep on the ground beneath blankets, though Isabella had thoughtfully provided a little rolled mattress to give some comfort to Eden's tender bones. They would eat largely cold food, dried meat and fish and the delicious sweet known as rahat locoum, whose sugary, gellid substance gave energy as well as pleasure. Sometimes they would build a fire and cook what animals they could shoot, rabbits or perhaps a goat.

During the first morning they had made good time. The horses were fresh and the country not too difficult. They had rested briefly in the vicinity of the Hospitaler castle of Belvoir, although des Moulins would not seek entry on account of the fierce hospitality of the castellans. He did not want to lose the time they had made. However, they lay in the shade of a rest house near to a well of pure, refreshing water and waited till the noontide haze had shimmered away to nothing, secure in the knowledge that they were doubly safe from attack in such a place.

During the afternoon the sun seemed even hotter than it had at noon and the terrain became more hazardous. Eden found her head swimming at times; she had not ridden out into the desert beneath the hammer of the sun before. She was grateful to find des Moulins frequently at her side, a guiding hand steady upon her bridle as the palfrey stumbled over a rocky patch on the narrow, winding, hillside paths. The grizzled, deeply tanned knight said little, holding the opinion that conversation did not exist for its own sake, but rather for that of orders and questions . . . and the latter only when they were sensible questions. Although Eden felt that perhaps her captain might, if allowed to do so, disapprove more than slightly of his present task, she nevertheless developed a swift confidence in the gray-haired knight, feeling that her safety was in careful and conscientious hands.

Their way was through the fertile valley of the mellifluously named river Litani. They kept close to the slopes of its enclosing mountains with their cover of trees and scrub, for however attractive were the comfortable flatnesses and however strong the lure of the clear-running water, they would not risk being seen by some Saracen patrol as well concealed as themselves. Des Moulins had decided to make camp for the night on the upper heights of these same Mountains of Lebanon and the climb was gruelling. Eden had feared that the highly-bred Balan might tire too quickly upon such a forced march, but to her pride and delight he showed no such sign. He followed staunchly in the tracks of the great, heavily muscled destriers of the knights, picking his delicate way judiciously among the stones and roots as surely as if he had been mountain-born.

His mistress was excessively glad, however, when she was at last permitted to dismount. Jogging to Canterbury in the old days had been one thing; scaling tortuous goat-paths with the continual bumping and sliding, and even the occasional undignified fall, was quite another. Every bone in her body seemed bruised, and every complaining muscle stretched. She was grateful to the thoughtful knight who caught her in his arms to break her fall as she slid from the saddle; one more jolt and she would certainly have come apart. Making camp was a merry affair. Even the taciturn captain relaxed and smiled a little when they had built a fire and sat about it, roasting a young roe they had shot during the climb. Its flesh was delicious, with a sweet dryness to it, somewhere between the meat of a pig and a fowl. They washed it down with water from a pure mountain stream and a little precious wine. Afterwards they watched the sun go down in its usual flamboyant exultation of color. Even though this was the least likely spot in which to be surprised by wandering infidels, des Moulins did not encourage unnecessary noise; their talk was brief and desultory. They would rise at dawn. They needed their rest if they were to continue to follow these mountains. Soon every man had subsided beneath his blanket except for the four who took the first watch.

Eden, encircled by the bulky shapes of the four knights at a distance of about three yards, wrapped herself in her cloak beneath her own rug and hoped that when it came the piercing cold would not prevent her from sleeping. Staring between the crags that reared about her into that handsomely dying blood-red sun, she could not help but think of another like it. Was it only two nights ago that she had lain in Tristan de Jarnac's arms and found that the world had been made over again in an instant, just for them?

She closed her eyes, as though by shutting out the sight she could also shut out the memory. But though she no longer saw the sunset, she saw again the dawn of that unspeakable happiness in Tristan's eyes and opened her own once more, for she could not bear such torment.

She thought then of what she had done to him in that hour of weakness and self-deception, of what she had written to him in her stark, curt message. She had held out no hope, no love, not even friendship, nothing. It had been as remote and impersonal as a military order; it had been worthy of Coeur de Lion at his least humane.

She crawled with self-loathing. She had known it would be so, but that letter had been necessary. Their shared wound was slight, surely, and if it were given no chance to deepen, must surely heal?

And yet, and yet . . . if they never met again in this

life, how much she would regret this manner of leave-taking.

She brooded into the thickening darkness and prayed in pain and sorrow to the Magdalen whose land this was, to help her to erase the presence of Tristan de Jarnac from her mind and her heart forever. And as she prayed, she also wept.

She must think only of Stephen. Stephen, to whom, with luck, every stumbling step that day had brought her close; whom, very soon, she might find at last.

She was disconcerted to realize that with that thought, with its prelude to triumph and relief, there came also a shadowy sensation of something very much like fear; not fear of Stephen; that could never be. But of the strangeness that there might be between them now. So much had passed since last they met. Their young world at Hawkhurst now seemed as far removed from reality as the little pictures of castles in the margins of an hour-book.

As for herself . . . he must find her greatly changed. Were they changes that he would be able to bear, to accept, to live with?

Darkness enfolded her and lay heavy on her heart.

She was unaware that she had slept until she woke suddenly and sat up, her ears pricking. She strained her eyes into the blackness, conscious of something subtly altered in the cragged, alien shapes about her. Then she fell back again, her instinctive scream muffled in her throat by the cruel hand that gripped her jaw.

Cold sweat prickled at her rigid flesh. She felt the icy touch of steel against her throat and knew fear of death in all its terrible surprise. Guttural commands passed above her head. A rough hand encouraged her to rise. There was soft movement all about her. There were sounds, too, all of them slight; a rustle, a thud, a half-uttered cry. She could not see the man who held her arms pinioned at her back, but she began to make out the dim shapes of his collaborators, swift, slender shadows filled with a sinister purpose. The moon came suddenly out from hiding and she saw, with awful clarity, the whole hideous truth. As the small, neat figures of their murderers efficiently stowed their few possessions upon the backs of their now masterless horses, her brave escort sprawled where they had lately slept, their stillness far deeper than sleep. Des Moulins was quite close to her; he lay peacefully, gaping at the moon, an open gash spread like a dark scarf across his throat. His silence was now grave indeed.

Eden felt the shaking of her body; it surprised her for already she had accepted death. The knife still caressed her skin. If only it were swift! Unbelievably, the blade was removed. She turned to face her captor who now held her by one wrist.

White teeth gleamed in a face that was part of the darkness; a white turban was ghostly above it. A hand touched her breast but did not linger. There was a spurt of laughter followed by a summons. The lean shapes gathered round her and she became the center of a circle of questioning murmurs. The man who held her thumped his leather cuirass with a definitive thumb, making clean his claim to ownership. There was a sharp chorus of disagreement. Oh, sweet Jesu, Eden thought. Not all of them. Let me die first.

They seemed, however, to be in no particular hurry to rape her, settling instead, so far as she could tell, to a detailed argument upon their relative rights to do so. The man who held her, it became clear, was not their leader, for he regretfully released her wrist at the command of a taller figure, bearded and turbanned in some rich cloth that glinted in the moonlight. He came close to Eden and stared carefully at her. His shrewd black eyes contained no emotion. He asked her a question.

She shook her head. He spoke again; this time it seemed he wanted her name. Hopelessly, she obliged. It could mean nothing to him. Almost abstractedly she wondered who they were, these quiet, busy men who had brought death so swiftly in the darkness. She wished that she could see them better; so shadowy were they and so terrifyingly tranquil, with their soft voices and noiseless steps, that she would almost have thought them unreal, figments of a waking nightmare . . . were it not for the even quieter shapes upon the ground.

The leader was still speaking to her, but she could make nothing of his muted, faintly growling speech. Then she remembered another occasion when this had been the case; had she not saved herself from the questing hands of Isaac Comnenus's palace guards by stating a claim on the only name that had meant something to them? Surely there was one, now, perhaps two, that would mean a great deal to these masters of ambush?

She touched the bearded leader on the arm and gestured urgently toward the north, along the black crests of the ridge. "Ayub Ibn Zaydun," she said clearly. "Friend to Salah-ed-Din. I go to seek Ayub Ibn Zaydun." Again she repeated the name, injecting her voice with counterfeit confidence, pronouncing the words in his own deep-throated accent.

The Saracen made a startled exclamation, echoed by several of his troop. "Emir Ibn Zaydun?" It was obvious that he recognized the name, though his surprise was large.

No one touched her now. She felt her courage returning slowly as they stood in bewildered silence, pondering this unexpected turn. Then the talk began again, low and voluble.

The horses had all awoken and now Balan stood close behind the little group, nuzzling at her shoulder. She turned and laid a hand on his saddle, pointing again toward the north.

"Now! I must go now . . . to Emir Ibn Zaydun!" she cried boldly, making it seem that she demanded their escort.

They moved closely together for further discussion and she saw how few they were; there could not be a dozen of them . . . to have killed all her fine black and silver soldiers . . . Seeing them so deep in colloquy, she half considered leaping on to Balan's back and

taking her chances of escape . . . but she knew this
would be only to invite an arrow in her back. In an
agony of trepidation, she waited.

She watched while a man was dispatched to examine
the contents of her saddlebags, returning to his leader
with her precious hauberk over his arm. Her lip
twisted over their cries of admiration as Master Hugh's
handiwork was admired.

"This is yours?" was the leader's obvious question.
He stared in fascination at her nod. He then pointed
at the shortsword which hung from his own shoulder
in the infidel fashion. This time she shook her head, but
indicated, instead, the small sharp basilard at her belt,
and then the short bow carried by one of his men, together with the quiver of brief, black-feathered arrows.
She knew that Saracen women could be warlike
enough . . . she had heard their blood-chilling
screams as they had swarmed from the hills seeking
vengeance for the massacre, along with their men.
She would not have these murderers think she, too,
could not use a weapon if she willed it. But, although
she had shot many a deer and rabbit on her own
purlieus, she had never yet killed a man . . . though
there still lived one she should have killed. She thought
that now, if she had to do so, she could.

The leader was looking at her in deeply puzzled
calculation. She cursed her lack of the Arab tongue,
without it, she could neither hope to influence him nor
to discover what it was they would decide to do with
her. At last the bearded man gave out orders. His
men began to lead away the horses of the dead Christians. Others, to her disgust, swiftly deprived the
corpses of their arms and hauberks and their splendid,
blazoned tabards. Master Hugh's mail was rolled and
replaced in Balan's saddlebag. She showed no surprise
at this but obeyed the leader's signal to mount and follow close to him.

Dawn was lightening above the dark ridge as they
prepared to leave the rocky clearing and the sky fading to gray-cold. The inimical crags took on a more
neutral aspect and their tips were washed with what

would soon be color. As they rode out of that desolate place, Eden raised her head to gaze in steadfast, silent tribute at the twenty men they left behind them upon the ground, their white shirts crossed with the proud scarlet emblem of Christendom and bordered from shoulder to shoulder with their blood. An innocence invested them now, like that of sleeping children. They would lie thus, undiscovered, she thought, until they were dust; there would be none to speak at their funeral save the watchful, wheeling birds who already waited overhead, their dark wings holding back the day.

She had taken all that they had, even unto their life's blood and had nothing to give them except her prayers. She vowed that she would spend every second of whatever fearful journey was before her in prayer for the safe housing of their immortal souls. They had died with all their sins upon them, but they had been soldiers of Christ and must surely find eternal rest in his forgiveness. She bowed her head, her lips already moving, as she turned toward the path that would take them away from the strange and secret mausoleum of the knights and soldiers of Montferrat.

After one faint whicker of uncertainty, the little horse seemed content to follow the fierce, short-legged bay in front of him, glad, no doubt, to dismiss the scent of death from his nostrils. He was well rested and kept up without hardship. Eden, thankful that they had not made her ride upon an infidel's saddle, drew what little reassurance she could from Balan's familiar presence.

As the day dawned she could look more clearly at her captors. At first they all looked much alike, small, compact men with dark skins and sharp features, their noses curved and predatory, their eyes strangely soft beneath black, heavy brows. Some had small, pointed beards. All wore intricately wrapped turbans. Their mail was light and shorter than that affected by Christians; over it they wore embossed leather cuirasses after the Roman style. Their legs, which were short and sturdy like those of their muscular little horses, were covered in narrow white breeches, tucked into their unheeled boots of goat- or cowhide; some rode barefoot. They were as eager to look at Eden as she was to observe them. More than once she looked quickly away to avoid the white flash of a smile. She found their friendship no less fearsome than its opposite.

They must have been riding for half an hour before it suddenly struck her; they were heading straight for the rising sun. Wherever they were taking her, it was not to the northern fastness of Ibn Zaydun. She pulled up short and demanded, with graphic gestures, to know their destination, waving toward the north like a demented thing.

The leader looked at her from beneath diplomatically lowered lids. He sighed. For all she knew, they were simply taking her to some stronghold of their own, the better to have their way with her. Grimly she faced the prospect of serving each man's lust until they had tired of her at last and slit her throat like those of her companions.

Thick consonants clamored senselessly about her ears as their leader told her what he thought of her halting the horses on the precipitous path.

Mutely she refused to budge until her demands were answered. "Emir Ibn Zaydun," she insisted, pointing north once more.

The leader sighed again. Then he smiled; it was a pleasant smile, not that of a murderer, one would have said. Eden felt vaguely foolish, like a weathercock that would not heed the wind. But she did not lower her hand. The bearded man spat. He stabbed a mailed fist into the disk of the sun. "Qasaba!" he declaimed, firmly incomprehensible. "Damascus!"

Damascus! Eden dropped her reins. Saladin's capital! Her heart sank. If they took her there, so far from her way, surely she would never again see a Christian face. She tried to protest, but the leader ordered her to silence, his hand on his sword. They rode on.

She would have wept a great deal during that harsh and fearful journey had she not disdained to let them see her tears. Tears could bring her neither comfort nor relief; she had done with tears. She prayed fervently, however, as she rode, both for her dead and for herself, begging that she might be delivered from the hands of the infidel to complete the quest on which Christ himself, she had been so sure, had sent her. The Saracen turned and smiled at her as she completed her beseeching . . . and then it was as if the Savior had cast back her prayer in her face.

The journey became a daylight nightmare. She sun reached its most terrible intensity with a devastating speed and bored into her forehead without mercy. Weary and oppressed with sleeplessness and sorrow, her mind fought to release itself from reality in the only way possible. She began to sway in the saddle. Suddenly she slumped across Balan's neck; the man behind her came forward, reaching for her bridle.

After this she was unaware of the greater part of the day. Sometimes she would swim down from where she floated, without sight or feeling, far removed from her unwanted, suffering body. She would be conscious then of lying on the ground, of a scented shade and quiet voices. She knew that sometimes she drank water; at others a fiery liquid.

Of her precarious descent of the mountain pathway, supported against the shoulder of the bearded leader, and secured to his saddle lest she should slip, she knew nothing at all.

Seeing her predicament, the leader, whose name was Kamal, decided it might be better this way. She should remain asleep until they had crossed the next range of mountains, the Anti-Lebanon, which now lay before them. He knew the paths better than any man; it would be but one night and one day's journey. It would be kinder thus, since the green-eyed girl was unwilling, and they would also make better speed toward their mistress, who expected them daily. A concoction was infused, involving certain herbs and a substance that Kamal had in the leather purse that hung at his belt. This was administered to Eden, who stirred only a little and then slept on.

Kamal saw the lines of weariness and tension leave

her face as she sank into this deeper sleep. She was indeed most beautiful, with her exotic Frankish coloring and her perfect woman's body. He felt the stirring in his belly and frowned at himself. She was not for him, he knew it. The mistress would say that he had done well; that would be his reward. He had the men construct a litter for their captive, out of sweet-smelling cedar branches from the oasis where they rested and a close-woven Egyptian rug. He gave orders that she was not to be jolted; he did not wish her to awake.

As they set out once more, Kamal thought it a pity that she could not enjoy the beauty of these mountains, where the cyclamen clung among the rocks, mocking the thorny ilex with its delicate pink and white blossom. On the lower slopes the red anemone and the hibiscus vied in scarlet and the yellow and crimson tulips bloomed among the fruit trees and the olive groves. Such a heavy heart would not be attuned to beauty, however. It was understandable but equally regrettable, for this was a land that surpassed all others. He would ensure that she was fully awake before they reached the flower of all cities. Surely the loveliness of Damascus would make her smile a little? He wanted the mistress to see her at her best.

In the event he chose his moment well. When they had reached the lower slopes of the hills he had Eden carried in her litter up onto a rocky outcrop that looked over the plain. He stood before her holding out a cup of light wine and spoke to her softly and urgently until she murmured a little and opened her eyes. Awake, she instinctively reached for the cup and drained it, for her thirst was strong. She was surprised at the feeling of well-being that was with her. A vague sensation that she should not have such a feeling was immediately dissipated by the Saracen's cheerful smile. Inexplicably, she gave way to the temptation to return it.

It was late afternoon. The air was pleasantly warm and the light breeze delicious. There was a lightness too, it seemed, within her own slightly dazed head. She was conscious, in some previously unexperienced way, of the bones of her skull, of their slight weight, their brittleness and hollowness. It was not unpleasant, merely a discovery. Her eyes felt astonishingly clear and her mouth pure and sweet. She scarcely was aware of her body, so total was her relaxation. She had never been so deeply rested. She stared at Kamal, questions dawning in her eyes. He nodded and continued to smile. Gently he took away her cup and helped her to sit up. Then he stepped out of her view.

"Behold! Damascus!" he said with infinite pride.

Even he was satisfied by her gasp of pure delight.

The city seemed to float above the plain like some exquisite mirage compounded all of light and whiteness. Slender minarets, swelling, triumphant domes and graceful towers rose through a wide reach of rolling foliage that was a deep, dark green and filled with peace like a still sea. There was a quality to the light that is seen in England only after rain, when every hue is deepened and enhanced to an almost surreal intensity. Eden felt that if she were to reach out she could grasp the vision. Such an intimation of beauty possessed a spirituality that was almost tangible. She felt her soul fly toward it as it might fly toward God. The perfection of Damascus pierced her heart. For timeless moments she forgot herself, her interrupted quest, her fears, her present situation, everything—while she gazed upon it in wonder and joy. Her eyes washed still clearer by her involuntary tears, she exchanged a glance of complicit understanding with Kamal. It must be wonderful indeed to have such a city welcome one as home.

It was the time of the Muslims' afternoon prayer. They could hear the chant of the adhan, the muezzin's call to the faithful, soaring from each delicate minaret like the cry of strange birds. There was a stream nearby where Kamal and his followers performed the ritual cleansing of face, hands, arms and feet, before kneeling upon the mats they carried beneath their saddles to face Mecca, the birthplace of Mohammed.

Eden had been surprised by the strictness with which they kept their religion; each day they had prayed, at sunrise, at midday, afternoon, at sunset and in the evening. Even as she had slept she had sometimes been aware of their murmuring voices as they recited verses from the Qu'ran, which all seemed to know by heart.

She had found herself, somewhat painfully, wishing that she were as good a Christian. Her prayers, of late, had been confined to beseeching, regret and desperate pleas for forgiveness, with little of joy or praise. And if she could not drive from her mind the way Kamal and his men had so coldly and quietly murdered her escort, neither would she ever erase the cruel memory of Richard's slaughter of the hapless garrison at Acre.

CHAPTER TWELVE

Damascus

Their descent to the plain was swift and smooth. Eden, riding Balan again, reveled in the enclosing shade of the stately, dark-hued trees, cedar and cypress, oak and poplar. But for the sand beneath her feet she might have thought herself in England, so familiar was the green cover. It was refreshing, too, to encounter other human faces . . . though these were far from reminding her of England . . . After the desolation of the hills it was good to see the swarthy men riding about their business along the broad avenues, or to catch the flicker of a curtain upon a closed litter that might hold some veiled beauty. She watched a train of sulky-faced camels with delight; their disdainful faces would never cease to amuse her.

She was also aware of frequent curious glances as they rode; she supposed her looks to be as foreign to the inhabitants as were theirs to her. Also it was not customary in Syria for women to travel unveiled. They had not come far into the city when Kamal took a left-hand turning and they were climbing a gentle slope once more, still beneath a roof of interlaced trees that recalled the nave of the great cathedral at Canterbury. They reached a high, sheer, white and windowless wall over whose top they could see yet more trees. In it was a great bronze gate, carved with a complexity of interlocking lines forming a pattern of stars.

Kamal pounded upon the heavy, moon-shaped knocker. The gate was flung open and all was noise and movement. They were in a large, oblong courtyard surrounded by a covered cloister like that in the palace at Acre. It was filled with restive horses whose outstanding breeding was immediately apparent, and with turbanned, smiling men, all of whom fell upon Kamal and his party in vociferous welcome. Their amazement at Eden was comic to behold. But although each one stared at her as though he had never laid eyes upon a woman, their looks were in no way disrespectful, much less anything approaching the unabashed lechery of the average Frankish soldier.

Kamal was impatient. He shook off his friends and, bidding her to follow, strode importantly along the cloister and beneath an arched doorway. His pace was so fleet that Eden received little more than brief, interrupted impressions of surroundings that were prodigally ornate. There was color everywhere, notably a great deal of gold and of the clear, singing blue that was like the breast of a kingfisher. Every wall was glossily tiled and every doorway decorated as if it might be the gate to paradise. There were numberless fountains giving vivid life to each brilliant court or garden, even without the company of the hundreds of feverishly bright-colored birds who shrilled their sunset prayer in every tree.

With a sense of having reached the center of things, they came to a walled garden of immeasurable beauty.

Scent and color flew to meet her in a flurry of blue and green and violet; at the same time she was conscious of an order within the apparent chaos of flowers and foliage, fountains and feathered creatures, of symmetry in the overflowing beds and paths. She followed Kamal, past a fountain whose tall jets sprayed them with a welcome coolness, toward a little blue-domed edifice beneath fruit trees at the end of the garden. This was an octagonal platform with low walls tiled in blue and green, inlaid with silver; several slender wooden pillars, enriched with a cursive design in black and azure, supported the silvered, turquoise dome. The floor flowed over with soft-textured carpets, cushions and bolsters in the same blue, green and violet hues that filled the consciously rioting flowerbeds.

At its center, quite alone, a woman sat, playing up-on a full-bellied instrument resembling a lute.

She did not look up as they approached. She sat cross-legged upon the cushions, her back straight as a spear, her head bent in concentration. A cloudy fall of hair, a dense black with one startling streak of silver, hid her face. She wore a white robe of thin, em-broidered silk and a violet shawl hung loosely over her arms. Her hands were very long and narrow, their nails filed to perfect half-moons which plucked the double strings without a single dissonance. Their skin was a smooth, dark gold and their backs were painted with intricate arabesques in some sepia coloring.

Kamal halted three yards in front of her and fell to his knees, his forehead touching the ground.

Eden stood behind him, motionless and straight.

The careful notes fell into the late afternoon like pebbles into a still pool. The melody was unlike any-thing Eden had heard; its scale seemed to have no beginning and no ending, the music spiraling, descend-ing and spiraling again to attain, it seemed, an irre-mediable excess of pain and longing and loss. It was impossible to be unaffected by it.

When it was done, the woman lay down the instru-ment and raised her head. She had the face of an idol, of a pagan goddess, of a mystic saint. The black hair sprang back, its silver wings arching from a perfectly oval, golden mask, where eyes of fierce jet dominated and demanded. She lifted the fingers of one hand.

Kamal rose, bowed and began to speak.

Occasionally, the woman asked a question. Her voice was low and mellifluous with a slight harshness to it that did not grate. Eden caught the name of Ibn Zaydun and saw a flicker of interest invade the mask. After a brief exchange Kamal was dismissed, having received certain instructions to which he had bowed in instant submission. Once more his head touched the ground at her feet before he left the garden.

"Eh bien, mon enfant," pronounced the woman surprisingly in near-perfect southern French. "Let me discover who you are and where you come from."

Eden was conscious of a blinding relief. If the woman were French, all would surely be well. She gave hasty details, concealing nothing, telling of her home, her quest, her capture, emphasizing her position at Berengaria's side.

"And now," she finished courteously, "that I have made myself known to you, lady . . . will you not do the same for me?"

The crescent brows arched with the faintest suggestion of surprise. Kamal had been remiss.

"My name is Al-Khatun . . . the Lady of the Moon," she announced with exquisite pride. "I have the honor to be the chief concubine of the mighty Sultan Yusuf Ibn Ayyub, Salah-ed-Din. I rule in this palace in his absence. I am the mother of his first son, the Emir Al-Afdal."

Saladin's concubine! And yet so proud. And Kamal, the leader of an armed troop, had abased himself to the ground before her. Clearly such concubinage was in no way to be compared with that of the bathhouse favorites of the Emperor of Cyprus. With what, then? Nonplussed, Eden scoured her experience. She thought of the Fair Rosamund, mistress of the late King Henry, whom it was said Eleanor had poisoned in her palace of pleasure at Woodstock; but she had been, by all accounts, a poor, clip-winged, fragile thing . . . whereas this imperious woman was gilded all over with the lustre of power.

"Why have they brought me to you?" she asked, still courteous, but with a brave bid for equality in her tone.

Al-Khatun smiled lightly. Her lips were full and finely shaped, stained with deep crimson. "Because Kamal knew that I had need of a Frankish slave," she said with gracious condescension.

"A slave," Eden cried involuntarily. "No!"

"Your duties will not be strenuous," the Sultan's concubine continued as if she had not spoken. "It is very well that you are of high birth and station. That is what I should have wished in one who will instruct my youngest son, el-Kadil, in your tongue and the

ways of your people. My Lord Yusuf desires there
should be greater understanding between Moslem and
Christian in the land they share; only thus may we
put an end to strife between us."

Eden was filled with wonder, herself forgotten.
"You can speak thus," she pondered, "after what has
passed in Acre? You do not seek the death of every
Frank in Syria in revenge?"

Al-Khatun sighed deeply, her brooding eyes far
away. "I think as my Lord Yusuf thinks . . . in this,
as in all things," she said softly, the pride displaced
by open sorrow. "There have been too many such
bloody pages in the history of our land. And I know,
as you must know, that the blood has not all been the
blood of Islam."

Eden hardly knew whether to feel admiration or contempt for such fatal acceptance. She tried to imagine
Richard Plantagenet speaking thus had Saladin slain
three thousand English troops.

"I thank you for the honor you show me in your
willingness to entrust your son to me," she declared
formally, a prayer behind each word. "But I would
ask you . . . out of the love and duty you clearly bear
the Sultan . . . to set me at liberty to continue my
journey. *My* duty is to my husband, whom the Sultan
has promised to set free . . . and has not. It is known,
even among Christians, that Saladin is a man of his
word. You would have him keep his oath, would you
not?"

Al-Khatun smiled her serene, elliptical smile. She
tossed a cushion at Eden's feet and bade her sit. Eden
did not want to do so, feeling that her height and
ceremony gave her some slight advantage during this
gentle duel. But she did not wish to seem churlish, so
she sank down, keeping her back as stiff as possible.

"If the Sultan has promised it, your lord will be set
free," the husky voice assured her. "If he lives."

"And how shall I know it, if I am a prisoner in
Damascus?" was the anguished cry.

The oval mask was imperturbable. "You will not.
Perhaps, however, if you please me, it might be made

known to you in time. I have many ways of gaining information."

Desperation grew. She would have to plead. "You are a woman . . . a woman who loves and is loved. Can you not find it in your heart to aid another such? I cannot, I must not stay here."

Al-Khatun regarded her closely, heavy lids lowered to reveal their outline of black kohl. "Do you, then, so greatly love your husband?"

The question eluded her guard, she flushed and murmured, "Lady . . . I have not seen him for two long years." She knew this should not have been her answer. Why had she not spoken a simple, heartfelt, "Yes"? Now it was too late.

"Then you may wait a little longer without harm," said Al-Khatun, with an ambiguous, gentle smile. "Perhaps I might have your lord sent here; you could find a new life, here in Damascus . . . if this were your wish when the time came . . ."

"It is not my wish! It will *never* be my wish!" Eden cried, angrily at last. "My only wish is to leave Damascus . . . to go home, with Stephen to our domain in England. Cannot you understand that?"

"I understand it very well." The delivery was cold. "But it is of no significance to me. You will stay here and you will teach my son. I do not offer you a choice."

Eden saw that she was beaten. The thoughts blundered through her head like confused birds trapped inside stone walls.

"Very well," she said dully, inclining her head without humility.

Resistance, she knew instinctively, would merely lead to lock and key, and that way, she would never be able to leave Damascus. If she were to accept her task with a seeming good grace, however, perhaps she might eventually be allowed a certain amount of freedom; even a slave might leave the palace occasionally. And when that came about, one day she would make her escape. She might be too late to find Stephen, but it was a better chance to take than that of their both ending their days in beautiful, alien Damascus, far from their own few acres of Christendom.

"It shall be as you demand," she said to Al-Khatun, unsmiling. "I will instruct your son as best I may." She made a private vow that she, too, would set herself to learning . . . in the Arab tongue. She hated the helplessness she felt without it.

"There is one more thing," said Al-Khatun dismissively. "You must receive your own instructions . . . in the faith of Islam. I am duty bound to your conversion. There can be no Christian in Saladin's palace."

"That, lady, will never be." Eden looked her determinedly in the eye. "You have power over my body, I cannot deny . . . but you have none over my immortal soul. It belongs to Christ and will remain his."

Again the elliptical smile. "We shall see. I will send you a tutor." She pulled on a silken tassel hanging from one of the wooden pillars and a tiny, tinkling carillon was heard from a little bunch of silver bells suspended from the center of the blue dome.

At once a bevy of brightly clad servant girls appeared, in diaphanous robes, with delicate veils across the lower part of their faces. Watching their chattering approach, Eden was suddenly surprised that their mistress herself went unveiled. Was it because she had no shame . . . or because her power placed her far above such shame?

The dusky girls were silenced by a finger and stood cheerfully to receive their orders. Then, smiling and chirping, they led Eden away. Remembering Xanthe, she found herself returning their smiles. She did not need to understand their ceaseless talk; no words were needed to express food, shelter and a change of clothing. Indeed she was grateful for her rose and green gown, though its stuff had weathered the mountains and was in sore need of cleaning.

She chose a blue-gray robe from the closet she was shown, but determinedly refused the foolish little face-mask that went with it; she would not be able to bear the irritation of the flapping gauze over her nose and mouth. It appeared that she was to sleep in a curtained-off cubicle in a large dormitory chamber occupied by, perhaps, twenty girls. She could not tell whether they were more of Saladin's concubines, his harem, or merely house slaves. As for her own standing in the strange household, time would describe it to her. But she did not think that life was going to be altogether unpleasant for as long as she must remain in this new, beautifully set jewel of a prison.

Al-Khatun's youngest son was a grave boy of twelve with his mother's deep gold skin and a thoughtful, sensitive face. He was a tall, slender child and did not look strong but his speech was punctuated by frequent, energetic gestures, as if his body were a mere vehicle for a restless and inquiring mind. When they met, in a map-lined room filled with precious books and parchments, he treated Eden with careful courtesy overlying deep curiosity. Already he had learned a few halting words of French but his accent was comic and his intonation had a rhythm all its own.

He had prepared a short speech with which to greet his new tutor. "Learned lady, I am happy to learn your tongue. My mother has said that we may speak together of all things that are of your country . . . but it is forbidden to speak with me about the Christian faith."

Eden thanked him solemnly for his welcome; the stricture was only to be expected. She intended to go about her lessons as she had done when, once, at Hawkhurst, she had taught one of the Saxon-speaking children a certain amount of French. The child had been intelligent, the second son of the miller, who wanted to leave the land and take up a trade in the town. She had persuaded him that he would better himself more easily if he mastered the tongue in which all matters of moment were conducted. El-Kadil was of a different station in life, but one willing and ready-witted child will learn as happily as another. Her common-sense methods had borne fruit enough with young Mat to give her the confidence she needed now.

When they had seated themselves upon the carpeted floor she commenced by pointing at various objects in the room, giving them their Norman names. Like most of the chambers in the palace, it possessed very little in the way of wooden furniture. There was no table, for instance, but two of the small, folding writing-desks which could be set at various levels, depending on the wishes of the scribe. Eden found it very pleasant to live much of life sitting on the ground, although it would have been unthinkable in the draughty homes and castles of England.

When they had exhausted the furnishings, the hangings, the rich rugs and cushions, the rolls of parchment, the maps and fine miniature paintings heaped in a small chest, they came to give names to each of the astonishing array of colored inks with which El-Kadil was making his own painstaking and decorative map of the city of Damascus. Eden was enchanted by the clarity and strength of the colors. She had seen and used black ink many times, of course, and green and sometimes red, but never the azure, the sapphire, the violet, the saffron, the cyclamen which the boy employed with such controlled ease.

El-Kadil smilingly held up one of the little glass jars; it was a deep leaf-green, tending toward olive, with a tinge of gold.

"This one . . . you . . . eyes!" he achieved shyly, his own full of approval. "Here . . . eyes black, brown . . . no green!" Then he pronounced several words of Arabic, which, though she could not understand them, she imagined to be complimentary.

"May I help you, Lady Eden? He says that your gaze is as the beauty of green leaves glimpsed behind a waterfall . . . a fine judgment for one of his tender years!"

She turned in surprise at the light, masculine tones of the smoothly spoken French. The smiling young man who leaned against the arched doorway was of middle height and wore vivid robes of scarlet and blue beneath a magnificent golden turban. His skin was very dark and had a bloom on it like mulberries. His face was eager and sensual, but lacking neither in authority nor strength.

"Forgive me." He came further into the room and salaamed with liquid grace. "I am Al-Ahkis, dragoman and councillor to the exalted Al-Khatun. I do not speak your language as well as I would wish . . . but if you have need of an interpreter during your first steps with your pupil . . ."

She saw that he stared at her with almost as open and frank an appreciation as the boy had done. She felt discomfited by her position on the ground. Seated at his feet, she could hardly return his bow.

"I thank you. It is good to hear my own tongue; you pronounce it excellently," she said without flattery. "But the boy learns quickly and our lessons are not yet difficult. I think we shall progress favorably without aid for a time." She hesitated. She did not wish to refuse him. It was good to speak French after the incessant chatter of the dormitory. His splendid robes betokened a high position in the household and he seemed disposed to be friendly toward her, but there was something in his candid and admiring gaze that made her unwilling to continue the lesson beneath it.

"Perhaps," she added pleasantly, "when there are deeper notions to be expounded than mere names and actions, I might then call upon your assistance?"

His smile was white, assured and lazily attractive. It was evident that he wished to put her at ease.

"Indeed, I hope that you will do so. But I trust we shall see much of each other for another reason. I should explain . . . the gracious Lady of the Moon has ordained that, when my other duties permit, I am to supervize your instruction in the faith of Islam. It will give me great joy to do this."

"Indeed." Eden was suddenly cold. "I have already made it clear to your mistress that I will have none of such teaching."

Al-Ahkis seemed unabashed. He smiled, as one might smile at a child whose conduct has been disappointing. "Al-Khatun has commanded it," he said with gentle finality. "It is for us to obey."

"It is not your Sultan's whore who is my mistress, but the Queen of England!" Eden flashed with studied insolence. "You may speak as many words as you will, but they will blow upon the wind. I will not forsake Christ who is my comfort and my strength."

"The words will not be mine, but those of Allah," the steward replied with unaltered courtesy. He nodded dismissively to El-Kadil who was watching the exchange with wide-eyed interest. "Kamal has a horse for the boy, outside in the stable court. You permit him to finish his lesson?"

"It seems I have no power to refuse," said Eden icily.

With a worried glance at her shut face, El-Kadil left in search of his horse, and the handsome Arab smiled at her reprovingly.

"You must not confuse your pupil with your anger. He is prepared to love and to trust you."

There was good sense in his words. "It is of no consequence to me whether or not he loves me," she retorted less than truthfully, for El-Kadil was an engaging boy and she, who had no children, loved to be in their company.

Uninvited, Al-Ahkis sank down with consummate economy of movement into the child's vacated place opposite Eden. He sat cross-legged and straight-backed upon the carpet as all of his race seemed able so effortlessly to do for long periods. He reached within his robes and produced a small, jeweled casket which precisely covered the palm of his hand. He held it out to her.

Half suspicious, half ashamed of her show of anger, she demanded, "What is it?"

"Take it."

Curious despite her annoyance, she took the box. It was made of soft leather in the ubiquitous brilliant blue of Islam, embossed with gold-leaf and held in an outer setting of pure gold, crafted into an intricacy of arabesque shapes whose delicacy amazed her eyes even as it tempted her exploring fingers. On one side a tiny key was set into a lock. She touched this, then drew back her hand, doubtful.

She felt his gaze upon her, amused and provocative. "Open it. It is yours."

She turned the key and pushed up the lid of the box.

Only it was not a box . . . it was a book . . . an inestimably valuable, inordinately lovely copy of the words of Allah to his prophet, Mohammed . . . the holy book of Islam, the Qu'ran.

"The workmanship is outstanding," she said with careful disregard of the contents. She felt that, in some subtle way, he was attempting to trap her. "I am desolated not to be able to accept such a gift," she said firmly, holding it out to him.

He made no movement toward it, only smiled gravely. "A gift, once given, cannot be returned. Among our people, to do so would be a great insult." His brown eyes rested on her in regretful sorrow. "We have been acquainted for less than a single hour; I have offered you only soft words and a gentle gift. Why then, woman whose eyes are green as leaves glimpsed through the waterfall, why should you wish to pay me insult?"

Without waiting for her answer he abandoned his strict posture for greater ease and arranged himself elegantly among the cushions, leaning against a striped bolster. Languid and assured, he prepared to listen to her.

She would not allow him to make her feel foolish. "It is a precious gift," she said earnestly, "and if I must keep it, I will indeed treasure it for its beauty . . . for I cannot do so for the message it contains."

Again the blossoming, easy smile. "Enough. It is a beginning," he murmured. The subject was closed. She saw that he would not press her further for the moment.

"How is it that you speak my tongue?" she asked

then, as he had obviously no intention of leaving her.

She was rewarded by the kindling of interest in eyes which would otherwise have been content merely to gaze and gaze upon her as though she were some public spectacle. "For two years I spoke little else," he told her ruefully. "I was a prisoner of the Franks until I was ransomed two years ago by the Sultan personally."

"He must set great store by your talents."

He inclined his head neutrally, but did not enlarge.

"Where were you imprisoned?" she asked, curious.

"In a city called Tyre. Perhaps you know it? I was the prisoner of the Marquess of Montferrat."

Eden's cry was almost one of joy; his casual words had dropped precious familiarity into the alien day. "I had just left the Marquess's household when I was captured," she told him. Then, in a sudden angry and bitter recollection. "The men Kamal slaughtered all belonged to him!"

Al-Ahkis's frown was swift and deep. "I did not know that," he said with genuine regret. "I am very sorry for it."

It was difficult to be angry with him. Besides, he was not, it seemed, himself a soldier, but some kind of administrator.

"If Conrad of Montferrat is your friend, lady, you have been fortunate. He is a strong man, and perhaps in time may be a great one."

"And your enemy, surely?" she asked, surprised by his praise of the Marquess.

He shrugged a blue-clad shoulder. "I developed a respect for him; there was time. He treated me well. We became friends . . . insomuch as it was possible. We played chess together. I taught him a little Arabic. He is a good soldier, and a brave leader, but he would prefer, if he were able, to build up the trade of his land rather than spend its blood. My master, Salah-ed-Din, was favorably impressed by what I had to say of him."

"So much so that now he will treat with Conrad, apart from the rest of the Christian leaders," said Eden thoughtfully. "I, too, admire the Marquess . . . but I hope he may remain on the side of Christ."

Al-Ahkis showed his surprise. "Are such treaties common knowledge? Then Conrad had certainly better step carefully."

"There are many in the Christian camp who already call him traitor," she agreed.

"But he is not?" He scrutinized her carefully.

"No. I think not," she said slowly. "But you have known him longer than I."

"He was all ambition at that time. And then he took Tyre. He has kept it."

"He is still ambitious, nevertheless." She thought, with a sensation almost like homesickness, of that tall, dominant figure defying the Lionheart.

"For the crown of Jerusalem," affirmed the Arab quietly. "But we do not intend to let the Cruciati have the city of Jerusalem. Without that, its crown is but a mirage, a poor thing of no substance."

"We will take Jerusalem with or without your let; be sure of that!" she declared proudly, lifting her chin.

The alertness and interest drained from his face, to be replaced by the previous lazy amusement. "You must no longer concern yourself with these things. Your life is now here in Damascus where there will be no echoes of the far-off struggle. It will be a better life than you expect," he added as her face clouded.

"The life of a slave? How can that be?" she cried furiously. "I, who have ruled in my own domain in England, as Al-Khatun does in this palace!" She despised the sympathy in his look.

"You must learn to forget the past; it is behind you; there is no way back. It will be better for you if you try to accept this," he said with deep earnestness. "A slave in the palace of Al-Khatun is not a slave in the household of Richard of England. Here, slaves may rise to considerable fame, to great riches. Many of our esteemed scholars are slaves, our philosophers, our scribes, our engineers. The Lady Al-Khatun is herself a slave, in a manner of speaking. The children of slaves are educated above those of free men; it is one of our prized principles. It ensures the virility of the race, for new blood begets new ideas . . ."

Here his eyes covered her with a slow, fastidious appraisal, so intimate and deliberate that it was as if he had drawn his slender, sensitive fingers over her body. She shuddered slightly, not with displeasure.

"If you were to marry in Damascus . . ." he continued suggestively . . .

"Have you not been informed? I have a husband," Eden broke in.

"Ah yes, that . . . I was aware of it." He sighed. How was he to make her understand? "A slave to Islam has no rights or duties beyond Islam," he explained with careful relentlessness. "Your marriage by a Christian priest is meaningless here. You may marry when and to whom Al-Khatun commands."

A stabbing cold invaded her. She had been right, then, to sense a more terrible prison than that of white walls and silken hangings. Not only did they have her unwilling body in their keeping but they would make what use of it they wished and put her soul in danger to do so. And beyond this, they would try to take that soul and corrupt it with the foul heresy of Islam.

This last she did not fear. Her allegiance to Christ was as real and as clear to her as her duty to Hawkhurst or to her father had been. This soft-spoken councillor could not hope to destroy it with his infidel doctrines, no matter how persuasively he argued. Her spirit was her own; it was safe in Christ.

But her body . . . how if they indeed united her in some heathen ceremony to a lustful Saracen? What would her life be then?

She felt panic rising within her and stifled the impulse to cry out, to run from the room, to try, against all the obvious checks and hazards, to escape from the trap which had closed about her.

Al-Ahkis, sensing something of what she must feel, inwardly applauded the calm with which, after a space, she answered him.

"It is considerate of you, sir, to trouble to make my

situation more clear to me. Is there, perhaps, more that I should know? I do not like surprises." She hesitated. "Am I to live behind locked doors, for example? Is a slave regarded as a prisoner . . . or as a menial member of the household . . . like my own serfs, at home in England?" She determined to insist upon her noble status at every turn; it might gain her some as yet unknown privilege that could be turned into an advantage.

Al-Ahkis smiled, understanding perfectly. "At present you are both slave and prisoner . . . because if given the opportunity, you would undoubtedly seek, foolishly, to escape."

"Then I shall always remain a prisoner," she averred.

"Perhaps not," he said gently. "You will soon discover that it is not possible for you to leave either the palace or the city without surveillance. All gates and walls are well guarded; the Sultan's most precious possession lies in Damascus. The guards will be given your description; a woman of your unique coloring is not hard to recognize. But one day, sooner than you imagine," he added, with his brilliant, caressing smile, "you may find you no longer wish to leave. All things are possible. And then . . ."

"Then," she broke in dryly, "I shall be no longer a prisoner . . . merely a slave!"

He shook his head in mock despair at her sarcasm and rose to his feet with the spare, flowing motion that seemed characteristic of him.

"You are the Lady Eden, gracious tutor to my mistress's son . . . and as such are highly honored amongst us." He stood looking down upon her, his rich robes brushing her shoulder, one hand resting elegantly upon the jeweled dagger at his hip. With the other he reached out and touched her hair, so lightly she could not be certain that he had done so.

"I will come to you again, tomorrow . . . after the evening prayer," he told her. Although he had shown her nothing but kindness, she found she was afraid of his coming.

The next day she dedicated herself to her small pupil, making an effort to redeem his goodwill and win his friendship which was readily received. El-Kadil insisted upon showing her his fine new horse which he now proposed to name Franjik in her honor. She found, to her delight, that the pony shared the same stable as Balan, and so was able to introduce her own beloved palfrey to the boy. El-Kadil instantly suggested that they take both horses and go hawking together.

The sensitive child found himself wondering whether he had been kind to do so when, later, they rode among the foothills with the bright-eyed goshawks hooded at their wrists and a small detachment of the palace guard ever at their backs; for he watched with pity as her green eyes dissolved in tears of hapless envy of the birds' free-soaring flight.

"It is not . . . truth freedom," he said, hoping the words approximated his thought. "Hawk . . . come palace . . . to eat." His brown eyes regarded her anxiously.

She managed to smile at him though her heart was sick. "No . . . it is not a true freedom," she acknowledged, seeing his wish to comfort her.

But the palace hawks were tamed and trained to the lure, and, although that would never be the case with her, there was some wisdom in the reflection that if she were, by some miracle, to escape, she would not find food and shelter, helpless among these hills, as simply as a hawk may take its prey.

In the evening, however, she had an intimation, had she but recognized it, of what a Damascus lure might be.

On her return to the palace she found that a chamber of her own had been assigned to her, close by the library where she would take her lessons with El-Kadil. All her possessions, taken from Balan's saddlebags, had been distributed in a closet set in the wall or in the sandalwood chest that was the one piece of furniture in the room, apart from the low, boxed mattress which was the Saracen bed and the usual multitude of cushions and soft carpets. The predominating color was a deep rose-chestnut, echoed upon rich wall hangings. There was no door, only a heavy tapestry across the pointed archway, while one wall consisted of curtained embrasures looking on to a pleasant court boasting two fountains and many bright flowers. Although it would give her much relief to escape the tittering inanity of the slave-girls' dormitory, Eden's first reaction to her new chamber was a wild and bitter laughter.

No door. Could there ever have been such a paradoxical prison? Or such comfort in any chamber, even in a palace? She felt, with reason, that fate was playing some deep, deceiving game with her, and for a long while she sat brooding in resentment, staring at the wall, unable, perhaps even unwilling, to take comfort from prayer. She lay down and closed her eyes; sleep would shorten the day.

And then, as he had said he would, Al-Ahkis came again, on silent feet, pushing aside the tapestry as if he were in his own territory and coming to stand beside her, sliding his warm gaze over her where she lay, half seduced into sleep by the comfort of the deep mattress.

He wore only white, with the glint of gold about him, and his black hair, without its turban, curved about his dark face.

"I have ordered refreshment," he said softly. "I was told you did not eat."

"I have no wish to eat," she returned shortly, wishing that she too were on her feet.

"As you desire, naturally."

It would, as it happened, serve his turn better if she did not eat. The servant who appeared was told to take away all except one tall jug of fragrant pomegranate juice and a damascened tray of tiny, dark sweetmeats.

"These, at least, you will not refuse."

He knelt beside her and she took what he proffered, hardly caring whether she did so or not. She wished only that he would leave. The rustle of his robe seemed unnaturally loud to her overwrought senses and she was foolishly conscious of her own uneven breathing. She did not yet know why she was afraid of him. There was no threat in his sinuous, deliberate movements or in his soft voice which expressed only courtesy and concern. Nevertheless, she did not want him here.

She lay back against the pillows with a faint moan, one hand to her brow, and closed her eyes, trying to shut him out.

"You are not well," he said at once, his tone solicitous.

"My head aches a little, that is all. Perhaps if I were to try to sleep . . ." The lie came easily, though, truth to tell, there *was* an unaccustomed pressure behind her temples.

"Drink this," he murmured. "You will feel better. And eat. These are small, but there is much good in them . . ."

He held the cup to her lips and to prevent herself from being treated like a child she had to take it from him and drink. As she did so their hands touched and she gasped as though she had been burned.

If he noted the small sound he ignored it. He spoke quietly to her of El-Kadil and his talent for drawing in inks, his unusual sensitivity to others, his love of horses and all animals. He told her of Al-Khatun's pride in him, and her hope that this youngest, perhaps last child of the Sultan would be spared the need to follow the fortune of his brothers, all in arms at their father's side.

Al-Ahkis did not seem to require answers of her and slowly, gradually, the tension behind her brow abated and she herself to relax. She sipped at the luscious juice of the pomegranate and ate two of the small, sticky sweetmeats which were strongly redolent of some pungent herb that she did not know. In an effort to establish its nature she ate several more. Soon she found herself adding her own impressions to the Arab's shrewd judgments of the child, even laughing over his tale of how El-Kadil had once set off on horseback to join Saladin on the eve of a battle, determined to be every inch the warrior that his brothers were.

Time slipped away. She no longer wished for him to leave.

She lay back in the throes of a delightful, drowsy numbness; she felt no compulsion to talk, nor even to listen, though she did both intermittently, between, it seemed, long lacunae of drifting timelessness when she neither slept nor was fully awake, though she was constantly aware of the gentle monotony of his voice as an undertow to the current that rocked her so sweetly. And then it was as if they were, in truth, in a scarcely shifting boat; they were floating, directionless, far out to sea. They lay together in the bottom of the craft, couched in soft silk, and his hands moved slowly upon her suspended body in the ceaseless rhythm of the waters, caressing, receding, stroking, lulling . . . and yet insisting that she did not sleep.

She let the dulcet, flowing motion of the dream take her, aware of her body's blissful weightlessness and yet also of its heavy, dormant quality where his hands touched her, as if it attended his signal to bring her to instant, pulsating, sensual life.

There was an ineffably delicate movement at her throat. A tiny flame shot through her, deep into her loins. With half closed eyes she looked down and saw that her breasts were naked; he had untied her robe and laid them bare and now lifted his dark head from where he had laid his lips upon them. Al-Ahkis saw comprehension dawning in the green eyes with their diminished pupils, with fear following close behind. He drew back and knelt upon the ground beside her.

"You have no reason to fear me, Eden," he said clearly, though his voice was vibrant with desire for her. "I take nothing from a woman that she does not willingly give."

He reached out and covered her breasts.

"This I swear to you, and you will recall it when the time comes . . . I will do to you nothing that you have not wished me to do." With these quiet words he rose and left her making no sound as he glided across the carpet-strewn floor.

Her last sensation was a strange, aching deprivation as consciousness faded back into dreaming and she floated once more upon her limitless, gently moving ocean.

She slept as she had not done since she was a child and awoke with an inexplicable sense of elation. When she tried to recall the events of the last evening, she found it difficult to tell what had been dream and what, if anything, reality.

When next she met with Al-Ahkis he gave her no help. There was nothing in his grave, correct manner to suggest that there had been even the slightest intimacy between them. He merely asked, with perfect solicitude, if her headache were now quite gone. Since they were in the presence of El-Kadil, it was impossible for her to raise the suspicions that crowded her mind . . . and the next time they were alone together the dragoman's manner was so remote and formal as to make her blushingly certain that she had been the victim only of her own errant and sinful dreams.

She began a rigid and demanding ritual of daily prayer and penance, with the object of banishing all such impure thoughts from her mind and confirming her steadfastly in her religion. As a further punishment, in the absence of Father Benedict, she removed the seductively comfortable mattress from her bed and slept upon the hard, cedarwood base, hoping to prevent her body's further betrayal. She was disconcerted to notice, during the first of these uncomfortable nights, that the wood had a heavy scent, no longer smothered by the bedding; it was stimulating and alluring and she wished heartily that it could have been otherwise. There seemed no way to avoid the Godless luxury of Islam.

CHAPTER THIRTEEN

▼▼▼▼▼▼▼▼▼▼▼▼▼▼▼▼▼▼▼▼▼▼▼▼▼▼▼▼▼▼▼▼▼▼▼▼▼▼

Damascus, Al-Ahkis

And indeed, her personal privations apart, Eden was not allowed to avoid it, for it appeared, as the days passed into weeks and she learned to know her prison better, that beautiful, drowsy Damascus was the most sybaritic city on earth. Proudly called the Garden of the World, the Bride of the Earth, by its besotted inhabitants, it lay at the very heart of profane Islam as Mecca lay at its sacred center. Eden could not fail to admit its virtues as she rode among the shady groves and elegant residences; in and out of the labyrinth of suks that proliferated off the old Roman road stretching from the East to the Western Gate that was known as the Street called Straight. The beauty of the city was an expanded version of the tiny, jeweled Qu'ran that Ahkis had given her—an exquisitely wrought setting for the finest the Sultanate had to give.

Her tours were frequent, for El-Kadil was a restless boy, endlessly seeking new stimulus outside the palace walls, insisting upon Eden's company, for he loved to show her Arab ways and treasures in return for her teaching. Al-Khatun, too, claimed more and more of her captive's time, finding her a more rewarding companion than the light-minded women of her entourage. The Lady of the Moon proved to be a far more energetic woman than her long-eyed indolence gave witness and she went about her lord and lover's business with a single-mindedness that was hard to fault, whether in the courts of the law or of the merchants, among the palace musicians or the astronomers in their fine observatory.

Since Saladin had made the city his own in 1174 it had become the flourishing capital of an empire, burgeoning with trade, commerce and culture of every kind. The Sultan's interest in the sciences, especially that of medicine, in the education of his people, in the proper administration of his land, had attracted men of knowledge and genius from every part of the Orient.

In Damascus they worked, walked and talked together in a climate of mental freedom not to be found elsewhere, while the results of their deliberations reverberated through the knowledgeable world. No less thriving were the artists; the music-makers, the poets, the miniaturists who brought their finely detailed work from India and from Persia. As for the makers of textiles, the rugs, the tiles, the wonderfully decorated buildings—they were taken for granted and asked for no praise in praising Allah with their skills. Nor yet did the armorers, whose sultry little shops brought back poignant memories of Hugh of Winchester, and whose breathtaking designs and workmanship would have brought tears to his eyes. A damascened blade is a beautiful thing, perhaps the most beautiful in a city dedicated to beauty in all things.

Al-Khatun took care often to be seen about the streets; like the Sultan himself, she made herself approachable by all, high or low. Eden was forced to admire her lucid and logical methods of handling whatever problem might arise, whether it was a plea for justice by some trader who thought himself cheated, or for work for a poor peasant who had lost his land and had a family starving in the hills.

It was difficult, insidiously so, as she rode about the unfolding city, for Eden to remember she was a slave.

She caught sight once, as she trotted beside Al-Khatun's canopied litter, of a chained gang of Christians, ruddy-skinned, laboring beneath the harsh sun upon some immense building. They were very thin, though muscular, and the back-breaking work was unceasing. Al-Khatun, seeing her expression, leaned down to her, the scent of jasmine clouding about her.

"They have no need of your pity. They are well-fed and they do useful work so that we do not pay our taxes to keep them in idleness. They are building an addition to the hospital. And if one of them falls ill that is where he will be cared for, like any other man."

Eden said nothing. She thought of free men, back in England, who died daily in their stinking hovels without so much as an old crone skilled with herbs to tend them. The only English hospitals were kept by monks and if he wanted to be their patient, a man generally needed money.

Saladin had built two large hospitals in Damascus, both of them free to all in need of medical care. There were also no less than twenty colleges, some for lay studies, some rising out of the *madrasans*, the ancient schools for religious study. A promising student could further his education without lack of money standing in his way.

It was a new way to Eden, but she saw at once that it was a good way. Indeed the whole smoothly functioning city was a new world to her, one much resembling what, she had unwillingly learned during her increasingly self-conscious conversations with Al-Ahkis, was the Moslem vision of Paradise. "Reclining there upon soft couches . . . arrayed in garments of fine green silk . . . and adorned with bracelets of silver . . . they shall feel neither the scorching heat nor the biting cold. Trees will spread their shade around them and the fruits will hang in clusters over them . . ."

His warm, golden tones had, she found, an almost compulsive ability to make her remember his words. He did not try to teach her, for she would not stay with him if he did, but she had not forbidden him to read to her from the great writings of Islam, and much of what he read was from the Qu'ran. Also, he was engaged in the task of translating the holy book into Frankish and often sought her help in finding the exact word or the most apt phrase. She saw the fine-spun web; he did not attempt to hide it from her. It did not matter; she would not walk into it.

Eden gradually became almost accustomed to her well-filled life. She did not in any way deceive herself that she was not enjoying much of it, while that part of her mind that she kept closed to her surroundings took its sustenance from her private prayer and the unflagging determination to make her escape when the opportunity arose.

And then, one morning, while she supervised El-Kadil in a dissertation on horsemanship, written in a French which, though simple, was near perfect, she was summoned to Al-Khatun's blue and green garden.

The Lady of the Moon was resting in her shady kiosk, though the pen, ink and parchment at her side betrayed her previous labors.

"Come . . . sit beside me, Lady Eden," she invited, honoring her captive. Eden obeyed, folding her long legs beneath her now as easily as any native Syrian.

"My son has made excellent progress. I am greatly pleased with your talent as his tutor," the exalted concubine began. "Also, Al-Ahkis tells me that although you stubbornly adhere to your mistaken faith, you have not shown yourself ill-disposed toward Islam. He finds you to be a woman with an interest and intelligence beyond the ordinary. My dragoman is a man of judgment. I hold him in high esteem."

She hesitated as if expecting Eden to make some comment. None came, and Al-Khatun abandoned the subject of her steward for the moment. There was another matter that must, of necessity, come first . . . "I have some news for you," she continued with more gentleness than usual. "It concerns your husband."

Silenced by the hectic pumping of her own heart, Eden waited.

"It has come to my knowledge that the man you seek is, as you supposed, still the prisoner of Emir Ibn Zaydun."

"And the ransom?" Eden gasped. Her life in Damascus fell into dust, leaving her as she had been in Acre,

raw with waiting, wound to breaking point. And then
that too was shattered by the shock of Al-Khatun's
next words.

"He has been withdrawn from ransom; the Emir
does not wish to part with him."

"No! It can't be true! He *cannot* do it, surely!"

"He may do as he wishes; the man is his prisoner."

"But the treaty . . . Saladin's promise!" Eden be-
seeched her, her body contorted in desperation.

Al-Khatun spoke softly still, but with a terrible note
of finality. "You will not have forgotten Acre . . . the
Sultan will hardly trouble a faithful vassal to give up
his booty to a foresworn enemy. No. The business is
finished. You too must let it rest. Your husband is
dead to you."

Booty! A dead man! Was that how they saw him?
How they would have her see him? She would not
weep before this proud woman, but she cried aloud
inside, cursing Saladin who had not kept his promise,
but far more deeply cursing Richard of England whose
foul inhumanity had made him break it.

"But he is not dead; he lives," she whispered fiercely, when she could speak, challenging the imperious
face before her. "And if he is alive, he may yet escape
. . . or be rescued."

Al-Khatun smiled with obvious pity. "If he es-
capes he will be caught and killed, be sure of it; or he
would die in the mountains. And who is to rescue him
from the Emir's eyrie? Yourself, perhaps? Who else
would try? No, Eden, it is senseless to think on it. We
shall not let you go. And you will forget him in time.
You have much to concern you here, and I think that
in the past weeks you have not been unhappy . . ."

For an instant Eden hated her for the bitter truth of
those last words.

Saladin's mistress saw that this was not the time to
speak further of the virtues of her handsome steward.

Later, having set her stone-faced captive the task of
classifying her large collection of French and German

silver, a labor from which she should find it difficult to detach her unhappy mind, the Lady of the Moon sent for her most valued servant.

Seeing that they were to be alone, the dragoman lifted his lady's hand and kissed the inside of the wrist, a caress known only to the two of them. Several years ago, when he had first come to the Sultan's palace, her eyes had fallen upon the ambitious and comely young man. He had raised his own to meet them and had not been afraid, despite the indignity and death that awaited any who dared to fill Saladin's place in his absence.

What had passed between them was over, finished long ago, and was locked in no heart other than the two that beat now in the glowing garden. Neither, however, were small enough in spirit to pretend it had never been, and now they shared a deep and mutual respect.

Now Al-Ahkis sat in Eden's vacated place. They drank wine together like old friends and Al-Khatun asked him if he were of the same mind in a certain matter.

"Yes, Princess," he sighed lightly, "it must be this woman and no other. Her strangeness has a rare potency for me. I am enamored of her green eyes and her golden hair . . . and of her spirit which is strong and lovely."

"So deep in love," murmured Al-Khatun innocently, "and yet you have not conquered her body. How is this . . . you who have so many women languid with love for you?"

He bore her teasing with a smile, sensing the merest iota of jealousy behind it, and was glad for the sake of what was past and because she was beautiful beyond all women save one.

"She still cleaves to her husband's memory," he observed regretfully, "but this cannot be for much longer; it is not in the nature of women that it should be."

"No. And there is a thing you should know . . ." She told him how it stood with Eden's husband.

His eyes gleamed with expectant pleasure. "Then in truth it cannot be long . . ."

"I think not. Court her, my friend. Has she had drugs?"

"Hashish. Once. A little."

"Then give her a little more. While she thinks of the past . . . and she does not only think of her husband, I am certain . . . she suffers. As soon as you have made her yours, she will suffer no longer, but cleave only to you; she will become enamored of your body . . . as others have done . . ." Her look was warmly reminiscent, but there was no invitation in it, and he knew that, whatever else she might feel in the secret recesses of her singular being, she wished him well with the Lady Eden as she wished him well in all things.

When he was about to leave her at last, he kissed the hem of her robe in gratitude and reverence.

"One thing more . . ." Her slight movement of the hand arrested him.

"Lady?"

"This young Marquess of Montferrat . . . my lord's letters say much of him. He respects the man, but fears he may one day present a threat to us with a united Jerusalem at his back . . . if Allah should permit such a tragedy to occur. He once said it were good if such a man should die young. Are you of this opinion?" Her voice was light, but she held his eyes in a long look.

Slowly, Al-Ahkis shook his head. "No, lady. That is not my Lord Yusuf's way."

He could not have described her smile. "No, it is not," she agreed softly. "Sometimes a man such as my Lord Yusuf has need of others . . . and other ways . . ."

Al-Ahkis stood before her in silence. He knew her; he had never feared her; but he feared her a little now.

"My ways are my lord's ways . . . and cannot change," he said with quiet certainty. Then he salaamed, but not to the ground, and left the garden.

El-Kadil was excited. He was to visit, together with Eden and a few chosen members of the court, the glorious palace that Al-Ahkis had built among the foothills upon the generous grant of land the Sultan had given him to mark his successful embassy to Baghdad. There had been several knotty points at issue between the Caliph and the Sultan, and the young Al-Ahkis had shown unusual perspicacity and delicacy in his smoothing of the threads that so tenuously joined them. Also, despite tempting offers of land and fortune in the Caliphate, his ambassador had shown unswerving loyalty to Salah-ed-Din. Such loyalty was a treasure that, since it could not be bought, must be rewarded. Magnanimously, the Sultan had doubled the Caliph's offer.

The small, bright cavalcade wound its way through the outskirts of the city and into the foothills, passing the gray mud dwellings of farmers and herdsmen and the black goatskin tents of the wandering tribesmen. Occasionally they left the track to make way for a laden camel train.

"That one has come from Samarkand, with silks and spices," volunteered El-Kadil as he watched it enviously. "How I wish I could travel back with it." He wanted to travel widely almost as much as he wanted to be the world's greatest warrior general.

"How can you tell where it has come from?" asked Eden, to whom one caravan resembled another.

"By the patterns woven on the rugs that clothe the camels' backs; each tribe works them differently. I have learned many of them, but not yet all. I suppose there are such things in your land, too?"

Eden grimaced. "Alas no," she admitted. "In England we would hang such a thing upon the wall for all to admire; our horses do not go so finely clad."

"I have heard that your noblemen, instead of rugs, put rushes on their floors, like peasants. Surely this is not true?"

"It is," she replied shortly.

"Even you? Even in your castle of Hawkhurst?"

"Even so."

The boy said no more on the subject but she was ruefully conscious of his pitying gaze.

He was right. It was they who were the barbarians, in so many ways; she would not deny it. She felt disconsolate and homesick, all at once, for the rush-strewn floors of England.

These thoughts were driven from her mind as they rounded a curve between two sloping hills and saw before them, in a secluded valley watered by a willow-banked river, the small but perfect palace of Al-Ahkis.

It was built of honey-colored stone and set back into the hillside among broad gardens. Behind it a magnificent waterfall fell in stages to the river it fed. She saw the dome and minaret of its miniature mosque and the patches of clarion color that betrayed the existence of the exotic roof gardens so beloved of the country.

The heart of the palace, its master told her, was its splendid library. Here, while the other guests strolled in the gardens with which they were well acquainted, Al-Ahkis showed Eden his collection of fine, decorated manuscripts in the bold, Kufic script. Eden admired the strong, ornate characters, but found them impossible to recognize as those she was beginning to know in her lessons with the boy.

"It is almost as though the scribe wished the writing to keep his secrets," she said slowly, tracing the fierce rectangular lettering which Al-Ahkis had said was a poem of love and wine.

"It is the lettering in which the teachings of Mohammed were first recorded. It is therefore much revered," the Arab explained. "We use it in this exaggerated fashion to ornament our books . . . much as a Christian monk might do with flowers, birds and animals. Islam does not make use of such figures. What Allah has created is perfect; it is not for his servants to attempt to emulate that perfection."

She considered the truth of his words. Though she had not realized it, she had missed the appearance of animals and human figures amid the cursive arabesques and alphabets of her Damascus surroundings.

"What would it profit me to commit your beauty, for instance, on to cold parchment . . . when I may enjoy it in all its bountiful reality?" His hand came down over hers upon the bright page and she drew a sudden swift breath.

"You should give thanks to Allah for such beauty . . . as I do . . ."

She felt his breath upon her cheek, warm and sweet. His closeness raised sensations in her that she could only repudiate in self-contempt as she moved quickly away from him, her courteous smile unaltered.

Seeing the motion of her breasts, Al-Ahkis smiled inwardly.

It would be today.

For the afternoon, he had arranged a polo tournament upon the maidan, the green square of well-kept grass hidden among the trees in the valley. He himself would not play; he had been careful to invite only the most dedicated players, exactly enough to make up the teams. The few women of the party were concubines, who would either watch their lovers play or amuse themselves among the gardens, gossiping and drinking tisanes. In his own rooms he knew he would not be disturbed.

There remained El-Kadil, who, surprisingly, did not want to watch the polo. "I saw a match in the city yesterday," he explained regretfully. Then, shyly, "I have heard that you have the Mardi Ibn Ali's famous treatise on war-machines? I would be eternally in your debt if . . ."

Al-Ahkis beamed and gave the boy's head a fatherly pat. "Certainly! I had intended to show it to you. I also have a translation of the *Shah-nama,* if you will promise not to be influenced by its railling against the Arab!"

The great Persian masterpiece was fiercely Iranian in concept, but contained a wealth of heroic myth and legend that would keep the boy enthralled for hours. They left him bent over one of the Mardi's drawings —of a remarkable shield which was also a bow. He wondered if his father knew about it.

"Come with me," said Al-Ahkis to Eden when he had assured himself that El-Kadil had all he might need. "In my palace are many treasures."

He led her into room after room of proportional and decorative perfection until the forms and colors mingled and coalesced and her head swam with a satiety of splendor. She saw lustrous tiles, fine glazed ceramics, glorious hangings, a roomful of unknown musical instruments, sculptures from Byzantium, carvings from Kashmir.

"Your palace is richer than the Sultan's," she observed wonderingly when at last he allowed her to rest in a cool chamber hung with green silk.

"The Sultan would give away all he owns if Al-Khatun did not prevent it," shrugged the steward, placing wine on a low ebony table which he drew up to the velvet-covered divan where she reclined in the relaxed position that was by now natural to her. "It is said that the Lord Yusuf seldom rides a horse that is not already promised to another; if he values anything in this world, it is thoroughbreds, so you may see that he cares little for possessions."

"But you care for them a great deal?" She accepted the rosy wine he offered, taking long, welcome draughts. It was spiced with an herb she half recognized.

"I love beautiful things; it is not forbidden."

"Does the Sultan, then, care nothing for beauty?"

"He finds it in the things of the mind, in music, in conversation with learned men, in the written word, among the stars. My Lord Yusuf is a man of fine and noble intellect."

"Then he must be sadly disappointed in his henchman's need for possessions," suggested Eden lightly, wondering why she should feel so free of heart as to be able to mock the exquisite Arab.

"He does not approve of unnecessary luxury," Al-Ahkis admitted, grinning ruefully. "I fear when he sets eyes on my palace he will council me to give all I own to the poor for the good of my soul."

Eden found this slight jest inordinately amusing, surprising herself by her own ripple of laughter. The day suddenly seemed very pleasant.

Al-Ahkis laughed also, with a curious satisfaction. "When you have rested you must play for me upon the ud; my lady tells me you play well."

She had almost mastered the vibrant, lute-like instrument and was happy enough to comply when he brought it to her.

"Give me a song from your native land . . . a love song if you will."

Avoiding his warm, provocative eye, she swept the strings experimentally before beginning the plaint of Guiot de Dijon, "Chanterai pour Mon Courage." "I sing to comfort my heart . . . so that I do not become mad or die in my deep sorrow. I have seen none come back from the savage land where is the one who can give peace to my breast."

Meeting his mellow gaze with open challenge, she continued, "God help the pilgrim for whom I tremble . . . for treacherous is the Saracen."

Her low voice shook a little, in keeping with the sombre chant and the Arab saw that she had gone far away from him. He regretted his impulse toward music.

Eden finished the song, filled with passionate longing for absent love, and lay back, her eyes closed against the threat of tears. She had intended the ballad only to be an expression of defiance in the face of all that surrounded her, so that he should not think she had already forgotten her quest, her name, her purpose.

She had not counted upon the visions she had conjured for herself with the music . . . of the laughing girls who had sung together at Winchester, of marching men singing the same song in Cyprus and in Acre . . . and of the man whom she did not, now, expect to see again, though her whole spirit yearned toward him, together with her blasphemous, ungovernable body. She moaned aloud, letting the lute fall discordantly from her hand. The man whose image tortured her was not Stephen. Perhaps it could never again be Stephen, though she still owed and would give him all her duty.

Was it for this great sin that God had punished her with this captivity . . . that despite her duty, her striving and her prayers, she still dwelled, day and night, upon the tormented eyes and the fierce, sweet kisses of Tristan de Jarnac?

Al-Ahkis saw that she wept and knew that some great sorrow had overtaken her. He slid onto the velvet coverlet beside her and took her in his arms, holding her only with kindness and wiping her eyes with her pale scarf. He brought the wine-cup to her lips and made her drain it.

Her weakness and above all, her emotion, could only aid his cause. Slowly he pressed her back among the cushions and lay beside her, biding his time, stroking her brow with a delicate, disinterested hand, forbidding his excitement to rise before the moment was full and ripe.

Eden was aware of a growing heavy weariness . . . but it was no longer a weariness of the spirit; indeed, she was surprised at the lightness that was in and about the passages of her mind. Her nerveless body seemed now to be floating, scarcely resting on the green coverlet, on the green waves of a green sea . . . floating, rocking, far away from her own pain, her own regret, her empty, echoing mind . . .

A shadow moved across her clouded vision and the face of the Arab closed over hers.

His kiss, slow and subtle, seemed to draw her up to him, to drain her of the dregs of thought and will. His hands were moving upon her breasts beneath her robe with a light, brushing touch that was almost unbearable and there began a slow, dull aching in her loins.

He murmured her name over and over, his voice catching in his throat, as he freed her from her robe and opened his own garments, and then there were only the hot, Saracen phrases falling about her eyes and lips and breasts as he took possession of her beauty. She saw brown hands upon her pale gold skin, a long, dark thigh pushing aside her whiteness, the slow, voluptuous movements of a dream. Then there was the sudden, exultant flaming of his eyes as he came into her and the deep, dark assuaging of the ache that was within her. He brought her, with relentless skill, up to a pitch of ecstacy bordering upon agony and held her there, her master, until consciousness threatened to leave her. Then at last he brought her triumphantly to a culmination that surmounted even the pinnacles of that ecstacy, so that then she clung to him, drowning, in an anguish of pleasure, consummation and . . . loss.

Gently, later, he moved from her and began to fasten his clothing. He heard her murmur "Tristan" once and saw that there were still tears upon her hectic cheeks.

Her eyes opened but there was no understanding in them and the lids fluttered down again as she fell into a deep, absolute sleep which owed as much to exhaustion as to his careful measure of hashish in her wine. He fastened his gold cincture about his slender hips once more and stood brooding over the prize he had taken. She had been more splendid even than he had expected. Even as he stared at her he felt a new stab of desire for her white, superlative body, the swelling breasts so vulnerable as she slept, the parted thighs glistening, seamed with his tribute. He longed to take her again but it pleased him, as always in these matters, to exercise control. Thus the pleasure would never pall, never being permitted satiety. He pulled the coverlet regretfully over her nakedness.

When, hours later, Eden awoke, it was with the same inexplicable sense of elation that she had felt when she had previously been given hashish. Then she remembered.

If, on that first occasion, she had allowed herself to believe that she had merely dreamed the events of the night before, she had no such easy dispensation now. Her body bore unimpeachable witness to what her mind almost refused to accept. She was just as he had left her, her thighs still open where he had lain between them . . . so deeply relaxed had been her sleep. She shudderingly recalled that dark, sinuous body welded to hers and made the sign of the cross in terror upon her naked breasts.

She had no escape from the hideous truth; she had committed the terrible sins of lust and fornication. She had made herself a filthy thing, apart from all virtue . . . and she had done these things with an Arab, an enemy, an infidel who surely would one day take her perjured soul down with her into the depths of hell.

Racked with terrified sobs, she tore at her body with her own avenging nails, as though she would pluck out the sin rooted deep in her treacherous flesh. Then, in an agony of repentance, she threw her crushed and discarded robe over the long, scarlet scratches and fell to her knees on the ground. Never had she prayed with such an anguished concentration.

If only there were a Christian priest to give her council. How could she know whether there might be forgiveness for such a sin? If so, how to award herself a penance harsh enough to earn it?

Gradually she became calmer, telling herself, as she had done before, that the blessed Magdalen had sinned in this same way and had been forgiven, even unto becoming one of Christ's precious saints. Now she too was a Magdalen indeed . . . a whore, a blasphemer, a willing vessel for an infidel's lust.

The path back to righteousness must of necessity be long and torturous . . . but surely it existed, it lay before her? She could only wait and pray and hope that God would make it clear to her.

With his customary delicacy, Al-Ahkis failed to accompany his guests on their journey back to the Sultan's palace. He had not seen Eden again before she left. Satisfied that he had awoken her body's need for him, he would allow her time to reconcile this discovery with her natural reluctance. Al-Khatun would do what else was necessary.

During the journey Eden sat stiffly in her saddle, gazing unseeingly ahead of her, giving curt, automatic responses to El-Kadil's enthusiastic chattering of two-way lances and Persian kings.

As soon as they arrived she sought out Al-Khatun in her evening resting place in the little kiosk in the blue and green garden. She knelt at her feet as she had trained herself to do, clasping her hands to signify the request of a favor.

Al-Khatun took note of her set, expressionless features. Here was a woman turned to stone. She gave Eden the signal to speak.

"My lady . . . I beg of you most earnestly, if I have ever pleased you, to send me away from your palace. I may continue to serve you, may I not, in some other place? In some other function? If I were elsewhere in the city . . . perhaps El-Kadil might come to me still for lessons . . ." She was halted by the amazed affront on Al-Khatun's face.

"Has it come to this, then? Am I to hear my own slave dictate her wishes to me? This is insolence, Christian! Do not tempt me. I do not often use the whip, but always when I think fit!"

Desperately, Eden attempted to explain. "It is on account of the dragoman, my lady. Al-Ahkis has . . ."

"What has he done, slave? I know that he covets your body as is his right. Has he then forced you against your will?"

Eden crimsoned. "No . . . he has not. That is . . ." She spoke so low that Al-Khatun did not hear her. However, she knew well enough what must have taken place.

"He has not. You have allowed him to use you as many women have," she suggested with the faintest hint of contempt, "and your Christian conscience troubles you. It is of no importance. I had, at any rate, decided to give you to him as his concubine. But he has said that after you have accepted the faith of Islam he will make you his wife. You are fortunate; there are many who will envy you."

Eden stared dully up at the flawless mask of a face. The long, implacable eyes told her that more words would merely be wasted. She bowed and asked if she might leave the presence.

Al-Khatun inclined her head, then added, "You will accompany me tomorrow when I visit the Ommayad Mosque to pray." Her voice was cold with command. "And every Friday henceforth, as is our custom. I will have one of the Imams prepare you for this marriage; he will also assist you to perfect your Arabic. You must be fluent if you are to rule in the palace of Al-Ahkis."

Outwardly, during the long weeks that followed, it must have seemed that Eden acknowledged herself to be beaten. She obeyed her mistress in all things and regained her approval of her grave, respectful manner toward the old Imam who came to bring her the teachings of Islam. Mohammed Ibn Hasib was a remarkable teacher from one of the great madrasahs of the city. He possessed both patience and the gift to impart knowledge, and Eden found his disinterested absorption in his task both relaxing and rewarding. He also taught her Arabic, since she had sworn herself incapable of learning from Al-Ahkis. Al-Khatun, surprisingly, had accepted this, supposing, Eden thought bitterly, that his charms were now sufficiently made known to her.

With the dragoman himself, upon those occasions when she could not avoid his company, she adopted an attitude of attenuated awareness together with a distant courtesy that diminished him to the status of a handsome vase or a silken hanging. She both accepted his presence and ignored it. When he spoke to her, it seemed to him that his voice crossed vast, icy distances only to arrive shorn of impact.

He did not know that, each time they met, his beautiful promised possession trembled at his step, at the softly grating timbre of his voice, at the feline control of each studied movement; for still her renegade flesh remembered where her spirit recoiled and she viewed herself with loathing and disgust. She would like to have blamed him, to have blamed her conniving mistress, to have indicted the whole opulent metropolis . . . but her sins sat, silently accusing, outside her own door and she could not deny them. She felt fear at the terrible realization that her body had a dark strength of its own, that although she could have wished the lustrously handsome steward dead for what he had made of her . . . her loins still quickened when she saw him. She would neither eat nor drink with him, indeed would touch nothing that she had not first seen others take.

At first, he had sought her out alone; once he had even tried to take her in his arms. She had snatched the dagger from his belt and would have plunged it into his heart. He had disarmed her at once, only to find that she had forged her own weapons of silence and contempt. He had left her soon and now did not attempt to visit her alone, but chose moments when he knew her to be with El-Kadil, so that she was forced to treat him at least with courtesy.

If his pride was fired by her rejection he gave no sign; once more, as he knew well how to do, he was biding his time. Soon, the Imam had told him, he hoped to broach the all-important subject of Christ's heretical divinity . . . the beating heart of all the differences between Islam and Christendom. If he was successful . . . and her receptive manner led him to hope . . . then the marriage might take place at last.

She would be his, the crown of his collections, her beauty his to treasure and take his pleasure in for the rest of its days.

At first he had not thought of marrying her, only to make her his mistress, but gradually it had come to him that this was a way in which he, a man of the pen, could match the man of the sword in his conquests; his converted Frankish wife would symbolize throughout Syria a triumph over the Cruciati and over Richard Plantagenet whom she had served. There would be

rejoicing at their wedding among the tents of the
Sultan . . . and the celebration would not fail to come,
with its reason, to the ears of the enemy.

Eden, sensing much of this, was grateful to an otherwise malign fate for the importance attached to her
conversion. The Imam had indeed found her meek and
compliant, full of interest and intelligent questioning.
She had gone with Al-Khatun to the mosque every
Friday where her bowed head at least indicated respect
for a holy place.

There would be no subsequent conversion, however,
and soon this must be discovered. She had seemed
compliant because to do so gave her precious time.
Neither did she feel that she sinned in listening to the
old man in his undoubted wisdom. Indeed she was
surprised and strangely comforted to find how deep in
accord were the teachings of Mohammed with those
of Christ himself, despite the Muslim blasphemy
against his godhead.

She learned of the five Pillars of Islam, which are
faith, prayer, pilgrimage, charity and fasting, and are
symbolized by the five fingers of an open hand which
she had often marked carved into a keystone or a
doorway. She knew that the holy writings of the Qu'ran
in addition to the Hadith, the collected words and
deeds of the Prophet, made up the Sha'ria, the
Holy Law of Islam, with which she was now almost
wholly conversant. Yet while, daily, she increased in
such knowledge, by night she also increased in faith
. . . in that Christ in whom she had placed all her
trust and who rewarded her with the tiny seed of hope,
which, carefully nurtured, had grown again, by his
miracle, out of her despair and her ceaseless, repentant
prayers. In this manner, through the changing seasons,
she lived each day for its own rewards and dangers
and did not number it as it passed.

She became more proficient in the Syrian language.
She had mastered the delicate ud and the many-
stringed cithara and was now engaged upon the nay, a
flute whose clear, round notes embraced two and a
half octaves. The surface of her life regained its pleas-

ant, even tenor, and, if she did not encounter Al-Ahkis for several days, she permitted herself to enjoy it. In the mornings, if she did not teach the boy, she would ride about the city with his mother; or perhaps as the summer lengthened, they would take a hunting party into the hills, and fly the fierce hawks or run down the graceful, succulent gazelle and mountain deer. Sometimes they would return, triumphant, with a lion or a leopard whose masked skins would grin at them afterwards from the tiles of the courtyards. Often they dined off the boar or hyena they had taken. Eden, who herself loved to hunt, was amused to watch the indolent courtesan become a keen-eyed amazon as Al-Khatun rode each racing creature relentlessly to its death, her dark eyes bright with the desire for their blood. Was it this in her, she caught herself wondering, that the gentle Sultan had required to feed his warrior's resolve?

In the softer afternoons they might watch the courtiers play polo on the maidans of the city, surrounded by the eager populace, crying its encouragement to each side. Eden learned to appreciate their swift skill, after an initial hesitation about the usefulness of such a peaceful male pursuit. She could not imagine the knights of England leaving their quintain to ride furiously up and down a field wielding a wooden mallet after a ridiculously tiny ball.

The best days were those of the summer that had now faded almost into memory; the Lady of the Moon would ride with her maidens into the hills to gather herbs. The slave-girls, shrill as always, would compete to collect the most of the bitter myrrh, the fragrant thyme and frankincense or the henna they used to paint their hands and feet and give lustre to their swathes of dark hair. They would invariably gather armfuls of lilies, although the palace courts were filled with them; and frequently they piled woven baskets with all manner of luscious fruits, grapes and quinces, figs and fresh dates, peaches and pomegranates from the Sultan's well-watered orchards. And then there were the spices, precious beyond gold dinars; saffron, calamus, cinnamon and the tough little nutmegs, all to be taken home and dried and ground so that their seductive scents pervaded the palace and set all appetites on edge.

While Al-Khatun, enthroned like an idol in her cedar palanquin, lazed and dispensed silver dirhems to those who collected the most, Eden joined in with the laughing girls, knowing herself welcome. She had gained great stature with them in being chosen by Al-Ahkis and her popularity increased as she became more fluent in their language. They were, however, at a loss to understand why she did not wish to discuss her forthcoming marriage; had it been any one of them, they would have longed, sacrilegiously, to cry the good news from the minarets. Truly, the Frank was strangely modest. Happily, those among them who had been lucky enough to share the bed of Al-Ahkis were only too pleased to feed their companions' curiosity.

Yet, despite all the pleasure and beauty that filled her days, Eden's only true happiness was in the hours she spent with El-Kadil. She had come to love the boy dearly and his joyful enthusiasm and deep-sprung love of life seemed to bring the lost innocence of her own childhood almost within her grasp again. In his company she forgot both sin and sorrow and reveled in the discoveries of each new day as the world unfolded before the boy in words, in music, in paintings, in concepts so numerous and so imbued with excitement that it was as though she herself experienced all for the first time—as, indeed, on many occasions she did.

Throughout the summer and the autumn the shadow of the impending marriage seemed far from her, but during the surprisingly cold winter, when snow clothed the mountains, the chill began also to brush cold fingers across her heart.

When spring came the Imam spoke softly to her of Jesus Christ and she knew that very soon, though it brought her death, she must find a way to leave Damascus.

▼▼

CHAPTER FOURTEEN

Kingdom of the Blest

In the cool, dim interior of the Ommayad Mosque, lit only by hanging, star-shaped lamps of jewel-colored glass, Al-Khatun knelt with her hand-maidens. The mistress, in her golden robes, a little ahead of the slaves in their own Friday finery. They occupied the Maqsura, a highly decorated area reserved for the princes of the land. This lay before the quibla wall at whose center was the sacred niche known as the Mihrab, which faced toward Mecca and so designated the direction of all orisons. The Mihrab, richly carved in wood and precious stones, with its pendant, jeweled lamps and its single pair of gold candlesticks, was the heart of the sanctuary, though it contained no saintly bones or holy relics as a Christian altar might.

The sermon, upon charity and blessed poverty, had already been delivered, together with the customary oath of alliegance to the Caliph in Baghdad. Eden, seeing that the other maids, like their mistress, were now engaged in the swaying ritual of their private devotions, was able at last to turn her head toward the wall on her left, where there stood an object of far deeper significance than any Christian might have expected to find in such a place. So deep, in fact, was this significance that its presence in this shrine of Islam had frequently brought tears to her eyes. At the head of an ornamented staff, secured by a mounting of red gold and encrusted with rubies, emeralds and sapphires, stood the fragment of blackened and splintered wood known throughout the Christian world as the True Cross.

It had fallen into Saracen hands at the disastrous battle of Hattin and been brought to Damascus to be exhibited as an object of contempt and a symbol of victory over Christendom. Eden recalled the rejoicing in the Crusaders' camp when, at the time of the treaty of Acre, Saladin had promised to restore it to them. Even to the most cynical, time-serving mercenary, the relic had the spiritual and emotional power of the Holy Grail itself. And then Richard Trichard had committed his atrocious act and the Cross had returned to Damascus, together with Saladin's unredeemed prisoners. Often, Eden had longed to fall upon her knees before the precious fragment, restraining herself only to protect her pretense of interest in Islam. Now, as the three slave girls undulated toward north and south, bent their brows to the tiled floor, moving silent lips, eyes closed, praying with their fluid bodies as much as with their minds, she was able to look upon the Cross for several seconds and to address herself to it directly. She had no doubt that she would be heard, even in this heathen temple.

One of the worshippers, an Arab, swathed from head to foot in the manner of the nomadic tribesmen, approached the jeweled staff. He was unusually tall for a Syrian and though the staff was two yards high it was blocked from her view. The man stood before it, briefly, and did not spit upon it as she had seen so many do. Then he turned away and Eden, not wishing to be seen staring in his direction, did likewise.

If she had not done so she would have seen the tall figure check suddenly and subject her small party to a searching scrutiny before turning once more toward the Cross and then striding out of the sanctuary.

Eden waited until Al-Khatun had finished her devotions, and made sure that she was the last to walk behind her as they processed down the domed aisle that led from the Mihrab to the central door. Thus she was able to fix her eyes upon the Cross and to concentrate upon it with a deep reverence, drawing strength and comfort from its holy presence.

She was smiling as she came out of the cool sanctuary into the sunlit square where the worshippers now gathered to exchange greetings and news. Almost at once, Al-Khatun was importuned by the Imam who had given the sermon. The two girls in front of Eden followed her into the shade of the arcade of archways and clerestories that surrounded the crowded courtyard. Eden, with her companion, was about to do the same when she felt a light touch on her arm.

Turning, she saw a tall Arab shrouded in a dark burnoose, his head swathed to the eyes in a complex turban, so that their dark glitter was the only visible part of his countenance. As he held out his hand to her in the universal plea of the mendicant, she recognized him by his dusty robes as the man she had noted in front of the True Cross.

"I am sorry. I do not carry money," she told him. This was a constant source of embarrassment to her, for Islam was rich in beggars, as being a living exhortation to charity. There would be many in the square after today's sermon.

"No . . . but you wear a cross of gold about your neck," was the astounding reply, in a dialect that was not that of Damascus.

Before she could demand an explanation there came a repeated pressure upon her arm.

"Do not speak. Live your life as you are accustomed to do. Change nothing. I will find a way to come to you."

Then he had melted into the milling crowd, leaving her, white-faced and reeling, to clutch at the gray stonework of the sanctuary lest she should lose her clouding senses.

For his last words had been spoken, softly but clearly, in the lucid, urgent French which she had half-incredulously recognized to be that of Tristan de Jarnac.

Afterwards, as she paced her chamber in a fever of excitement and soaring, inexpressible joy, Eden could not understand how she had kept from crying out aloud when she had heard that familiar, beloved voice so close to her. For what seemed many minutes she had leaned, dazed, against the cool walls of the mosque, searching the crowd for that tall, vanished figure.

Then she had collected herself and rejoined Al-Khatun. Not even the talkative slave girls saw fit to comment upon the soliciting of a beggar; they had encountered twenty such before they had crossed the square.

Tristan. Here. In Damascus. It was not possible . . . unless it were one of Christ's holy miracles.

Why had she not sensed it was he as he stood before the Cross? Surely she should have known those straight shoulders, that proud stance? She was weeping and laughing all at once as she paced the confines of her chamber in an agony of happiness combined with an impatience that must surely resemble the longing in the blood for some necessary drug. When would he come to her? How long must she wait? That he would somehow save her, she was certain, and gave thanks as though it were already accomplished.

She could not be still. When she had worn herself out with pacing she tried to distract herself with the music of the ud, but the passionate, triumphant love songs became gales of trembling laughter as she realized anew that Tristan was here, that her captivity would be ended and life start anew.

The days stood still. Mornings, evenings, afternoons stretched out their hours to the limits of all patience, only to turn into eternities of sleepless, reasonless night.

It was in the night that she feared that he would not come, that he had been a vision sent by the Devil to tempt her, or worse, a punishment from God to lure and then cast down. By day she looked for him everywhere, in the streets, in the labyrinth of suks, on the maidan, among the hill slopes, clad with spring flowers. Wherever she followed Al-Khatun she sought for him with burning, secret eyes, until the concubine acidly rebuked her for daylight dreaming.

Two weeks passed and he did not come. She became thinner, her eyes large and bright. The waiting stretched her upon a rack of days.

And then, one morning, as she sat with El-Kadil over his books, trying to file her mind for his instruction, one of Kamal's soldiers came softly through the curtained doorway and salaamed deeply before them. He was dressed in the brief hauberk, tight breeches and rose-colored turban affected by most of the palace guard, his shortsword slung from his shoulder and a dagger at his hip. As he rose from his courtesy she met the red-depthed, gleaming eye and knew at once that it was Tristan.

His face and hands were stained to a walnut darkness, his lips to a mulberry warmth; he wore a short, pointed beard in the manner attributed to the Prophet. There was nothing about him to deny the Arab and the Muslim. But this time he had not covered his face, and there was no way in which, having kept its image before her for so long, willing and unwilling, she would not have known him.

She rose from her cushions, her smile surprising El-Kadil.

"What do you want?" the boy asked mildly, looking up from the quatrains he was attempting to compose. Such interruptions were not unwelcome. "Have you come about the mare? Kamal said I might watch her foal," he explained pleadingly to Eden.

Tristan did not reply at once. He looked closely into the boy's thin face, apparently weighing what he found there.

"No," he said quietly, "I have come to take the Lady Eden back to her own people."

"Are you her husband?" inquired El-Kadil excitedly, for he knew her story.

"No, I am not . . ." began Tristan regretfully.

"But you will take her to him? You know where he is to be found?"

"I know."

The Prince nodded, satisfied. Then he favored Tristan with a regard as careful as the one he had received. "You are not a Syrian," he announced at last. "Nor, I think, a Turk or an Egyptian. Are you perhaps a Persian?" he wondered hopefully, the tales of the *Sha'nama* galloping in his mind.

Tristan decided to trust him. He would be able to bear such a burden. "I am one-half English, one-half French," he told him gravely, "and I am a commander under El Malik Rik."

The boy blanched with amazement. "I should call my guard," he said slowly. The pleasure had faded from his face. "It is my duty."

"Please . . . no!" whispered Eden, biting her lip, knowing she was bargaining with the child's love for her.

"I regret I cannot allow you to do that," said Tristan smoothly. "But there is something else that you must do . . . at swordpoint if necessary."

Eden made a small, protesting noise.

"The Lady Eden has need of your clothing. You see . . . she, too, is to be disguised . . . as yourself."

The Prince was now plainly distressed. "I cannot! If I help you I am a traitor to my father."

Tristan's eyes hardened. Suddenly he pulled the boy to his feet and jerked his hands behind his back. "The lady will undress you," he said softly, "and if you take breath to cry out . . . I will draw my dagger across your throat. I do not want to do it . . . but be assured that I will."

Eden's eyes fell beneath the scorn in El-Kadil's. "Put up your dagger," the boy said contemptuously. "I do not permit a woman's hand to touch me."

She met Tristan's faint smile above the proud head. He had saved the pride of Saladin's house.

"The djellaba, the robe and the turban only," the knight ordered. "Eden, you may give him yours. The great advantage of the Saracen method of dress is that it is no great matter whether the wearer be male or female. No . . . do not unwind the turban; there isn't time."

Eden saw that El-Kadil's cheeks flamed like her own

as they stumblingly exchanged garments beneath Tristan's amused eye.

"Excellent! And now your face. I have a preparation here which will turn you into a veritable Moor in two minutes . . ."

"Sweet Jesu!" Eden remembered. "Xanthe's box! The money and my hauberk! I cannot leave them here." She fled to the door, the boy's robes flowing about her as becomingly as her own. "It is only a short distance . . ."

"I do not think you will be successful," El-Kadil said severely and almost sadly as he tied his departed tutor's girdle about his slender waist. He looked at Tristan, man to man, honesty to honesty. "I wish I did not have to give the alarm, but . . ."

"Then I had better tie you up," suggested Tristan, dropping a hand to his dagger once more.

El-Kadil looked considerably brighter when he found himself resting again among his cushions, bound hand and foot, inescapably but not, Tristan hoped, too uncomfortably.

"Don't gag me yet," the boy begged. "I won't cry out while you have the dagger. I am not brave enough."

"You are your father's son," said Tristan gravely and he bowed deeply to his captive.

When Eden returned with her possessions bound up in a cumbersome bundle in a silk scarf, her face and hands were as black as her savior's own. Kamal's unsolicited lieutenant nodded approvingly at her artist's work but eyed her burden with disfavor.

"I won't leave them . . . or Balan," she stated, her chin going up. "I had planned to take the Prince's horse, to aid the deception . . . but he has often ridden out on Balan; it will not be marked."

She turned to El-Kadil, her face soft with love and regret. Wordless, she bent to kiss his smooth cheek.

"I know we shall not meet again," the boy said tremulously, "but I shall never forget you . . . And if ever there is peace between Saracen and Christian, be sure I shall seek you out in your manor of Hawkhurst."

"May God permit it," whispered Eden fervently.

"As Allah wills it," replied El-Kadil with the ghost of a smile.

Eden left the chamber, her throat tightening, while Tristan used her scarf to stifle the cries the son of Saladin must make.

A sense of unreality assailed her as they made their hurried way toward the stables. Eden was astonished to find that Tristan was well acquainted with the courts and passages of the palace.

"I have been one of Kamal's troop for three days now," he explained. "He takes me for a Circassian. Try to move as the boy does. And tell me, does he ever run?"

"Sometimes, when he forgets his dignity." She looked at him wonderingly.

"Then let us by all means run past the three slave girls who are coming toward us."

Eden's blood ran cold as she saw that Yuldiz, Fat'ma and Scheherazade were idling toward them from the other end of the chamber they traversed. There was no hope but to obey him, and attempting to achieve El-Kadil's loping stride she ran, remembering just in time not to pick up her skirts. The three girls wafted into giggling courtesies as their young master flew past them in his purple robe, doubtless in the direction of the stables. Yuldiz ogled the handsome new recruit she had marked before. Tristan readily grinned at her, a promise in his eye, he would not, he hoped, be able to keep.

At the next test, Eden almost turned and fled back toward the library, her heart in her throat, for there, crossing the yard from the stables to the arcade down which they came, was Al-Ahkis, his handsome face breaking into a smile at the approach of his Prince.

A second's numbness. Then, affecting not to have noticed him, she cried "Race you!" in the boy's half-broken tones, and fled past the surprised dragoman, her head determinedly turned away from him.

"His father should have been a horse-trader," observed Tristan cheerfully, sketching a salute toward the splendid figure as he strolled unconcernedly in Eden's wake.

He found her huddled against Balan's side, her breast heaving. "We shall not escape. I know it. This is madness!"

"This is not the time to lose courage," he said tartly, tossing Balan's saddle across his rug and saddlebags. "Compose yourself and try to look like a prince."

With an effort she thrust down the rising nausea and stuffed her possessions into the bags. Then she climbed on to the horse's back.

"Oh, Tristan . . . if we fail . . . ?"

"We won't fail." He gave Balan's rump a lusty slap.

Somehow it was accomplished. Eden rode, her head turned inward with interest toward the companion who rode so closely beside her, discoursing loudly upon the relative merits of their mounts. They crossed the stable yard toward the great, starred bronze gates, which the guards opened for them, with a salute but without a second glance, and then they were through them and she heard the dull metallic clang as they closed behind them. They rode swiftly along the route to the hills. Already she could feel the coloring on her face run into rivulets of sweat. The road was clear; she massaged it back to smoothness. The unreality had increased a thousandfold. Each second she expected to hear the sounds of pursuit, to be surrounded by Kamal's avenging horde, see them become again the merciless slaughterers they had been upon the bare mountaintop.

But they did not come, and in fifteen minutes they were among the foothills.

"We shall make for a gorge I know, to the north. It is well-hidden and far up in the hills. They will not expect us to take that direction, but will ride south as soon as the boy tells them who I am. Richard is at Jaffa. We can sleep there and make for the south in the morning."

Something stirred at the back of her dazed and obedient consciousness, but it did not fully wake and she nodded her agreement to his proposal.

"How long do you think it will be before the boy is found?" he asked later.

"Not for an hour or more; our lessons are rarely interrupted. Unless . . ."

She flushed and he looked at her closely. "Unless?"

"Perhaps the dragoman . . . the man you saw crossing the courtyard . . . he sometimes visits the library at such times."

"But he has seen, as he thinks, the Prince go across to the stables; why, then, should he seek him out in the library?"

She stared ahead of her, rigid with an old pain. She could not tell him that it would not be the Prince that Al-Ahkis would seek out.

Again, she simply nodded, praying God that it did not happen. She had hardly spoken to her threatened bridegroom in the last few weeks; and being much occupied, he had not looked for her. Perhaps he would not do so now.

"Then we are safe," said Tristan, smiling. He wondered why she would not raise her head.

They rode in silence for a space until she said, with a strangely shy curiosity, "You have not told me how you came to be in Damascus. You could not have known . . ."

"That I should find you there? Ah no; that must be accounted a miracle."

Her eyes softened. "I think so too."

"I had other business. I will tell you of it, later, when we have reached our destination."

"As you will. Tell me, instead, of the fortunes of the armies. I have been sadly kept in ignorance; it was Al-Khatun's intention that I should forget the past. I heard rumors, sometimes, among the slave girls. It was said that Richard has not marched on Jerusalem?"

"First he needed Jaffa, the port which commands it. Saladin and his mounted ramieh and Turcopoles harried us down the coast and destroyed the walls

and the harbor before we reached it. But we had
the better of him at Arsuf, some few miles out of the
city. It was a great victory for Richard. The arrows
fell so thick and fast we scarcely saw the sunlight and
those damnable ramieh were everywhere you looked.
Richard's plan was to wait until their horses tired
and then charge en masse; but the Marshal of the
Hospitalers couldn't wait. His force charged too
soon, scattering our own protective infantry. There
was nothing for the King but to make his grand
charge at once. As it was, we routed them soundly,
but only because Richard had the sense to stop and
reform before the Turks could do so. It's no easy task
to stop an army in full spate . . . but he succeeded
and we won the day outright. There is no better general than Richard when he is thus. The Lion roared
and all obeyed. It was magnificent."

"So you are again enamored of the Lionheart?" murmured Eden.

"I have never denied him to be a great leader," he
said with reserve.

"And after Arsuf?" She would not dwell on the
King.

"We took what was left of Jaffa; the town was
gutted; we camped in an olive grove. Saladin had
marched to Ascalon; it's the key port to the road
linking Syria to Egypt and the Sultan made it useless
to us in the same manner as Jaffa. He couldn't afford
to hold it himself; he needs all his troops to defend
Jerusalem. We took his leavings as before, and now
we're rebuilding."

"Surely *we* have no shortage of troops? Why does
Richard not follow Saladin and lay siege to the Holy
City?"

He regarded her with a soldier's surprise. "Too far
from the sea. We rely too heavily on our navy to
chance being cut off by one of the Saracens' relief
forces. We have made our way safe, slowly, rebuilding the fortifications between Jaffa and Jerusalem that
the Sultan has pulled down. The problem remains; if
we attack, Saladin will send for reinforcements and we

shall be outnumbered. Therefore," he finished heavily, "we sit in Jaffa and in Ascalon and play political games with the Sultan . . . or rather, his brother, Al-Adil."

"Games?" She was disapproving.

"What else would you term a suggestion that peace should be considered on the marriage of Al-Adil to Joanna Plantagenet?"

"Sweet Heaven! What did Joanna say to that?"

"She flew into a royal Plantagenet rage and refused to wed or bed with a black infidel."

Eden's smile held a particular wryness.

"Undeterred by her refusal, Richard proposed his niece, Eleanor of Brittany, in her place. The Saracen swore eternal love for Joanna and no other and the plan languished. The King and Al-Adil have become mightily close. They hunt and hawk together, play chess, make music and talk deep into the night. Richard wanted to meet Saladin, but the Sultan disapproves of leaders who make merry together while their troops kill each other. His brother is a fair ambassador. He may have done much toward procuring peace."

"Peace!" She was stupified. "What of Jerusalem?"

Tristan sighed. He signaled a stop to rest the horses, for the going was rougher now and they must not become winded.

"Jerusalem," he said quietly, gazing across the stony slopes as though he saw the towers and domes of that disputed city, "Jerusalem was the brave standard that guided us forward. It was the bright cause for which we fought, to which we dedicated our souls . . ." He broke off and faced her and she saw the pain he had kept from his voice.

"And it is to be lost to us?" she breathed, unable to believe it.

"I fear it greatly. It cannot be forever. Others will make the pilgrimage . . . but I think it may be lost to Richard Plantagenet. Already he has wept over it as lost."

Eden could not repress a certain amount of bitter

satisfaction at the thought. For her, the King would never again be worthy of the Sepulchre.

"We went up, one day, on to a hilltop," Tristan continued softly. "Someone called out that from the summit you could see Jerusalem. Richard rode up in eagerness, his face made young again . . . and when he reached the spot he looked once, then threw his shield before his eyes, crying out, 'Dear Lord, suffer me not to see your Holy City, who cannot deliver it from the hands of your enemies!' And then he wept. I think all of us wept. It was a moment of knowledge from which we could not turn."

"And yet you will not try to take the city?"

"You do not know how it has been," he said wearily. "We were camped at last at Beit Nuba . . . a mere twelve miles from Jerusalem. The rain did not cease. The storms were so terrible that our tents were torn from the ground. Many of the horses died; food perished; our mail rusted; our clothing rotted. Many of us are sick. Yet, despite all of this, we could endure, sustained by the knowledge that we were near to Jerusalem." He caught her gaze in sudden, swift challenge. "It is as a lover who is conscious of his nearness to the beloved . . . she is not his, but the siege lies always in his mind . . ."

Eden paled, her mind flooding with a thousand reasons, regrets, desires; he had taken her too much unawares.

"But you did not take the city," she reminded him, trembling, "because it lay in the hands of another."

Their look now was charged with a bitter sweetness. Inwardly she accused herself in anguish. Who was she to love this man—for she could not be with him and not know that she loved him—she who had defiled her body and been defiled, who had betrayed the husband God had given her and who did so continually, ever and anew, by the existence of this love that she longed to call pure. God forgive her. It must be, it *should* be extinguished.

"I have . . . much to thank you for, yet again," she said distractedly, avoiding his eyes. "I have deserved

it . . . less, even, than before. You do not know . . ."
But she could not tell him of the Arab. Not yet.
Perhaps never.

She began again, hastily. "My letter . . ."

"Let us not speak of it," he interrupted fiercely, turning to tighten Gorvenal's girths.

Neither of them, she thought, would dare to speak of what had gone before that letter. Yet there was one thing she must know.

"The Lady Alys . . . I trust I did not wound her severely," she asked, embarrassed.

He turned back, smiling slightly now. "I believe you damaged her pride beyond repair. You will doubtless suffer for it when you reach Jaffa."

Again there was that faint fluttering of something behind the curtains of her mind.

"The Queen is in Jaffa?"

"She removed from Acre; the plague was brewing. And it is not far removed from Ascalon where Rich- and is supervising the rebuilding."

She felt a swift, intense longing to be with Berengaria, to take refuge in her gentleness and courage. It would be so good, too, to see the restless Joanna, and Mathilde, and even proud Alys, for she must ask her forgiveness.

"Come," said Tristan kindly, sensing her thoughts. "Our way lies north, for the present."

It was evening before they reached the summit of their climb. Eden had come to the end of her own recital of the events of the past months. She had kept it light and uncomplaining, though she was heavily conscious of what she had left unsaid. Tristan, with an almost boyish determination toward secrecy, had still refused to explain his presence in Damascus.

The diminutive valley he had chosen to be their hiding place was little more than a surprising, green hollow in the hillside, screened from view by trees and crags. It was watered by a narrow stream which fell from the curtain of rock surrounding it in a series of narrow cascades. A single tree stood at its center, its new spring green strung with golden blossoms like tiny, stemless goblets.

Eden cried out in pleasure as they came into it. "How did you find it?"

"I looked for it," was all he would say. He had found it at a time he no longer wished to remember; it was dead to him now.

They relieved the grateful horses of their loads and spread their saddle-rugs upon the ground. Tristan had brought food—fruit, meat and even wine—and Eden quickly prepared a small feast while the animals cropped the watered emerald grass.

"It is a perfect sanctuary," she said contentedly. "Even if we were pursued, no one would find us here."

"It is a greater sanctuary than you know," Tristan replied, his smile brilliant. "Turn away for a moment. There is something I want to show you."

Obedient, she heard the clink of metal and presumed that he was removing his sword. His face had been as bright as a happy boy's.

"You may turn back now."

She did so, smiling. And then her incredulity rang out between the close, reverberant walls of the gorge. Before the green and golden tree, gleaming and triumphant as the natural beauty that surrounded it, was the long staff and the surmounting red-gold monstrance that held the True Cross.

"Now we are in a sanctuary indeed," observed Tristan quietly.

Automatically, Eden sank to her knees.

Behind her, the tall knight stood, his head bowed as he saw the two strong threads of his life come together in this peaceful place.

A great stillness fell upon the valley. At last, when she could trust herself to speak again, Eden let loose her flood of questions. How had he taken it? Why was he in Saladin's capital? How had he penetrated Al-Khatun's household?

"One question answers another," he said. "I came to Damascus to take back the Cross for Christ's followers. I was able to enter the palace because I was already in disguise. I have spoken Arabic for some years and I am a soldier of some professional skill. It was not hard to convince Kamal that I merited the honor of serving the illustrious Al-Khatun."

"If we had not come to the mosque that day . . ." Eden shivered. Chance, that had been so kind, could have been equally cruel.

He shrugged. "Then you would have come another day . . . and I should have been there. I came there often. At first I thought to take the Cross in broad day, in full view of the worshippers . . . but a staff as high as a man is not easy to conceal. I had to give up the pleasure of audacity for the certainty of success. I hid in the mosque and remained throughout the night, exchanging the Cross, at my leisure, for the excellent work of one Simon of Acre . . . mere brass and glass, but an effective likeness; the important difference being that Simon's staff was in three convenient sections. I had to file this one in order to carry it beneath my cloak."

"You have done a wonderful thing for Christendom." Eden's voice was as filled with pride as if he had been truly her own.

"I did no good, kicking my heels in Jaffa," he said dismissively. "And there is much need for such a gift among our men. There has been a falling away, a diminution of spirit, especially since . . . Acre. Some of them are like to give themselves over to acedia, others too wholly to the flesh. They are in need of comfort. The Cross may bring it to them."

"Surely it will also bring new hope!" she cried gladly. "If the Cross can be retaken, snatched from the very heart of Islam . . . may not Jerusalem be retaken also?"

He would give her no answer to that.

A silence fell between them now. It was compounded, not of emptiness, or even of the shyness that each of them felt from time to time at the extraordinary gift of the other's presence, but rather out of all that they longed to say to one another and must now, though the words pressed about them, as close and as substantial, it seemed, as the stone walls that sheltered them. So that their hands might be occupied at the center of this strange stillness, they ate and drank, their eyes meeting from time to time, although their hands, even when they might have done, did not.

They smiled and were blessed, the Cross standing over them as a guardian. At last Tristan said reluctantly, conscious of introducing the serpent into this primal garden, "There is something I must tell you. You should know it before you enter Jaffa. God knows it is not a matter of which I would wish to speak . . ."

She saw that he thought he might cause her pain and held out her hand toward him, bidding him to continue.

"Before I left Richard there was a new addition to his following; a man whom he greeted as an old friend. He is no friend of yours. It is Sir Hugo de Malfors."

Eden cried out as memory rushed to attack her. The name was blasphemy in this blessed tranquility; she had not known how deeply she had buried the shame until this painful exhumation.

"He has taken the Cross to regain his fortune," Tristan continued steadily, seeing that she struggled for control. "He and the King were very thick together, though de Malfors remained but three days. Richard would tell me nothing of the man . . . but then, he and I are not so close as we have been . . ." Nor ever should be . . . but that was another tale.

Eden had schooled her features to a mask of composure. "I give you thanks for your warning."

"You had to know. He will return to Jaffa and you will encounter him. I am told he may inquire after you. But be assured," he moved instinctively toward her as the fear flared in her eyes, "he will not live long, Eden. I have already challenged him on your behalf." His eyes caressed her face and saw the beloved green eyes widen into surprise and then close as if she could not support the thought that had followed.

"I seized the right; the Queen supported me. Rich-

ard did not care and your husband was not there to
stand for you. De Malfors refused the fight. He said
he had business to perform and would not risk a
wound at that time. We are to meet again when that
business is complete. And then I shall kill him."

Eden was very still. She sat staring at the ground,
her head bowed, and did not speak for some moments.

When she looked up at him he felt, with shock, that
he had never seen such sorrow sit upon a human
countenance. Pity overwhelmed him as he returned,
ignorant of its cause, her despairing, ravaged gaze and
saw the tears fall unchecked upon her breast.

Suddenly she sprang to her feet with an incoherent cry, a mere rag of anguish and contrition. The
Cross, between them, caught fire from the sinking sun
and glowed like a whole, compacted cathedral among
the watching rocks. She forced forth the words that she
had carried within her so long, casting her hideous
gift of pain and disillusion to him who had given her
back her life. Which she must inflict and witness as her
penance and her punishment.

"My lord . . . I am not even worthy that you
should speak my dishonored name," she cried in desolation. "You should give me over gladly to Hugo de
Malfors rather than seek his life on my account. I
can no longer be defiled by such as he . . . nor yet
by any man. In Damascus I have sunk as low as to
encompass a far greater destruction than even my
overlord could wish . . ." And steadily, without taking
her wild, suffering eyes from his, she told him how
she had lain in fornication with the dragoman of Al-
Khatun and had made no attempt to escape his demands or those of her own drugged and degraded
body. She tried to read his face as her relentless voice
went about its wounding but every feature was frozen
into an unnatural stillness, as though he had commanded his very blood to stop.

She had done at last. The silence lay about them like
a shroud, though nothing within it had been laid to
rest.

After a long time he said remotely, "Why do you tell me this? I am not your confessor."

Her voice was low and trembled greatly. "I had to. I could not ride beside you, eat with you, talk with you . . . God's Holy Passion, *laugh* with you . . . and carry that burden. Every moment I was deceiving you . . ."

"Perhaps I had rather remained deceived!" The pain was naked in his wild cry.

"You must not say so!"

"Why not? Are you the better, now, for your undeception? Am I? Shall we be able to laugh together from this day forward?"

She thought that he looked as if he wanted her to die.

"Tristan . . ." she moved toward him, her eyes half mad with pleading. "There is no penance that can be greater than the loss I bear now . . . the loss of your . . . friendship . . ." She dared use no other word.

He stared at her brutally, so coldly that she moaned with pain. Then suddenly his face came to life again in a vivid blaze of contempt. "You say so?" he demanded scornfully. "But is there not, perhaps, a better way . . . since you have such need of expiation? I can think of a manner of your doing it that will most excellently suit the sin."

He grasped her wrists and violently pulled her to him, crushing her breasts against his hauberk and grinding his mouth upon hers in a savage kiss that left it raw and throbbing. Breathless, she stared into the garnet depths of eyes that were a stranger's, gleaming, feral with lust and the will to hurt. She closed her own against their raging and her lips were engulfed again, at the center of a storm of sensual frenzy that swept them both to the ground. He twisted cruel hands into the length of her hair and rent the clothing from her breasts, covering them with brutal, biting kisses that seared her flesh.

Then, with a low, exultant laugh, he pulled up her skirts around her waist like a back-alley whore's and held her beneath him, controlling her feeble attempt at movement with one iron-muscled thigh. She felt the hot strength of his desire flame along her loins, and although she knew he meant to crush her, to degrade her and bruise her spirit, she could not quell the shameful answering of her flesh to his. He hurt her as he kissed and caressed her into a desperate, swelling need for him, his hands, his lips, his tongue searching the secrets of her body and making use of them without kindness, without mercy. He wanted to wound her so that all previous memories were erased, flayed from her body and dashed from her mind by this black, abrasive passion that knew nothing of love. The pain was exquisite then, when his beautiful, damnable hands had done their work, he thrust apart her thighs at last and possessed her like an enemy. His coming into her was like a sword. He moved within her body with a relentless, watchful vengeance, never taking his eyes from hers, holding her in a grim, inescapable regard. And although it was her undoing, nothing less, that he craved, she could not help but go with him on his harsh, havenless journey, for beyond his cruelty she sensed the terrible void of his loneliness, a thing that she had created. And as she stared into those dark, unhappy eyes, her own torment became nothing. The humiliation which he had sought to bring her was consumed, made dust and forgotten, among the harrowed, empty reaches of his hurt.

At the ending, as they fell together through desolate wastes of space, she cried out to him in the only words that remained to her, with a desperate wish to give him comfort. "Tristan . . . forgive me. I love you!"

There was nothing that he could do that would ever make it otherwise. His eyes widened in a sudden, sharp horror and he threw himself away from her. Lying on his back, arms outflung, he stared up at the deepening sky, rosy with the innocent glow of evening.

He saw nothing.

Eden sat up where they had lain, trying to mend

the torn fastenings of her robe with shaking hands that would not obey her. She wished violently that he would simply rise at once, take his horse and ride away from here, out of her sight forever. There was nothing either could say to the other, now that it was done, that would not be a prolonging of pain. Though she was sensible of her body's dull aching, she felt no emotion other than this desire to be free of his company. Something was now completed between them. Perhaps what had taken place had even been a strange kind of justice.

She did not know. She wanted to be alone.

All at once Tristan groaned and turned on his belly, pressing his brown face deep into the grass. Eden saw that his shoulders were shaken by great, silent sobs and that his outstretched fingers clawed at the ground like a man clutching at a crumbling cliffside.

Insensibility fled and pain rushed back upon her as she saw his contorted, soundless grief. She could not witness this and remain still. She pulled herself over to him and lay down her head close to his, her arms about him and her body across his like a shield.

She said nothing, letting her love flow into him, unaltered, sweet and sorrowful. She acknowledged then, with a bitter foreboding, that this was the truth that lay at the center of her life.

He did not move. She murmured over and again that she loved him. She twisted her fingers into his, where they lay upon the grass. At last he accepted her gift and caught her hands in a desperate grip that ground the fine bones painfully.

"Tristan," she whispered soon, "will you not look at me, my love?"

She felt him stir beneath her and sat up so that he might rise to his knees and face her. His eyes were dry and wild with suffering, all anger gone. He had not been granted the relief of tears.

"Look at you," he muttered. "How shall I look at you? There can be no forgiveness for what I have done . . . neither here nor in purgatory."

Fear touched her at the tragic intensity of his look. He was no stranger now.

"There can be no question now of forgiveness between us," she cried. "It is of no account. Believe that I love you truly . . . whatever I have done . . . whatever may be left for me to do. God knows well I have not wished for such a love . . . as I know you have not. As for my body, you have made it yours as no other has done . . ." Was it possible that she smiled? "And my punishment shall surely not be in your taking of it—but in the leaving that soon must follow." How could she have thought that she wanted him to go?

Tristan, dazed by such words that could cut through pride, hurt and hatred to the simple, miraculous truth, looked at her, rapt, as though seeing her for the first time.

"Can this be true?" he wondered. "Can you have such strength? You can love me and tell me so, after . . ."

She shook her head gravely. "Indeed I could not have told you before." She would not tell him that it was his grief had made her speak.

They looked at each other for a deep, silent space and then he rose to his feet and pulled her to him with a delicate gentleness that hurt her almost as much with its poignancy as had his previous violence.

"My dear love," he murmured, his lips in the wilderness he had made of her hair. "The rest of my life is yours. I have no other allegiance."

She raised her head, her eyes glorious, and he kissed her lips, caressing their soft swelling with a lightness that fired her to instant passion. Her arms went about him and she pressed her body to his as if she would become one with him, lips, breasts, belly, thighs, while her hands sought with a sweet urgency for his naked skin.

Tristan gave a low, incredulous laugh and swung her up against his chest, holding her there for a joyful, exultant moment.

"I have shown my lust, my lady . . . let me now show you my love."

He laid her down once more upon the green grass, himself her coverlet. For minutes passing, they lay as close as two can be unless they are one, and spoke in low, intimate voices of everything and nothing as universal lovers do—as *they* had never dared hope to do. They gave each other comfort for the storm that had passed and slowly, with no more shadow of sin or shame, each discovered the other's beauty with eyes, lips, hands. Their touch was tender and tentative at first, but both were all the time aware of the desire that waited their pleasure.

His caresses this time were gentle, as subtly insistent as before they had been brutal. He kissed the bruises that flowered already on her breasts. His hands on her belly were like the soft breath that fans the flame. Once more her desire flew up to meet his and she parted her thighs for him with a sigh of delight, arching her back so that there should be no part of her that did not touch him, worship him, please him. They had entered into each other. It seemed now a desire as much of the spirit as of the body. Though it grew stronger as they moved slowly and powerfully toward the culminating ecstacy, it would not weaken at their coming apart but would glow within them with an unquenchable flame that would be with them all of their days. She cried out at the climax and seemed to feel her heart fly up into the rose-streaked dusk like a captive bird set free. She was a part of him now, as he was of her; they could never again be separated, by life or by death.

They slept afterwards, a warm exhaustion stealing through them, his cloak flung over them, hers rolled beneath their heads.

Above them the Cross kept watch. Neither had thought of it in the hour that had passed. Had they done so, they would at first have accounted themselves blasphemous, defilers of sanctified ground . . . but at the last, perhaps, they would have been led by the joy in their hearts to expect a measure of forgiveness from the Christ who forgave the Magdalen because she had greatly loved.

It was near dawn when Eden awoke. She felt him at her side and moved her head to kiss his hair. She gazed contentedly upwards for a while, allowing no thoughts to cloud her drowsy appreciation of the green branches spread above them, their yellow cups still closed in sleep.

For the first time in her life she was aware of perfect happiness. If only they might stay forever in this tiny paradise. She would ask for no other company all her days.

A bird sang out and it was as though he had given a signal, perched upon his waking branch. For now the thoughts came, all at once, an ambush of them, swift and confusing, at odds with the softness of the morning.

They whispered to her that she had not yet deserved paradise. She must not stay there, not even for another day. They reminded her insidiously that she had a quest to complete, that there was a man to whom she owed her duty even if she could no longer give him her love . . . perhaps all the more because of this fact.

Tristan had known this, of course, but he had not spoken of it. He had taken it for granted that she would go back with him to Jaffa, to bear the Cross in triumph to the disheartened Crusaders. She knew, as she knew herself, that he would hear of nothing else— and that, when he awoke and she heard his beloved voice, she would ask for nothing else.

Certainly, she knew too, he would see to it that there was a search for Stephen, a questioning of the ransom; Tristan would do that as much out of his own iron honesty as out of love for her. That, however, would not in any sense be justice. There was only one person who must find and tell Stephen what his wife had become . . . Eden herself. This must be; there was no escape from it. She must go, now, alone.

Slowly, agonizingly, she slid her body away from her sleeping lover, covering her place with the still warm cloak. She washed herself in the bright pool at the foot of the cascade and dressed in her hauberk and soft riding boots. She plaited and wound up her hair beneath her scarlet cap, quietly loaded Balan, and was ready to leave.

She had not permitted herself to think, had engaged in blind movement, accomplishing one small, necessary action after another. Now she stood still and looked down at Tristan, lapped in the peace of the cradle or the tomb. Nothing of the world lay upon the quiet planes of the face that her fingers had so lately traced in loving knowledge. He did not know, how could he, that his paradise and hers must be so brief. She thought how he must wake to find her gone. The realization stabbed her so that she nearly cried out. He moved in his sleep and flung a hand across her pillow. He would know why she had gone; he would not doubt, now, that she loved him. She longed to leave him some token of that love, but she had nothing, no rings, no ornaments . . . only Stephen's cross that was drawing her away. She could have wept at such poverty.

And then the bird sang out again and she had her answer; it was more fitting than any gold could have been. She reached up and took a blossom from the tree that had sheltered them and laid it gently on the pillow near his hand. When he awoke its golden heart would be fully open.

CHAPTER FIFTEEN

Zaydun's Fortress

For two days and nights Eden knew what it was to be afraid. She taxed her own strength and that of Balan to the limit, riding almost without rest through the inhospitable hills. What sleep she did snatch was light and filled with nightmares, for she lay down in a wretched fear of wild beasts. There were bears among these mountains, lions and hungry wolves, and she had nothing with which to defend herself but a single small dagger. Though she saw none but the brightened gazelles and other deer, she heard the wolves cry at night and once she found what she knew to be the spoor of a leopard. Her fear was magnified by her loneliness. She had never in her life traveled alone for more than the twenty miles or so from Acre to Tyre, and she was driven to a nervous desperation by it, talking incessantly to Balan as the only sensate being in a desolate and unfriendly universe.

There was also the very real terror of losing her way. The map which she had taken from the guardroom at Acre was little help among these stony ravines and desert valleys. She set her course by the sun and the unfamiliar stars, and knew thus that at least she was making gradual progress northward. The one charted landmark that she recognized was the ancient fortress town of Baalbek. It had been known to the Greeks as the City of the Sun, whence had come the gilded dome over the mosque in Jerusalem known as the Dome of the Rock. The citadel was a second home to Saladin. Here, his forerunner, the bloodthirsty Zengi, who had captured it from the Saracens, had crucified its entire garrison after promising them their lives. El-Kadil had told her this once when she had confessed her shame on behalf of Richard Plantagenet.

She rode around the ill-omened city in an elaborate half-circle and turned toward Tripoli.

Just before noon on the third day, as the sun beat its relentless drums upon her brow, she had her first welcome sight of that blessedly Christian city, viewed from the hilltops across the plain beneath. It was no Damascus; its towers and domes would not haunt her memory. But after the terrible loneliness of the last two days the sight of it brought tears of relief. Within the hour she was at its gates. Here she received an unpleasant shock. The great wooden gates were closed despite the daylight and grim guards were posted about the walls.

"What's your business, lad?" one called. "It must be pretty pressing to risk the plague for it."

"The plague! The Arnaldia?" she asked. His nod confirmed it. She had seen enough of the scourge in Acre to know that the risk was indeed great, but she must buy food, and more important, she must visit a mapmaker. Persuaded by her urgency, the soldiers let her in; their orders were not yet otherwise, though they expected them hourly.

They bade her cover her face in a vinegar-soaked kerchief to avoid breathing the rising miasma from the swamps that carried the disease. Willingly, and because it added to her disguise, she took their advice.

The mapmakers had their premises all about the harbor and it was in this direction that she turned Balan's head, promising him a rest and some good grain while her chart was drawn.

Alexander the Greek, in his spacious chambers on the first floor of a house overlooking the harbor, was a master of his craft. Eden discovered to her embarrassment that he was also a lover of attractive young boys and a great deal of prodigal charm flowed about her crimson ears beneath the scarlet cap before he had finished his work and agreed to set her, reluctantly, on her way back toward the mountains. His work was swift and certain. He used a ready-prepared outline containing the main features of the landscape, filling in what was necessary for her own journey in addition to these.

"These mountains are notoriously difficult to follow, and a harsh terrain. Your master will take a guide, of course . . . I happen to know of one . . ."

"It is most kind, Kyrie, but . . . my master . . . already has a guide." She shook off his detaining hand, bowed hastily and took up her map, rolled in its hardened leather cylinder. She hung it around her waist beneath her tunic for it was the most precious thing she had . . . her only means of finding the well-hidden stronghold of Emir Ayub Ibn Zaydun.

And even when, later, she could feel its reassuring weight knocking against her hip as she rode, her heart sank as she came again to the foothills of those frowning, desolate mountains.

Before daylight dimmed, she exchanged her scarlet cap for El-Kadil's turban and stained her face to the complexion of a Persian or a Circassian. Thenceforward, if she were to encounter any of her fellow men, they would again be Saracens. The territory of Tripoli ended with the plain. And although she had scant fear for her Arabic, nevertheless she prayed that such an encounter would not occur. The mapmaker's evident interest had unnerved her; it could take so little to penetrate her disguise. If she had let him continue when he had run his plump hand over her thigh . . .

In his map, at least, she soon developed complete confidence. He had included each small landmark along the way—a disused keep where the foothills gave way to steeper slopes, a welcome stream with a pool at its base, a strangely shaped rock with a face like a bear's —all guaranteed that she was still on her road. The Greek had estimated that the fortress was somewhat less than twenty miles from Tripoli and she hoped to accomplish them before the next dawn. She would do without sleep. She could not have expected it to come to her, in her heightened state, so near to the end of her journey.

She was increasingly grateful for Balan's familiar company as they climbed in the lowering darkness. She could not ride. The path had diminished to a mere rutted track and she had to lead the horse slowly. The highly bred palfrey was sure-footed but he could no longer see his way and had to trust to his mistress to be his eyes. Once he started at a hideous snarling among the rocks nearby and Eden was hard put to it to hold him in his fright. She dared not contemplate the consequences if she lost him. They continued in an eerie silence, moonlit now. She was startlingly conscious of every twig that cracked, every bird that rose, or stone that fell about them.

The night stretched endlessly, aimed, it seemed, for infinity. At one point Eden shook her head suddenly, realizing with a cold terror that for several paces she had been walking in her sleep. She might have led Balan over a precipice, or stepped upon a viper or had her throat torn without warning by the murderous leap of a night-stalking panther. The sweat of her fear kept the cold from her throughout the terrible night and she wept, as though to welcome a beloved, prodigal friend, when she saw the promise of dawn streak the sky.

They stopped at last in a small clearing among the secondary heights, where horse and rider could drink from a stream and Eden could consult her chart. The two peaks whose inimical black shapes she had kept in sight throughout the night were softened and colored by the sunrise and she saw from their nearness that she had not much farther to go, perhaps only two or three miles. She began to make her metamorphosis once more, washing away the walnut stain in the stream, scouring her face with her hands until it glowed. She took the much-traveled rose-colored gown from her saddlebag and shook it hopefully to free it of the worst creases; it had been laundered in Damascus and did not look too ill. It was fully fifteen minutes, however, before she had made sense of the cuckoo's nest of her hair and braided it upon her breast. She then replaced the turban, for the sun would be cruel later, and in the same cause added a line of Xanthe's kohl to her lower eye lids.

She was blinking it into place when she caught a slight sound behind her. She whirled in instant apprehension. Three men stood there; Saracens. Their expressions were those of fascinated surprise and their hands were upon their swords.

Her immediate feeling was that at least they were not wild animals, and if they had sought her death, they would have accomplished it ere now. She stared at each neutral, astonished face; no one moved. She felt her courage return. If they were men, they could speak and she could understand them.

"Good day," she said in Arabic, forcing a smile. "Allah is all-merciful; I have need of such as you."

Their appearance did not inspire such bold confidence. They were dressed much as Kamal's soldiers had been, though with a certain flamboyant carelessness that did not advertise the professional. Their amazement deepened into rank incredulity as their fair-skinned, beautiful woman, who treated the mountain fastness like the harem, addressed them not only in their own tongue, but in the polished, metropolitan accents of Damascus.

"Lady, in the name of Allah, the almighty and merciful, who are you and how do you come to be here?"

The man in their midst had stepped forward. His dark face was lined beneath its violet and silver headdress and she saw the glint of gold in his ears.

She lifted her chin. "I come from the palace of the illustrious Al-Khatun in Damascus," she said imperiously, "and I seek the Emir Ibn Zaydun on a matter of the utmost urgency. My name and title are not your concern. I take it you are the escort sent by the Lord Zaydun?"

Her heart beat at her own grandiloquence but she saw that they would not question her pretense. She was in a situation where truth was as unlikely as false-hood.

"Not so, lady," the older man said slowly. He looked a question at his companions, but got no answer for they still stared open-mouthed at Eden. "Our master is a friend to the Emir, may his name be blessed, and his wishes are ours; however, we have seen none of his men among the hills . . . and none from Damascus either."

"My escort was not large," she improvised, "and men trained by Mustapha Kamal know well enough how to make themselves invisible." She gave a brief, impatient sigh and cast her eyes unfavorably over the three silent swordsmen.

"It cannot be helped," she said disdainfully. "I can wait no longer. If you are truly friends to the Emir, you will act in his interest in guiding me to his fortress."

Each man looked at the others. A shade unwilling-ly, their leader bowed his head. "Very well, lady. It is written that we take you there, in the name of the munificent Lady of the Moon, to whom Allah be ever bountiful. You may mount your horse; the path is not difficult."

Hardly able to believe in her success, Eden gra-ciously inclined her head and waited for them to lead Balan over to her. As she mounted she added a pri-vate Christian blessing upon the name of Al-Khatun.

The road, as her guides had indicated, was neither long nor arduous; it was merely completely concealed. The Saracens revealed paths that a moment earlier had been a seemingly impenetrable screen of foliage. Upon one occasion they rolled away a vast rock to show the way beyond it. It would have been impos-sible, she realized soberly, for her to have discov-ered it alone. This seemed to her a token that God had not forsaken her, that once again she was fol-lowing her course according to his will.

The path broadened, then rose to join a highway chiseled out of a deep curtain of rock. Balan hugged the cliff, keeping even his rolling eyes away from the emptiness to his left. The curtain of rock was convex, a long curve which extinguished all that lay ahead.

And when it ended, and became concave, even my Lady of Hawkhurst, self-styled ambassadress to the Princess Al-Khatun, could not prevent a gasp of un-prepared wonder. Where the rock swept inward in a jagged curve, a miraculous edifice clung to it. It seemed part of the stone that bred it and yet greater, rearing its astonishing towers and battlements close to their matrix like some grandiose bas-relief.

"Qal'a Zaydun," muttered her guide with almost superstitious respect.

She urged Balan forward and took the head of the brief cavalcade. Her back straight, she looked neither to left nor right as she clattered across the narrow causeway that crossed the concavity of the cliff face and made the stronghold of Ayub Ibn Zaydun mag-nificently impregnable.

Outside the towered gates, the man in the violet headdress reined forward, crying out, "Open in the name of the Sultan and of his illustrious consort, Al-Khatun." Eden suspected he showed more confidence than he felt. The wooden gates were flung open, to reveal a second pair, of iron, within. Eden indicated that she wished to speak at once with the Emir and one of the impassive-faced guards padded across a small, interior courtyard to relay her demand.

After a short time, the man returned and asked her to follow him, ordering her companions in another di-rection where they understood they would find food and drink. Thinking they deserved a greater reward, Eden delayed long enough to extract twenty gold besants from her saddlebag. They could well have robbed and killed her and thrown her body down a ravine for the wolves; instead they had led her faith-fully here. Their wide grins proclaimed them grati-fied, despite the Christian coinage, and their salaams as she left them were very low.

The armed guard now led Eden into the main part of the fortress. The dim, lofty interiors, with their great reaches of barbarically furnished space, lacked the soft, sybaritic splendor of a Damascene palace, but were no less imposing to the viewer. She had an impression of wood and stone, worn to the forms of man, of huge, unkempt rugs of wool and hide, of walls festooned in wicked-looking weaponry. There were tables large enough to seat a horse troop and the chairs were carved and blazoned like the thrones of emperors. Huge presses stood against the walls, too large ever to have entered by any door. The roofs were high and beamed like those of a Saxon castle and equally blackened by fire from the vast open hearths. Everywhere there was color . . . not the muted, glowing shades of Damascus, flowing into each other with a careful rhythm that rested the eye, but flaring, brilliant primary hues, raw and intense, a challenge to nature.

Eden felt her features freeze into a mask of pure, personified suspense as her guide stopped before two of his fellows who guarded immense doors from behind which came the wild notes of a flute above a deep buzz of talk. The guards exchanged words and the doors were opened.

Slowly, her eyes fixed ahead of her, Eden walked into a great chamber filled, it seemed, with dark-skinned, fierce-eyed men, outlandishly garbed and loud-spoken.

Ayub Ibn Zaydun, mercenary chief, robber-baron, territorial despot under the goodwill of the Sultan, kept his hall in state. At first it was not clear to Eden, staring ahead so that she might not look in every face for Stephen, which, among the dozens of splendidly dressed figures, might be the Emir, but as she walked forward a way was cleared before her and she was swept on a cloud of murmurs and flashing-eyed, curious looks toward a long, low seat, lit from above by one of the narrow slit windows that perforated the tall walls.

Ayub Ibn Zaydun was a vast monolith of a man, near fifty. His strong features, slant-eyed, full-lipped, with wide, oblique cheekbones, betrayed Slavic origins, while his bracken-colored hair could have been that of a Scot or a wild man of Ireland. He wore loose breeches, tied at the ankles, in fluid scarlet cloth, together with a breastplate and harness of leather embossed in gold, closely following the virile contours of his superbly muscled body. His arms and shoulders, bronzed and rippling with oil or sweat, were magnificently naked and gold glittered all about him. His neck was hung with medallions and bizarre, woven ornaments of bright thread. His arms were covered with bracelets and the rings in his ears were jeweled with rubies. Three large hunting dogs, a long-haired breed that Eden did not recognize, crouched at his feet. Behind him a huge cloak of saffron velvet was spread out across the settle, one of its corners cast negligently about the shoulders of another figure, equal in magnificence and, if anything, more barbaric.

It was hard to tell, upon cursory inspection, whether the Emir's couch companion was boy or woman. The slight shoulders and graceful posture were those of a woman, as were the heavily lidded eyes, kohled and outlined in gold and turquoise, the painted lashes, the lips carmined to a pouting fullness, the blushing cheeks curtained in a mass of tightly curled and hennaed hair whose perfume hung upon the air. The clothing was that of a man—the white, loose breeches like those of the Emir, the silken djellaba slit to the waist to reveal a fine-skinned but undoubtedly masculine breast. The rings, the beads, the scarves were a woman's; the dirk, the soft leather boots, the seamless coat of cloth-of-gold belonged to a man.

Realizing that she was staring, Eden returned her attention to the Emir who was regarding her with evident masculine interest. There was amusement, too, in his bold, brigand's visage, though its cause was indefinable. She felt a keen wariness as she sank into a graceful curtsy. She needed this man's friendship and must study how to obtain it.

Ibn Zaydun was the first to speak. "They tell me two things of you, lady," he said lazily, his voice deep, resonant and filled with authority. "Firstly, that you come from the Lady of the Moon, whom Allah preserve in all his ways; secondly . . . that you are the Lady of Hawkhurst and wife to a certain one of my prisoners. I find these facts to be strangely conflicting. My Lady Al-Khatun does not customarily use Christain emissaries. Perhaps you are able to enlighten me?"

The tone was light enough but Eden stiffened, knowing she must not fail this test. She had considered, too often, what she must say.

"The Princess Al-Khatun is a magnanimous and high-souled lady," she began fervently. "It is true that I have been her handmaiden, for I was a captive, like my husband . . . but, having heard my story, my gracious lady was pleased to release me so that I might seek out my lord and beg you to ransom him, in her name and my own."

The Emir gazed at her speculatively, one hand tapping rhythmically against his curving mouth. Again she sensed a dark amusement in the man.

"You would ransom your husband? But I have already told the Sultan that he is no longer for ransom."

"I know this, Emir . . . and I beg that you will find it in your heart to alter your decision. I have journeyed from England to find my husband . . ." Even as she forced herself to plead she had the impression that he was laughing at her behind those tapping fingers.

"I have a great deal of gold laid by," she persevered, "and I myself am content to be your hostage while you send for it to the Queen of England."

Ibn Zaydun smiled openly.

"Do you not believe," he suggested caressingly, "that there are certain values that have a greater worth than gold?"

"Certainly." She distrusted his amiable tone. "It is simply that you have the right to his ransom." She allowed a tinge of acid into her own.

The Emir continued, musingly, "What, then, do you suppose that those values might be? The things that are worth more than gold?"

"Why . . . kindness. Loyalty . . . love . . ." Eden did not care for this. He was amusing himself with some esoteric, personal diversion at her expense.

"Ah! Love! That, indeed!" His tongue dripped saccharin, his smile tantalized. "And do you love your husband very greatly, Lady of Hawkhurst . . . that you think him worth much gold?" There was insult in this, she knew.

"I have said that I have traveled far to find him," she said quietly.

"True. You are a woman of purpose," the Emir allowed, "and of great beauty."

His eyes moved over her with a peculiar detachment.

Eden began to be afraid. It was obvious that he would not permit her to reach him, that her plea was less to him than the dust at his feet. "If you will only allow me to see my husband," she began again, fighting the impulse to weep.

Ibn Zaydun's smile became an unholy thing. She saw, too, that the faces around them wore expressions of obscene glee.

"Is this your great love, then, lady?" the Emir demanded with a limitless contempt, stretching his glistening body with a deep, animal enjoyment. His hand fell casually upon the shoulder of his painted companion, the fingers then sliding deliberately beneath the thin stuff of the shirt and possessively caressing the soft, naked skin. He put his lips close to one ringed ear and his foul whisper was loud enough for her to hear.

"How can it be . . . this great love? She does not even recognize you, Stephen."

It seemed to Eden later that she should have cried out, lost all consciousness, run mad perhaps . . . and yet all she could do was to stand, fixed and rigid, letting the terrible arrows of the truth shaft home as her shocked system registered the reverberations of his words.

Somehow she found the courage to turn her eyes upon that outlandish figure. She might almost have believed it at first to be a cruel joke. There was nothing of Stephen in that painted face, neither of his look nor his manner.

And then, slowly, the blackened lashes lifted and the eyes were bent upon her. They were blue as the summer skies over Hawkhurst.

She cried out now, in agony.

The blue eyes checked for a moment as if puzzled. Their pupils were large, dark and dilated; there was no comprehension in them.

"What have you done to him?" Eden cried. She staggered and would have fallen had not a hand steadied her.

"Ah . . . so you do know him after all?" The Emir's voice was honeyed gall. "But it seems that he does not, at present, recall who *you* might be . . ." He moved his caressing hand to the long, inner length of the white-clad thigh. "This is your wife, Stephen, my beautiful one. This is the Lady Eden."

"Eden?"

He rolled his curled head dully toward her again, the heavy perfume reeking from it. "Eden," he said again as though it were a word known long ago and since forgotten.

"Oh Stephen!" She moved toward him, held out her hand. "What has happened to you, Stephen?"

He smiled vaguely but she could not feel that he knew her. His hand was cold to the touch and he did not return her pressure.

"You will have to forgive him," purred Ibn Zaydun. "It is the opium . . . he is always so *excessive* . . . but then, in other ways, his excesses are his greatest charm . . . are they not, my sweet, white-fleshed dreamer?"

And before Eden's horrified eyes, the half-naked Emir pulled Stephen into his mastering arms and kissed him full upon the lips.

Retching, beside herself, she rushed at them, her

arm raised to strike. Ibn Zaydun caught it lightly before the blow could fall and tightened his grip into a cruel tourniquet.

"Thus . . . I now have you both!" His laugh was echoed lasciviously by his minions. "Never fear," he added, seeing her eyes wide and horror. "I have no taste for woman's flesh." He leaned toward her, his musky odor hideously sweet in her nostrils. "And neither now has he!" came the loathsome whisper.

Her anger overcame the horror and her voice was strong and accusing. "How have you done this?"

The Emir waved a disclaiming hand. "Not I, but the fruit of the poppy. It is a wondrous substance. It can make a reality of what, heretofore, were nothing but half acknowledged dreams. So it has been for Stephen. I have not made of him anything that Allah has not made before me; you deceive yourself if you think otherwise."

"You blaspheme! God did not make man to mate with man."

He sighed. "So beautiful and an innocent. Open your eyes, lady. Look at the world as it is . . . not as you would have it be."

Her laughter was harsh and bitter. "Innocent no longer. The world I have seen is not as I would have it . . . nor yet are the men within it."

But the Emir was becoming fatigued with such fruitless observation. "That is your misfortune, since you will have it so," he said curtly. He stood, stretching to his full, imposing height, and looked down at her without mercy. "You are not wanted here, Lady Eden. Stephen of Hawkhurst is not for ransom. He is mine."

She recoiled. Surely he would not dismiss her at once. "I would not leave until I have spoken with him . . . alone," she begged, miserably aware of his power over her.

Ibn Zaydun shrugged, uninterested. "Very well, since you wish it. You have, as you say, come far. Tomorrow he should be himself again—or what is left of himself, but do not expect to find the boy who left you. He is gone forever."

The towering figure strode from the chamber, his lieutenants washing about his heels and Eden was left to sink down on the vacated settle, her head bent in her hands. Now that they were gone, she would let herself weep; she would break the hard heart of heaven with her weeping if she could.

Alone in the echoing room, she lifted her voice in anguish to the God who had forsaken her.

"Was it for this, Lord, that you sent me forth? Sweet Jesus . . . I implore you . . . why? Why have you permitted this degradation?" What heinous sin had she committed unaware, during that long sleep of childhood at Hawkhurst, that she should be heaven-sent half across the face of the earth, not, in the end, to find the reward of her faith, but this bitter, unimagined punishment? Or was it that Christ had changed his design for her when she herself had fallen from his grace? Were the sins of Damascus to be expiated in Qal'a Zaydun? And at the terrible expense of Stephen's soul?

She could not believe it. All was confusion. All was loss. Almost, she would have found her way at once to the cliff-hung battlements and cast herself below, as Jezebel had been cast down, to be carrion for dogs. And yet she must see Stephen once more, must speak to him, make him understand . . . There was a light touch on her arm.

"Lady . . ."

A tall boy stood beside her, of perhaps eighteen years, his dark eyes filled with pity.

"My name is Abdul. I wished to say to you that I will show you somewhere you may rest and be unmolested. I would bring food to you there—if you would follow me. It is not good to sorrow so much."

Touched to repeated tears by such kindness in this unkind place she summoned the weary relic of a smile and nodded gratefully.

"You have suffered a deep shock," the boy continued as he led her slowly from the hall. "The Lord of Hawkhurst is much changed since first he came here . . ." He hurried on as she made a small, choking sound. "But you have seen him at the worst, I think. That is something."

"Truly," she agreed with a shuddering horror of recollection, "there can be no worse, surely, than that I have seen." Ibn Zaydun's impure kiss upon Stephen's painted lips would stay with her all of her days. Like the kiss of Judas it had been a sign of betrayal, but what it had betrayed she did not yet dare to know in full. She must live each minute as it came.

"Tomorrow," said Abdul gently, "I will tend him if I can. We are friends . . . I, too, am a prisoner. I will see to it that he has only a small amount of the opium."

"Must he have it?" Her voice was low and trembled.

"It has become necessary to him."

"How is that?" She knew little of such darkness.

The boy shrugged sadly. "It is not known how. It is no matter. The thing is accomplished. Many use it here, but your lord . . . did not take advice. Now he must have the opium. Without it he is mad; he suffers."

Eden gave a moan of pain. She had not thought there could be greater depths to this pit of misery wherein she fell unendingly in a black vortex, amid hateful whispers and without her God.

The room that Abdul showed her was in one of the towers, with a door giving on to the tempting battlements. It was cool, quiet, and bare save for the straw palliasse the boy had brought. He left her to fetch wine and food though she denied all desire for them.

"You will need strength, therefore eat," he advised when he returned. She obeyed like a half-sleeping child, though she could not have named what passed her lips. Abdul remained with her for most of that day, walking with her upon the walls, talking to her softly of Stephen when he first came to the fortress, fearless, strong in his faith and bitterly resenting his captivity.

"He used to speak of you then, my lady. He held

your memory very dear. There was a medal you gave
him; he used to . . ."

"Pray do not!" she cried. Then with sharp control.
"How has he come to this pass?"

The boy bowed his head. "The Emir Ayub is a . . .
most persuasive man," he said in a voice tinged with
his own private hurt and shame. He looked at her
carefully, weighing his next words. "Whatever it may
appear . . . he is not . . . unkind to the Lord of
Hawkhurst. On the contrary—I think him to be the
only man who can influence the Emir with his lightest word. I know you perhaps cannot . . . will not wish
to . . . understand, but there is great affection between
them."

But she had cast her hand before her eyes. He said
no more.

The night that followed was the nadir of her life.
How willingly, now, would she have faced the wild
beasts of the mountain, rather than this remorseless
dismantling of her spirit.

She could not pray. Her lips would not form the
words. Nor would God hear her voice. He had cast
her into the outer darkness and Stephen with her
. . . poor Stephen who had never done harm and had
loved his Maker all of his life, even unto taking his
Cross. It was beyond her understanding.

Toward the dawn she began to think that perhaps
the Devil had greater powers than man had yet discovered. He could inspire weakness to evil despite all
prayers, as she knew to her own, irreparable loss.
Perhaps, Satan had even risen from his pit and cast
out God. Confusion would reign throughout the earth
and it would soon be wholly given over to evil. The
strange heresy did not even trouble her as it should;
at least it provided that which she most needed after
the long, anguished night . . . an explanation of
Stephen's terrible, undeserved fate.

When morning came she had not slept. Hollow-
eyed and deathly pale, she braided her hair to make
work for her shaking hands. She could not stop the

trembling of her whole body, so filled was she with trepidation at the prospect of her meeting with her husband. She had scarcely gained control of herself when Abdul appeared. She would not touch the bread and wine he had brought, but begged him to lead her at once to Stephen.

The room where he was reeked and gleamed with luxury. He lay upon a damask-covered couch, inhaling dreamily from a brief pipe whose purpose she could only guess. He lay on his side, holding the upturned bowl of the instrument over a small lamp on the table beside him. The table also held a pearl-handled spatula and a delicate porcelain box of miniature proportions.

He looked up and his eyes filled instantly with pain. There was no doubt now that he recognized her.

"Eden. Dear God!" He laid down the pipe.

His face, without its paint, was ashen and terribly strained, the eyes huge and wild within their dark sockets. There were lines upon it that did not come to a man until old age.

"Do not gaze at me so; I cannot bear it!" He threw his arm across his ravaged countenance for she was burning him with her pity.

"Stephen. You know me. I am glad." Her broken whisper was almost too low to hear. He let his arm fall and nodded vehemently.

"How could I not? You have not changed. You still have that beauty that catches at the heart."

Her agony ached in her eyes. He half rose from the couch and made as if to take her in his arms. Then he faltered and fell back, a wave of shame flushing his pale cheeks.

"I would have given my life to have avoided this," he muttered despairingly. "It is not right that you should see what . . . I have become."

"Oh my dear . . ." She stepped toward him.

He shook his head with a wretched violence. "Don't speak so. I am lost to you . . . and you to me . . . do you not know that?"

She could not speak. It was the truth. Ibn Zaydun's kiss had betrayed nothing but the truth.

"Why have you come?" he asked dully, after a long time.

"'I came to bring you ransom," she said simply, her weariness weighting her words.

He laughed, an empty, ghostly sound. "My body has already found its ransom . . . in the opium. As for my soul . . ." He suddenly began to shake uncontrollably. "I fear that it is condemned to eternal hellfire . . . if such there be. I no longer care whether there be or no."

"Do not say so!" she cried in instinctive horror. She did not see the irony of this, that she, who had denied God three times over during the solitary, tormented night, should fear for his lost faith.

Suddenly the strength came into her and she realized her purpose anew. "It is no matter what you have become!" she cried with a note of desperate hope in her voice. "You must leave this place, now, with me. We will find our way back to the Christian lines and you can take your leave from King Richard. And then we will go back home together, to Hawkhurst. It cannot be too late to mend . . ."

He would not let her go on. "It is too late . . . by a long, long space, not in time alone. It is not time that divides us now." His voice was very gentle, and his smile was suddenly, agonizingly that of the young Stephen who had been her mentor so long ago. "There can be no way to mend . . . the marriage that was once between us. I can . . . no longer . . . love you as you deserve. Nor, when you came to know the man I have become, could you love me."

She covered her ears, shouting her denial.

"It is no use, Eden. Leave this place. Go home. Forget me. Have the marriage annulled. I'll give you any . . . evidence you need . . . but go! Go quickly!"

She stood her ground, tears washing her cheeks. "Why? Why will you not escape?"

He shook his head slowly, then crossed to take her

by the shoulders, looking down at her with kind, haunted eyes.

"Very well, since you force me; I will not leave because I do not wish it. I wish to remain with one who loves me . . ." He ignored her sharp cry, going on relentlessly, "and whom I also love . . . not with the learned love of unawakened children such as was shared between you and me . . . but with my whole, discovered self. It was hard for me to accept it, believe me; almost as hard, perhaps, as it is for you at this moment. I suffered, both for my body and for my soul. And because I suffered I sought relief in this insidious friend . . ." He indicated the little box of raw brown opium. "I did not heed the warnings of others who had come to know his ways, and now I have my punishment. That, too, must keep me here. So you see, beloved shadow from my long-distant childhood . . . there can be no leaving here for me. Hawkhurst was ever your true home; mine is Qal'a Zaydun."

Her heartbroken cry wrenched at his breast, but he put her from him and called for Abdul, who kept watch at the door.

Then, taking up his pipe of opium and placing it in a fold of his robe, he was gone from her sight, forever.

Many hours, it seemed, and many tears later, Abdul touched her shoulder where she lay across the couch in Stephen's vacated chamber and told her that the Emir wished to speak with her.

"He says he will give you an escort, for Stephen's sake, to take you safely wherever you wish to go."

Every sense dulled and leaden, she dragged herself slowly to her feet and followed the boy like a mindless thing.

The Emir was alone, in a small chamber off the hall. His eyes no longer glittered and there was no malice in him as he spoke to her.

"Lady, you have found great suffering here. I regret it, for Stephen does. You will know by now that you must leave here . . . but there is one thing more that you should know. I will not keep it from you. Stephen does not realize it, but he has abused the drug that sustains him for too long. The opium is killing him. He will die . . . quite soon . . . another year at the most."

The quiet words were insupportable. She felt herself transformed into a monster of vengeance; her nails were claws to tear out his eyes. She cried, "It is you alone who have done this thing!"

His blood was streaked upon her hands. Weeping hysterically she lunged for his dagger, but he caught her hand in his iron grip as before and shook his head, smiling grimly.

"No, no, lady. You must not take me from him. He would die the sooner, believe me, if you did." He released her with a sigh that was almost a groan and she fell at his feet, defeated. He did not speak again and she heard him leave the chamber softly with his rhythmic, animal's step.

There was nothing for her to do but to take the road, a score of armed men once more at her back. When their captain asked her where they were bound she did not know, at first, what to say. Her course had for so long been so firmly set toward this terrible place that she hardly knew how to consider the leaving of it.

At length she told him, "We ride for Jaffa." She must make her peace with Berengaria before . . . Before what? Going home alone to Hawkhurst, to sit in front of her fire and gaze into its shadows as before, down the long days until death should deliver her? It was not to be borne.

She thought now of Tristan as she rode out again across the narrow causeway between rock and rock. Although the knowledge of his love had lain against her heart—for nothing, not even deepest sorrow, could change that—she had not dwelled upon him with the surface of her mind as long as she was in Qal'a Zaydun. What could there be for them now, she wondered wearily? One day she would be free from marriage, yes . . . but how could they take for themselves a freedom won at such a price? She must not even ask the question; she could not think about the future. Her heart was too heavy with her failure, her mind still too bemused with shock.

She addressed no word to the Saracen captain, attired as if for battle, who rode quietly at her side, but fixed her sad eyes upon the narrow path ahead and tried, from out of the destruction of her life and Stephen's, to find her stumbling way, through prayer, back to God.

▼▼▼▼▼▼▼▼▼▼▼▼▼▼▼▼▼▼▼▼▼▼▼▼▼▼▼▼▼▼▼▼▼▼▼▼▼▼

CHAPTER SIXTEEN

Masyaf!

Perhaps it was the subdued demeanor of their charge that had impressed itself upon Eden's outriders, making them sluggish and inattentive. Whatever it was, they were in no way prepared for the event that overtook them in the high-walled pass which would lead them, that afternoon, out of the mountains.

At one moment they were riding in orderly fashion, two by two behind Eden and their leader, the last of them filing down the harsh hill path into the welcome ease of the valley floor; the next, the twenty men and horses were thrown into flailing, wild-eyed rout as a force of twice as many men, some ramieh, some on foot, crashed down upon them from out of the rocks and trees. They fought bravely but the surprise was too great. Armed *cap a pie* and in their own territory, they were ignominiously cut down by the swinging axes, struck dead in their saddles by the upward thrust of a sword, felled to the dust by the murderous blow of the spiked mace, their brains let out upon the sand. It was all over in seconds. Eden, after the first horror, her overstressed faculties incapable of accepting any more of tragedy, lay senseless in their midst beside the decapitated body of the quiet captain.

When she came haltingly back to herself her first thought was that perhaps she was in hell. Her head hung dizzily downwards and something firm and oddly warm was beating rhythmically against her temple. She could not feel the lower half of her body. It

369

didn't seem to matter anymore. Again she relapsed thankfully into unconsciousness.

When she next returned from darkness it became clear that she was, in fact, not in hell but hanging across the saddle of a horse. She groaned and the steady motion ceased; her head no longer knocked against the warm flank. There were hands about her waist and then she was uncertainly upright on the ground.

Numbly she stared about her. The faces which surrounded her were not those of Ibn Zaydun's men, though certainly of a similar cast, being uniformly armed to the teeth and for the most part very young. She frowned, trying to understand. Then she remembered.

Seeing her pale, one of them stepped forward to support her, his grin not unfriendly.

"Who are you?" Eden managed to ask, suddenly aware that her throat was on fire.

The man offered her his water bottle. "My name is of no importance. I am, as we all are, but a servant of my master."

"The Sultan?" But he would say no more. Recovering his canteen he stabbed a brown finger toward her horse. She was delighted to realize that at least she had not lost Balan and she mounted gladly. The cavalcade proceeded.

It was not long, however, before she noticed that the direction in which these unknown soldiers were taking her was almost exactly due north, according to the sun's height, and that they were already climbing among the foothills of a new and gloomily forbidding range of mountains.

Her captors did not appear to mean her any harm, nor yet, on the other hand, did they intend to converse with her. Every attempt to question them about their mysterious master was ignored, and demands as to why they had not killed her along with her previous escort were met with a peremptory, "Be silent, Frankish woman!"

Realizing that she could gain nothing by irritating

them, she receded into her withdrawn state of the morning and again addressed herself to prayer. But she found that the familiar words meant little to her. Life had become unreal—as insubstantial and irrational as a dream. It no longer seemed to be of any importance what happened to her, for she scarcely had existence save when she was jolted into physical awareness by the savage intricacies of the path. She sat upon Balan's back and simply stared at the stones ahead, without thought, without emotion.

She traveled in this fashion for nearly thirty miles. They made two stops but during neither of them did she emerge from her suspended, almost catatonic state.— It was her body's healing gift, did she but know it, to her dangerously over-burdened mind.

In the end what brought her to herself was the sunset. She could not see the sun go down among mountaintops without feeling Tristan close to her. It seemed that she would always see him with that blood-red halo . . . on the roof of the palace at Acre . . . in the paradise garden above Damascus. And now she was again among mountains, a wild and jagged range of boulder-strewn passes and echoing canyons, more threatening in aspect than any through which she had yet traveled.

This was one question that they consented to answer. "It is the Ansariyah Range, woman, which lies between the rivers Homs and Orontes."

She seemed to catch the echo then of something previously heard or known, but it was gone at once and did not return.

"Is there far to go?" at last she asked wearily, almost spent.

"Not far." A young man pointed upwards into the dark mass of the mountain.

"I can see nothing. Only rock upon rock."

Then, straining her eyes into the gloom, she saw that there *was* something more. Against the black, ill-favored face of the mountain in its aureole of flame-streaked cloud, there appeared several tiny, all but invisible points of light. They were widely spaced and they grew as the party approached them. The path changed direction and she saw suddenly that the lights were not a part of the hillside but of a huge, shadowy mass that loomed upon its lower slopes, its uneven, towered and castellated outline proclaiming it to be another vast stronghold such as the one she had left.

"That is the fortress of your master?"

"That is Masyaf!"

Again it seemed to Eden that she should know that name. "And your master himself?" she tried again.

"You will be taken before the noble Rashid, who will do with you as he desires." Rashid? The name was nothing to her.

She prayed that he was not another despot as depraved as Ibn Zaydun.

The Master of Masyaf was at his meat when his troop of ramieh returned. His dining hall was at the heart of a castle built like a labyrinth, its only entrance through an insignificant gateway in the foot of one of its massive walls, double-doored and heavily guarded. A password was given, echoed and reechoed to lead Eden and several of her senior companions toward this central chamber, whose resounding din, before they reached it, guided them through corridors hushed with heavy hangings and rich carpets spread negligently underfoot. The Master of Masyaf shared one thing with Ibn Zaydun; Eden saw clearly that Rashid, whoever he was, was a master of great wealth. As she entered the hall, she could almost have fancied herself back at Mategriffon: there was the same heady roar of conversation, the same shrieking plaint of pipe and timbrel, and insistent beat of the drum; the same clatter of tableware; the same energetic movement of men who did not long sit still.

There must have been one hundred and fifty fighting Saracens in the hall, seated at four long tables arranged in the familiar E-shape of understood hierarchy. This time there was no mistaking the Master, for his bearing distinguished him above the ordinary.

His figure was neither tall nor broad and he was the

only one among them of any great age, though this itself was indeterminate. Like Eleanor of Aquitaine, the man who commanded the center of the board might have been any age between forty and the grave. His intelligent and patriarchal face was deeply lined, but his eyes, as they took note of the pale-skinned woman accompanying his captain of ramieh, were clear and shrewd, and his gestures as he conversed were swift and alert. He was dressed with a simple magnificence in black and gold. His aspect was that of absolute authority. This much Eden had realized of the man before she found herself suddenly thrust forward and unceremoniously thrown down upon her face before him.

"Abase yourself, Frankish woman, before the legendary Rashid-ed-Din Sinan . . . Prince among the Hashashin!"

She lay with her face pressed against the chill stone floor, her chilled blood pumping a warning within, as she recalled, from some distant cell of memory, a golden, purring voice which cracked, laughed suddenly and cried, "Bring down the Assassins upon him!" And another voice, the one to which her heart was attuned, offering its stern and meticulous account of the nature and ways of Islam's murderous and heretical sect.

As if to mock these voices from tired memory, there came another, close at hand it seemed, that belonged to days even longer departed. Indeed it could have no place here, either within her own swimming, weary head or outside it.

"Go gently, Faisal; you should have a greater care for such beauty."

She did not believe it. She was possessed of devils. The voice, harsh, grating, unforgettable, was that of Sir Hugo de Malfors.

"You may rise to your feet, Lady Eden. My Lord Rashid permits it."

Slowly, still in her dream, she rose. It was no mere devil in her head. There he stood in truth, grinning, black-avised, triumphant . . . the Baron of Stukesey that was overlord of Hawkhurst, swaggering before the Prince of the Assassins in ruby velvet, his face seamed from brow to chin with the livid, puckered memento of young Gilles's vengeance.

"They have captured a rare prize, Excellence," he observed, his hog's eyes gleaming with joy. There followed a swift exchange in which Sinan was apprised of Eden's birth and station and her position as Sir Hugo's vassal.

He held up his hand to silence the black knight in mid-flood. "I would hear this woman's story from her own lips." He did not speak loudly and yet his voice was clear enough to be heard throughout the vaulted hall. When Sinan spoke thus, no other did so.

Eden found herself swiftly propeled to a more intimate antechamber where there were soft couches and tables set with wine. She was permitted to sit and to drink and shortly Rashid came into the room. Sir Hugo, to her immense relief, was no longer with him.

"And now," that calm, abstracted voice stated, "you will tell me all. I am intrigued by your presence . . . and by the extremity of coincidence that brings you here so soon after your close countryman."

She sensed no particular kindness in him, but neither was there cruelty, so she took courage as she wove the brief, truthful outline of her quest. Although she felt a great fear in the presence of this all-powerful satrap whose evil reputation exacted even Saladin's respect, it was not a fear that existed upon a personal level. He would not harm her; she was not of any importance to him, unless he held her to ransom. She relaxed a little and sipped at her wine as she told her tale.

"And so you have found that your husband is not to be ransomed," the quiet voice said thoughtfully when she had finished. "And you have left him in the hands of my old enemy, Ibn Zaydun?"

"That is so." She lowered her eyes. The bones of truth would suffice.

"And what would you do, were I to allow you to leave Masyaf?"

"Journey to Jaffa, to seek the Queen of England whom I serve."

There was a faint inclination of the black silk turban and its gold crescent pin shimmered with the movement.

"It may be that you will do this . . . but not yet. Meanwhile you are my guest. None here will do you hurt."

"Sir Hugo . . ." she began, now knowing what she would say.

"None will harm you," he repeated, his clear eyes holding hers, yet looking far beyond them . . . and at the same time into them as though they saw through the fragile flesh into her thoughts. His eyes, she saw, were almost colorless, a mere wisp of smoky gray floating behind them. She could not rest from his eyes. It was an experience quite unlike any she had known. His low voice seemed, despite its weight of authority, to smooth away the care that bound her up, so that she was filled with an almost euphoric sense of well-being. She nodded obediently when he told her to leave him, that she was to rest, to sleep fast until the morrow.

Then she was gliding weightlessly from the chamber, the exhaustion gone from her bones and the furrow of sadness from her brow. She was as insubstantial as the confused dream her life had become and her thoughts drifted away from her, so that all she knew of that night's passing was the amazing sensation of hovering, bodiless, above the feather pallet to which they led her to rest.

The next day her strength and vigor had almost fully returned to her and she was able to look rationally at the world for the first time since she had entered Qal'a Zaydun. A heavy calm pervaded her, perhaps the gift of the enigmatic man who ruled this fortress. If so, it was not the gift of this world. What he had performed last night upon her tired body and racked spirit had been nothing short of magic, she was certain. And magic was the work of Satan. Was this, then, the root of the temporal power of Rashid-ed-Din Sinan?

Even so, she could not help a sense of deep relief at her own return to herself on this pleasantly cool day at Masyaf. It was soon apparent that she had the run of the castle. Though every door was guarded, none prevented her entrances. She was even permitted to walk in the courtyards between the tall, long-windowed walls where the sun slanted downwards upon a tiled pool or fountain.

It was in one of these that Sir Hugo de Malfors discovered her, shortly after noon. "Well found, my lady."

She neither shuddered nor looked askance but gave him a long, contemplative look. Her revulsion from him would never change, but there was a familiarity about that very feeling that reminded her, ludicrously, of home.

"What is your business here, Sir Hugo?"

He arched a quizzical brow. "Is that the sum of your curiosity? Do you not long to hear of the adventures that brought me here . . . a penniless baron, beaten from his own doors, with scarce a man to follow him?" He was bitter and he found her to blame. She must be careful of him.

"It is not my concern. I ask you only what you do here?"

He frowned. "Still proud? Well, you may hold to your dignity, lady . . . but remember I once brought you low enough. To your back, where you belong! I had good sport of you; I was not best pleased to find you gone."

Had she been at Hawkhurst she would have found him terrifying, but somehow the looming walls of Sinan's fortress and the power they enclosed had the effect of belittling him so that his angry insults hardly disturbed her.

"But all shall be set right between us, Lady Eden, I promise you!"

If he had hoped to arouse her he was disappointed. She sat down on the edge of the fountain and trailed a hand in the water, her look still clear and thoughtful. It seemed that he could no longer reach her.

"If you will not tell me why you are here," she said, as though he had not spoken, "then you will not. It is only that, like the lord of this stronghold, I am curious as to the coincidence of your presence."

Hugo bared his excellent teeth. "And you are sure it means mischief? You want to know, too, whether my business touches yourself or your capon of a husband? Well, want must be your master," he said unpleasantly, "for I shall not tell you. Only one thing will I say to you . . . when my work here is complete and I journey home, I shall not go alone. We shall go back to Hawkhurst together, my lady, and take up where we left off. How like you that?"

Still she did not betray a reaction, though the deep bile rose in her throat. Her calm look enraged him as much as her silence. He stepped nearer to her, his arm raised.

"Tread warily, Sir Hugo. Sinan has said that none shall harm me here. I do not think that you are the man to go against his word."

His arm fell and he made a contemptuous sound. "Not for a whore I've used already," he blustered. "There's fresher meat to be had in Masyaf." Then he leaned into her face, his hot eyes hating her. "And I suspect I am no longer the only one who has enjoyed these golden charms. There was a certain knight in Jaffa who blew very warm in your cause. Indeed, I have an appointment with him on my return . . . I tell you so that you may pray for his misguided soul, for I shall kill him when we meet."

Now, at last, she could not hide her fear, but raised startled eyes toward him, one hand stretched instinctively to plead.

"God's Holy Bones! So that's how it lies?" His

laughter was triumphant. "Then you may commence your prayers now, my lady, for I will enjoy this death better than if he were a Saracen."

Mightily pleased with himself, he threw her one more look of contempt and strode from the yard, leaving her to her shattered peace.

Her disquiet grew until it filled the quiet place. She had forgotten Tristan's challenge, buried deep beneath the anguish and the love that had followed its revelation in that timeless place among the mountains. Now it seemed that it must be taken up . . . and she could not but fear for her lover's life. Again the fear of God possessed her. Was this, also, to be part of her punishment . . . that Tristan should die as well as poor Stephen?

She tried helplessly to control her terror that wanted to take wings, telling herself that Sir Hugo need not be the victor, that perhaps the two would never meet. God knew that these were unpredictable times; there could be other circumstances . . . Sir Hugo might be killed.

She toyed with the thought of enlisting Sinan's partisanship, but this was soon discarded. Whatever there was between Rashid and de Malfors, it would have more claim upon him than the personal cares of a Frankish woman prisoner. She must leave this place; find Tristan and beg him to avoid the meeting. But, even now, she could see the gentle smile behind his eyes as he would refuse her. The challenge, she remembered, had first been his. There was nothing she could do. Fate would take its course and she must only wait, for she could not alter it.

She was disturbed, suddenly, in her unhappy reverie, by the unexpected sound of a woman's shrill laughter. Despite Sir Hugo's hint, she had seen no women about the castle and the sound intrigued her. It had come, she thought, from the round tower behind the inner battlements which enclosed the courtyard. Thinking it better than sitting still in her sadness, she rose, shook out her skirts and set off to investigate.

She left the yard by its narrow doorway, crossed another, smaller court, and entered the tower that stood at one of its corners.

There were three rooms, one above the other, joined by a twisting stair. All were deserted. All were in various stages of silken disarray that confirmed the presence of women. Perfume hung in the air, musk, roses and patchouli. Here were their instruments, a lute and a rebec, here their boxes of cosmetics, here their diaphanous garments of gauze, ribboned and braided, gilded and silvered like the wings of butterflies. Their owners must still be close at hand. Eden listened, but did not hear the bright, metallic laughter again.

And yet it seemed that there *was* a sound, a faint but insistent murmur carried lazily on the air, but whether of music or voices, she could not tell. She left the tower by the only other door and moved toward the sound. She found herself behind the castle where it roosted in the hillside. There was a covered way before her, formed of stone pillars wound about with rose and thorn trees that met and entwined above them, together with a dark green creeper bearing intense violet bugles made translucent by the sun. At the end of it was an arched door in the foot of a wall whose summit was hidden in foliage. From beyond the door came the sounds that she had heard, muted and dulcet, the strings of instruments and a low-pitched singing voice. She turned the iron ring that opened the door.

The lofty, vine-covered wall enclosed a garden that had been caused to bloom, by some miracle of husbandry, out of the sterile mountainside. Its grass grew as green as the eye could bear, laced with watercourses flowing over patterned tiles. Flowers were few and therefore the more precious, their vibrant colors piercing the air in great gashes . . . vermilion azaleas, cyclamen, creamy lilies, the warm golden spread of the saffron crocus, some already reclaimed from the sun by the deepening shade of the fruit trees . . . fig, quince and orange . . . and one immense dark cedar beneath which stood the scarlet and gold striped pa-

vilion of Sinan. The satrap himself was seated outside
it upon a couch spread with silks and bright kelims,
stroking the glossy head of a nimr, the small, elegant
leopard of these regions, which lay stretched across
his lap.

Before him, extended upon the grass in attitudes of
deep sleep, lay two youths, clothed in green silk. The
Master brooded over them, his countenance serene
and watchful, while several young girls, their curved
bodies visible beneath iridescent robes that shimmered
as they moved, played softly upon the ud or the
cithara and one of them sang in a gentle, lulling tone.
Eden checked and would have retreated, so intimate
and yet so strangely expectant was the scene; but the
colorless eyes had seen her and a girl hurried toward
her, a finger to her lips.

"Al-Jabal welcomes the new addition to his garden. You may be seated, but make no sound, only
watch and listen."

Eden signified her willingness and was given a place
near the foot of the Master's couch. It seemed that all
called him Al-Jabal . . . the Old Man of the Mountains
. . . without disrespect, though it had been a name
first given to him by the Franks whose lands and
camel trains he had terrorized in his preying swoops
from Masyaf upon the exposed plain.

As Eden allowed herself to float upon the warm,
persuasive waves of the music, she became gradually
aware of a scent that clung about the sleeping youths
. . . a spicy, pungent aroma that she had known before . . . in the sleeping-chamber of Al-Ahkis. They
had spoken little of hashish in Damascus, though
she had, of course, known of its existence, and she
had remained unaware of the nature of the substance
which had so heightened and released her perceptions
in the dragoman's exquisite palace.

Now her spine tingled as she watched the two young
men, smooth-faced and entirely at peace in sleep.
How much of the drug had they been given . . . and
for what purpose? Looking around at the perfect
beauty of the garden she found it hard to believe that

what she saw could be a part of anything that was
evil, yet she had heard it said of Sinan that he was a
demon with the face of a man, and she knew that he
dealt in destruction and death. Time passed. The
peace of the place weighed so heavily that she did not
think she would ever find the purpose to move from
her present position. Then one of the sleepers made a
small sound. He moved his head a little, then raised
his knuckles to his eyes like a child. The other, too,
was soon stirring. Sinan ceasing his rhythmic caressing
of the nimr and leaned toward them, concentrating
all his great power and strength upon them. They
gazed into his eyes and seemed to see nothing.

"Arise, my sons. Sit. Listen to my voice for I
would command you," he invited, his voice a mere
wisp of smoke in the charged afternoon.

They obeyed him at once, rising to sit, cross-legged
and grave-eyed before his splendid couch. Eden saw
that their pupils were dilated and dense as Stephen's
had been, but the whole eye was very bright and
their young faces fresh with health.

"This day you have woken to find yourselves in
my paradise, and all its delights shall be yours, even
as Allah has promised. For it is written," quoted the
light, steel-smooth cadence, "for those who fear the
majesty of their Lord there are two gardens planted
with shady trees. Each is watered by a flowing spring.
Each bears every kind of fruit in pairs. They shall
recline on couches lined with rich brocade and within
their reach shall hang the fruits of both gardens. They
shall take to themselves young virgins who are un-
touched, as fair as coral or rubies. Shall the reward
of goodness be anything but good?

"But Allah has also said," he continued, his voice
suddenly terrible, "for the Unbelievers I have prepared fetters and chains and a blazing fire. The time
has come, my sons who have found favor with me,
for the Unbeliever who has been chosen to depart into
that fire."

Eden caught her breath, afraid, as he reached into
the breast of his robe and brought forth two daggers,

which he held out to the youths, handles foremost. Both rose to their feet and stood before him.

"Beloved sons," Sinan intoned, "go thou, in the time when it shall be accomplished, and slay for me the Unbeliever from whom Allah has turned his face . . . and when you have slain him, return to me and you shall know paradise again. And if you do not return . . . nonetheless Allah will send his angels to bear you up into paradise. And this shall be your reward when you have slain the Marquess of Montferrat."

No heed was paid to Eden's gasp. The young men put out their hands and took the daggers, carried them to their lips, then knelt before Sinan. He gave them his blessing and then rose to leave, gliding with noiseless motion across the grass.

A girl signaled to Eden to follow and she did so, her clamorous thoughts fermenting what she had heard.

Al-Jabal turned slightly and allowed her to fall into step with him. "So . . . you are not to be a part of their first taste of paradise? As you will . . . though your beauty fits you for it. You may come to change your mind." There was no threat, scarcely even suggestion in his words. It was obvious, indeed, that he honored her with the idea that she should become a houri to gratify the drug-heightened lusts of his Hash-ashin.

For the two youths in the garden, paradise had already begun. They would continue to eat the hashish until they had done their leader's will, so that afterwards, even should they be caught and killed, only their bodies would remain earthbound . . . bodies that they would gladly leave behind, knowing that such a death, in the service of Allah and Al-Jabal, would take them straight to the eternal paradise of the two gardens.

Conscious of Sinan's guards, waiting for him at the end of the covered alley, Eden dared to question him before he should be gone from her.

"My lord . . . if you will . . . what has the Marquess of Montferrat done to incur your punishment?"

He surveyed her with a calm lack of surprise. "He

has committed an act of piracy against one of my ships."

Eden could well believe it. "And for this he must die?" A petty reason, surely, for one so powerful.

"Not for that. You asked me a question."

"Then for what?"

His expression told her nothing. "Is not the Marquess the enemy of your King?"

"Perhaps it were better put the other way."

"Either way, he is a man with many enemies. It is because of this that he will die."

"But surely . . ." She broke off, her instincts telling her she must not show sympathy for Conrad. "Surely . . . this . . . execution . . . is none of King Richard's doing?"

"A king is not an executioner," was the bland, neutral reply. "Not even when it is a king who must be executed."

She frowned. "Your Excellence is pleased to speak in riddles."

"Perhaps you do not yet know . . . it is two days since the Marquess of Montferrat was voted King of Jerusalem by an international council of the Franks. It is the zenith of a bold career," he observed impartially. "He will not long wear his crown."

They had reached the first courtyard. Abruptly, his guard surrounded him and Eden was left alone with what she had learned.

She stood still for a moment, shocked in a way that no miseries of her own could have contrived. Soon, she made her way, without thinking, back to the courtyard where she had sat earlier. She stood staring into the rippling fountain as if its movement could clear the confusion in her mind. Conrad to die at the hand of the Assassins! A man with many enemies, Sinan had said. But which of them would fill the striking hand with gold? Richard of England? Would the King, even he, stoop so low? And besides, had he not still need of Conrad as an ally?

Guy of Jerusalem, the displaced monarch . . . that would be nearer the mark. The man was weak and little-hearted; he would not have so far to stoop. And he had so cravenly feared his own murder at Conrad's hands. "Two can play at that game," Richard had mocked, "but only one can strike first." Guy it must be. He was fearful enough to set his own risk before his allies' need of Conrad's strength.

But there was also Saladin. Al-Ahkis had said the Sultan feared the day when Jerusalem should be united under a strong hand. Would he kill Conrad so that the Christians would continue to quarrel amongst themselves? Such ignominious guile fitted no description she had ever heard of the fair-minded father of El-Kadil.

And yet, perhaps there were those among the Sultan's following whose scruples were not so strong. Although the Hashashin, even apart from the territorial power they wielded from their string of mountain fortresses, were hated among Saracens as a heretical sect, a foul stain on the purity of Islam, they were also widely used as instruments of hidden justice. And then, like the bolt from a crossbow, she was struck by another, closer suspicion. Sir Hugo de Malfors!

What better reason for the unlikely presence of that arrogant baron than murder . . . and the murder of a man by whom he was outshone in this world as is the candle by the star? Her mind raced back to Tristan's words: "He and Richard were thick together . . . he only remained three days . . ." And then had come the revelation of his challenge and her own most wretched confession . . . But she must not think of that now. She must speak with Sir Hugo, find out if her terrible suspicion were justified.

After a brief agony of impatience, she was able to seek him out in Masyaf's great dining hall. She waited again, until he had finished his meal, before she waylaid him as, belching heartily, he left the chamber.

"By the Rood, lady, you sing a new tune! What can have caused such a sudden strong desire for my company? Do you come to plead for your paramour?" His eye darkened. "For I shall show no mercy there, I swear."

She shook her head with a vehemence which intrigued him.

"If you will step into my privy chamber, I will send for wine. I honor you, for at Masyaf, one does not take meat or drink with a woman."

She thought of refusal. It was possible, perhaps likely, that he would force his attentions on her as he had done in the past. She decided to take the risk. She must learn all she could of this planned murder. The Baron occupied a small chamber on the ground floor of the fortress, furnished in the surprising luxury that belied the stern surroundings throughout that grim pile. There were several carved chairs in the western style, as well as a table and the customary divans and cushions. A black slave brought wine and she could not repress a shiver when the door clanged shut behind him.

Facing her in his own upright chair, Sir Hugo held out a cup across the table that separated them. "I recall when you poured wine for me at Hawkhurst," he mused suggestively. "It shall be thus again, very soon. We shall make a companionable pair yet, my lady."

Eden let this pass.

"It is not Hawkhurst that is my present concern, but Jerusalem," she began.

He showed surprise.

"What can you tell me of . . . the probable future of Conrad of Montferrat who is to ascend its throne?"

This time his surprise was absolute. When he spoke, however, his words were carefully chosen and his expression bland. "That it should be as bright as so talented a man can make it."

"If he lives!" she said fiercely, watching the blank features.

He lifted an interested brow. "Have you reason to doubt it?"

She leaned forward, holding his eyes. "Do you not *know* that I have?"

He frowned. "Tell me more."

"I know that Sinan will have him murdered . . . and I know that you come here from King Richard."

Again that look of surprise. Was it at her words, or at her knowledge?

He considered her narrowly. "It is well to be ignorant of Sinan's affairs," he warned, his tone flatly sincere. "The Assassins are successful for the very reason that those who pay their hire can never be traced, for they will die rather than reveal their names. This knowledge can bring you nothing but danger, Lady Eden. Sinan must not discover that you have it."

She smiled wryly. "It was he who told me," she said simply.

Sir Hugo stared at her, clearly disturbed. "Then you will never leave Masyaf alive," he said heavily.

Amazingly, she had not thought of this. Nor would she do so now.

"Why will Al-Jabal cause this murder to be committed?" she asked passionately.

"He is wise. He must see that Conrad brings a new hope to Jerusalem . . . a hope that Christian and Saracen may live in peace together. He must know, too, that Conrad has treated with Saladin."

Sir Hugo brooded, his black brows furrowed. "Look about you. How is such great power and show maintained if not by great wealth? It takes much gold to kill a king."

"Especially if a king is paying?"

But he would not be caught. "I did not say so."

"As for treaties," he continued, "they mean little. Al-Jabal also has a treaty with Saladin . . . since the day when his Assassins penetrated to the heart of the Sultan's court and made it known to him that they could have struck him dead at any time. That is the kind of power wielded by Sinan. His followers think him a god. There is no man alive he could not kill, and no man who would dare to point the finger at him."

"Then do you not fear for your own life, Sir Hugo?" Eden cried, seeing a chance to wrest the truth from his eyes, if not his lips. "You, who are the secret messenger of a would-be murderer."

It was enough; she had caught the flicker of doubt

before he had quenched it. "I am in no danger from Sinan," he said quietly, smiling now. "I have served him well, and will do so again."

But she had bowed her head. The taste of her little victory was bitter in her mouth. She had not known how she had longed to find that Richard was innocent. He was indeed a wretched man, unfit to be England's King. God would see it and God would surely cast him down.

She was surprised to find her cheeks wet with tears.

"For whom do you weep, by the Cross?" demanded Sir Hugo, much puzzled.

She did not answer him for he would not understand. She saw that her tears had shaken his even mood and was on her feet before he could realize it. He opened his mouth like an angry fish as she lifted the latch of the door.

"I thank you for your time and your wine, Baron," she said coldly and was half down the corridor before her overlord could realize that his prey had escaped him again.

For the next few days Eden was careful to avoid him, though once, at a distance, she saw him close at Sinan's elbow, smiling his mischievous, confident smile as they talked. No matter how deep he was in Al-Jabal's affairs, Sir Hugo would find a way to save himself.

It seemed that he had done so when one day he rode out of Masyaf and did not return. But there could, as he had said, be no such safety for her. Daily she expected to be cast into a dungeon, or worse, pitched from the battlements as she had heard it said was the satrap's chief punishment. And yet daily, in the face of her fears, her life continued its placid pattern among the gardens and courts. Occasionally she would be asked to sing and play for Al-Jabal's delight, for he liked to hear music that was foreign to his ears. She was given sewing to do, with the other women of the castle, though they were not those she had seen in Sinan's secret garden, where she had never entered again. Upon blessed afternoons she was permitted to ride among the hills, wearing her hauberk in case of an enemy ambush, and guarded by half a dozen sturdy ramieh. Balan, it seemed, was as well cared for as she was herself. His coat gleamed and he frisked on the hillsides like a foal.

Most often, however, she was simply left to herself and to the unquiet company of her thoughts. Her sorrow was boundless. Day and night she dreamed complex, impossible dreams of escape, that she might warn Conrad of his terrible danger and come to be with Tristan when he and the Baron should meet. But she knew well that there was no escape from Masyaf. The attempt would not be worth so soon a death. And yet she did not know why she still wished to live; for though she had comfort enough, she had nothing to hope for . . . she had already had her miracle, in Damascus.

One afternoon as she sat in her preferred courtyard, sewing the torn sleeve of one of Sinan's mercenaries, she became aware of an insistent, rhythmic sound beyond the walls. She was accustomed to the return of mounted men from some nameless foray, but these did not gallop their horses, whooping, up the slopes as the ramieh did, in a triumphant, homecoming paean. Their march was disciplined and tranquil and they halted outside the gates. Curious, Eden ran up to the battlement which looked over the only approach to the entrance of Masyaf.

What she saw sent her reeling, her hand clutching at the parapet. Drawn up in perfect order before the walls, their banners clearly marked with the sign of their order, was a company of the black-clad Knights of St. John of Jerusalem. Before them, upon a powerful, white destrier, their leader looked up and cried out sternly for entry.

Eden, too, cried out, in incoherent disbelief, though she was too high up for him to hear her.

Below, the gates were flung open, the knights rode into Masyaf, and at their head was Tristan de Jarnac upon Gorvenal.

Still clasping the warm stone of the parapet for

support, Eden attempted to gather her scattered wits and to control her foolish body that was trembling all over for pure joy. The miracle of Damascus had come again. God had relented and had sent Tristan once more to be her savior.

Every instinct told her to run down at once and throw herself into his arms, but caution laid a cool finger on her arm and she stopped to consider. She could have no notion of Tristan's errand here, or of what would be his reception. It seemed likely that he came to Masyaf in the guise of friendship to Sinan; even so, it might not be wise for Eden to lay any claim upon him. Whatever his cause, it must not be prejudiced by her. She must be circumspect, must wait, watch and listen and seize upon what chance she could to make Tristan aware of her presence.

For the moment it was enough that she knew of his beloved, impossible presence. She felt weak with delight, her whole being translated into happiness as she stood clasping the crenel as if part of it. It was as though she had been given new life.

Her ecstacy was broken soon by a purposeful tread behind her. Two guards appeared, obviously seeking her out. Although there was no especial menace in their lean faces, her pulse quickened when she was told that Sinan wished to see her.

Al-Jabal was seated in the smaller of his presence-chambers, a comfortable room which, looking as it did into the impregnable inner court of the castle, could afford the luxury of large windows, their triple-arched spaces filled with smoky, thick, yellowish glass. The sheik was alone apart from servants.

"Sit, lady. I will be very brief." She had never seen a man who possessed such a quality of stillness. She wondered why any scene so peaceful as that of this tranquil man, with quiet hands folded before him, should provoke irrational fear in her.

"You have seen certain things at Masyaf that perhaps you would find it more convenient to forget," he said serenely, as though he spoke of weather. "Especially in the company, should you meet it, of our present visitors from Krak des Chevaliers. It would not be a matter, merely, of your own death, but that of each one of theirs." The voice was clear and unconcerned, yet even now she did not sense evil in him, only a monstrous detachment, as though he played at checkers with the world and would sweep clear the board for a single mistaken move. She was broken and isolated in his presence. Even the sly and violent lechery of Sir Hugo was preferable to this; it was, at least, human, and therefore comprehensible.

She veiled her eyes and bowed her head with acceptant grace. "These things are already forgotten, Excellence."

"Then you may leave, Lady Hawkhurst."

Still she found the courage for a question, "Excellence . . ."

"Speak."

"It is only that . . . womanlike . . . I would know what the future holds for me."

"I am no soothsayer," observed Al-Jabal with faint acidity. Unfolding his long, parchment-thin hands, he held them toward her, palms upward. "I have not yet considered your uses," he told her with an honesty that reduced her to a cipher. "It will be made known to you when I have done so."

She must be content with this. She made her courtesy and was about to leave when he spoke again, his tone tinged with a slight warmth.

"There is one thing, however, which I would have you do this night. I have taken pleasure in your singing. It would be a compliment to our guests if they were to hear the songs of their own countries. You will come to the hall to entertain us while we dine."

Eden had to stifle a cry of joy. She would see Tristan, be close to him perhaps. She smiled as she went to her chamber to prepare.

As she dressed her hair, with more care than she had taken for many days, she considered how she should behave. He must not acknowledge her and she, in turn, would not be able to speak with him; there was no necessity for a mere singing girl to address a noble guest. Nevertheless she must somehow give him her urgent news.

It came to her as she began to turn over in her mind the songs she might perform. They would all know the songs of Provence and of Aquitaine, the popular ballads of love and of chivalry . . . but only one among them, she was sure, would have any knowledge of the language of Old England, the Saxon tongue spoken by serfs and villains, that Hawisa had taught her in childhood. Tristan, too, had learned it in his Cornish youth. Her course would take a steady nerve and a flawless pretense, but it was the only one open to her. Their meeting was to be public, and so must be their communication. There might come no other chance. She tuned the cithara they had given her and went down, with a racing heart, to the hall.

The feast was almost done and the wine flowed freely. Sinan's personal musicians, seduced, most of them, from the colleges of Damascus, were playing the wild laments of the mountain tribes, the drums mournful and the rebecs passionate and desolate. She would ask the drummer to accompany her singing; his insistent rhythm would gain her an audience more swiftly. She had entered the hall from the back and stood behind the players, who were placed opposite Sinan's central table at a distance that was pleasant for the satrap and occasionally purgatorial for the lesser beings close-by. Looking round, she caught her breath as she saw that Tristan sat on the right of Al-Jabal in the place of honor, and was deeply engaged in conversation with him. His beauty overcame her as if he were a stranger, seeing him so remote from her. His presence was as commanding as that of Al-Jabal himself. He wore magnificent white velvet, extravagantly jeweled, and the light from the sconces gleamed upon the fall of dark hair whose every curve raised an ache of desire in her.

He lifted a cup to his lips and his face was turned toward her for a fraction. Her longing to touch him was unbearable; to gaze endlessly into those stern yet alluringly lazy eyes; to feel the seeking pressure of his lips that now mouthed pleasantries to the subtle potentate beside him . . .

The musicians had come to the end of their melody. She tore her gaze from Tristan and spoke to them hastily. She would begin her singing at once. She commenced with the much loved "Pax in Nomine Domine" which Crusaders had sung as they marched across many lands to their destiny. She kept her eyes upon the Master of Masyaf and his honored guest as courtesy demanded of a minstrel. Tristan, turned toward his host, gave no sign of having noted either song or singer, but continued his conversation, enlarging on the talk with elegant, descriptive gestures.

It was one of the younger knights who first set up the cheer, "Bless you, mistress!" thumping the table with his hanap in disheveled appreciation, a streak of spilled wine disfiguring the white cross on his breast. "Now give us 'Ah, Amour!' for the sake of your fair gold hair!" She smiled and complied, although she saw that the boy was reprimanded by the older knight next to him and listened to his song with downcast eyes.

Still Tristan did not seem to be aware of her presence. Her next song was a little wilder as she willed him to look up. Yet, surely, he must know her voice. They had so often sung these same ballads together in Acre, their voices tuned together as then their bodies could not be. She took space to breathe and gulp a mouthful of wine. This next was to be the song that would tell him all.

As if he had sensed her need, he turned a little in his seat and allowed his gaze to wander inconsequentially around the hall. His eyes did not rest for even a second as they passed over her yet she knew that their movement was entirely for her. He had known from the beginning . . . and knew far better than Eden how to be truly circumspect. He had turned his head back to Sinan now, a charming smile upon his lips, but carelessly he raised his cup in her direction, then threw back his head and drained it to the depths.

He had given her the courage that she needed.

She had chosen an old Kentish love song that told of

a country maiden seduced by a nobleman. Its melody was lilting and graceful enough to keep the interest of the knights though neither they nor their Saracen table companions would, she trusted, comprehend the words . . . which bore a startling difference from the original.

Eden told of a young wife who had found her husband a captive in a Saracen castle not to be ransomed, and of how she herself had become the prisoner of another castle, where she must remain because she had discovered the evil secret of its castellan; that he had arranged the bloody murder of a certain merchant prince who had once saved the lady from an unpleasant fate. All was conveyed in the gentle, tender notes of the love song, in the soft, guttural Saxon, with no hint of the menace at its heart.

Tristan, occupied now with the bearded emir at his right, did not appear to be listening. His conversation flowed uninterrupted and once he leaned back in wholehearted laughter, his black eyes rakish.

Eden sang once more, a hymn that she knew to be well liked by the knights, and then made her courtesy, placing a delicate hand on her heart and then extending it in submission toward Sinan . . . or to the figure that gleamed, while amidst darkness, beside him.

There was one more thing she might do before leaving. Court musicians were well known to have open ears for other notes than music. Gracefully she thanked the boy who had beaten out her rhythms upon the copper-bowled nakars, the double drums favored above all by the Saracens, and used as often in battle as at table. He smiled and, in turn, complimented her singing.

"What brings such unusual guests to Sinan's table?" she asked idly, giving much attention to the retuning of the cithara.

"It is a deputation seeking peace between the Al-Jabal and the Knights of their order. They have been at each other's throats for many months." He grinned. "But while the Knights cannot take Masyaf, neither, alas, has Sinan been able to conquer Krak des Chevaliers. This way we have but wasted good lives on both sides . . . so there is to be a truce between us. The Chevalier in white is their spokesman. He is neutral, not being a member of the Order. A fine man, it seems, for a Christian!"

Eden smiled.

"Forgive me, lady . . . you speak our tongue so easily . . ."

"You are forgiven," she said and left him, laughing at his confusion. He was a fine boy . . . for a Saracen.

In her tiny chamber under the parapet she schooled herself once more to waiting. She longed for Tristan to find some way to come to her, but knew the risk to be too great. She had made this clear enough in her song; indeed, she had made herself no part of his duty . . . only dwelt upon the imperative necessity of getting word to Conrad of Montferrat.

It was no surprise to her, therefore, when the next day Tristan rode away with his knights from Masyaf and she had not come near him again. She stood, as before, upon the battlements, and though she lifted her hand in a loving farewell, no head turned as the twenty-one men clattered down the rocky slopes of the Ansariyah. It cost her much courage to see him go and she could not prevent a sinking of her heart.

Within hours it was as if he had never come there and the uncertainty that underlay her days returned again to torment her. What disposition would Sinan eventually make of her? Where did Sir Hugo de Malfors enter into any such plans? How would Tristan determine to take her out of Masyaf . . . and how soon?

For several suspended days her life continued upon its slow surface, as it had been. She sang and sewed and chattered to the slave girls who did domestic duties about the castle, all of whom were consumed with curiosity upon the subject of El Malik Rik, whom they believed to possess not only the heart of a lion but also the indefatigable sexual prowess of that fearsome beast. Eden regretted that it would scarcely profit the Christian cause in Islam to disabuse them.

Her restlessness led her to an erratic movement about the courts and passages of the fortress that she almost feared would give away the added stress under which she existed. Then, realizing she had not been allowed to ride out in the afternoon for some days, she took her request to do so to the soldier who had captained her guard on the previous occasions.

He checked with a high authority and, to her relief, permission was given. Wearing her hauberk for protection as before, she descended with her six outriders to the valley below the fortress, her one desire for a gallop that would stretch both her own and Balan's resources. She had always been active, and the long days of indolence and uncertainty had made her nervous and irritable. The ramieh paced her amiably, indulging in the curious, high-pitched calls with which they always accompanied such high speeds. They rode as though they were part of their short-legged horses, fierce grins of pleasure splitting their dusky faces.

Eden was in fact riding so fast that she did not understand what took place as they rounded a slope to enter the next long pass. At one moment the ramieh were whooping and skirling about her while she matched Balan against their leader's proud speed . . . the next the man was riding with the steel of an arrow protruding from his neck, the sounds curdled horribly in his throat. The cry went up for ambush and someone seized her bridle, dragging her round in an attempt to aim her back toward safety. Willingly she let herself be guided, for it was hard to hold the terrified horse who understood, no more than she, the desperate changes around them.

"Masyaf!" howled the man beside her. She pulled up the hood of her hauberk and dug her heels into Balan's side, expecting, at any second, to feel the blow of an arrow in her mailed back.

Then, behind, a voice cried incredibly, "Eden! Back!" and the moment dissolved for a second time into lunacy as, recognizing the voice, she tried to turn again. Balan leaped and ran wild, breaking the Sara-

cen's hold on his bridle and all but throwing his rider.
He pelted pell-mell for Masyaf, ignoring her frenzied
pulling on the reins.

The ramieh had fallen back, but now another figure
rode up beside her, his great white destrier gaining
inexorably on the palfrey. Soon he had passed them,
his grin of concentration giving him the air of reckless
enjoyment. Yards further on, he slowed and wheeled
a pawing Gorvenal so that he stood across their track
at the narrowest part of the road.

"Hold, Balan! Easy, old friend, easy!" he cried as
the frightened roan faltered in his headlong panic. He
caught at the rein as they approached and brought the
horse, shuddering, to a halt beside his old stable companion. "If you do not *desire* to leave Masyaf . . . ?"
suggested Tristan with a wicked lift of his brows, "I
can give the creature's rump a slap that will send him
back in seconds. I daresay he knows his road. So, unfortunately, does the single man who has escaped us
. . . and pursuit will therefore be swift. And so . . . if
Balan is quite reconciled to it . . ."

"Tristan . . ." She smiled and wept and panted for
breath, her face streaked with dust and sweat beneath
the hot mail of her hood.

"We'll talk at Krak . . ." he said. "It's fifteen miles;
can you do it?"

She nodded, saving her breath for one question.
"Conrad . . . have you . . . ?"

"I sent messengers. He will be on his guard." She
gasped with relief.

He could give her no respite. They turned at once
and hurtled down the valley, where she scarcely had
time to note the five bloody corpses upon the sand nor
to count the number, well above twenty, of the black-
clad knights who surrounded them in a protective
phalanx as they rode on into the dry nightmare of dust
and pounding hooves and throbbing, inimical sun.

Like the knights she stood in her stirrups and leaned
low along Balan's stretching neck to give him his head.
The strain on the sinews at the back of her knees
would soon become insupportable but she knew she

must not slacken, for pursuit was as certain as was
the death they would die if they were caught.

They had not long in which to be apprehensive. At
a bend in the track similar to that at which they had
made their own ambush, Sinan's warriors swept out
from the rocks and crevasses of the mountain side. A
hail of arrows came down on them from the outcrop
that was their vantage point and Eden felt herself
suddenly propelled forward over Balan's straining
head as one of them knocked the breath from her
body with a brutal and unlooked-for force that must
surely mean her death. Despite the agony, she somehow clung to her reins and managed to regain her seat
as the terrible ululating shrieks broke out behind them.
She did not think the horse capable of more speed
and yet he found it as they were hounded in a whine
of arrows through the pass, Tristan never leaving her
side, his face grim as he glanced at the black-feathered
nock angled outward from the back of her hauberk.

"It hasn't penetrated," he yelled, seeing her terrified
look. "The bruise will hurt . . . but it will heal." Relief flooded her, though it did nothing to allay the
abominable pain. The disloyal thought plagued her that
it would have been so much easier had she been truly
hit . . . She longed to be unconscious and to feel nothing.

Little by little, though it seemed impossible, they
were gaining ground. Now their leader turned off into
the hillside again, tracing one of those hidden paths
that are known only to those who have forged them;
the winded animals blew heavily as they welcomed
the changed terrain. But even as they took blessed
cover among the rocks and scrub the hellish cries came
close behind them. Tristan drew rein, thundered an
order and several of the knights fell back, their
swords drawn, while others drew their bows from their
saddles, notched arrows and waited, tense as their taut
strings. Tristan urged her on and they struggled up
the shifting sands of the path after their unhesitating
leader. Eden looked back only once, through the inter-
vening foliage . . . and wished, sickened, that she had

not. One of the knights, the eight-pointed cross on his breast bloodied and rent, was engaged in a death struggle with one of the spotted beasts that had seemed so decorative in Sinan's paradise garden. But now the graceful nimr was a slavering horror of teeth and claws, both blood-red as the disfigured cross. It was the boy who had stained that self-same cross with wine, for whom she had sung of love and longing. The leopard gathered its haunches for a last spring and the boy plunged to the ground beneath it; his bowels strung bright across his trunk as he lay, dying slowly beneath the pitiless jaws.

She had hardly assimilated this hideous sight when she heard the baying of the dogs. They were to be hunted through the hills like game. Transfixed, she felt Tristan's impatient hand upon her rein and then they were scrambling for their lives up the backsliding, graveled slope, their hopes sinking with the laboring hooves.

Quite suddenly the path was whole again and they were able to outdistance the howling huntsmen and gain the cover of the next pass.

"How far have we come?" gasped Eden, her back a throbbing agony, her limbs numbed in every muscle.

"Four miles at most," cried Tristan.

She wilted in her saddle.

"They'll not follow for more than another three," he rallied her. "Then we'll be in Krak territory. We'll have reinforcements. Come—you have done well so far."

He smiled for the first time since they had met, and even now, amid this mortal fear and pain, she melted at the beauty that could conceal such an iron determination. She returned his smile with a sudden shyness, remembering . . . But he had turned away and was forging ahead so that she must use her heels to keep up with him.

It was, in the end, as he had said it would be. The baying of the pursuit, both human and animal, kept up its terrible concert for perhaps a league more, and then, as they climbed a sloping ridge under a white hot sun and it seemed that, any second, the loping pards must eviscerate the last of their hard-pressed horses, a swirl of dust appeared on the edge of the ridge and black silhouettes rode up against the dazzling light. Thirty knights from Krak des Chevaliers, with a deep-throated roar of "God and His Cross!" hurled past them and bore down upon the astonished Saracens like mounted angels of death, the bright tips of their spears sparkling and thirsty. This time, Eden did not look back, for Tristan urged her onward, but the sounds which receded behind her were many and dreadful and her prayers were fervent as they rode over the ridge and down into the next, peaceful valley. Soon the only disturbance was the iron echo of their alien hooves as the black band moved triumphantly homeward among the clanging crags. It was not yet dark when they came to Krak des Chevaliers.

The greatest military stronghold in the history of Christendom was also an achievement of austere and compelling beauty. Crowning a deep spur whose steep sides gave protection from every side save the powerfully fortified south, the massive citadel needed no absent, flaming sunset to flatter its brooding command of the valley. Eden was conscious of great awe, despite her spent body, as they left the northern road and came under its mighty lee toward the single eastern entrance.

Upon the walls a steel-clad garrison gave them a bristling welcome, but inside they were swiftly reminded that, although primarily a barracks housing near two thousand men, these men were also brethren of the Hospital and could provide as homely a rest for a weary traveler as the most welcoming hostelry in Europe. Their grim fortress was also a monastery with a serene inner life revolving about its vaulted chapel, its comfortable chapter-house and its calm, contemplative cloisters.

There were no women in this immense, disciplined household and Eden was given a tiny, white-walled cell of her own, where a lay brother with downcast eyes brought her water. Gratefully she washed away the grime and sweat that had accumulated upon her to as great a degree almost, as they had done upon poor Balan. Like the horse, she found tide-marks upon her flanks, though hers were of dust rather than foam. Her face was likewise rimmed about the edges of her hood and her hair dark with sweat. She bathed with the frantic pleasure of a bird in a spring pool, though the luxury was rendered somewhat piquant by the searing pain of the wound on her back. Afterwards, the young brother who had brought the water—his eyes now almost turned back into his flaming face—dressed the great, blackening contusion with a trembling care, using unguents of herbs very similar in aroma to the betany and thorough-wax she was used to at home. The monk brought her food and drink to her cell as she was still in too much discomfort to attempt to sit at table, let alone to face the curious gaze of two thousand stalwart knight-monks.

She was lying on her belly on her bracken pallet with its wooden bedframe when Tristan, who had dined in the great hall that was said to be the finest in any fortress standing, came to visit her. He wore a plain black tunic and hose and was without his mail. His black hair hung in damp, curling strands about his neck.

She looked up in welcome, her frown of pain banished in a smile of pure happiness.

He knelt at her feet and kissed her hands as though she were his liege lord.

"Come!" Her voice trembled. "Sit here, at the bed-head, so that I may look at you."

He did so, his bearing strangely grave.

They looked at each without speaking. There was so much to be said, to be learned, between them that neither knew where to begin. They had not spoken together, in any true sense, since that luminous night above Damascus. She saw his eyes upon her breasts and realized that they swelled, naked, upon the pillow where the blanket had fallen open. And although she had let him enter the secrets of her body as no other had done, she found herself rosy, now, with an untoward shyness. She covered her breasts and sought hastily for words.

"Tristan . . . I must beg for your forgiveness. I did not leave you . . . that dawning . . . because I wished to, but because I had to do it. There could be nothing but the truth between us . . . and for me the hard truth was that I must keep faith with the quest that brought me to this land . . . and to you."

He nodded quickly as if it hurt him to agree. "You need no forgiveness. Certainly you were right to put Stephen first. But you were wrong to think that you must do so alone . . . to think that I, too, would not learn to put him first . . . eventually. I had promised this. Your leaving wounded me, Eden. It was the second time. It became hard to hold to my . . . faith." He would not say love.

"Never doubt that," she said fervently. Then, since he did not reply, "You have not told me how you came to Masyaf. It seemed a miracle."

"I knew that I would find you there." He hesitated, then explained, "There are many watchful eyes among the hills; I was able to trace you and to follow in your wake. Eden . . . I too have visited Qal'a Zaydun."

She met his unwavering eyes. "Then you have seen Stephen . . ."

He shook his head. "Only the Emir, who refused me your husband's ransom as he had refused you."

His face was intent with pity and a deep relief flowed into her. He knew, then . . . knew all. She did not have to speak, now, of the macabre travesty that had become Stephen's life.

"Your mission with the knights of this order," she asked, "this was already planned?"

"Perfectly genuine. I had originally thought to engage their aid in a more warlike fashion, if necessary, but this treaty with Al-Jabal was protracted and an impartial envoy needed. I fitted their requirements. It was an easy matter to persuade them to keep a watch on Masyaf for a time beforehand. Thus we learned that Sinan follows the civilized custom of allowing his more marketable prisoners regular exercise."

Eden shuddered. "Blessedly for me . . . and for Conrad of Montferrat."

"May God grant it so."

"You think your warning will reach him in time?"

"It looks hopeful. Like myself the Hashashin like to establish the habits of their subject before they strike. They might take a week or more to learn Conrad's ways. I sent two messengers. One or both will have arrived by now."

"Christ be their speed," she breathed. "Tristan . . . why is it that Al-Jabal will do this thing? What can he gain from the death of the Marquess? I cannot believe it is for gold alone."

"Not gold, but power. Sinan is unrivaled in these hills, in the whole of northern Syria, at present; but if Conrad, as king, were to bring about a lasting peace between Christian and Saracen then Saladin would have both the time and the resources to root out the heresy of the Hashashin, and cast Sinan into the dust."

She told him then of the presence of Hugo de Malfors at Masyaf and of what he had scarcely denied of Richard of England.

"It is a happy fortuity for Sinan," Tristan said contemptuously, "that Richard and the wretched Guy de Lusignan also seek Conrad's death . . . and will pay him richly to carry out his own will. And in Hugo de Malfors they have the perfect harbinger of murder. I hope to serve him in a similar fashion myself . . . very soon." His contempt was like a burning glass.

"He has said he will seek you out," she told him, alarmed. "Has he not yet done so . . . for he left Masyaf some days before your arrival?"

He shrugged. "He will find me . . . or I him. Do not concern yourself with it."

"But how if he should seek an underhand path? He would not stop at murder if the notion took him."

"Do not think of it. I am well guarded. Krak is the strongest fortress in Outremer . . . and will be stronger when we have added the outer ring of fortification we have planned."

"But . . . you will not remain long at Krak . . . you will go back to Jaffa . . ."

His gaze faltered and fell. When he lifted his eyes they were stern and brilliant in his strained face and his lips, for once, were thin as knives. He leaned forward and took her hands, resting clasped upon the pillow, into his own.

"Once, above Damascus, I promised to serve you all my days," he said softly, "and it is a vow I shall keep . . . though not in the fashion that I then intended . . ."

A sudden, intuitive foreboding was born in her. She moved her hands into his, grasping them tightly, trying to stem the fear that waited for his words.

"But I have also taken other vows, Eden . . . for I could see no other way to serve you now without endangering both our souls and, in the end, degrading our bodies . . ."

He saw that her eyes were lit with unshed tears and turned away from them, hating what he must do.

"I cannot cease to love you," he cried, anguish burning in his throat, "cannot root it out of me like some heresy out of the truth . . . for it is no heresy, as God is our judge, but truth indeed."

She let her brow fall upon their twined hands and allowed the tears to fall. She had not the courage to look at him while she must hear him.

"But if we cannot quench the love of the spirit, we may . . . we must . . . adjure the union of our bodies. Oh my dear love, I do not say that this was not sweet beyond the dreams of heaven . . . but your husband lives . . . and has his place, and his rights with you . . ."

She raised a ravaged face. "But Stephen is not . . . he will never . . ."

"It may be that he can be saved," he cut her off swiftly. "It will not be long before Al-Jabal stretches out his powerful hand to crush the impudent serpent, Zaydun, at his gates. When that happens, we have the treaty, and I think that Sinan will release the Lord of Hawkhurst to us."

She gazed at him in bewilderment. Stephen to be set free? But Stephen was dying. He did not wish for freedom.

Before she could phrase her confused reaction Tristan continued hastily, "In that matter I will serve you, and in any way that I may do so as your sworn knight . . . but for the rest . . ." His pain leaped out to meet hers. "My duty belongs to the Order of Saint John of Jerusalem. I have already become a lay member. In a year or so . . . if I have proved worthy, I shall take the full vows."

"No! You cannot!" Her cry was that of a wounded creature.

His look was relentless. "It is done."

"But to give up your whole life . . ."

"What life is that?" His tone was bitter now. "I have served a master whom I can no longer respect. I love a woman whom I cannot have with honor and may not take without. I have already done you great harm . . . perhaps great wrong."

"Not so!"

He stared, frowning, through the little iron grille that served as a window onto the inner ward of the castle.

"I have already caused the death of one woman who loved me; I would not bring any further hurt to you."

Dimly, Eden remembered the talk, in Acre, of a lady who had died. "At Hattin was it not?" She did not know she spoke aloud. It was an old memory, not relevant to this present pain.

"Claire," he said dully. "She had followed me to war and I had allowed it. I was young and selfish and bitterly foolish . . . and bitterly I care to regret my foolishness. You will know of Hattin. It was a butchery. She was taken by Turks. I searched for her throughout the battle and found her afterwards stretched upon the field. They had raped her and cut open her belly. She still lived. I plunged my sword into her heart. Her eyes still haunt me."

She was by his side then, and took his head to her breast, stroking the damp hair with gentle fingers.

"My love . . . you must not think of it. It is long past and God has long forgiven you. You cannot bear so much suffering." Feverishly, she kissed the black strands, twisting her hands amongst them, her love an ache in her that she could not compass. Somehow, she must relieve him of this burden, for she saw that now, all sins were become as one to him and he saw himself universally condemned.

"I tell you now that you have given me the greatest happiness my life has known," she said triumphantly. "If it is wrong, then God absolve us, for I do not regret a single moment of it."

He rose then and put his arms about her, pressing her face against his breast. They stood thus together, for a space, sorrow eroding all thought, and, for a time, all sensation.

Then Eden raised her head and looked into the carven purity of his face, her lips trembling apart as she traced the beloved contours with her eyes. With a passionate moan she fastened her mouth on his and hung upon it as though it succoured her very life's blood.

The answering tide of passion rose within him and for a time his lips were urgent and demanding upon hers in turn, his body pressed fiercely against hers. Then he had taken his arms from around her and put her from him, bereft. He stepped back and continued only to hold her hands.

"Eden, we cannot. It is finished. I must leave you. It is better I do so now. We may perhaps meet again . . . in Jaffa. I do not know."

Her small cry seared his soul. He kissed her soft hands for the last time and then the iron control was with him again and his features hardened before her despairing eyes into their customary lines of cold command.

"I have arranged for a company of the knights to escort you tomorrow to Tyre . . . where you may reassure yourself as to Conrad's safety." He spoke with careful, unstressed gentleness, adding, "I will send to you at Jaffa . . . if there should be news of Stephen."

It seemed fitting, at this pass, that mention of her husband should be his last word to her.

She was left then, to stare at the meaningless cross, carved into the dark wood of the door that he had closed upon her.

That night, the Emir Ibn Zaydun, with his army of howling, black-skinned mercenaries, descended from his mountain fortress upon the peaceful campfires of an unusually large Christian caravan, laden with rich merchandise and bound for Tripoli. Their guard was large, but not large enough to be effective against the caterwauling fiends that fell from out of the darkness. A spent messenger fell from his dying horse at the gates of Krak some fifteen miles and as many minutes after the attack. A hundred men rode out of the ever-vigilant citadel. Eden listened as they galloped away in a clatter of steel beneath the thin moonlight. In the morning they had not returned and she learned that Tristan had been one of the first among them.

▼▼▼▼▼▼▼▼▼▼▼▼▼▼▼▼▼▼▼▼▼▼▼▼▼▼▼▼▼▼▼▼▼▼▼▼▼▼▼

CHAPTER SEVENTEEN

Tyre, Jaffa

It took four days to reach Tyre. Her escort was two full convoys of Knight Hospitalers, a hundred men of mixed cavalry and infantry due for a period of duty under Conrad. The pace was hard and the protection guaranteed; they no longer had to fear Al-Jabal and nothing short of a similar force was likely to attack them. They reached the city during the late evening. The gates were opened for them though it was later than curfew. The knights departed to their various hostelries while their leaders went with Eden to the palace.

She was glad to have finished the journey. She had suffered more weariness as a result of the confusion and sorrow within her than of any physical hardship. Words and images, both of Tristan and Stephen, had passed and repassed through her derelict mind until the words became mere mockery and the images false and threatening of her reason. It would be a sweet relief to confide in the warm and practical Isabella, who perhaps could advise her somewhat as to how she must live in the empty, haunted place that her life had become.

The palace gates were open and there was a great mass of people thronging the outer ward.

"Can there be some festivity?" wondered Eden tiredly as four knights-banneret shouldered a path for her and their commanders.

A man next to her spat vigorously. "God's blood, lady, but I wish it were! Do you not know? This very

night they have murdered our Marquess. Cut him
down in the street like a ruffian."

It seemed that her own heart had ceased to beat.
She stood quite still and closed her eyes. She did not
heed the Hospitaler's concerned plucking at her sleeve,
nor the crowd's angry murmur swelling about her
ears. She made no movement, gave no cry, only
stood and tried to shut out the truth with blindness.
And in the darkness in her heart and behind her lids
there hung the calm, ascetic vision of a face at rest,
a lined and knowing countenance in which the only
live feature was the compelling, colorless, utterly emo-
tionless eyes.

So . . . the warning had been of no avail. The instruments of Rashid-ed-Din Sinan had consummated
his will.

When she could open her eyes she thought only of
Isabella. She whispered swift, insufficient thanks to
the Hospitalers and hurried desperately through the
crowd to the main door of the palace where she demanded entry to the Marquessa's apartments.

"She will see no one," stated a beleaguered major-
domo.

Eden gave her name. "There are things I must say
to her. Ask her if she will see me. It concerns . . . the
death of your master."

Instant suspicion flared in his eyes but the message
was given and minutes later a respectful attendant
brought her to the long room which she had last seen
in bright sunlight, filled with laughter and talk of love.

Now the chamber was a catacomb of darkness, all its
illumination concentrated in the pale aura of the hundred candles that surrounded the couch at its center.
Upon the couch was disposed all that remained of the
master of the house. Even in death, Conrad of Montferrat presented a picture of surpassing magnificence.
His still face, white as silk against black surcoat and
crimson coverlet, lacking the permanent possibility
of humor that had lightened it in life, was austere and
patrician, the eyes shuttered, the mouth implacable.

Across his breast, her black hair flowing like a river of tears, lay Isabella, her slight body in its golden dress shielding his as though she would warm it back into life. There were others in the room but they were of no consequence.

Drawn without awareness of her body's motion, Eden walked softly to the bier and stood looking down upon its tragic burden. Isabella made no sound and moved no more than did her husband. With a sudden horror, Eden thought she might have taken her own life. Then the faint rise and fall of her breast reassured her. She made no attempt to touch her. There was no comfort that she could bring. She could only be with her, nothing more.

She kept this motionless, silent vigil while minutes turned to hours, undisturbed by the hushed comings and goings in the room about her, as one by one Conrad's loyal subjects came to assure themselves that there was no truth in the terrible rumor that was bruited . . . and left, in twos and threes, talking together of vengeance, their faces streaked with unashamed tears. The Marquess had been a good master . . . and, take him all in all, a good man, as the world goes. They had looked upon his corpse and now they longed to look upon his murderers.

It was not until the middle reaches of the long night that Isabella stirred at last. Eden, sitting now, huddled where she had stood, her head upon her knee, caught the heavy rustle of damask and looked up. The Marquessa stood unsteadily beside the catafalque, her eyes dark gashes in a bloodless face. Unable to speak, she extended her hand toward Eden. Going to her, Eden wrapped her arms about her.

"Isabella . . ."

There are no words for what cannot be borne.

She led Conrad's wife away from her dead husband. The faint, regular quivering of the slight frame reverberated against her arm.

"My dear . . . you must rest. You will need great strength."

If strength was forged out of suffering, and Eden had some reason to believe it was, then surely it would come to her.

Isabella would not leave the room but allowed herself to be placed on a couch at a distance from the body. She seemed to come to herself a little and made a small, dismissive gesture toward the women of her chamber who still sat, drooping with weariness, in the shadows.

"I am glad you are here," she said when they had gone, her voice hoarse with fatigue and unshed tears. "It was good of you to come to me."

Eden clasped her hands. "I did not know of . . . this, when I came," she said, low.

"No?" There was a faint frown of bewilderment, gone at once. All facts, save one, were immaterial to her. "They felled him in the street. I did not believe it when they told me. And then they brought him home. He was not dead." Isabella spoke in swift, disconnected snatches, her voice taut and breathless. "It does not seem possible that he can be dead!" She stared at the corpse feverishly, as though she doubted its reality. "But a few days since, he was triumphant. It was the crown of his life! The Count of Champagne came here to lay Jerusalem at his feet. It seemed that he must have the goodwill of all the world. Why, Richard himself sent the young count as his envoy; he is his own nephew and the King of France, too, is his uncle. He represented in his person the hope of healing all breaches between true Franks in Palestine. We were so gay together, so debonair, and Count Henri so handsome and gallant. I even flirted a little . . ." Eden saw that, at last, tears began to glisten in the agonized and uncomprehending eyes.

"When Conrad heard that he was to be king," Isabella continued, now conquering the wavering of her voice and speaking out with trenchant pride, "he fell upon his knees in true humility and said, 'If I am not worthy of this, then be sure that God will not permit it!' It is not God who has prevented it, but Satan," she cried then, "through the hands of these bloody executioners!"

She rose now and stalked the chamber, the undammed torrent of her words carrying her out of death's stunned silence and back toward the shores of reason and strength. "It was such a foolish, unnecessary chance! If I had not lingered, as I ever do, at my bathing . . . Conrad lost patience. He was eager to dine, having ridden far in the day. At last he said I should dine alone as a penance for my sinful luxury. He would visit his friend, Philip of Beauvais, who would not refuse him a meal at his table. I laughed and did not take it amiss . . . he is much with the Bishop of Beauvais. He leaned to kiss me and he left with his tunic and his hair all dampened from my tub . . ."

Her brave tone faltered but did not break. "It seems that the Bishop had already dined, for Conrad had turned for home again when it happened." She was standing beside the body again, looking tenderly into the dead face. She put out a hand to touch the broad shoulder, cold beneath its black velvet. "Turning a corner, he was met by two monks, one of them carrying a letter for him. As he reached out to take it they stabbed him to the heart!" She threw back the cloak that covered the immobile breast and Eden saw the deep, trenched gashes, aslant amid the blood that rusted his tunic.

"God have mercy on his soul!" Eden whispered. Then, seeing that Isabella had fastened her eyes upon the wounds with a fixedness that would become obsessive, she gently drew back the cloak to its previous position.

"It is done," Isabella said with bare, sad simplicity, "and cannot be undone." Her expression changed to one of stark ferocity. "But it can be avenged! If only they had not torn one of them apart in the street where he stood! But I have the other safe in my dungeon. He will live until he has confessed to the hand that fashioned him into a blade for murder. He will live and live and long for death."

"Do as you will with him," said Eden, knowing that now her time had come to speak, "but it is needless. *I* can tell you the name."

She saw puzzlement snap at the heels of disbelief in the wan face. She had known, as they had watched through the long night, that this moment must come. She had deliberated, suspended between the desires for vengeance and for truth, the exact compass of the words she would speak. She would tell what she *knew* . . . but she would not, however much she longed to do so, mention that which was, although almost certainly true, still within the bounds of conjecture.

"The Sheik Rashid-ed-Din Sinan," she said quietly, "the leader of the Assassins." She said nothing of Richard Plantagenet, nothing of Guy de Lusignan. She would leave it to the wretch in the dungeon to speak further . . . if he could.

Isabella, after showing an initial surprise, remembered Conrad's triumphant laughter over his capture of one of Sinan's richest galleys and accepted the knowledge with desolate fatalism. And even in her grief, she could not prevent her curiosity as to the manner of Eden's possessing it.

And so, with the dawn dispersing the shadows in that sorrowful chamber, choosing her words sparsely and sufficiently, the Lady of Hawkhurst told her tale of attempt and failure. "If Tristan had not lingered on my account, if he had come himself to Tyre . . ."

Isabella shook her head. "If I had chosen another hour to bathe," she said. "It is no matter now. His death was determined."

When it was fully morning the steward and the people of the household came softly to beg that they might take their master's body and prepare it for burial. Eden cast a fearful glance at Isabella, thinking that so final a moment might destroy her hard-won, delicate balance. She saw that this was not so, however, for the Marquessa lifted her head and gave clear, proud commands to her servants, ordering the disposal and promising to visit the body once more when they had laid it out in the vault of the palace chapel in a splendor and pomp which she insisted should be absolute.

Then, controlled and imperious, she gave Conrad's last orders to the captain of his garrison.

"The keys of the city of Tyre are to be surrendered to none save the envoy of Richard of England . . . or of Philippe of France."

When the man had gone, his jaw set to betray no emotion, she turned to Eden, a bitter irony in her look. "He held fast to his allies to the last . . . even while he was dying. Would Richard Plantagenet have done as much for me?"

Eden lowered her head, ashamed, and held her peace.

"He also made me promise," Isabella continued in a subdued tone, "that I would soon marry again . . . a strong man who could hold the city. It was hard for him . . . and for me, to think of that at such a time . . . Oh, Eden," the cry demanded satisfaction of God himself, "he would have made an incomparable king!"

The servants had pulled back the curtains from the long windows and Isabella stood for a moment, her fists clenched before her, looking out over the brightening sea as it lapped about the great causeway built by the city's first great conquerer, Alexander of Macedon. He too had died too soon, though in his lifetime he had subjugated half the world. After a time her tense figure relaxed and her hands fell to her sides.

"We will take rest now," she said, her tone calm again. "I would not have my weak body betray me later, for I must show my people that there is still a ruler in Tyre. Only . . . come with me to my chamber, Eden. I do not think I can lay down upon that bed alone."

Their sleep, though it brought renewal, brought also that terrible, inevitable first moment of waking, when what had seemed mere demonic visions of the night remained to taunt them with cruel reality. Isabella rose, hard-eyed and determined, from the bed where she had known all that she now expected of love's joy, and dressed sumptuously in stiff black and gold, the keys of the city slung heavily from her chatelaine. To Eden she gave a gown of deep gray edged with vair and a silver veil to cover her hair.

They descended once more to Conrad's presence-chamber, where, as sole ruler, the Marquessa seated herself in the vast chair of state, filling it with the nobility of her presence if not with her slight body. There, she was immediately engaged by her steward, her chamberlain, her chaplain and all of the chief lords of the city. The funeral would take place that day, at the hour of prayer called nones.

It was into this room, filled with grave ministers and sober courtiers conducting their business in the subdued tones of mourning, that a servant entered and announced, in tones too shrill for the circumstances, for he had failed to take them into account, "I beg entry, Highness, on behalf of Sieur Tristan Damartin, the Chevalier de Jarnac!"

Eden blanched and swayed where she stood beside the throne, then nodded speechlessly to the surprised inquiry of Isabella's brow. No thought took recognizable shape in her mind, only a whirling miasma of trepidation and dismay. It was over between them. Was that not enough? Must he follow her here and begin her torture anew?

She was grateful, when the broad doors swung open again, for the preoccupation that took no note of her and the busy murmur that drowned her horrified cry, as across the threshold, his bearing grim and stark, strode not only the mailed and booted figure of Tristan de Jarnac, but another, staggering under a weariness that had become insupportable, his light weight bent beneath a too-large hauberk, his eyes well-nigh senseless in his wavering head. And yet, as they wandered the crowded room, they came unerringly to where she stood. It was Stephen de la Falaise.

Seeing the shock stab through Eden, Isabella spoke. "My lords, I crave your indulgence. There is a matter I would attend to alone. With your goodwill . . . you may continue your convocation in the antechamber."

The chamber emptied quickly though there were many curious looks cast at the stern-visaged knight and the crumpled figure who had sunk down upon a settle set against the wall.

"Your companion seems ill . . . perhaps he has need of my physician?" asked Isabella without formality, her dark eyes sweeping the knight whose alabaster countenance had once put her in mind both of Lucifer and of the Archangel Michael.

De Jarnac sketched a bow. "I have the only medicine he needs," he replied courteously, "though I would ask the favor of a private room in which to administer it. It is not in the common run of remedies."

Isabella considered swiftly some of what she had heard from Eden.

"Then this, Chevalier," she said with a glance of agonized sympathy for her friend, "is the Lord of Hawkhurst?"

"He is." Tristan, too, turned to Eden who had now moved. Her eyes accused him.

He met them squarely. "You did not tell me of the opium," he said.

He saw the green gaze widen then drop, confounded.

Cold fingers reached toward her heart. She regarded him with a weary fatalism. "I thought that you knew. That you knew . . . all," she said.

They heard Isabella give a soft moan of pity.

"It is my deep regret that I did not know," he said, "though I would still have brought him to you." His voice was cold but his look pleaded for her absolution. "I thought only to bring you the husband for whom you . . . and I . . . had searched so long. I could not have known, when I found him, that I would also bring you . . . this."

Slightly, she shrugged. The world held no further sense. "It is all one," she said.

Tristan tried to gauge how near she was to breaking.

"When we reach Jaffa," he said with great gentleness, "I will give him into the care of the hospital there. They are skilled in such matters; it is likely they can cure him."

A sudden gust of leaden laughter sounded from the

settle. "And can they also cure death, Chevalier? Have they a cure, too, for love?" Stephen's voice was wild and harsh with pain. His eyes rolled, huge, in his translucent brow. He resembled the witless, chalk-faced clown in a play, only, for him, the mask had become the reality.

Eden could not bear to look at him.

Seeing her stricken face, Isabella said softly to Tristan, "This day I will lay my husband in his tomb; it seems that you have taken Eden's lord from his grave. Do you not question, my lord, whether you have done him wrong?"

A ruby spark flew in his eye. "Highness, I mourn the Marquess, who was my friend, as deeply as any man, as you must know if you have heard Eden's story. However, it is you who are wrong to think Stephen ready for the grave. He can . . . and will . . . be cured of his craving, as others have been."

Isabella disdained to answer him. He knew she spoke of no corporeal grave.

Eden dragged at the reins of her own control and crossed the room to seat herself at Stephen's side. She took his thin hand in hers and sought hopelessly in his face for the boy she had known and loved.

"I know you did not want this," she said painfully, remembering her departure from Qal'a Zaydun, "and I do not make any demands upon you, save only that you will let them try to make you well."

He turned his brilliant, vacant eye upon her, involuntarily tightening his grip upon her hand. "Did they tell you that they have killed him?" he asked dully, his body quivering like an arrow gone to ground.

"The Emir?" She stared at Tristan. "Is it true?"

He nodded wearily. "It was during the raid he made on the caravan. The fool had let Stephen come with him. Zaydun himself died in the battle. Stephen we found among the wounded. Oh . . ." he stemmed her concern, "it was slight; he was hit on the head. He was unconscious when we found him. I did not even know who he was until he awoke. It seemed then," he added with a tired irony, "as though I had been suddenly granted the means to make . . . some amends to you. He was perfectly lucid. I had no suspicion of his need for the drug, no more than I had when I visited Qal'a Zaydun and the Emir told me with such cold courtesy that his prisoner lived and was not for sale. That was *all* he told me. So, too, unfortunately, was it all *you* told me."

Eden caught her breath and turned from him.

"When he discovered that Ibn Zaydun was dead," he continued relentlessly, for she must know all now, "he took leave of his senses and raged like a caged animal. He continued thus for many hours, longer than the strength of most men would allow. It was then we began to realize that there was something other than grief that fed his frenzy. In the end he told us that it was opium. We gave it to him and he became quiet."

"So you too would feed his frenzy?" demanded Eden, horrified.

Tristan wished he had time to be kind. "Let me tell you something about opium," he said quietly. "When a man craves for it he must have it, as he must have blood in his veins. If he does not get it, he suffers terrible pain. Every muscle is insufferably cramped. The bowels ache all along their length. He trembles unceasingly and feels an empty, retching nausea. In addition to this there is the agony of the soul. He is a man alone in the universe, desolated by a loss greater than that of every friend, every love he has ever known; for that is what it is like to be without the thing he craves." He looked over at Stephen, now huddled, his arms crossing his breast, his hands clawing at his shoulders, eyes seeing nothing. "Already the trembling has begun. I will take him with me now, if the Marquessa will be so kind as to give us a room."

"Of course." Isabella shook a small bell.

"Why did you not leave him at Krak? Surely there were physicians enough in the community of the hospital. Why drag his poor body upon such a journey?" Eden was overcome with pity.

"Because I did not know where you might be if we

had delayed so long. You have an unnerving capacity
for disappearing. I did not want to arrive in Jaffa and
find you had set sail for England. Stephen was well-
attended on the journey. You must not mind his looks.
He has been thus for many months."

She made a gesture of defeat.

"Nevertheless I would wish to travel on as soon as
possible. The sooner he is in the hands of the Hospitalers the better it will be for him. They will see that
he sleeps for some time before attempting to with-
draw the opium. He should not waste what strength
he has. I wish to leave in, perhaps, two hours' time."

"No!" cried Eden. "I must stay, at least, to see Conrad laid in his grave."

She turned to Isabella. "You cannot think I would
leave you to bear it alone."

Isabella crossed the room to embrace her warmly.
"The Chevalier is right, my dear. As to the rest, well
. . . I shall have to bear the weight of this great city
alone. And, then, I think I would prefer to make my
final farewells to Conrad with an undivided mind. If
you were to remain, I fear I should not easily dismiss
your troubles from my thoughts."

Eden saw that there was truth as well as kindness
in her speech. She looked toward Tristan, meeting his
gaze as calmly as she could.

"Then I will go with Stephen to Jaffa," she said.
Then, clearly: "But there is no need for you to in-
convenience yourself further on our behalf. We shall
be secure in the company of an escort. You must wish
to return to your fortress." Even had he been a stranger it was poor recompense for all he had tried to do.
She knew it and was ashamed, but would not let him
see it. She could not bear, added to all else, the agony
of a shared journey with Tristan.

His faint smile recognized her purpose and hid his
hurt. "I too have business in Jaffa," he said neutrally,
"both with the King and with the Baron of Stukesey.
There is also the matter of the men I shall leave. They
do not yet know I am no longer their commander."

Eden caught at one name only. "Sir Hugo? But surely you do not still . . ."

"I said the business was mine," he replied curtly.

Isabella's servant appeared at the doors. Tristan directed the man to the settle where he attempted to coax the lolling figure upright.

"You will be ready to leave in two hours?" was the sharp reminder to Eden before he assisted the impassive-faced servant to pull the semi-recumbent Stephen from his seat and support his dragging steps from the chamber. Eden looked after them and thought that she hated him.

"God's Holy Name!" declared Isabella softly as the doors closed upon them. "But there goes a man indeed!"

"By the same Holy Blood," Eden swore tightly, "I wish upon my soul that I had never seen him . . . that I had never left England!" Her face was drawn as though it were her effigy.

Isabella saw that her heart was near to breaking. She took her in her arms and held her close, murmuring gently above her bent head. "I can offer you no comfort, for, as with myself, there is none. We can only live from day to day, accepting what we cannot change. For me there has been an ending. It seems as though it is all there will be . . . but I am twenty-one years old and my good sense beats down my sorrow to tell me that there must one day be a new beginning." Her brave tone gained conviction as she stepped back to gaze into Eden's pale face. "For you, the ending is not yet accomplished. I do not know how far you have yet to go, but know that my prayers are always with you. I wish that you could stay with me, Eden, but your duty lies in Jaffa, as mine lies in the great keys that drag at my waist. It is a pitiful tangle in which you are caught, I know . . . but there are many years ahead. Time must solve it."

She wanted to say, "You are young; your husband is young; he may be a man yet, when he is cured," but there had come to her the near-forgotten vision of poor, inconsequential Humphrey of Toron, whom once she had thought she loved. If she had known Conrad during that first marriage, had loved and lain with him as Eden had with Tristan de Jarnac, how could she ever have taken Humphrey into her heart and her bed again? She could not. For a moment, reading the destruction in Eden's face, she longed to take a dagger and plunge it into the slender back of Stephen of Hawkhurst. What demon of righteousness had possessed that man with the beauty of an angel to make his mistress, whom it was clear he loved, a present of her husband's rejected life? Did he truly think God could demand of him such cruelty? And yet the ways of the Almighty were inscrutable. It was beyond understanding that He could have taken Conrad from the earth in his full flowering, leaving a wife who loved him and a land and people who needed his sure hand, and leave that wretched, unnecessary creature who had just left the room. She pitied Eden with all her heart. She hugged her with a fierce protectiveness that excluded her own grief.

Eden, overwhelmed by such a gift of friendship, took from it the hardiness needed to avoid tears and return Isabella's warmth with her own grateful smile.

"I wish I did not have to leave you," she said, "but we will meet again perhaps. I will not go home until Stephen is well. If I can, may I visit you again?"

"You will be the most welcome sight I could hope for!" Their embrace was lighter this time, as though they already felt the pull of parting.

Yet, two hours later, when the time came for Eden to leave, the wrench was as painful as though it were unexpected.

"We have traveled a lifetime together throughout a single night," Isabella whispered as she stood at Eden's stirrup before her doors, "and, if we should not meet again, we will nonetheless always be sisters."

Eden, with Tristan silent at her back, Stephen close on his right, and the long line of black knights behind them, remembered another day in high summer when a girl who had thought herself a woman had ridden from these doors with part of the youth of Tyre at her wayward heels . . . Neither they, nor she, had come back. As she raised her hand in a last salute to her friend, she saw that the brave smile of farewell flickered a little and that Isabella too, remembered.

The fifty miles to Jaffa flew beneath their determined hooves. The roads were good and the day fair. Their menie of mounted knights traveled gaily, singing as they went. Eden rode silently at the center of the cavalcade. She had been unable to accustom herself to the strangeness of riding next to Tristan, his hand ever and again at Stephen's bridle to guide his loose hand. It was as though she traveled with the ghosts of her past for company. She could not even begin to think of the wasted, indifferent figure of her husband as representing her future. She did not dare to consider, yet, what form that future might take.

Tristan, at first, made some attempt at conversation, speaking to her, she thought, in the courteous, easy tones of a respectful stranger. At last, cut beyond endurance by this inconsequential pretense, she looked up and shook her head at him, her eyes resentful.

After this they rode in silence, though Eden longed to speak with Stephen, to find the words to break the heavy enchantment that seemed to hold him. He rode carelessly, slumped inert in his saddle. Now and then he would mutter to himself in quick, indistinguishable Arabic. He seemed neither to know nor care whither or with whom he was bound. At one juncture she had reined in on his other side, but one glance at his apathetic countenance assured her that he would find any present words of hers as unwelcome as Tristan's had been to her.

There was nothing she could do to reach him, the boy who had grown at her side since she was ten years old and he sixteen. Unable to support her part in this moving chain of negation and humiliation, she let Balan drop back amongst the following knights, seeking shelter in their cheerfulness. She did not rejoin the head of the procession until they had reached

Jaffa. Here she took leave of Stephen outside the gates of the noble building that now housed the Queens of England and Sicily. He would go with Tristan to the precincts of the hospital.

"Farewell, Stephen," she said, as though he might, at last, speak to her. "I will visit you tomorrow." She stood hesitating while he dragged his tormented eyes from God knew what unhappy phantasm to rest on her.

"I do not wish it," he said coldly, the words all too lucid. "The woman was right. You do me wrong to keep me from the grave. There is nothing for me here, nothing in me for you."

She recognized nothing that she had known of him in his looks of chill distaste. An echo of Ibn Zaydun's bittersweet tones mocked her. "I do not care for woman's flesh . . ."

Suddenly she seized his bridle urgently, willing him to hear her. "Think of Hawkhurst, if not of me!" she cried. Surely that name, of all others, would reach him? He had been so proud of his gentle domain.

But he said nothing, only turned his horse's head and ambled steadily away from her.

"I will come to you despite this," Eden said softly, though she despaired.

"Leave him for a few days." Tristan spoke warmly at her elbow as though there were no barrier between them. There was pity in his voice. There was also guilt. "He will understand better when he has slept for a day or more. Though he still has his bare physical strength, he is not in his rational mind. You must not mark what he says. I will have them send to you when you should visit him."

"Very well." She kept her tone neutral and did not look at him. "Perhaps that would be best."

He watched her bent head with a longing that he had fought hard to master, but it was master of him yet. "Then . . . farewell," he said unsteadily, "I am for the hospital also."

Because he would be absent from her again, even though she devoutly wished it, she allowed herself

to look at him now. His wary eyes brushed hers for an
instant as they had done in the days before they had
been friends. Then each turned from the other, sharply, as though they had felt the sudden prick of a dagger.

Eden did not watch as he rode away with his
knights but gave her horse to one of the grooms who
had run out from the royal residence. Turning her
mind resolutely, she felt a lifting of the spirit that
was almost like hope as she went through the gates and
crossed the dusty stableyard, then entered this latest
makeshift palace and went to look for Berengaria.

Although the house had not been built for great nobility, it had belonged to a merchant of some fortune
and was a cool and spacious building set among fragrant orange groves and carefully tended gardens of
palm and bright shrubs. The room which the Queen
had made her own looked inward on to an arcaded
court where scarlet hibiscus and oleander were reflected in a blue-tiled, octagonal pool. Eden had
crossed the court and now stood, unobserved, looking
in upon a scene that, only now, she knew she had
not hoped to see again. Her blood raced at the dear
familiarity of it.

Berengaria, in blue samite, was seated with her back
to the window, her sewing held close to short-sighted
eyes. All around her were her women. There was
Mathilde, not an ounce thinner, though her hair was
lighter and her skin rose-bronze. The eternal dish of
sweetmeats was at her side as she strummed tentatively on her lute. Nearby, Xanthe, her dark hair fallen
about her shoulders, sent a swift and certain needle
through the circle of her embroidery frame and murmured the tune that Mathilde sought. In a high-backed
chair, opposite the Queen, sat a straight figure from
whom Eden shrank a little. Lady Alys was as marble-
cool as ever, her lips taut over the tapestry that lay
across her lap, a wrinkle of concentration between
her brows. Save for one beloved absence, they might
have been at Winchester.

Eden stood frozen, only half wanting to make herself known. There was a contained completion about this quiet picture framed in the window's arch that caused a rag of fear to flutter about her heart. Was there still a place for her amongst them? Or would she come, unwelcome, to destroy their peace? Alys, for one, could hardly fail to be her enemy. Berengaria she had deserted and caused, she did not doubt, endless worry and distress. Xanthe, her servant, she had left behind, making no provision for her, relying upon others to do so in her place. Mathilde . . . well, Mathilde was always kind, but perhaps, after so long, even she . . . It was eight months and more since she had left them.

The Lady Alys looked up from her tapestry.

The empty embrasure perfectly framed the woman who stood among the flowers, the evening light falling upon the golden crest of her head. Quietly, Alys put down her tapestry. Sighing once, she crossed to the window and leaned out.

"Eden of Hawkhurst, is it you indeed?" she called.

The peace was shattered into the corners of the room. Berengaria gave a faint, birdlike cry, her fingers flying to her mouth, while Mathilde and Xanthe shrilled like frightened peahens. The sewing fell to the floor with the lute. Eden had just enough time to catch the glint of an ironic smile on Alys's smooth face before she was weeping in Berengaria's arms.

"I knew you could not be dead, *mi corazon*," the little Queen cried amid her own tears. "I would have known it! I would have known my prayers were useless. But it was not so. They sped like arrows and have found their mark. I give thanks to God, who in his mercy has brought you back to us."

It was long before Berengaria had ceased to hold her and she could look about at her old companions. When she did so, she saw that each of them, even Alys, had tears in their eyes. How could she ever have doubted them? Her smile, as she hugged each one in turn, was one of pure happiness. No matter now what she had suffered, or what was still to come. She had come to her safe haven, she was home. And though she did not deserve it, she was beloved, for love takes no note of deserving. She was their prodigal and she had returned.

Soon the questions began to fall about her ears like warm, longed-for rain and it was clear that the answers would reach far into the night before she might ask any of her own.

There were many things that she did not tell them. Perhaps, later, she would confess herself to Berengaria. Certainly she would do so to a priest. Nor would she expect to find the kindly indulgence that her own Father Sebastian had for his small flock.

She was wretchedly conscious of the repeated echo of Tristan's name throughout her convoluted tale. She was careful to attach no especial warmth to it, or otherwise, but she felt their curiosity. It was Mathilde, of course, who gave it thoughtless voice.

"I think it is the most chivalrous story I have ever heard!" she cried, her eyes alight with old legends. "The Sieur de Jarnac is a more perfect knight than any who served King Arthur. It is almost too sad to bear. He must love you beyond life, and yet he must not have you. And for it to have been himself who brought Stephen to you at the last . . ." She broke off, choked with sympathetic tears.

Eden felt suddenly older than time. "You must not confuse the truth with minstrels' tales," she said gently. "The Chevalier and I do not talk to each other of love."

This, at least, out of the sad collection of truths and half-truths she had given them in her weakness, was simple fact.

"If it satisfies your desire for a romance," she added wearily, "then you have your end accomplished as you would wish, surely? For I have done, with Tristan's help, what I came to this land to do. I have found my husband." Her voice had become cold and tight as she steeled herself against the long scream that she could feel beginning deep within her, for this was black falsehood. The man she had found was not Stephen. Stephen was dead. And Tristan, because he loved her, would try to give him resurrection. Why did she lack the faith that said he would succeed?

There came an urgent need to talk of these things no longer. Abruptly she swung toward Alys. "What I did to you, before I left . . . I want you to know that I have been ashamed of it."

This one, small shame she could confess, for this venial sin ask forgiveness.

Alys smiled, not unkindly. "You were most resourceful . . . as always," she said. A light shrug dismissed the subject and Eden knew she had best count herself forgiven, for it would not be raised again.

Berengaria, who had watched her closely throughout her recital, saying little, leaving the questions to Mathilde, now came close and took her hand.

"There are to be no recriminations," she said firmly, "and you are to sleep now. We all shall need our rest," she went on with a suggestion of humor that was new to Eden, "for tomorrow Richard comes visiting."

"From Ascalon?"

"We are much honored. He rarely tears himself from his latest beloved building project. I have lately thought he would have been as happy had he been born a stonemason. The city was reduced to rubble. Already it promises to surpass itself." There was pride in her voice and an affectionate resignation had taken the place of the confused and desperate questioning of the early days of their marriage. Although there was no sign of the thickening of her slight form that would have gladdened the heart of Queen Eleanor, there was a matronly look about her that bespoke a certain contentment. Eden only wished that she, too, could look forward with such obvious satisfaction to the arrival of Richard Trichard.

"Does it go better, Berengaria, between you and the King?" she asked next day, seated in the inner court with the Queen and a thinner, more restless Joanna Plantagenet, who had already extorted from her far more of her history than the romantic Mathilde had been able to do.

"We are as well together as we ever shall be," replied Berengaria without regret. "Richard is as he is and I no longer hope or seek to change him." She raised compassionate eyes to Eden. "He too . . . no longer cares for the love of women. I think he never did, save for Eleanor."

Bitterness shivered over Eden despite the equable, passionless voice. It had held no surprise for her. It seemed that some part of her had long ago recognized Richard's nature. Was it, perhaps, because, unknowing, she had also recognized it in Stephen?

"He visits my chamber from time to time." Berengaria no longer flamed as she spoke such words. "And one day, please God, we will give England an heir. Otherwise we are good friends and do not deter each other from our chosen pastimes. Richard has his rebuilding . . . when he is not tearing down some city. And his treaties . . . when he is not plotting to wage some new war. I have my household, my music, my friends. If I once expected something different, I have learned to do so no longer." She sighed, but not deeply, and smiled cheerfully at Eden. "Eight months has been a long time, in many ways. We have missed you, Eden."

"Longer than a flagellant's scourge in this hellhole!" Joanna offered, making broad sweeps of her pen at the drawing she was making of the scene in the courtyard.

"Jesu! How I long for Richard to finish this peace, so I may go safe home before he weds me with a camel or a Turk."

Eden smiled. "Has he made no more acceptable suggestion?"

"Not since I refused the infidel ape. I am in deepest disgrace with my brother, as I assure you he is with me."

Berengaria looked at her with affection. "You will marry whom you please, Joanna. You know it. But if you don't look about you swiftly, I believe little Mathilde will beat you to the church door."

"Who is it?" Eden was surprised.

"Can't you guess?" Joanna mocked. "Who is it has as great a staying power with his trencher as her own? And a far heavier hand with the wine?"

"Sir John de Wulfran!" cried Eden at once. "I am delighted for them both. It is an excellent match. As for the matter of eating . . . I hope they may better discipline their children than themselves."

"I like fat babies," declared Berengaria. Then her face darkened a little. "The business of Lady Alys," she said with a faint, regretful hesitation, "is none so happy. I had hoped . . . many of us had thought that she would at last make a match of it with young Will Barret. He has courted her up and down the days whenever he had a moment free to do so. They were a great deal together. Richard was in agreement it should be a match. All was arranged and Will set to be a happy man. Then, when I told Alys, thinking she would thank me for it, she turned upon me like a wild thing, that lovely, calm look of hers all distorted, and said that if the King insisted on the marriage she would take her own life. She would rather lose her hope of heaven than take second best."

"Second best?" Eden met the quiet gray eyes.

"She was beside herself. She didn't know what she was saying."

"You mean, sweet, charitable sister, that she would have slit her throat rather than so incontinently have spoken the truth!" Joanna said trenchantly. "If she could not have Tristan de Jarnac . . . and he had made it quite clear that she could not, poor lass . . . she wanted no man. Why do you bow your head, Eden? This coil is none of your making. We do not *choose* whom we may love . . . as I think you know . . . neither Alys, nor the Chevalier de Jarnac, nor Berengaria, nor yourself. We shall all, I am certain, choose more wisely."

"And what of yourself?" asked Eden quickly, covering her distress.

"Ah! I make do with what comes my way," said

Joanna, smiling mysteriously, and attracting a look of reproof from the Queen. "I find the excellent Xanthe an experienced and invaluable aide in such affairs of the . . . for want of a better word . . . heart. She has had a long apprenticeship. She has become my inveterate messenger. She is also useful as a companion to the Comnenus child, who gabbles away to her in their execrable Cyprus Greek. I don't know what I'd do without her. I'm afraid you've lost your tiring-maid, Eden."

Eden laughed, remembering Xanthe's tireless efforts to render her exciting to the jaded appetites of the unlamented Emperor. "After so long a time I can scarcely complain of theft. But I had thought to lose her to young Gilles in the end."

"Alas, no." Even Joanna's mordant tone sobered. "I very much fear that we have lost Gilles himself."

"How so?" Alarm tinged Eden's question.

"It was because of Richard," Berengaria interrupted with a sudden, determined resonance. "It seems that he became . . . too attached to the boy and your esquire was not flattered. I don't know what took place between them, but Gilles flung out of the King's household and swore he would never go back. Richard had him sorely whipped for the insolence. He was not seen after that."

"Dear God . . . must he now corrupt children?" Eden's tone resounded with contempt. "And was there no one to care what became of Gilles then?"

"Do not accuse us, Eden. It was the boy's pride that took him off." Berengaria was quietly firm. "He left the palace in Ascalon during the night. Will Barret himself took a party of knights and rode out after him. They did not find him. It was thought he might have tried to reach the Chevalier de Jarnac, whom he admired . . . and trusted."

"I beg your parden. Of course I accuse no one . . . no one save myself," Eden said subdued. "Gilles came to Outremer in my service, and if he is truly lost, the responsibility is due to me." To her and to the living legend of Richard Lionheart which had drawn ten thousand boys like Gilles to dedicate their lives to its false lustre.

"He may return if he should discover that Sir Tristan is here," comforted Berengaria, "though I trust, if he does so, he will not then decide that he, too, is meet material for a Hospitaler."

"The boy would make as good a poor, chaste and obedient knight as ever that proud gentleman would," pronounced Joanna scornfully. "Lord, what utter fools men are! I have more than half a mind to drag the handsome Chevalier by his fine, dark curls into my own bed rather than have him make such a sorry end of his manhood. You say nothing, Eden. Have you no sorrow that he may prove the last of his noble line?"

Eden looked at her stonily. "By all means take him to yourself. Why not go further? I am sure his noble line bears blood as high as Plantagenet."

The hot, mischievous eyes snapped. "Believe me, I would . . . if I thought I had even the faintest chance of faring any better than the luckless Alys. No, you must face the bitter truth, my dear, like it or loathe it. You and you alone can claim the iron Chevalier's heart. I only hope," she concluded thoughtfully, "that your precious Stephen is worth the loss."

"If only some compassionate entity would likewise claim your vulgar and insupportable tongue," said Berengaria with unexpected venom, "we should perhaps all manage to love you better."

It was at this inauspicious moment that Richard's comely young herald chose to announce his master's imminent arrival.

Berengaria's look changed and she laid a hasty hand on Eden's arm.

"Do not speak to him of Sir Tristan. He has been much angered by him . . . Best he should have time to forget . . ."

"Angered . . . for what reason?"

"The Chevalier became the champion of Conrad of Montferrat, God rest him . . . and tried to turn Richard's mind toward him before the whole Council.

Richard called him traitor and ordered him from the board. They have not met since that day. It was before he came to you in Damascus."

Eden was silent. So Richard had thrown his gauntlet at last.

As the chink of mail and the sound of brusque, male laughter came toward them along the arcade, she assumed an expression of bland, dissembling courtesy, while her blood pounded out its tattoo of hatred.

Richard Plantagenet appeared taller, broader, more bronzed and gilded than she remembered. He looked tired, though his eyes and his step were as restless as ever. He strode across the courtyard with unswerving directness, his hard long sword barely skimming the uneven flags, and enveloped Berengaria in a good-humored embrace.

"How are you, *ma mie?* You look content."

"Thank you, Richard. I am content enough."

Eden thought now that every time she saw Berengaria look at her husband as she did, it would cause her a small shock of surprise . . . also that nothing hereafter could occur that would change either the look or the surprise.

"Sister! I hope you keep well . . . and quiet. How do you like the life of a spinster, eh? Have your thoughts yet turned to taking the veil?" His bright eyes shone with malicious amusement. They did not change as he swung round to Eden.

"My Lady of Hawkhurst, by all that's Holy! Becket's bones! But we scarcely thought to see you again. I conjectured you had run off with a Saracen, but I hear you have retrieved your missing husband from the Emir's lair. I wish I might train my bitch as well! He does poorly they tell me? The infidel has given him opium."

"It is very kind of your Grace to take such interest in his welfare," said Eden icily. "The news of his return has traveled quickly."

"Indeed yes, I assure you your husband has his friends in high places," the King said silkily. "I'll send him my physician if you like . . . though I'd not recommend him. He has not succeeded in ridding me of the accursed Arnaldia. However, with opium it is more a question of denial than treatment . . . painful, but effective. If it is not already too late. If the addiction is far gone, they can do nothing." He cocked his eye at her like an inquisitive blackbird, gauging her response.

She surveyed him calmly. "I have great faith in the Knights of the Hospital. If it is possible to do so, they will cure him. We must pray that it is so."

Richard made a sound much like a snort. "If God wills it, it will be so. Otherwise, my lady, I'd advise you to think long and well of Hugo de Malfors' suit. I know you have not liked his somewhat hardy manner of courtship, but he seems determined still to have you, and you'd go far before you found a better match. The man is your overlord after all, and if young de la Falaise dies you'll owe him something. You must have a husband; your lands demand it. I'd like to see the marriage myself. You may bear that in mind."

"Richard! You cannot mean this!" Berengaria was horrified.

Eden drew a long breath, regarding her Sovereign with the curiosity usually reserved for exotic and loathesome unknown species. She longed to reveal the depths of her contempt but she knew that Stephen, if he recovered, would need every crumb he could get of the King's goodwill if he were to be allowed to return safe to England. Accordingly, she sank into a graceful genuflection. "I will think upon your words, should the need, alas, arise. I am, as always, your most humble vassal."

As he smiled like a fox and waved her to rise she seemed to feel pincers of steel sink into her soul, as though the two arms of some fatal circle closed upon her. It was a trap that Satan himself must have devised . . . for it had been the Baron of Stukesey's manner of courtship that had sent her across the world to this place and to Stephen . . . and now her King, who should be her protector, waited only for Stephen to die before he flung her back into Sir Hugo's arms. God could not let it happen. Stephen must recover. He must!

"I hear your friends at the hospital have a new recruit," Richard continued with a fine dislike. "The Chevalier de Jarnac, having ill served his King, now proposes to do the same, no doubt, for God. Milk of the Mother, but he's lucky he still has two hands to clasp together in prayer . . . and he'd best pray we do not meet again. They tell me it was he who discovered your lord and decided he was more live than dead?" So . . . Stephen too must suffer for Tristan's disgrace.

Eden inclined her head, expressionless while Berengaria clicked an impatient tongue. Richard, catching it, rounded on her.

"Oh, I know, my lady. I insult your chosen favorite, your *preux chevalier*. The very flower of chivalry, de Jarnac . . . will rescue any fair dame with a will . . . and betray his liege lord with a greater one. Well, you may languish after him as you please, but I have named him traitor. He is as much a traitor as his comrade the Marquess of Montferrat." His smile grew evil. "And you are doubtless aware by now of the reward that treachery has brought to *him!*"

For her life, Eden could hold her tongue no longer. "He was no traitor! Has he not left his kingdom in your hands?" Hatred sparked her glance.

Richard appeared not to notice. "The final wisdom of one whose soul stands in peril," he declared smugly. Then he laughed harshly, his face seaming suddenly with disillusion and weariness, all malice fled. "Who else remains save Richard? Philippe has long since slunk home. His jackal, Burgundy, has lately followed him, now that I can no longer afford to keep him in meat. De Lusignan is worse than useless. Conrad's choice lay between myself and Saladin." He laughed again, briefly. "And I wonder he did not pick on the Sultan!"

"Still so much choler, brother?" Joanna was airy. "I thought you had made your peace with Conrad?"

Richard smiled softly then, suddenly content again. "Aye. He is well at peace now, is he not? So perish all traitors!"

Berengaria stiffened with rage. "You should be ashamed!" she said scornfully. "I will not have you talk so in my presence. If you have no respect for the death of your ally, you should honor the grief of his wife."

Richard looked down, musing into her angry face where there was no longer any trace of indulgent affection. He took her small chin in his hand. "You have been too much with my cross-grained sister, *ma chère*. Do not let her sour your sweet nature, I beg you. You need not concern yourself with Isabella of Tyre. I assure you she will not wear her mourning above a day or two. She will soon change it for a wedding gown."

Their concerted gasp seemed to please him. "What? You don't clamor to hear the lucky bridegroom's name? You disappoint me sadly."

"A strong man . . . who can hold the city . . ." quoted Eden tremulously. "I make myself your questioner. Who is it, my Lord King?"

Richard threw himself down upon the wooden settle next to Berengaria. He looked at Eden sharply, without mischief, his tired, drawn look more pronounced, the skin tint yellowish beneath the bronze. "You are right, Lady Hawkhurst, and there is but one man who can fit the description. Thank God he is with us still. Henri of Champagne bears a stouter heart than any of his kin. I send him, within the week, to claim the keys of the city . . . and the lusty widow. They say she is beautiful and has a high spirit. It promises to be a fine match."

"She has been a widow for only two days," said Eden, her voice pitched past pain.

Richard grinned. Her pain eased his own. "Then her bed will scarce have time to grow cold," he said.

"Suppose," said Berengaria controlledly, "that she refuses him. She is the Marquessa of Montferrat, and the heir of Jerusalem."

"Then we shall have to persuade her otherwise, for the good of her inheritance. But I am willing to wager that she will not. Henri is young, handsome, a popular leader. The city of Tyre will welcome him for his youth and his strength. She will take him, you'll see."

For Isabella, too, there was to be no choosing. She must be given away as the chief jewel in the crown of Jerusalem. At least, Eden reflected amid her compassion for her brave, imperious friend, she would wed a man whom she had found to be attractive and in whose company she had, upon a single, poignant occasion, rejoiced. Henri of Champagne, though he had not been chosen, must be a thousand times more welcome as a husband, to any woman, than Baron Hugo de Malfors.

"Let her take him tomorrow . . . if it will put an end to even one of your eternal, senseless quarrels," said Joanna fiercely. "Tell me, Richard, how stands the treaty with Saladin? You had best be quick and call it completed, for little John has got his sticky fingers on your crown. Our mother sends a list of grievances against him from up and down the country. As long as your vaunted sword."

Richard ignored her querulous tone. "Will Longchamps sends another," he brooded, wiping a hand across his brow, "and Cousin Philippe gnaws at Normandy, despite his oath to me. God rot his bilious gut! John has a hand in that too, I swear. He is as thick with Philippe as they were before our father died. God knows it's true . . . the time has come to look to my own kingdom. But which is the greater cause . . . Jerusalem or the empire of the Angevins . . . if it still stands? Who knows," he cried in taut, fearful frustration. "During the weeks it has taken for such unquiet messages to reach us, perhaps brother John has come to sit snug and soft upon my throne already, dangling his scarlet heels above the ground."

"Poor John! If only he had been taller. He might not have needed to take your throne to prove himself?" said Joanna unkindly.

"Joanna, you are a fool. Hold your tongue." For

once, Eden agreed with him. He rose and paced the yard, his face filled with desperate striving, as if the truth he sought after were before him but beyond his understanding. "We have come so close to Jerusalem," he said with a humility that she had never seen in him. "Could Christ forgive me if I did not make one last attempt?"

Joanna sighed. She wished Jerusalem would crumble to the ground.

But Berengaria laid a gentle hand on his sleeve, her anger passed away; her eyes shining with conviction. "If you should succeed you would be hailed as the greatest monarch in Christendom, the new Charlemagne. None would dare stand against the conqueror who had restored to Christ his Holy City. This was always your vision, Richard. Hold fast to it."

He went to her, took both her hands and kissed them. He did not hide his gratitude. "God bless you, Berengaria. My heart tells me that you are right. I have seen the city from far off. I did not think it would be given to me—but it may yet be so." His brow cleared and the high color flowed back to his face. "By the Virgin, it cannot be otherwise! Why, only yesterday, one of my esquires brought to me a holy and miraculous gift. I had meant to tell you . . . it is the fragment of the True Cross that was taken at Hattin. The boy found it beneath the pillow that holds my crown. Neither he nor any other knows how it came to be there. They are calling it a miracle. And why not? A miracle, though it may not be what we deserve, is surely what we need. Perhaps, indeed, God has sent us his sign. Miracle or not, I shall take it as such and fight to the utmost to restore the Cross to its true home."

His face was alight with purpose as it had been during the early days in Sicily and Cyprus. Seeing him thus once more, Eden's long nurtured hatred failed her and she felt herself betrayed by an insidious willingness to believe in his legend afresh, to see in him the Golden Warrior of Acre's harbor, the unconquerable champion of Christendom that Berengaria had recalled.

Then Joanna gave her deep-throated chuckle. "Splendid, Richard, quite splendid . . . but I think there is something you should know . . ."

"No!" The Queen and Eden cried out as one.

Richard was bemused.

"Joanna . . . you are not to trouble him with your selfishness just now," said Berengaria threateningly.

Her meaning was perfectly clear. This was not the time to reveal Tristan de Jarnac's place in this most necessary miracle.

The King smiled with true kindness for the first time as he kissed his sister on both high-boned cheeks. "Not much longer now, Joanna. Help me, too, to hold fast to my vision, will you not? Put away your mockery for a time. You will like it well in Jerusalem."

Joanna sighed resignedly, but returned his kisses. "Then I shall like it exceedingly well in France," she said dryly.

When Richard had left them, bound for a soak at the bathhouse, she turned impatiently on Berengaria. "Is my brother a child, to be deceived in this fashion?"

The Queen looked at her coldly. "Must one be a child, then, to be permitted the gift of hope?"

Her dignity confounded Joanna for a brief moment. Then her eyes narrowed and she continued stubbornly. "He has offered scant hope to me . . . or to Eden. And for de Jarnac's sake he should be told the truth. He cannot fasten the appellation of traitor upon the man who has recovered the True Cross."

"Joanna, how can you be so obtuse," demanded Berengaria without courtesy, "you who are also a Plantagenet? Can't you see that Sir Tristan has wounded Richard's pride? He loved the man, loved him dearly. The only way that he can accept his defection is to harden his heart against him. Thus he has done, and that is how it must remain for the present. Perhaps, in later days, we may be able to do something to heal the breach . . . but not now, Joanna, not now. Jerusalem must come first."

Joanna frowned, brooding. "De Jarnac has restored the Cross to Richard, has brought it to him as a gift. Is this not enough to return him to favor?"

Berengaria shook her head, smiling a little at such naiveté from such a self-confessed mondaine. "He has brought the Cross . . . but in secret. And he does not also offer back the gift of himself and his allegiance. He has given that to the Knights of Saint John."

"You are too subtle for me, Berengaria, but perhaps you are right to see it so. One day Richard's pride will be the death of him. But the matter of Jerusalem," she looked searchingly into the face of her sister-in-law, "do you truly believe we shall take the Holy City?"

"I believe, as Richard himself feels . . . that we must make one last attempt. For God, and for ourselves. It will pull us together as nothing else can. There is much need of it. Men still desert us daily as they have done ever since the executions at Acre."

"When Eden was the first one to defect," said Joanna with grim humor. "You should have stayed away, my dear. Or, since you needs must return to our crabbed company, you should have slit the throat of Hugo de Malfors, up on those heathen hills, as a precaution against Richard's unpredictable ways."

"It may be I shall do so yet," returned Eden lightly.

But the Queen's face was ridged with pity. "I will speak to Richard on your behalf, when we are alone," she promised. "Be sure that he will not hold to such bararity. Why, surely he must know that it would anger his mother, whom he best loves, most grievously."

Joanna sighed, her eye cynical. "Eleanor," she remarked, "is in England."

It was almost a week later, when, on a morning of hard, brilliant light, cooled by a landward breeze that tossed the sand in gusts about his horse's hooves, a boy in the black tabard of the Knights Hospitalers rode into the merchant's stableyard with a message for Eden.

He did not bring good news. Stephen, after appearing to make excellent progress during the early part of the week, had passed a night of delirium and frenzy and was now, though tranquil for short periods, in so weak a condition that he was not expected to live out the day.

Eden called at once for her horse and accompanied the messenger back to the hospital. This was a long, low, dun-colored building that had once been a Christian monastery. There were no windows on to the street and the place had that blind, secret look that seems to offer nothing of hope.

They rode through the postern and as Eden slipped from her saddle another black-clad figure hastened toward her.

"My lady, I am glad to see you, though I sorrow at the cause that brings about this meeting. I am Brother Martin." It was the same knight-surgeon to whom she had come, so many months ago, for news of Walter of Langford.

"It is certain that he cannot live? You are quite sure?" Her voice trembled. Brother Martin shook his head in perplexity. "I regret that I must say so. He is barely with us at this moment, though there are periods of lucidity . . . And yet, but yesterday, I swear I had considered sending for you with happier news. He seemed so much the better; one could begin to see the man he must once have been."

Eden bit her lip, visions of Hawkhurst crowding in on her. "And can you determine no reason for such a notable change?" she asked as they hurried through the long, cool corridors and the pungent herb gardens, past chambers filled with the low, harsh hum of masculine voices.

"None that seem possible," Brother Martin said. "In a single night there has been a monstrous regression in his condition that I cannot explain. It is as though

he were suddenly back at the stage where he most
depended on the drug, rather than having been totally
deprived of it as he has been here. It is beyond comprehension. None of us can account for it . . ." He
broke off as he approached and drew back the curtain
from the doorway of a small chamber set off one of
the larger halls.

"He is in here, my lady. We have made him as comfortable as may be."

The emaciated figure of Stephen lay sleeping beneath
light cotton covers, his breathing disturbing their surface less than a child's.

The light from a latticed window fell upon his thin
face and the soft flame of his hair so that he resembled the portrait of some ascetic, aureoled saint.
So stricken was Eden by his gaunt and cavern-eyed
features, their color curiously heightened, the lips unusually swollen and scarlet, that she did not see the
other figure at the bedside until he spoke her name.

"Eden. My lady . . ."

Recognition breathed through her like a sigh. She
stepped across the threshold, staring dazedly from one
to the other, and once more, as she did so, she was
aware that the three of them, together in this little
limbo of a room, were held in the incomprehensible
grasp of some great, living, fatal circle.

"Tristan," she managed to say clearly, "it is you
who have sent for me?"

"Yes. As I promised."

She noted then that his body was tense with some
tightly controlled anger; she had never seen his look
so grim. He was cloaked and booted and had the air
of one who has ridden fast and far.

Though he spoke to her, he might just as well have
addressed Brother Martin, or conceivably, the wall.
"I am glad you are here. I cannot, myself, stay now,
my Lady Eden. There is one thing I must do as soon
as I am able. I will come to you later. You will guard
him well, I know, till I return."

So abrupt were his words and so evident his intention of leaving at once that she felt her presence to be quite insignificant to him. The cause of his anger, whatever it might be, was consuming him, and his concentration was far beyond the inhabitants of the cell.

He took up his gauntlets which lay on the bed, pulling them over the long hands which now wore the white-crossed ring of the hospital as well as the black, spurred ruby of Jarnac. "They will have told you he will not recover. I am very sorry for it," he said, his eyes scarcely brushing her as he strode past her through the doorway.

Without turning, she moved to take his place beside Stephen as his swift steps receded along the echoing flags.

It had been as though he had never been a part of her life, her blood, her body, and yet, too, there had been that strong sense, beyond the natural, of the three of them being knit together, inextricably, by a fate that they could not comprehend, must only follow to the bitter working-out.

Guilty, she wrenched her thoughts back toward Stephen, so still and small upon the white bed. She wondered again at the hectic color that sat so strangely on his hollow cheeks, at the turgid, reddened mouth, disturbingly sensual in the ravaged face.

As she looked, the inert body gave a sudden, convulsive start and the eyes flew open, hot blue and crowded with terror.

"No! No, you cannot! Do not hurt him! He must be saved!" A fleck of foam appeared on the pouting lips. She bent close to him, holding fast his hand.

"Stephen! You are dreaming, nothing more. Wake now. It is Eden; it is I!"

He shuddered and brought a shaking hand up slowly to his head. She saw that a heavy sweat had broken out upon him. He shivered, his breath coming in deep, uneven gasps. His hands clutched at hers like a claw. "Eden? It is truly you?" He was shaking now, uncontrollably. "It is so cold, Eden, cold." His eyes filled with tears. With a cry of pity she took his trembling body into her arms, cradling him against the warmth of her breast, wrapping the covers tightly about him.

"Bring more blankets, for the love of God, Brother Martin. He is chilled to the bone."

Behind her, the monk gravely shook his head. "Blankets cannot avail him. He will immediately be on fire with the fever, my lady. These cold sweats and the fever that follows torment him equally."

She looked at him wildly. "Is there nothing you can do?"

Her desperation touched him. He hated his own words. "No, nothing."

Stephen suddenly flung himself away from her, his eyes glittering and excited. To her horror she saw his swollen lips part in a jerking, rictus grin which tremored into a violent laugh, the precursor of a harsh gale of senseless mirth which he could not or would not control.

Horrified, Eden endured the paroxysm, ignorant of how to help him.

Brother Martin laid a compassionate hand on her shoulder. "Try not to distress yourself too much, my lady. This, too, is part of his sickness. It is the same immoderate laughter that occurs if one takes too much of the drug . . . but never before have I seen such a response to its withdrawal . . ." He sighed in deep regret. "It confounds us all. We know so little, it seems . . . so much less than we, in our pride of learning, think we know."

"Don't berate yourself for ignorance, Brother surgeon," the grating whisper traveled from the pillow, the hideous laughter done. "I would not embarrass your science with my equivocal case. I have a confession to make to you . . . now that I am safe beyond the lasting penance you would lay upon me. It is not your denial of the opium that affects me now, but rather my own liberal consumption of it. Last night I received an amount which will soon take me where I wish to journey . . . Indeed, I wonder greatly that I am still here to puzzle you . . ." Stephen's bright eyes were turned upon them with a gentle, teasing humor that bore no resemblance to his primary, moon-mad laughter.

"How has this come about?" Brother Martin was stricken. "Each man here is under the strictest instructions."

A boy's mischief lighted the drained face. "Perhaps, brother, it would be best if you were to think of it as a miracle, and most welcome . . . as I do."

Eden wanted no more of miracles. "Miraculous . . . to bring you to your death! Oh, Stephen . . . do you have so little use for life?" She was choking with pity and a rising, vengeful rage that as yet could have no object.

Stephen looked at her kindly, as he had used to do when, as a child, she had found some passage in their books too difficult. He reached for her hand and smiled and she saw that, after all, he had remained the boy she had loved, and now looked out at her clearly from behind the mask that circumstance had made for him.

"Eden . . . how can I explain to you . . . you who were my wife . . . in whom I was once so content?" A reflection of her anguish crossed his face and he carried her hand to his breast.

"We were happy, were we not, at Hawkhurst, when we were children together? You will remember that we were happy? Perhaps, if I had never left you, never listened to Hugo's tales of the Crusade . . . if I had stayed with you upon our domain . . ." His sigh was so attenuated that it seemed only to come from his glistening eyes as he pondered at last—in the way of those who know well that they are dying—on the things that might have been.

Eden held his hand in hers and did not speak, for she could not. She felt the bones beneath the faintly pulsing flesh with the same sense of helpless, angry tenderness that comes when we handle a small bird.

"It is strange," the half-extinguished whisper continued, "but there is a fatal justice in it . . . that Hugo

... should be the one ... the one to send me forth ..."
His voice faded, his breathing was swifter and more
shallow.

Alarmed, Eden bent over him. "Rest, love. Do not
talk." She could hardly see him through her tears. He
wavered before her like the image in a pool when rain
comes. She turned again to the monk, standing, pillar-
like, behind them, his lips moving in prayer.

"Even now ... is there *nothing* we may do for him?"

"My daughter ... we may pray."

She nodded, she had known. "I should like to be
alone with him, if you will permit it? I will watch with
him as long as ..."

The knight bowed. "It is a small thing to ask. You
will call me if I am needed. I shall hear you. There is
one thing ..." he hesitated. "Try, if you can, to learn
who it is who has given him what he sought."

She inclined her head again and he left her on the
silence of roped soles. She saw that Stephen had closed
his eyes. He lay quiet now, his limbs relaxed and
peacefully disposed, his hands loosely clasped above
the covers. Beyond his excessive leanness there now
seemed to be no sign of the extremity of his condition.
His lips and cheeks had paled and the turbulence
had left his breathing as it had left his limbs. He
looked so tranquil that Eden almost allowed herself
to fall a prey to a new, deceiving hope.

Then he opened his eyes and she saw how their
feverish brightness had diminished and still ebbed
with the candle-glow of his strength. Still he held fast
to her hand and pressed it faintly as he spoke to her,
his voice now nothing more than a moving breath on
the motionless air of the cell.

"Forgive me, if you can, for seeking death so gladly
in the face of your beauty. We do not choose what we
must become. I never sought to hurt you, God knows;
you must believe me ..."

"Yes, yes! Do not tire yourself so ..."

"I thought you would count me dead. I was so
sure of it. So many are lost who take the Cross." He

smiled, a movement of will rather than muscle, the trace of mischief again incredibly present. "I made sure you would have wed again by now . . . perhaps with Hugo." Her gasp did not reach him. "I know he once thought to have you . . . asked your father. Think of him, Eden. He has been a good friend to me . . . better than you will ever know. He would care for you, and for Hawkhurst . . . as he has cared for me . . ."

Pity and irony burned like a bolt of steel beneath her breast.

"The other . . . Sir Tristan. You must give him my thanks also. He has done what he thought was right, within his lights." The mischief flickered again and went out. "And, in truth, it was he who has helped me from this world at last . . . I owe him much gratitude. You . . . must pay my debt . . ." Panting, he closed his eyes as her cry rang out, ragged with pain and disbelief.

"No! You cannot mean it! It was not Tristan!" She shook his hand, unaware what she did. "Stephen, for the love of God, say it is not so!"

His white lids fluttered and the pale lips parted once more. The effort was very great. "It is not . . . Eden . . ."

He could not summon the strength to finish. He lay silent for a space and then suddenly started up toward her, his eyes wide with an excitement that shook his exhausted frame. He gave a single great cry of "Ayub!" his arms outstretched as if in welcome, then fell back upon the pillow.

Although he was smiling still, she saw that he was dead.

When Brother Martin returned he found her kneeling beside the pallet, her head upon her husband's cold breast. She looked up when he touched her gently, and he saw that her grief was dry in her eyes. It would be the hardest of all to bear. He did not trouble her, therefore, with the question he would have asked. There would be time enough for that.

As for Eden, she spoke to him of no one save Stephen himself.

They would bury his body in the sepulchre of the monastery, where the knights of the Order were laid in rest. He had not confessed before he died, but had not the great Abbot Bernard of Clairvaix, that piercing intellect that had forged itself into the arrowhead of the first Crusade, promised, when he had called to arms the youth of each generation, that the soul of a dying Crusader should fly straight to heaven, every sin fallen away?

Brother Martin was certain that his promise must hold good for Stephen, whom the Crusade had called and also, after this aberrant and singular fashion, killed; Eden, responding automatically to his repetition of the Christian prayers for the dead, could only trust in the infinity of God's mercy . . . and hope, for Stephen's sake, that Christ's heaven and the green paradise of the two gardens were, by some ultimate miracle incomprehensible to man, one and the same. Knowing such a hope to be nothing short of heresy, she prayed the more desperately, not only for the resurrection of Stephen's soul, scarcely departed from the slight, insulted body before her, but also for her own. She understood nothing.

She only knew, somewhere at the center of a weariness that clothed her spirit with its own, stifling shroud, that now it was all over.

Now she must go home.

Nothing that Berengaria could say would deter her. Eden longed for her home like a lost child. To go back to Hawkhurst was the one thing that made sense to her in a world made hideous with unreason. She would go there though the seas divided against her and she would go at once.

"Will you not wait, at least, until Sir Tristan returns to Jaffa? I know in my heart that he will be able to set your mind at rest upon this terrible matter of Stephen's death."

Eden stared up at the Queen from her place beside the chest she was filling with what was left of her worldly goods and fortune. "My mind rests. He is a murderer; that is all. I never wish to see him again."

"I will not believe it." The soft voice was raised in earnestness. "And, oh my dear . . . neither should you. You have nothing in evidence save the ravings of a poor, crazed and dying creature. I cannot believe that you will condemn Tristan on such a slender charge. He has been steadfast so long; how should he change at the last? Will you not reconsider, and stay until he comes again?"

"Stephen did not rave; he was perfectly clear before he died," said Eden coldly. "There is no question. Tristan has killed him. I do not wish to reconsider . . . lest I should start to consider *why* he has done so." She folded a gown with harsh concentration.

Berengaria sighed abruptly. "I could . . . forbid you to leave."

Eden rose to her feet and looked steadily at her friend. "I hope, my Lady, you will not do so, for then I would have to disobey you, and this would cause me much grief. I have enough of grief," she added cruelly.

Berengaria crossed to take her in her arms. During the days since she had walked behind Stephen's coffin to the gloomy vault beneath the monastery, Eden had become thin and pale, her gestures erratic and her speech swift and nervous. Berengaria's heart bled for her as she saw the torment that Tristan's name had awakened in her.

"Go then, if you must, *mi corazon*," she said, holding her close. "And let us trust in God that soon we shall meet again in England. For surely, when Richard has assayed Jerusalem, whether for good or ill, then all will be concluded here and we shall come home to our kingdom at last. Go then, Eden; go to Eleanor. She will know how to find words that may comfort you, where Berengaria cannot."

Eden returned the warm embrace. "You make me ashamed," she said. "If you cannot comfort me, dearest friend and Liege Lady, it is because I cannot be comforted. Nor do I deserve it. And yet," she added, a wild pleading in her eyes, "if there is comfort for me anywhere in this world, I know it will come to me at Hawkhurst. If I know that you let me go willingly, I shall sleep the easier for it."

"Then let it be so," said Berengaria with a sweet finality. Her tone then became brisk and workaday. "You will leave on the pilgrim ship?"

"I will. We set sail tomorrow."

"So soon!" The Queen felt her throat constrict. "Perhaps it is for the best. Long farewells are painful. We must send to Joanna. She will wish, as I do, to write to Eleanor . . . If you will be kind enough to act as our courier?"

"I am more than willing. I long to see the Queen Mother almost as much as I long for Hawkhurst."

She would lay her confused and sorrowing head in the lap of that brave, unparalleled lady and confess all anew. If there were a way through the maze of guilt and sin to some measure of peace in which to spend the endless days, then Eleanor would find it. In this she trusted. In this she placed her single, shriveled seed of hope.

"I must send at once to Richard in Ascalon," said Berengaria busily. "His envoy will have scant time to catch the galley before she leaves. Then there is Alys . . . and Mathilde . . . and perhaps some of Richard's knights may wish to send letters. And if only your Gilles would return! I shall send him home to you at once when he does . . . You will not mind being the bearer of so many missives? Eleanor will see that they are delivered . . ." Her voice ran on, lightly planning the happiness of others, while beneath her breath, far more fiercely, ran the desperate prayer that Tristan de Jarnac, too, would put an end to his sudden, inexplicable disappearance before the ship set sail.

Her prayer was not answered.

If this caused her despondency, however, she did not let it appear, but threw her energies into making Eden's departure a pleasant one, as far as this was possible. Indeed, the small cavalcade that rode down to the blue harbor amid an orange morning of sun and scintillating light was as gay and as brightly clad as the one which had gathered to say farewell to Eleanor herself when she had sailed from Messina, her duty as royal matchmaker done. Many of those who formed the group on the quayside among the scurrying, half-naked sailors and straw-hatted pilgrims of every station, were the same, now become friends to Eden where before they had been but unknown, vivid faces. Only the King's absence made the occasion less than glorious . . . while one other made it, though it was not to be admitted, less than happy.

Xanthe, her hand clasping that of an excited and voluble Minou, was the first to allow herself the luxury of tears, as her southern blood cried out at so much well-mannered control among her betters.

"Think of me sometimes, mistress," she cried, her brown eyes soft with affection as she kissed Eden's hand. "I will never forget that you were the one who gave me my fine new life!"

There was one, then, among those she had touched with her own blighted fate, who called herself happier for it. Eden humbly thanked God as she kissed the olive cheek. Mathilde, too, she could embrace without regret. In her sea chest lay the letter in which Sir John de Wulfran begged her father for her hand in marriage, closed with Richard's own seal.

"Be happy, *ma chère* . . . you deserve it. You have always made others so."

Mathilde burst into tears at her words, much to Xanthe's satisfaction, and wordlessly presented Eden with a stout wooden casket. "They are comfits for the voyage," she sniffed, smiling through her tears. "They are almond dragees. If you suck them you will not be sick. There are enough to last the journey." The voyage was expected, if all went well, to take six weeks. The laughter that greeted the gift brought Eden a relief which would help her to accomplish her next, more difficult farewell.

Alys was cool and stately, her dignified gaze serene.

"Well, Eden . . . we have not been friends, I think?" Eden acknowledged her courage. "But one day, I hope, we shall meet again and it may be that we shall somehow find our ways to each other. I wish you joy in your homecoming, truly. May you find the peace you seek. Go with God."

There was strength and warmth in the arms that enfolded Eden and she rejoiced in the clear sincerity of the words. For the first time, she too trembled on the edge of tears.

She bit them back as Joanna Plantagenet took Alys's place before her. She was dressed in a height of fashion that bordered delightfully upon indecency around her tawny breasts and was well aware of the effect upon every lusty man in the cheerful, milling throng alongside the little scarlet and blue painted galley. She allowed her remarkable bosom to heave in an exaggerated sigh and attar of roses mingled with musk in the warm air as she leaned forward for Eden to brush her rose-tinted cheeks with smiling lips.

"You cannot know how deeply I envy you! I have lain awake half the night, debating whether or not to stow away on this pretty ship. But then Richard would forsake my cause altogether and I should doubtless lose my fortune as well as my crown. Alas, so much the worse! Give my undying love to civilization, my dear Eden . . . And be sure to write to me if you should encounter any really personable baron of good character . . . not *too* good . . . and outstanding courage and fortune . . . And for God's sake let him have a sense of humor!"

"Joanna . . . you have no shame!" Berengaria laughed at her sister-in-law who stood tossing her ruddy curls with all the spirit of a high-bred mare. Eden was glad of the excuse for mirth, for this last leavetaking would be the hardest of all.

It was Berengaria who made it easy for her, as she might have known she would. There was no trace of moisture in the Queen's gray eyes as she took Eden calmly by the hand and walked with her across the quay and over the narrow gangplank to the deck of the crowded vessel. There, they faced each other, their hands still joined. There was a lightness of spirit between them that comes of the knowledge of shared affection. There was no place for tears. "See how willingly I set you on your way," the faintly accented voice said without a tremor. "And yet I do not part with you, for you will be always in my heart and in my prayers, as I know I will be in yours."

"Always."

"And pray for Richard, also, Eden." She sighed. "He has much need of prayers. I know he has not been kind to you . . ." The King had refused to listen to his wife's pleas against Sir Hugo de Malfors, now his close companion in Ascalon. "But we must hope that one day he will find his way back to himself . . . for he has been greatly changed in these last, long-drawn weeks. He needs accomplishment; without it, the Plantagenet devils reign in him."

"Richard shall have my prayers." If only for the sake of his Queen.

"Good-bye, then, Eden . . . until we meet again in England."

Their embrace was strong but brief, for now they feared the tears that would diminish that strength. "Be happy at Hawkhurst. I will send you comfort if I can," was Berengaria's promise.

"I will take it from the knowledge that the Queen of England is my friend," Eden replied proudly. They smiled, and Berengaria turned away.

Eden watched the small, indomitable figure cross the gangway. At once the plank was taken up and the sailor's cries rang out to get the galley under way. This too, Berengaria had planned.

Standing, very straight, at the wooden rail, Eden raised her hand high in response to the small forest of waving arms that saluted her. A sense of unreality prevailed as the crowded brightness of the quay receded slowly. She saw Berengaria call for her horse and mount it. She reined toward the departing ship and put her fingers once to her lips, scattering her kisses across the sparkling water. Then she turned and was gone, the little band of courtiers trailing behind her like a flaunting, many-colored scarf. Now that she could see them no more it was as if, suddenly, she had left no life of her own behind her on those blue and gold shores. Fear shook her like a freakish wind; she seemed not to know who she was or what her purpose. Then a woman of middle-age, a pilgrim, richly dressed, touched her arm and made some friendly comment. The moment of terror receded. She was Eden of Hawkhurst and she was going home.

She turned courteously to her companion and made her a bright, encouraging reply.

As the red and blue galley sailed out of Jaffa, two men faced each other, swords in hand, upon the hot sands of Ascalon. They were Sir Hugo de Malfors and Tristan de Jarnac.

De Jarnac had waited restlessly for nearly a week in Richard's camp while Sir Hugo was absent with the King on reconnaissance near Beit Nuba. Saladin had wind of the proposed movement on Jerusalem and his troops were massing in the area. Yesterday the King had returned and this morning Sir Hugo was sufficiently rested to take up Tristan's challenge. Richard, had he known of it, would have forbidden the fight. They had taken very great care, therefore, that he should not know of it.

They were in the desert, some two miles out of the city. There had been few words between them. Words were the business of the four esquires who attended them. Each knew that only one of them would survive the contest. Each had had his own compelling reasons for his brutal determination that it should be himself.

They began then, their steel struggle, *à l'outrance*.

Their swords were hard, long, newly sharp Damascus blades, Sir Hugo's broader and heavier than Tristan's, with his name carved deep into its length, its pommel of gold with the terminals carved into the boars' heads of Stukesey. Tristan's slender blade carried only the name of Christ inlaid along its length and terminated in a simple ebony cross, damascened, like the blade, in silver. Neither man used a shield or buckler, though both were helmed and both wore daggers at their belts. They stood some twenty feet apart until Sir Hugo's esquire called upon them to begin.

Without haste they moved toward each other, both faces calm. Within six or seven feet they began to circle, watching like hawks for any sudden movement. Each held his sword low before his taut belly.

Suddenly Tristan stepped sideways, judged his distance and lunged from the right. Hugo, swift despite his weight, swung his right foot deftly behind him and back, avoiding Tristan's blade and bringing down his own in a blunt, scything movement. He caught Tristan's sword near the tip and all but sent it flying from his hand. Tristan, recovering before Hugo could cease his weighty swing, had found his balance and moved in under the Baron's outflung left arm. He felt his sword point catch in the netted hauberk and saw the blood spring up as Hugo flung backwards, staggering but without losing his feet. As he sought to press home his advantage, moving in with his sword guarding his chest, Hugo gave a great beast's roar and brought his weapon swinging down in a terrible arc from sky to sand, cutting the very ground from beneath Tristan's feet. As he attempted to rise he found the Baron's boot pressing like a gravestone upon his ribs. He saw that Hugo was smiling.

"Rest in peace, monk!" he said as he raised his sword and hurled it down in triumph into Tristan's breast. The world rolled and receded toward darkness, rushing into a vortex whose center was pure agony.

Hugo looked down in satisfaction and carefully withdrew his blade. Setting it down, he knelt at his conquered enemy's side. "Be sure I shall guard her well, Chevalier, for the rest of her days," he said clearly. They would be the last words he would hear, and most fitting.

Tristan scarcely heard them, so intense was his concentration upon the will to move; to move the muscles that could guide his hand; to move his hand to reach his dagger. He need not die at once, not if his will were strong enough; he could and would reach the dagger.

He felt Hugo's warm, unwholesome breath upon his face. Now was the moment. He opened his eyes. Sir Hugo smiled into them. He held them with his own, pretending hatred, humility, defeat, while his hand went slowly, surely to its work.

"Guard her well . . . and love her well, and in no monkish fashion," Hugo growled, still grinning like a dog.

It was then that Tristan forced his body into its last, inhuman effort, raking upwards with the dagger from his belly towards the broad, pulsing throat . . . He thought he felt the flesh give way, the weapon jerk home . . . and then there was nothing . . . It seemed that he fell, though surely he was already upon the ground . . . he went on . . . falling.

Hugo stared down at the inert body, his hand at his gurgling throat. His eyes were hot with triumph.

Later, Richard Plantagenet looked upon the body they had brought him, his eyes hooded and sad.

He sighed and a great weariness passed across his face. "He was a brave knight and a good companion . . . whatever may have been his failings," he said, and he wept. "I shall not replace him."

▼▼▼▼▼▼▼▼▼▼▼▼▼▼▼▼▼▼▼▼▼▼▼▼▼▼▼▼▼▼▼▼▼▼▼▼

CHAPTER EIGHTEEN

Hawkhurst

The Lady of Hawkhurst was seated before her empty hearth. It held no fire because it was mid-June. Her chaplain and her bailiff had just left her after eating at her table. They had, as on most evenings, talked incessantly of the Holy Land. They spoke of mailed knights and veiled ladies, of Christian courage and Saracen savagery . . . and if, occasionally, Eden had intimated that these last were apt to be interchangeable, neither stalwart Saxon had taken a blindman's notice.

They no longer spoke of Stephen. These two, as before, had become the chief companions of her evenings. They would drink wine and reminisce with her, play backgammon or draughts if she had a mind, discourse with equal vigor upon religion, philosophy or the killing of a pig and walk with her as she loved to do in the intense green world outside the mellow walls.

Its color lay upon her tired eyes like a healing balm. It seemed that she had never known England was so green . . . massively, exaggeratedly green; green in great rolling swathes of mixed and mingled forest; in soft, lapping tides of watered meadowland; verdant, emerald, malachite, aqua, beryl, olive, pea-green, sea-green, apple-green and blessed, blessed every blade and flower. For days she thought she must have wept green tears as she walked about the sweet, soft lands of her domain.

As she did so a gladness had arisen in her that she had not thought to know again. At first she had put it down to the precious familiarity of her surroundings, the sane and secure sameness of her father's house, which Hawisa had guarded like a Cerberus against friend and foe alike, ruling over the household and over Eleanor's men with a rod as strong to break their backs as ever that stout queen wielded.

It had been Hawisa, indeed, who had told her the reason for the strange content that had fallen upon her, when she had expected only loneliness, a sad sense of unachievement and loss.

The journey home had been easy enough. Their little ship had been sturdy and her captain honest. There were few storms. The pilgrims had made each other good company, exchanging tales of Jerusalem and the river Jordan where they had broken off the branches of palm they wore in their broad-brimmed hats, for stories of Compostella in Galicia where the Spanish contingent that joined them in Gibraltar had been at the shrine of Saint James, whose scallop shell they wore in their cloaks. Several were hung about with enough extra leaves and medallions to insure them a small recompense for the monies expended on their pilgrimage. Most, however, were rich and traveled only for the good of their souls, like the noblewoman who had become Eden's companion. They had traveled cheerfully together, with much music and song and the gallant little ship had reached her haven before her time.

Within four hours of arrival, Eden and a joyfully released Balan were safe within the gates of Hawkhurst.

And what a welcome had awaited her there! A greater babble of weeping and laughing and frantic, incessant questioning broke out than the dignified manor had ever seen. Hawisa could not be persuaded to take down her apron from where she had cast it over her head in case, when she did so, Eden should no longer be there. Father Sebastian did not cease to praise God at the height of his considerable pulpit voice, while Rollo and the rest of the servants celebrated roundly in the only fashion they knew. They got themselves noisily, thoroughly and unashamedly drunk and roared about the house giving thanks. The women of the household, several of whom had infants new to Eden tumbling about their heels, held back until they had set these innocents safely in their wicker cradles, then joined their menfolk's revels with a will. Eden herself queened it at the head of her great oak table, with Wat the Bailiff on her right hand, glowing with a justified pride in his husbandry of her acres. Father Sebastian, on her left, prayed loudly and alternately for Stephen's soul and a good harvest. Several of Eleanor's soldiers, who had somehow never brought themselves to leave so comfortable a billet, possessed excellent voices and a makeshift collection of instruments, to which Eden added her own lute and the ud she had brought from Jaffa. Music rang out and dancing beat its rhythms through the wood and stone of Sir Godfrey's fine hall so that the din was remarked upon with envy, a mile away in the villa.

It was the next morning, on attempting to raise her head from the pillow, that Eden began to feel queasy. Hawisa muttered that everyone had been a little intemperate and no wonder, and dosed her with elder and wormwood. When the nausea occurred again the following morning the moment her mistress rose from her bed, the good woman put a hand on her hip, raised a single brow, then brought both brows down firmly, bristling around her forthright nose.

"Have you had your last month's courses?" she demanded, mincing no onions.

Eden tried to think, dismayed. "I can't remember," she said. "I don't even know when they should have been, Hawisa. So much has happened . . ."

"Evidently." Then the frown cleared from the broad brow like the wrinkled skin from warmed milk. "But surely this is the most blessed thing, my chuck! Poor Sir Stephen is gone from us forever, God rest his young soul . . . but he has left his seed in you, in his stead. Thanks be to the blessed Mother of God!"

And the apron went up over her head again, leaving

Eden to stare at her, clinging rigidly to the bedpost, while she tried to take in the meaning of what the old woman had said.

That she was with child! She had not thought of it, could scarcely believe it. But that she was with child by Stephen . . . this was not possible. The thoughts flew about her vacant mind like imprisoned, directionless birds. A child! The dearest wish of her heart. A child, but whose . . . ? And then the door opened and her thoughts were free. She had conceived. She knew it would be true. She had conceived in that green glade above Damascus . . .

But she alone knew that she had not conceived by Stephen. She would bear Tristan de Jarnac's child and bring it up as the heir of Hawkhurst. There would be no need for anyone, save her confessor, ever to know the truth. Even as she took the decision she closed another door upon those other unwanted thoughts that flew at once to torment her. The memory of Tristan's eyes upon her, his body close to hers, of his fire-sweet kisses on her lips, his skin beneath her hands . . .

She slammed home that door and locked it fast. The child would be hers. Let others name his father.

She shifted in her chair, a little heavy with the wine she had drunk, though the child was as yet scarcely more than a warm knowledge within her.

She was tired, for today she had ridden home from Winchester. She had seen Eleanor, had stayed with her for several happy, tale-drunk days. They had sat up each night until first light, for the Queen no longer had much use for sleep and she was too eager for Eden's news and history to break off until her visitor dropped with weariness.

"And so, my golden boy is all tarnished in your eyes," she had growled, sitting bolt-upright in her carved chair, her fine eyes still clear and penetrating while Eden's lids were heavy.

"Berengaria has not, from what you tell me, the kind of strength he needs. I confess I had not foreseen it. When I married them, I was thinking of his private

pleasure rather than his public face. I had thought
their temperaments a fair match of opposites. But then
. . . his private pleasures have been other than . . . I
had hoped he would change. No matter. I do not
claim to be surprised. There is too much of the woman
in both of my sons . . . though why, in the Devil's
name they should both be such arrant fools, when the
woman that is in them is myself, I cannot comprehend." She had finished on an explosion of irritation.
"May God give Jerusalem to Richard as soon as he
likes . . . for then Richard may come home and attend to John. I can no longer control him. He has
become devious and dangerous, a spinner of webs, a
weaver of nets. He speaks the whole world fair and
plots the downfall of half of it; and none knows which
half. Blood of the Lamb, but I sometimes think that
Geoffrey was the only child God sent me that I do
not wish I had strangled at birth . . . and him, God
himself took before he could do much damage in the
world."

They had talked, also, of all that had happened to
Eden since last they met. Eleanor had listened with a
grave, intent concentration, often asking a question,
never offering judgment. They had gone beyond the
dawn that night.

"And so my wheel has come full circle and I am
back at my beginning," Eden had mused, her somber
tone embracing both acceptance and defeat. "I have
gained a child and find much happiness in it . . .
though I should feel shame. But I have lost Stephen
. . . and not only to death. And I have found and lost
together all that I shall ever understand of love . . ."
Her voice trailed; she did not wish to follow that
road.

Eleanor looked at her with a mixture of tenderness
and irritation. "And how much, after all's done, does
that amount to, my child? It seems to me, concerning
these two who have ruled your thoughts and deeds
these long months, that your understanding has been
very little. Stephen, though you were wed to him, you
did not know at all. It was a stranger to you who died

in Jaffa. And Tristan . . . though you say you have known love with him . . . how far have you looked into his heart? You have judged him harshly."

Eden had been hurt. "How else does one judge a murderer? And how was I to see into so devious a heart as his? It is over, your Grace, over. I beg you . . . let us speak of him no more."

Eleanor thought of the contents of her daughter-in-law's letter. She nodded and said nothing, but rose from her, stretching the cramped muscles of her back.

She looked down at her sleepy guest with commiseration. "In the case of Stephen," she said with exquisite delicacy, "it is too late . . ." And then she had drifted from the room, leaving Eden to ponder her words.

Bitterly she thought that, whatever the Queen might suppose, she had understood Tristan very well, and she did not, even on Eleanor's beloved account, wish, ever again, to open that locked and bolted door in her life. The Queen had sent her home with many gifts. She would have jewels enough to found a substantial fortune for her son . . . for it would be a son.

"But don't spoil him; do not keep him too close by you," ruefully advised the mother of Richard and John. "Come back to me, soon," she had cried as Eden mounted her horse to leave. "You have brought a breath of spring to me . . . and a savor of spice. Come and see me often. I thrive upon your youth!"

"Youth!" Eden was startled. "I thought I had left that behind in Outremer."

"You flatter yourself," Eleanor had said dryly. "What you left behind was your innocence. You will see the world . . . and yourself . . . much more clearly without it."

For more than an hour she had drowsed upon her time with Eleanor, recalling each swift and certain strike home of that abrasive, unillusioned wit. She needed Eleanor. She would learn from her how to disdain the weakness that so often tempted her toward self-pity, despite the green summer and the coming child . . . or, perhaps, because of them.

Outside, the birds still sang in the trees that guarded the eastern side of the house, their evening hymn in concert with that of Father Sebastian who was teaching serfs and village boys to sing, among the resounding stones of the chapel. Eden leaned back and let the peace of Hawkhurst flow over her. Even as she needed Eleanor's hardihood to stiffen her spirit against herself, she also needed this blessed quiet to give her strength of a different kind, the strength that can endure and bend and never break, so that she might become, in time, the firm root of her son's future, passing on to him the heritage of that strength.

As she lay and allowed the music and the tranquillity to reach deep into her, she became suddenly aware of another sound, a rhythm beneath the piping cadences of birds and boys. It was the clatter of hooves upon clay, iron upon stone. Hawkhurst had a visitor.

Eden sat up, her hands grasping the arms of her chair. It was late. None came visiting at such an hour, unless for some grave reason . . . or for mischief. She listened. One man only and riding hard. A messenger? From whom? She subsided again in the chair and waited for the thundering at the door. One man alone could bring no harm. It was not as if it were like that terrible night . . . so long ago, and yet, ever since she had returned, she had unconsciously waited for it . . .

The hammer blows came. Where was Rollo? It was his business to see who knocked. He must then come to ask if she would receive him . . . Again the dull, repeated blows.

Her heart began to pump. What if Rollo were absent? There was talk of some village girl he was courting . . . and many of the serfs were out working in the fields in the late sun of summer. Panic rose within her, unreasoning, black with fear. It was foolish; she tried to thrust it down. Then she heard the great doors heave open, caught the fractured murmur of voices, and her blood drummed in her ears like a rushing torrent.

Beyond all sense, she knew that the man who would appear on the threshold would be Sir Hugo de Malfors, come to claim her body and her lands at the King's bounty. She had prayed that he would not survive the Crusade, although it was sin to desire a man's death. She might have saved her sinful breath. That man would survive the very heaving of the earth, fire, flood, windstorm, any cataclysm known to man. He was indestructible, like wickedness itself. And now he had returned, thinking to encompass her own destruction. The wheel had again come full circle, as with some, deep atavistic instinct she had known it must.

She rose to her feet and stared in fascinated horror at the curtained door. Then a deep and terrible anger was born in her, so that her shaking stopped and her blood stilled and ceased its pounding. She became very cold.

There was, as there had been before, a knife upon the table, with which she had cut her meat. She took it up and placed it in the deep cuff of her sleeve. This time she would not fail. God owed her this life.

She waited, marble-still, for an eternity. The firm step came beyond the door. It was opened and the curtain flung aside.

The knife clattered from her nerveless fingers to the floor as Tristan de Jarnac strode into the room. They stood, mutely, gazing at each other down the long length of the table.

Tristan made a small movement of his hand that stood for a greeting. "My lady . . . there is much I have to say to you . . . if you will hear me?"

She could not speak. His voice, his presence in the room destroyed her. Her trembling began again.

He came further into the room. "I am sorry I have taken you unawares," he said temperately, "but had I not done so, I had no certainty that you would receive me."

She tore her voice from its captivity. "I had not wished . . ."

"Ever to set eyes on me again. I know. But there are things that must be said between us."

She shook her head. A cloud of pain surrounded her. "There is . . . nothing . . . between us . . ."

Tristan loosed his dark red cloak and swirled it from his shoulders, throwing it down upon the table. He took a small packet from within his tunic. "From Berengaria. I come to you as her courier, as well as for myself." He came toward her, his hand outstretched. She trembled lest she touch his hand as she took the letter.

He saw how she suffered. "Sit down," he ordered gently. Obediently, she did so for she could no longer have stood.

He moved away from her and stood before the hearth. Silent, they looked at each other.

She noted distractedly that he was thinner, that his hair was longer. He looked younger, less the iron-clad knight in his plain green tunic. It occurred to her that he had moved, perhaps, a little stiffly. In his face she caught a suppressed restlessness, controlled as always, but betrayed by the deep, ruby gleam behind his eyes, the tension of his mouth.

In Eden, Tristan saw only agony and waiting. Her beauty pierced him like the first pain of his wound. "I know what you have thought of me . . . about the cause of Stephen's death," he began. He saw her eyes widen, her ordeal increase. "It is untrue," he said quietly. "I did not give him the opium that killed him. It was Hugo de Malfors. I have killed him for it. And for you."

She gave a cry like a child's.

He came to kneel at her side, his hand upon her chair. He saw the shock of understanding begin its work in her. His voice continued levelly, giving her time to bear it. "The Baron had visited Stephen, unknown to the knights, on the evening before he died. As you saw, Stephen, God rest him, was glad of it."

She fought to keep her clarity. Her words were gasping and disconnected. "But Stephen told me . . . he said . . . I was so certain . . ."

As the enormity of her error rushed in upon her she cried out again. Dark wings beat about her and her hands flew to her face in an attempt to hide herself from them, from Tristan, from his terrible innocence, her own heinous guilt.

"He told me," she repeated helplessly, an agony in her breast. "He said that you had helped him from the world, that you had done what was right, in your own lights. He thought, surely, that you had taken pity on him, would let him go . . . ?"

"I have heard these things from Berengaria," he said softly. "She has told me all that was said. Look at me, Eden."

She could not.

"Believe me, I would not have brought him so far, have caused him so much affliction, only to take his life at the end. He meant that I had helped him from the world by bringing him to Jaffa, where he met his end. I would not have killed him, Eden, even for you. Love cannot be built upon death."

She stared dully before her, tormenting words and visions crowding in on her. She understood all now, at last. It was a business beyond tears. She had scarcely listened when Stephen had smiled and said how fitting it was that Hugo should be the one to . . . send him forth. She had thought he spoke of the time when he first took the Cross. But later, surely later, for the love of Christ, she should have come to think again?

But she had not. She had remained steadfast in her vile assumption despite the pleading, even the tears of Berengaria, the acid contempt of Joanna, the outright disbelief of all who came near her. She had been well content to think of Tristan as Stephen's murderer.

She turned her agonized eyes and now looked upon his face. Bitter shame flooded her at the gentleness she saw there.

"Do you still believe it of me, Eden?"

Urgently she shook her head.

"Then why . . . how did you ever think it?" A note of wildness resonated at the end of his words and her heart grew more sick as she saw how deeply her false belief had hurt him. And as she looked at that proud, bitter yet still gentle face, she knew the reason for her faithlessness and she knew she must try to tell him of it.

It was not easy. "I found it possible to think it of you because . . . I was wounded," she began unsteadily. "I loved you and my love for you was wounded. It was because . . . you took your vows to the Order of Saint John. I felt that you deserted me. I know I had no such right." There was a faint wonder in her voice, for now she was making, for the first time for herself, the discovery that Berengaria had made almost at once, and Eleanor after her. It was an annihilation.

"No right," she repeated, "to feel as I did. I do not think . . . I see now that I was not even aware of my emotions. It was easier for me to think that you had evil in you . . . that way I could better support the pain of losing you." She finished on a leaden note of self-loathing. "Eleanor is right. I have understood nothing."

Tristan rose, with a certain difficulty and walked softly about the room.

"You are in pain!" Guilt stabbed at her anew.

"I had Hugo's sword through my side. I thought I was dead of it, but God decided otherwise. I give him thanks for strong mail and a stronger constitution."

She could not bear his nonchalance. "And I did not even know."

"It is well enough now. Only you must forgive a certain stiff-backed quality in my deportment." His smile tried to relieve her of too much grieving.

"And is Hugo truly dead?" she asked, the truth of it reaching her abruptly. "It is hard to believe it. I still feel he must come crashing into this hall." She laughed distractedly. "I thought . . . when you rode in at the gates . . . that you would be Hugo. Is that not strange? He had said he would come, and Richard had said I should wed him . . ."

"Even Richard cannot hale him from his grave to do so," Tristan said grimly.

"How does it stand," she said, with gradually returning control, "between you and the King?"

He had seated himself on the edge of the table, his pacing done. "Not good," he admitted. "He has not tolerated my company since I began to see eye to eye with Conrad. And since de Malfors's death . . . well, Richard did not like to lose his drinking companion. He calls me traitor, but he has not sought to take my life for it. He will not do so, I think. There are too many in the English camp who have come to think as I do." He looked at her covertly, seeing that her eyes held less desperation, that she listened to him with a calmer air. "A swift peace can be the only half-good ending to the Crusade," he continued. "Richard has failed again to take Jerusalem. Saladin will keep it now." He sighed with a mourning regret. "It has been an ill-starred affair. So many lives, so many illusions, fortunes lost. Which of us will come home with that for which he sought?"

He saw her bow her head and instinctively reached his hand toward her. She did not look up and he went on, "The great leaders, Richard, Philippe, Conrad, foundered in their own littleness. Richard, still worrying like a starved dog at Jerusalem, still believing he can recoup his former glory. And perhaps he can . . . for no man is more unpredictable." Again his faint smile lightened the heaviness in the room. "When all is done, it is the man who came for booty who will be best satisfied, the younger son who has stripped his fortune from dead ramieh, the foot soldier who obeys orders and prays when he remembers."

"And you . . ." she asked huskily, "will you go back to Outremer? Will you finish the Crusade beside Richard?" She dared not ask herself why he was here.

His smile was rueful now. "He'd not have me yet . . . though one day we may be reconciled. And then . . . I have other plans."

"Of course." She wanted to weep suddenly. "Your future belongs to the Order."

"I no longer wear their emblem," he said gently. "Had you not noticed?"

"No." She was startled. "I did not think. Will you not, then, take your vows?"

"No."

"What will you do?"

"When I joined the Order," he said slowly, letting his gaze rest upon her like a benediction, "I wanted nothing more of the world, if I could not have you."

For an instant he saw joy dance in her eyes. It was enough. It was the moment. He came and swept her up into his arms.

"I make no more vows, my dear and only love, unless they are to you."

She was weeping, gasping, her hands fluttering about his face. They kissed with a starved and feverish intensity, their mouths moving one upon the other with a bruising force that would immolate all pain. She fought for breath and tried to cry out for forgiveness, but he stopped her mouth with a kiss as suddenly tender as before it was fierce.

"Never say that, love. What need have we of forgiveness?" he muttered as he sought and claimed the sweet body for which his own had cried out with loneliness since the heights above Damascus. Her breasts were wet with her tears. He kissed them all away. Suddenly he raised his head and cried out with exultant laughter, "Have you a priest in your household, Eden? If so, call for him and tell him he has a marriage to perform!"

"At once?" Amazed, bewildered, overjoyed, she was laughing too, her hair all tumbling about her shoulders, only the trace of shadows in her face.

"Why not? Or would he prefer me share your bed unwed?"

He saw that she became, on the instant, suddenly quiet. Her great eyes slanted up at him with a new witchery, a mischief that he had not hoped to bring back to them for long days.

"What is it, Eden? Why do you look at me so? Do you not want me for your husband?"

She nodded gravely and folded her hands upon her stomach. "Indeed I do, and the sooner the better. I will send for Father Sebastian at once. Even so, we are a small, rural community here at Hawkhurst and you must forgive us if, despite the wedding, tongues will wag."

Tristan was mystified. "Perhaps it may be a little soon after they had become accustomed to your being a widow, but my name is irreproachable, my titles respected, my lands rich and wide in England and in France. I cannot see that the manor of Hawkhurst will have much to complain of."

"Only that its heir comes something swiftly into the world."

His face was as blank as a shield without scutcheon.

"Tristan . . . I'm telling you that we shall soon have a child."

He folded her so tightly in his arms he thought he would die with the pain.

"Damascus?" he asked, his voice muffled by her hair.

She nodded vigorously into his shoulder, trying not to hurt him further. "A child, of that night . . . and oh my love, you did not tell me!"

"I did not know until I reached home. I did not think of it. It was Hawisa who realized first."

His eyes caressing hers had the sheen of chestnuts. "You have given me such happiness." His face darkened. "But, if I had not come to you, what then? Would you have told me of it?"

She hesitated for only a second. "No," she said bravely, "I should have let them think it Stephen's child."

There was a silence, though they held each other still. Then he raised and kissed her hand.

"My courageous lady. That would have been the wisest thing to do, had it been necessary. Thank God it is not necessary. And thank God for Berengaria, for it was she who gave me the strength to conquer my broken pride and seek you here."

She looked at him with understanding. "So you did not forgive me easily . . . for what I had thought of you?"

He held fast to her, stroking her hair. "Not at first. But I would have come to it in time. I knew that you were not yourself, that you were distracted with sorrow and your own sufferings. I would have come to it, and to you. But Berengaria would give me no time and no ease. She had sent for me to tell me that your boy, Gilles, was found and that I should take good care of him . . . He's safe at Winchester by now. He will come to you soon."

"I am so glad. I would not have had his death at my door. Besides, I have missed his rascal's face."

"He's been good company. I might make him my squire."

"But Berengaria . . ."

"You will no doubt find all in her letter. She spoke to me of the nature of love and of what she had seen between us. Her words touched me to the heart. She said that few of us were blessed enough to find a soul that matched our own. There was a deep regret in her . . . for herself, for Richard, perhaps for the greater part of the world. But not for us. She had seen what we might be, what we are, to each other, and she would not let it pass. And so she sent me to you."

"I said to her," she told him softly, "that if there was comfort for me, it would come to me at Hawkhurst. She has sent me that comfort for she is wiser, far, than I have been."

"We will grow wise together," said Tristan. He bent his dark head passionately above her pale, grave face, the ruby depths flaming in his eyes. He brooded over her with his hawk's questioning, his lips close to hers.

"You do believe that I would have come to you at last," he demanded, hungry for her.

"If you believe it," she whispered, "what does it matter? You are here."

They came together and there was no more suffering. In a dark corner of the world, its fatal circle broken, the wheel of fortune fell into dust.

ABOUT THE AUTHOR

My Lady's Crusade is ANNETTE MOTLEY'S first novel, but she is by no means new to writing. Her stories have been appearing for years in an English magazine for girls. Born in 1944, she attended a convent school in Perth and after university embarked on a teaching career. As a teacher she had a ready-made audience for the stories she had been writing since childhood. But writing was her first love, and she gave up teaching to devote all her energy to it. Ms. Motley has discovered fiction as the ideal form for her vast knowledge of history and has several more historical novels in the works. She currently lives in Blackheath, England, with her two cats and says she plans to be thirty-three for quite a while.

A Preview of
BITTERSWEET
by Janis Flores

A sweeping story of relentless passion
and intrigue that swirls around a strange
beauty whose manipulated life leads her
from London's underworld to the Bar-
bary Coast. This novel will be available
in June from Bantam Books.

Chapter One

Ariel Drummond stood in front of the headmistress at Miss Appleby's School for Young Ladies, looking at this moment anything but the picture of a proper young lady. Her mouth was set in a tight line, her large, almost violet-colored eyes flashed dangerously in a show of unladylike temper.

"I won't go! Papa has no right to call me home in the middle of my last term. It isn't fair . . .

"I don't care! How can he be so cruel as to think I should leave—"

"Ariel," Miss Appleby spoke firmly. "I refuse to listen to such an ill-mannered tirade; it is most uncivilized. I suggest that you begin packing at once. I will send Daisy to assist you, for your father wishes you to be ready to leave at three. That is all." . . .

Staring blankly down at the terse letter in her hands, Miss Appleby remembered Ariel as a child of eleven when she had first come to the school. Even then she had shown promise of the beauty that was now hers: curly, blue-black hair and startling eyes surrounded by a thick fringe of black lashes, eyes that could change color from deep blue to violet, depending upon her mood. Her white skin was tinted with a natural blush, and her thin body had matured into a well-proportioned, if slender, figure. She had a quick mind, too, Miss Appleby admitted, although it was a shame that she preferred to use it so openly rather than hide it as a lady should. In fact, Miss Appleby recalled more than one occasion when she had had to admonish Ariel for her quick tongue . . .

And so it had gone for six years. In the beginning, Miss Appleby had tried to be sympathetic. After all, she would tell herself, the child's mother had died—and in queer circumstances, too. There had been something strange about a normally placid cart-horse suddenly going berserk and deciding to gallop down a crowded street, upsetting the cart and throwing poor Mrs. Drummond right under the excited feet of a temperamental two-in-hand, whose driver was nowhere to be found. But as Mrs. Drummond had been driving the cart herself, no one could be blamed, and eventually the incident had been labeled as simply an unfortunate accident . . .

Ariel, after running up the stairs in a manner that would have confirmed Miss Appleby's worst fears, had reached the room she shared with Clarissa Higgins and was pacing back and forth in a rage, her skirts whirling alarmingly about her ankles. Clarissa, a rather pale creature with brownish hair and a plump figure that indicated her love for bonbons, sat nervously in a chair, wincing every time Ariel flashed by. By nature a slightly timid and safely conventional girl, Clarissa had first been awed by, and more than a little envious of, Ariel's direct and forceful personality. In the two years she and Ariel had shared this room, Clarissa had never become accustomed to Ariel's outbursts of temper and her reckless vitality. In fact, she often consoled herself that Ariel would someday come to ruin because she had never learned the saving grace of control at all times. And as always, when this thought was uppermost in her mind, she smiled a sly, secret smile, feeling herself superior to her roommate, because after all, *she* was a lady, and Ariel most definitely was not.

Finally, after watching Ariel pacing furiously back and forth, Clarissa ventured a suggestion. "Would you like the smelling salts, Ariel? You look—"

Ariel looked at her as if she must be out of her mind. "Smelling salts! Whatever for?" She gave a short laugh and threw herself on her bed. "I don't need smelling salts, Clarissa. I need to smash something!"

And to Clarissa's horror, Ariel picked up a hairbrush from the nightstand and threw it savagely toward the dressing table mirror. It missed the glass by inches, clattering noisily to the floor, and Clarissa retrieved it and put it gently on the table, giving Ariel a long-suffering glance.

"I do wish you would tell me why you are so upset, Ariel," she began. "It—it doesn't do to throw things."

"I'll tell you why I'm upset!" Violently, Ariel threw herself off the bed and stood with her hands clenched. "My father has sent for me—that's what's wrong! I'm wanted at home because of 'family matters.'" Her lip curled contemptuously, and she repeated fiercely, "family matters! That means he is in trouble with his damn gambling again!"

"Ariel!" Clarissa, shocked to the core, protested. "Please don't use such language. It's vulgar—and—and disgusting. Not to mention—"

"Unladylike?" Ariel mocked. "Well, I'm sorry to offend you, Clarissa. But saying damn doesn't do justice to the situation at all. I don't want to go home."

Clarissa tried another tack. "Perhaps it's not—gambling"—she gave a delicate shudder. "Perhaps a relative or—"

"I don't have any relatives," Ariel snapped. "No, I know it's his gambling. And I'll be damned"—she looked hard at Clarissa, who in spite of herself drew back—"if I'm going to suffer because my father can't control his indiscretions."

"But—"

"Oh, for heaven's sake, stop acting like such a prig and help me pack. The carriage is coming at three, and I'm going home to tell him just what I think about having to leave school!"

Stung at the insult, Clarissa attempted to bring some order into the chaos of dresses, petticoats, and other paraphernalia a still-furious Ariel was now throwing in a jumble on the bed. But even as her hands were busy folding the garments, Clarissa thought that someday she would dearly love to put Ariel in her place—if she could only find the courage. A prig! How dare Ariel insult *her*, the daughter of a prosperous and respected lawyer, when her own father was such a ne'er-do-well! And as for Ariel, with her black hair that was never smoothly in place and those strange eyes that flashed dangerously instead of looking demurely from beneath lowered lashes—that gave her the idea she was better than everyone else? Someday, the proud and arrogant Ariel Drummond would be brought low, and she would be there to savor the fall. Clarissa's rather small eyes glittered at the thought . . .

From the moment her father's coachman assisted her into the carriage, Ariel forgot the giggling and tearful goodbyes and began to concentrate on the problem of persuading her father to allow her return to school. It was imperative that she return; the thought of being forced to live at home sent a stab of panic through her. If only she could depend upon her father's sympathy and understanding. But Father hadn't been understanding since her mother had died. In fact, Ariel felt he actually disliked her for he treated her with a cold aversion that she was at a loss to understand. Its roots went deeper than anger or disgust at anything she had done to displease him. It had something to do with her mother's death, but what, she didn't know. When immediately after her mother's death he had banished her to boarding school, Ariel had felt the first faint stirrings of anger at his injustice. As time went on, the anger hardened into cold contempt, especially when she was old enough to recognize her father's gambling and drinking problems. Now she wanted nothing to do with the father who had rejected her.

An hour later when the carriage pulled up to the front door of the Drummond residence, Ariel was in such a state of nervous anticipation at seeing her father again that she thought she was going to be ill. And as always when she was nervous or frightened, she could feel her face stiffen to hide her true feelings. She was too proud to admit her fear of her father, so she became angry. Her anger grew as she raced up the steps into the house. Better to face her father in a temper than to stutter with the nervousness she knew was too close to the surface.

"Papa!" she shouted, running into the house. "Papa, I must talk to you."

John Drummond emerged from his study at the end of the corridor, staring distastefully at his daughter. Hadn't that expensive school taught her *anything*? His dislike deepened as he saw that Ariel, with her thick black hair and her eyes blazing in a white face, resembled her mother even more strongly than she had the last time he had seen her. Was there no end to his torment? Why did Ariel have to look so much like her mother that he wanted to kill her?

"Kindly lower that ill-bred voice and stop your rushing about," he said sharply as his daughter reached him. "I can see that your time and my money have been utterly wasted if your education has not taught you proper behavior."

"I'm sorry, Papa, but I must know why—"

He raised an eyebrow. "I beg your pardon," he said sarcastically, "but did I hear you correctly? Do you dare to question me?"

"But Papa—"

"Go to your room at once! I refuse to discuss the matter further."

But Ariel was too upset to care. She said hotly, "But we haven't discussed it at all! Why did I have to come home? I have only half a term left, and it isn't fair—"

"I said, go to your room," John Drummond repeated, his mouth a tight line as he glared down at his daughter. "And do not come out until you can speak in a civil tone. Sometimes I find it difficult to believe you are my daughter when you act in such an uncivilized manner!"

"And I find it difficult to believe that you are my father if you have so little concern for my feelings!" she stormed at him, too angry to be appalled by her own words.

"There is no need for anyone else to be concerned with your feelings, Ariel, for you concentrate on them to the exclusion of anything else," he said coldly. Then he turned back to his study and locked the door behind him, leaving Ariel, helpless with fury, standing alone in the corridor.

Ariel had been home a week, alternately raging and sulking in her room, before she learned that John Drummond was far too involved with his insurmountable debts to be affected by her tears and pleas that she be allowed to return to school. A careless conversation between two servants was the source of this devastating knowledge. She realized that her father could no longer afford to send her to school. She was furious that she should have to suffer for her father's vices, and her dislike of him turned to scornful contempt for his weakness. Sullenly, she kept to her room, which was where he found her the night, that unbelievable, humiliating night, of his last card party.

It was late. The clock had just struck one, but she was still awake and dressed, reading one of the shocking new French novels that had so impressed all of the girls at school. They pretended to be horrified at the coarse language, the scandalizing conduct, the intimate details, but secretly they were delighted, envious, and just a little hopeful that something similar would one day happen to them. After all, it was *so* romantic! Looking back, much later, Ariel thought that her own life had been such as to make that particular novel pale in comparison, but at the time she sighed regretfully that her own experiences had been, and were likely to remain, terribly dull.

Hearing her father rattling the knob on her door, she tried frantically to hide the book, with its telltale yellow cover, under a chair. But then she realized he couldn't get in, for in a fit of rage at his injustice, she had locked it. She laughed to herself, picturing him, red-faced, on the other side of the door, outraged that any room in his house would be locked against him. She laughed, but not for long.

"Ariel! Open this door at once!" he thundered.

She recognized immediately that particular tone of voice. It meant that he had been drinking heavily, and suddenly frightened, she hurried to the door and un-locked it just as he began an uncharacteristic assault on it with his fists.

"Yes, Papa?" she said stiffly, to cover her feelings of impending disaster. She was shocked at his appear-ance, and suddenly, she wanted nothing so much as to slam the door in his face to blot out the sight of him. Even then, she thought later, she might have been saved if she could have brought herself to ask him what was wrong, but she was too upset to understand or to sympathize with the man standing in the hallway, his shirt-sleeves rolled up, his cravat askew, his hair falling over his forehead. His eyes were wild, and Ariel was frightened.

"What—what is it, Papa?" she stammered, trying to back away from those terrible eyes, glittering with drink, and that ravaged face so close to hers.

"Come with me!"

He grabbed her arm, pulling her from the room, dragging her down the stairs toward the library. He paused before the library door and took a deep breath, still holding her arm in a fierce grip.

She shrank back; a card party had been going on in there for hours, and suddenly she had a premonition of disaster. She looked at her father, opened her mouth to speak, and drew back again at the glance he turned on her.

"You're all I have left," he muttered opening the door. "I hope to God you're enough."

The library was suffocatingly close and cloudy with cigar smoke that hung above the circular table in the center of the room. The four men seated at the table looked up with surprise at their entrance. She noticed almost hysterically that not one of them had risen to their feet as was customary when a woman entered a room. But then, she thought wildly, she wasn't quite a woman yet. She was only seventeen.

She had time to notice that, though cards were scattered about the table, only one man had any quantity of chips. Risking a quick glance at this man's face, she almost recoiled. She saw him staring at her with a peculiar expression. He ran a thick tongue over his lips, glanced casually at her father, and shrugged. She felt her father stiffen beside her, and his grip on her arm tightened.

"Papa," she began unsteadily, "what—"

"Be quiet," John Drummond commanded sharply, moving jerkily to the table. He ran his fingers through his hair, threw himself into the empty chair, and with an air of desperation, picked up his cards. He glanced quickly at Ariel, who stood frozen, then at the big man to his left and said, "I'm ready, Mr. Metcalf."

Two of the men sitting at the table leaned forward, speaking urgently to her father.

"I say, John, you can't—"

"This business is insane. I won't allow—"

But the man with the chips, Mr. Metcalf, raised his hand and immediately the other two fell silent, one fingering his mustache nervously, the other staring down at the table. Ariel looked at the fourth man, who hadn't moved or spoken since she had come into the room. He was handsome, in a cold sort of way, with dark hair and long side whiskers outlining a lean, angular face that supported a hawkish nose and full mouth. He had an aura of assurance and controlled power that was all the more noticeable because he was by far the youngest man at the table. Why, Ariel thought in surprise, he can only be a few years older than I! She made an instinctive movement toward him, but just then he looked at her, and she stopped, frozen by the expression in his dark gray eyes. Their glance held for an instant, and Ariel could feel herself flushing at the cool appraisal he gave her before he impatiently turned his head and picked up the glass resting by his hand. He raised the glass to his lips, and as he did so, the ring on his right hand caught the light. It was a gold ring, heavy and intricately engraved in which was set a large opaque light jade stone shot through with varying shades of green. On the stone, the barest outline of the head of a snarling dog had been skillfully carved.

The man tossed down the contents of the glass with one swallow, threw down his cards into the center of the table, pushed back his chair, and stood. He was tall, so tall that he towered over the men still seated.

"Too rich for my blood," he said, looking down at John Drummond, who shifted uneasily in his chair. "Is this hand so important to you, Drummond?" he asked softly.

John Drummond looked up, his eyes glittering. "You don't understand, Fallon. With these cards, I can recoup everything. Everything!"

The younger man gave him a glance of contempt before shrugging and turning away. "I've heard you say that before," he remarked casually.

"Get out!" Drummond shouted suddenly. "Get out and don't come back!"

"Never fear, Drummond. I won't return. I won't be a party to this—"

The rest of his sentence was lost as John Drummond hurled a glass at him. The glass hit his temple, and he staggered slightly, the amber liquid that had filled the glass running down the side of his face. With studied composure, he pulled out a handkerchief, wiped his face, and bowed mockingly toward Ariel's enraged father.

"I have heard," he said quietly, in a deep voice under tight control, "that breeding tells. Now I realize that isn't always true." And before John Drummond could frame a reply, Fallon walked from the room.

Ariel caught the faint scent of the cologne he wore. It was pleasing, a masculine scent that suited him, and even in her fright, she wondered who he was.

The two other men were rising indignantly to their feet, only to be halted by Mr. Metcalf, who waved them back.

"Stay," he commanded softly. "You will be witnesses."

"No, Charles, I can't possibly—"

"I refuse—"

"Oh, do you?" he asked, staring at each man in

turn. "Have you forgotten how deeply in debt you are to me? I could ruin you both tomorrow if I chose. Are you willing to risk that for a chit?"

"But you can't possibly be serious—" one man began.

"Oh, but I am," Charles Metcalf interrupted in that same soft voice. "If Drummond is so insistent upon using his own daughter as a wager, why should I object?" His small black eyes turned toward Ariel, and the expression she saw there broke her horrified trance.

Her eyes flew to her father, sitting hunched over the cards in his hand, and she rushed over to him. "Papa!" she shrieked. "Papa, you aren't serious! Papa—say something!"

Frantically she clung to his arm, begging him to stop this madness. But to her utter disbelief, he behaved as though she weren't even there. He jerked away without glancing at her and stared straight ahead while Charles Metcalf laughed softly.

"Papa—Papa—" she sobbed, thoroughly terrified by now. But he ignored her again, and she backed away, staring at him in wide-eyed disbelief.

There was silence in the room. Someone cleared his throat, a harsh, rasping sound that died away abruptly as Metcalf began to speak.

"All that you owe me, Drummond," he said. "With these." There was a scraping sound as he pushed the pile of chips in front of him to the center of the table. "Enough?"

The words hung in the silence, and she knew without looking that her father had nodded. Her heart began to pound uncomfortably against her ribs, and she clenched her hands. What if he lost? But he couldn't lose, she told herself desperately. He wouldn't have made the wager if he thought he would lose. He wouldn't—he wouldn't—

The cards were slapped to the table one by one. Someone drew in his breath sharply, and the tension seemed to vibrate in the close, still air. Ariel forced herself to look at the table and saw that her father and Metcalf each held one last card. Beads of perspiration gathered on John Drummond's forehead and dripped slowly down the sides of his face. He reached out for a glass, knocked it over, and the contents sent a spreading stain across the table. None of them seemed to notice. Drummond closed his eyes briefly, took a deep breath, and laid down his last card. White-faced, he looked toward his opponent's impassive face and then at the remaining card held in his pudgy fingers. Slowly, torturously, Metcalf laid the card on the table and leaned back heavily.

Suddenly, Ariel was standing over the table, looking down at the cards. They were meaningless to her, and she turned frantically to her father. "What does it—" She stopped. Her father's face had taken on a grayish tinge, his lips were slack. The silence was almost palpable in the room as all four men stared down at the cards.

"Papa!" Ariel shook his arm, trying to make him see her, say something to her. "Papa! It was a joke, wasn't it? To make me apologize—to make me sorry for the way I've acted? Well, I'm sorry! Do you hear me? Papa!" Her voice rose to a hysterical shriek, but still he kept staring at the cards. Metcalf rose ponderously to his feet. The movement startled Ariel, and she fell back against her father's chair. Forcing herself, she looked defiantly into those small black eyes surrounded by folds of flesh. "It was a joke, wasn't it?" she demanded in a shaking voice.

Metcalf laughed silently, his huge stomach quivering under his embroidered waistcoat. He reached toward her, and instinctively she moved back, repulsed. His laughter stopped abruptly, his lips tightened cruelly. He reached out again, and before Ariel could move away, his sausagelike fingers had circled her throat, forcing her to look up at him.

"Three days, my dear," he told her in that soft, hateful voice. "Three days. Learn to accept it now, or it will be the worse for you."

He released her so abruptly that she staggered. She

turned to her father. "What does he mean?" she cried hoarsely. "Papa! Look at me! What does he mean?"

Blankly, John Drummond looked up into his daughter's face. She wanted to shake him, to wrench him out of that terrible apathy that gripped him, but it seemed that she was as unable to move as he. Father and daughter stared at each other in awful silence, until finally, John Drummond repeated tonelessly, "What does he mean? Why he means that in three days you're to be married. I—I—lost." He shook his head as if to clear it. "I lost," he repeated unbelievingly. "I was so sure—you understand, don't you Ariel? If I had won. . . . There wasn't any choice. You were all I had left. . . ."

The disjointed voice trailed away into silence as Ariel stared at him in horror. Her eyes went from her father to the two other men in the room. Both avoided her glance, making a business of gathering up their belongings, leaving quietly and quickly, ashamed of their own silence. Ariel looked back to her father, who was gazing down at the table in front of him, and suddenly she was too angry to think. How dare he sit there while her life fell into pieces around her feet! It was madness, an insane nightmare to expect this of her! Reaching down, she swept everything off the table. Cards, chips, and glasses went flying in all directions, and still her father sat there, motionless.

"I won't do it!" she screamed into his blank face. "Do you hear me? I won't! I won't! I won't!" Her voice rose higher and higher, and for an instant, she thought she would actually reach out and slap him out of his apathy. But suddenly, she felt herself jerked around to stare into Metcalf's bloated face.

Beside herself with fear and fury, she looked into those tiny little eyes and spat, "Never! I'll never marry you. You can't force me. You're horrible and repulsive, and I wouldn't marry you if—"

Calmly, deliberately, Metcalf raised his hand and slapped her. The blow sent her staggering toward the sideboard where she fell against the polished surface. So outraged that she didn't stop to think, she reached out and grabbed the first thing that touched her hand, her only thought being to strike back at the monstrous man who had slapped her. Her fingers tightened around the neck of a decanter, and she lifted it, intending to throw it as hard as she could into Metcalf's hateful face. Before she could act, he reached her side. Putting one beefy hand around her wrist he forced her arm back. Her fingers lost their grip, and the bottle crashed to the floor. Alcohol fumes engulfed them, and she coughed, eyes streaming.

Metcalf's voice was a hiss in her ear. "I like a bit of spirit, my dear, but only in certain things. You'll have to learn a little respect—"

Her arm was forced down and back, and she cried out, gasping with pain and fury. "Not yet, little Ariel," he said softly. "You aren't convinced yet." His grip on her wrist tightened, forcing her hand back until she thought the bones would snap. Her knees began to buckle under her, and still the pressure increased.

Looking up at him with blazing eyes, she said between clenched teeth, "You're—hurting me—you monster—"

He smiled malevolently. "Good. I suspect that's the only way you'll learn, my dear," he said, forcing her to her knees in front of him.

She bowed her head, biting her lip to keep from crying out and giving satisfaction to this hideous man, but he put his hand under her chin and jerked her head up.

"Look at me!"

She closed her eyes, determined not to give in. The pain in her twisted arm was like fire now, and she knew she would faint if he didn't release her soon.

"Look at me!" he demanded again.

She opened her eyes in time to see a huge hand descending on her, and then pain exploded at the side of her head. Knocked sideways, she would have fallen to the floor, but his grip on her wrist held her upright. Swaying, she felt a trickle of blood running from her lip and looked up in time to see him raise his hand again.

"All right—" she heard herself say, hating herself for giving in to him, but unable to call back the words.

Miraculously, his fingers loosened their grip on her wrist, and she sagged at his feet, rubbing her arm.

"That's better," Metcalf said. "Remember that little lesson when your temper threatens to overtake you again."

He turned away briskly. "Well, Drummond," he said to her father, who, unbelievably, had not moved. "I think I will take my prize home tonight. I wouldn't trust her not to run away, so I will take her for safe-keeping."

John Drummond nodded, still caught in his death-like trance, and Metcalf, smiling to himself, stepped out into the hall, shouting for his carriage. Returning, he tossed Ariel his cape and ordered her to follow him. She shrank back against the wall, praying that her father would rouse himself and refuse to let her go, but when he remained silent, she knew that any appeal would be useless, and she felt hatred for him rising like bile in her throat. It was a nightmare; it couldn't possibly be happening—her father had gambled her away!

"Ariel! Come along!" Metcalf ordered from the doorway.

Ariel turned and looked at him dully, unmoving, until Metcalf took a step toward her. She knew that he wouldn't hesitate to force her to follow him, and for the moment she decided to obey him, though it cost her an effort not to burst into tears of fury. Only her pride forced her to drag herself to her feet unaided. Once standing, she found herself in front of her father, staring down at him with narrowed eyes that held nothing but contempt.

"I'll never forgive you for this," she hissed at him. "Never! I hope you burn in hell forever for what you have done to me tonight."

"Come along, my dear," Metcalf said again. "And Drummond, remember that your notes are due tomorrow. I'll expect them paid in full."

The last Ariel saw of her father was a ravaged face,

haunted eyes, and shaking hands reaching for the bottle. Then Metcalf's hand was on her arm, and he was propelling her down the steps toward his waiting carriage.

This is but the beginning of Ariel's strange life of being sold and bartered by greedy men. It leads her into an underground world of shame, but toward the one man whose love for her is undaunted.

DON'T MISS
THESE CURRENT
Bantam Bestsellers

WE DELIVER!
And So Do These Bestsellers.

☐	2044	**CAVETT** by Cavett and Porterfield	$1.95
☐	2222	**HELTER SKELTER** by Vincent Bugliosi	$1.95
☐	11696	**GODS FROM OUTER SPACE** by Erich Von Daniken	$1.95
☐	11917	**LINDA GOODMAN'S SUN SIGNS**	$2.25
☐	11162	**THE DAVID KOPAY STORY** by David Kopay & Perry Young	$1.95
☐	2927	**THE MOTHER EARTH NEWS ALMANAC** by John Shuttleworth	$2.25
☐	10080	**LIFE AFTER LIFE** by Raymond Moody, M.D.	$1.95
☐	10150	**FUTURE SHOCK** by Alvin Toffler	$2.25
☐	11255	**GUINNESS BOOK OF WORLD RECORDS 16th Ed.** by the McWhirters	$2.25
☐	10251	**WHAT DO YOU SAY AFTER YOU SAY HELLO?** by Dr. Eric Berne	$2.25
☐	10277	**BURY MY HEART AT WOUNDED KNEE** by Dee Brown	$2.50
☐	10306	**PASSAGES** by Gail Sheehy	$2.50
☐	10436	**EVERYTHING YOU ALWAYS WANTED TO KNOW ABOUT SEX** by Dr. David Reuben	$2.25
☐	10565	**SOME MEN ARE MORE PERFECT THAN OTHERS** by Merle Shain	$1.75
☐	10759	**ALL CREATURES GREAT AND SMALL** by James Herriot	$2.25
☐	11001	**DR. ATKINS' DIET REVOLUTION** by Dr. Robert Atkins	$2.25
☐	11122	**THE PETER PRINCIPLE** by Peter & Hull	$1.95
☐	11291	**THE LATE GREAT PLANET EARTH** by Hal Lindsey	$1.95
☐	11400	**WHEN I SAY NO, I FEEL GUILTY** by Manuel Smith	$2.25

Buy them at your local bookstore or use this handy coupon for ordering:

Bantam Books, Inc., Dept. NFB, 414 East Golf Road, Des Plaines, Ill. 60016

Please send me the books I have checked above. I am enclosing $_____ (please add 50¢ to cover postage and handling). Send check or money order—no cash or C.O.D.'s please.

Mr/Mrs/Miss_____

Address_____

City_____State/Zip_____

NFB—3/78

Please allow four weeks for delivery. This offer expires 9/78.

RELAX!
SIT DOWN
and Catch Up On Your Reading!

☐	10077	**TRINITY** by Leon Uris	$2.75
☐	2300	**THE MONEYCHANGERS** by Arthur Hailey	$1.95
☐	2424	**THE GREAT TRAIN ROBBERY** by Michael Crichton	$1.95
☐	2500	**THE EAGLE HAS LANDED** by Jack Higgins	$1.95
☐	2600	**RAGTIME** by E. L. Doctorow	$2.25
☐	10360	**CONFLICT OF INTEREST** by Les Whitten	$1.95
☐	10092	**THE SWISS ACCOUNT** by Leslie Waller	$1.95
☐	2964	**THE ODESSA FILE** by Frederick Forsyth	$1.95
☐	11770	**ONCE IS NOT ENOUGH** by Jacqueline Susann	$2.25
☐	8500	**JAWS** by Peter Benchley	$1.95
☐	8844	**TINKER, TAILOR, SOLDIER, SPY** by John Le Carre	$1.95
☐	11929	**THE DOGS OF WAR** by Frederick Forsyth	$2.25
☐	10090	**THE R DOCUMENT** by Irving Wallace	$2.25
☐	10526	**INDIA ALLEN** by Elizabeth B. Coker	$1.95
☐	10357	**THE HARRAD EXPERIMENT** by Robert Rimmer	$1.95
☐	10422	**THE DEEP** by Peter Benchley	$2.25
☐	10500	**DOLORES** by Jacqueline Susann	$1.95
☐	11601	**THE LOVE MACHINE** by Jacqueline Susann	$2.25
☐	10600	**BURR** by Gore Vidal	$2.25
☐	10857	**THE DAY OF THE JACKAL** by Frederick Forsyth	$1.95
☐	11366	**DRAGONARD** by Rupert Gilchrist	$1.95
☐	11057	**PROVINCETOWN** by Burt Hirschfeld	$1.95
☐	11330	**THE BEGGARS ARE COMING** by Mary Loos	$1.95

Buy them at your local bookstore or use this handy coupon for ordering:

Bantam Books, Inc., Dept. FBB, 414 East Golf Road, Des Plaines, Ill. 60016

Please send me the books I have checked above. I am enclosing $_____
(please add 50¢ to cover postage and handling). Send check or money
order—no cash or C.O.D.'s please.

Mr/Mrs/Miss_____

Address_____

City_____State/Zip_____

FBB—3/78

Please allow four weeks for delivery. This offer expires 9/78.

Bantam Book Catalog

Here's your up-to-the-minute listing of every book currently available from Bantam.

This easy-to-use catalog is divided into categories and contains over 1400 titles by your favorite authors.

So don't delay—take advantage of this special opportunity to increase your reading pleasure.

Just send us your name and address and 25¢ (to help defray postage and handling costs).